BOULEVARD

BOULEVARD

STEPHEN JAY SCHWARTZ

A TOM DOHERTY ASSOCIATES BOOK
NEW YORK

BOULEVARD

Copyright © 2009 by Stephen Jay Schwartz

A Forge Book
Published by Tom Doherty Associates, LLC
175 Fifth Avenue
New York, NY 10010

www.tor-forge.com

Forge® is a registered trademark of Tom Doherty Associates, LLC.

Library of Congress Cataloging-in-Publication Data

Schwartz, Stephen Jay.
    Boulevard / Stephen Jay Schwartz. — 1st ed.
        p.   cm.
    "A Tom Doherty Associates Book."
    ISBN 978-0-7653-2294-4
  1. Police—California—Los Angeles—Fiction.   2. Women—Crimes against—Fiction.
3. Sex addicts—Fiction.   4. Los Angeles (Calif.)—Fiction.   5. Psychological fiction.
I. Title.
    PS3619.C4877B68 2009
    813'.6—dc22
                                                                    2009016626

First Edition: September 2009

Printed in the United States of America

0 9 8 7 6 5 4 3 2 1

For Ryen, Benjamin, and Noah: you are my everything.

ACKNOWLEDGMENTS

Thank you to Gigi Cutler, for always believing, always; Ryen, for your amazing sense of story and your ability to see the art in everything, even your pain; Susan Dane, for your friendship, your encouragement, your editorial expertise; Blair Hayes, for your inspiring talent and enthusiasm; Scott Miller, for your passion, your unflagging support, and for the hurricane force that is you; Eric Raab, for your editorial talent and your zeal in championing the book; Claire Roberts, for your drive and commitment; Kim Dower, for taking it all up a notch; Tom Doherty, for backing the deal; and the great team at Forge and Macmillan.

I would like to additionally acknowledge Steve Cohen, for the incredible support and for giving me such great opportunities; Elco Lighting; Dr. Larry Schwartz; Art Gardenswartz; Rennie and Frank Morian; Phil and Paula Friedman; Heather Rivera; Stephanie Sun; Katharine Critchlow; David Baird; Jerry and Annette Schwartz; Al and Dianne Hecht; John and Ruth Rauch; Art Lapin; Koli Cutler; Brock Winkless; Danielle Hill; Joe Jabour; Rosella Jabour; the Novel Café and every writer in it; Arthur Gren, PI; Roni-the-doctor; Penny Harker; Avi Lonstein; John Mendoza; John Otto; Dr. Leslie Palmer; Caren Bohrman; John and Carol Brown; Don Barbaree; Mike Barskey; Brett Battles; Dante Rochetti; Chief Craig Harvey at the L.A. Coroners Office; Officer Dennis Mesa; Officer Mark Alvarez (a real 10–8 cop); Sergeant Carl T; Inspector Antonio L. Casillas; Officer Kevin Martin; and the fellas of Company A for giving me the jump on Book Two.

The lines along which [the shattered vase] had broken . . . will always remain discernible to an experienced eye. However, it will have a certain wisdom since it knows something that the vase that has never been broken does not: it knows what it is to break and what it is to come together.

Salman Akhtar, Psychoanalyst

BOULEVARD

CRUISING

Detective Hayden Glass of the Los Angeles Police Department's Robbery-Homicide Division drove his old Hollywood beat, crossing Fairfax, heading east on Sunset Boulevard. The night was warm, encouraging nervous movement on the streets. Traffic stretched taillight to grill; kids heading to clubs like Dragonfly or Liquid Kitty or Club Lingerie, and coming from the Whiskey or Viper Room or House of Blues.

Quarter to two in the morning and the 7-Eleven at Sunset and Crescent was hopping. There were warrants on half the cars for sure. A long white limo sat in the parking lot with a half dozen prostitutes tucked inside—they'd make their move when the heat was off. Hit the street for twenty minutes and disappear in cars before Vice could nail them. Street signs along the Boulevard wouldn't let you make a left turn after 11 P.M. That's when the johns were cruising.

Hayden passed an unmarked sedan on the corner of Gardner and Sunset, Detective Emery inside. Not a big crew, just one division. Hayden remembered the task forces he used to run—three divisions with eight girls on the street, a field jail, foot officers, black-and-whites and motorcycles. He could net twenty guys a night with an operation like that. Emery glanced his way, acknowledging Hayden with a nod. There was Officer Cynthia Prava as a "trick decoy" a half-block down Gardner wearing a black leather miniskirt and boots. They'd hit their quota as long as Prava was on the hook.

Hayden passed tattoo parlors and head shops. Then a bus stop pay phone where the crack whores called their pimps or rides or drug connections or johns. The circuit girls that came down from Vegas kept BlackBerries and iPhones tucked inside their tall, red leather boots.

He saw two strip clubs in a row just before La Brea. This stretch of Sunset between La Brea and Highland was always backed up with hookers and crack addicts trickling out pretending they had someplace to go. The dealers had sentries who whistled when they saw heat. Hayden was driving a "brown paper bag," an LAPD Crown Vic without lights. He wasn't recognized.

He drove by Hollywood High School, which sat in the middle of it all like a tortoise on its back in the muck. Hollywood High made a kid grow up fast. Most of the kids looked like runaways. It was just a matter of time before they joined the ranks of players out hustling deals on the Boulevard just outside their classroom doors.

Hayden saw "cruisers" all around. Men driving alone, peering into the shadows, eyes straining, riding the brakes, weaving through traffic, not drunk, but intoxicated by a rush of dopamine pumping. They drove Range Rovers, Mercedes, Hummers, Jags, Volkswagens. Looking like anyone, anywhere. Bankers, studio execs, mid-level sales managers, schoolteachers, pastors. Monday morning they would likely sit at their jobs in a daze, nursing the numb feeling that they had done *something secret something shameful something wrong.* Some would wake up in county jail with their lives unraveling, contemplating suicide. Tonight they drove without thought of consequence.

Most didn't know what to call it. It was just something they did, a secret they kept from the rest of the world. A secret kept from themselves even, as they avoided their reflections in the mirror of the bathroom at Carl's Jr., where they would stop to wash the grime of strangers from their hands and cocks, panicking over drops of semen that stained silk shirts; running alibis through their heads to justify three hours lost in the night. They drove on autopilot, expressions fixed, empty, without compassion as they crisscrossed the same two-mile stretch of Sunset looking for a "hit."

It was Saturday. Vice Night. Hayden knew that most johns were aware of this. They seemed not to care. He watched a black girl in bright green spandex slip into the passenger side of a Honda Accord, her lips already moving. The girls had to get to the point quickly—they didn't have time for guys who were shy or didn't have the guts to act. Hayden knew the drill, had heard it a hundred times before.

Fuck, it's hot out there, it's Vice Night. You ain't a cop, are you? The john would shake his head, pulling out his cock as proof. Or, wary, he would ask the girl if *she* was a cop. *I wouldn'ta got in your car if I was, Jack.*

Why don't we touch each other at the same time, the john might suggest. This would get them past stalemate. She'd put her hand in his lap and he'd palm her breast. As they drove off, *What ya got in mind, honey?*

Twenty for a hand job, he would say.

Nothing less than forty or you drop me off at the next light. Or fifty for head. With a condom.

Okay, fifty.

They would leave Sunset for a quick side street. The residents of Hollywood peered through the bars on their living room windows to see strange cars with bodies bobbing inside. A dome light might illuminate the back of a hooker's head, an exposed breast, a pumping hand. Sometimes the flashing red and blue of a cruiser pulled alongside, his spotlight tagging the john stepping out, zipping up, reciting a tale he had practiced but never thought to tell.

The girls were always in and out of jail. Hayden knew their stories. *My boyfriend brought me out here from Kansas got busted jacking his boss's warehouse in jail now put me on the street I've only done this two months been in County three times already need an extra twenty for the bus can you spare you're not a cop are you?* The john might want to hear the sob story, depending on how lonely he was or how hard up for a connection. It was the preamble they were addicted to—the hours of cruising, the hint of blond on a girl walking the street, her eyes tracking his, the U-turn that brought them within range, pulling up alongside and rolling down the window, her quick walk to the passenger door, lifting the latch, the eye contact, the knowing smile, her hand settling into his lap to let him know that, yes, he had scored. After that, it got scary. *Where do we park? Am I going to get busted? How do I get this fucking whore out of my car?*

Hayden drove East on Sunset past Highland. The streets were mostly clear of pros until about Western, where the tougher, cheaper girls would be found. They were the street-scarred, knife-wielding drug addicts who would just as easily rob a john as get him off. Hayden didn't understand the attraction to these women, but he felt that any guy picking a girl off the street was looking to be punished for something he'd done, consciously or not, and he might as well take his beating sooner than later.

Hayden made a U-turn at Cahuenga, continued west toward Highland again. He watched fog hovering low in pools above the ground. He couldn't remember the last time he had seen fog in Hollywood. Instead of descending from above it seemed to rise from the street, circling manholes like urine-tinted cyclones in reverse.

He cracked the window and the fog poured in. For a moment he felt a cold terror that set his hands to shaking. It was a feeling he recognized, from some place, some time before. He could not recall it now.

He was almost to Highland. Up ahead, a line of cars. Through the fog, a glint of blond. He passed slowly, tapped his brakes. She looked up. She found his eyes and they shared a look. She took a step for his car with her hand outstretched. He stepped on the gas. Through the rearview mirror he saw her flip him off. Another car was there in a heartbeat and she stepped inside. The car, the corner, the Boulevard, disappeared in a haze as he turned north on Highland for the 101.

1

The apartment Hayden entered was unremarkable save for the twenty-year-old black female lying half-naked half off a sofa in a pool of her own blood. The once beige carpet was dark, wet, and thick like a sponge against her flesh. Hayden stared at the disfigured body. Seven or eight thrusts with a nine-inch blade, then a cello stroke to her throat.

He went to a corner and observed the body from a distance. Something was off, he thought. She hadn't landed half off the sofa, she was placed there. And the coffee table had been pulled out by a yard, making the body a centerpiece.

"Morning, Detective." Hayden turned to see Officer Nolan, who had been first on scene. "Her name's Lori Nichols. Ready for this? Pete Jackson's niece."

"Councilman Jackson?" That explained why the Chief of Police switched the investigation from West L.A. to Downtown Robbery-Homicide and why there was so much activity in the room.

"Who's the guy in the car?" Hayden asked.

"No ID."

Hayden moved closer. A sheer black bra barely covered her breasts. She'd bled out a long time from the chest and stomach wounds before the killer slit her throat. He pulled out his notebook to sketch the scene.

Hayden was aware of the many eyes watching him. His first prominent case without Rich at his side. He chewed the inside of his lip as he did when his nerves wore thin, knowing it would be a canker sore by day's end. It would burn in the mustard from the burger he would eat at Tommy's and be a white-hot reminder of the anxiety he felt at this moment, when the dead girl's eyes stared ahead and beyond.

Two uniformed officers peeked over his shoulder. His sketches enjoyed a reputation in the department, looking more like images from a graphic novel than the standard amoebic circle with the words "dead girl" etched inside. His drawings captured the emotion of the event. They gave the victim a voice that called out for justice, sometimes for vengeance. Hayden wanted to hear that voice, always.

He finished the sketch and observed the room. The party mess was in piles, as if the girl who lived here, the dead girl, preferred order over chaos. She liked neatness but acquiesced to the party on what most likely was her boyfriend's behalf. There were books quickly shoved under the coffee table—chemistry, social sciences, modern American history, and the speeches of Martin Luther King. A Yellowstone National Park wall calendar noted in neat, girlish writing the days which she worked two different jobs—the Los Angeles Public Library and Denny's Restaurant—and the times of her classes, dates of midterms and five consecutive skull-and-crossbones that most certainly symbolized her time of the month. There was an American History midterm at ten o'clock the following morning that she would fail.

The front door was wedged open and the ident technicians sauntered in. Hayden noticed the room number on the door—203—in browned-out copper, oxidized by ocean air. He added it to his sketch of the room. His gaze crossed the walls to view inspirational posters—"If you love something set it free" and "Happiness is wanting what you have," with photos of baby eagles launching off the nest and soft footsteps in the sand. Plastic flowers in vases from Target, a magazine holder with copies of *O, The Oprah Magazine* and *Ebony* and *Time*. This was her apartment, she lived here alone. But there was a strong male influence, a boyfriend who stayed often but kept his distance. Hayden saw it in the DVDs piled defiantly on the entertainment center. *Bad Boys I* and *II*, *The Godfather* trilogy, *Dead Presidents*, *Pulp Fiction*, *Boyz in the Hood*, *Alien vs Predator*. Pushed to the side were titles that shared a different voice, a voice of cautious optimism and hope—*Maid in America*, *Akeelah and the Bee*, *The Pursuit of Happyness*. This girl had dreams, a plan, and Hayden felt that if she had lived another five years her AA degree from Santa Monica City College would have matured into a BS from UCLA. She might even have followed in her uncle's footsteps.

Hayden ran through a series of questions in his mind. *Did the dead girl know her killer? Did the killer crash the party or was he invited?* The floor was a mess of bottles—Coors, Michelob, Mickey's big mouth. Someone with a little taste brought a six-pack of Moretti and two bottles were left unopened on the stereo. Hayden suppressed the urge to crack one, return this place to a party instead of a crime scene.

Did the killer spend the night? Were he and the girl involved? And who was the dead guy in the car?

The kitchen window looked out above the carport where Victim Number One, a black male in his twenties, sat hunched in the front passenger seat of a red Toyota Camry, a 9 mm hole in the back of his head. Hayden ran a scenario: The killer is a friend of the two victims. After the party, the three rode in the Camry to a convenience store. Girl's driving, killer in the back, Victim Number One in the front passenger seat. Something happens, an argument, or maybe the killer had it planned all along. Pops the guy, tells the girl to keep driving. Marches her up to the apartment. Maybe it was a love triangle. Maybe something else.

The apartment was loaded with prints from the party, but Hayden doubted the killer's would be found. This guy was careful. The seats and headrests in the Camry had been wiped clean and the 9mm casings removed. He was a cautious killer, but Hayden doubted he was a pro. A pro didn't fool around with rape, and he didn't take the time to stage a scene. This was a man who killed for the joy of it. And he would kill again. It wasn't about the councilman. It was about the look in this girl's eye when the knife went in, and the sound of her last breath exhaled. And if she hadn't been the councilman's niece, the case would've stayed at West L.A.

Det. Lawrence Wallace stood watching Hayden from the hallway. Hands in his pockets, leaning against a wall. This mess was his before the chief handed it to Homicide Special. Larry lifted one hand and made a tip-of-the-hat gesture to Hayden. Hayden gave a quick nod. He didn't feel comfortable taking a case away from Larry. They had known each other since the academy, when the two battled for top honors in the annual Police Action Pistol Shooting Contests. One year the gold medal went to Hayden, the next to Wallace. They shared a friendly competition for years, until Hayden pulled ahead fast, his star rising at a rate that few could match. Things changed after Hayden made Robbery-Homicide. Larry seemed bitter, and the rivalry wasn't friendly anymore.

Hayden measured the apartment with his footsteps, which led him to a little yellow Art Deco table shaped like a sunflower. Their only witness, the apartment manager, leaned belly-to-elbows on its surface with his butt anchored in a high-back wooden chair. He wore a sleeveless T-shirt, Bermuda shorts, and sandals. His eyes studied Hayden's Calvin Klein suit, Jerry Garcia silk tie, and burgundy Prada lace-ups.

Officer Ricky Sung, one of the too-many officers on scene, handed Hayden the old man's driver's license and a cup of Starbucks. "He lives next door. Shares the northwest wall."

"Any reason he's sitting in the middle of my crime scene, Officer Sung?" Hayden asked sharply.

Sung's eyes darted nervously to Wallace.

"He was in the scene when we found him. Detective Wallace didn't want him moved until Downtown arrived." Sung excused himself. Hayden could tell that he didn't want to end up in the middle of a dispute between two strong-willed homicide detectives.

Hayden looked over at Larry, who was easing his way out the front door, playfully slapping the backs of the patrol officers he passed. Larry was a broad-shouldered black man, a bit beefy around the middle, who seemed relaxed and confident among his peers.

There were stories about how Larry acquired the subtle limp in his left leg. Most thought he took an AK-47 round from Phillips or Matasareanu, the two Bank of America robbers who terrorized Van Nuys for fifty long minutes back in '97, firing over eleven hundred rounds of armor-piercing bullets into an unsuspecting crowd. But Hayden knew the truth. He remembered drinking it up with Larry at McGuire's Tavern, a pub they frequented back in the day, when Larry revealed how he got plastered in Pamplona, Spain, during the Running of the Bulls. How he fell into the street and was gored in the ass. It was a story Hayden respectfully kept to himself.

"I didn't see anything, if that's what you're thinking," the old man chirped from behind him.

"Were you at the party last night, Mister . . ." Hayden read the license Officer Sung had given him. "Sullivan?"

"Yeah, right." The old man coughed.

Sullivan folded his arms, stared across the table at a mound of grape jam caked on the kitchen wall. "I got a pass key. Nobody tells me I can't open a door."

Hayden was suddenly aware of a change in the room. He looked up to see a woman surveying the crime scene, directing the efforts of a male assistant carrying a stretcher. The assistant appeared uncomfortable viewing the nakedness of the corpse, seemingly drawn to it and repulsed at the same time. But she was all business and had no patience for his naiveté. When she turned, Hayden saw the large yellow letters that spelled out CORONER on the back of her coveralls.

She was petite, perhaps 5'2", with shoulder-length dark hair pulled back. Her shape was hidden for the job but she was attractive. On a different day, on her day off, she might be wearing a sundress or tennis skirt or miniskirt and tall black leather boots. Hayden could see the form of her breasts beneath the coveralls. They seemed firm and small and he imagined them very white, like powdered sugar.

He pulled himself back into the paperwork, focused on printing Sullivan's name and address on the field interview card. Caucasian male, age seventy-one. No known aliases. Hayden noticed that he had misspelled Sullivan's name twice. He took a breath, exhaled slowly, and corrected his mistakes.

He could sense her sensing him, and when she looked his way he released the thin practiced smile and nod that appeared both professional and inviting. She turned away before he could get a read, distracted by a question from her subordinate, and then she was all business again.

He left Sullivan for the time being and worked his way back to the victim. He pulled a tape measure from his pocket and triangulated the body, setting its measurements between two fixed points in the room.

He felt the excitement as he moved toward the coroner's arena, her workspace. The physical distance between them would now be reduced and their responsibilities would draw them together. If Charlie were the coroner investigator on duty, they'd be joking and making plans for their days off.

"Worked another double homicide about a month ago, just off La Brea and Third," he managed. She was taking her own measurements, maybe didn't know the comment was made to her. "Charlie took care of that one," he said.

She leaned over the body, strapping the lifeless black legs onto the stretcher, which was in its collapsed position and just inches above the floor. The back of her neck was sweating from the work. Her body moved under the coveralls like a Christmas present overwrapped, you could shake it and feel the contents slipping under the wrapping and wonder what surprise waited inside.

She turned abruptly when he touched her back. "I just need to get past you a minute." He excused himself as he stepped closer to the body. She turned back to her work, unsure. Hayden reached into his jacket pocket and produced an evidence collection envelope and a set of tweezers. He knelt beside the body and shoveled a sample of dark soil into the envelope, holding it open for her to see.

"This doesn't look like your typical garden soil, does it?"

She turned away. "I'm not a crime scene technician," she answered. Her voice was soft, deeper than he imagined. He sealed the envelope, used a black Sharpie to write its contents on the label.

"You know you look really hot, don't you?" he whispered, immediately wishing he could take it back. Still, he held his breath for her response.

The question stopped her for a moment as though its meaning, so out of context, might be understood after a little contemplation. He felt her stare on the side of his face as he made his notes. Then she slowly recoiled into herself. She whispered in her associate's ear and he nodded, glancing at Hayden. She left the apartment and her assistant assumed her duties.

Hayden avoided the man's look and returned to the kitchen to continue sketching the apartment.

He couldn't believe he had said that.

He felt his body covered in sweat.

It was starting off to be a long day. A long time before he would feel the burn in his lip from the burger at Tommy's.

He wondered when he would see her again.

2

Hayden pulled up to Parker Center, the impersonal cube of steel and windows that sat a short distance from the Art Deco monument that was City Hall. He wished the LAPD had been headquartered in City Hall, where the lobby and offices held the shape of serious architecture. Instead, Parker Center suffered the misfortune of utilitarian city planning. It had been built as an answer to the decentralized character of the Los Angeles Police Department in the late forties. It solved the problems of its day, but as a structure it wasn't built to last. Ceiling pipes leaked and draperies grew spores from dust and mold. The LAPD was destined to occupy it until the new corporate headquarters would be built in or around the year 2011, although Hayden knew they would never meet their deadline.

Parker Center housed the various sections of the Robbery-Homicide

Division, or RHD: Rape Special, Robbery Special, the Bank Robbery Section, and Homicide Special I and II. Hayden worked in Homicide Special I, which differed from Homicide Special II only in that it occupied a location eight feet to the north and across an aisle. Both I and II provided Los Angeles County with the city's best detectives experienced in closing complicated, often politically sensitive cases. O. J. Simpson, Robert Blake, Haing Ngor, Ennis Cosby—all were investigated by the detectives of RHD's Homicide Special.

Hayden took his seat at a broken metal desk that would have been rejected by most junior high schools, which was probably how it found its way to Parker Center. Except for the camaraderie of other detectives the squad room was a dismal place to work. Hayden would rather have been at a crime scene, any crime scene, than sitting in the discomfort of his desk at Robbery-Homicide.

The room was electric with the news of the murder of the councilman's niece. A dozen detectives worked their phones or milled about in discussion. Lieutenant Garcia was holed up in his office, on a cell phone, pacing, glancing his way. Hayden cracked a full set of knuckles and settled down to work.

He prepared a list of the things he would need for the murder book. Witness statements, crime scene photographs, coroner's report, ballistics, suspect interviews, blood spatter report, hunches, theories, and best guesses. If he didn't close the case in sixty days Garcia would make him write the "60-dayer," a lengthy explanation of why he was too incompetent to catch his suspect. Hayden hated 60-dayers.

He searched his desk for an empty three-ring binder, saw one neatly wedged under the pile of cold case files on his partner's desk. He grabbed it, careful to keep from disturbing the stack. Rich's files were an island of order among a mess of paper clips, pencils, and ancient Post-it Notes. They were like a hobby for Rich, his sport, and his devotion to their care had taken more time away from his family than his wife would ever admit. It began when the mother of a murder victim came to the station looking for answers, ten years after the fact. Rich solved that one. Then an investigator on another cold case sought his advice, and Rich solved that one, too. He would eventually solve twenty, return ten to the abyss of cold storage, and leave five on his desk to torment him. Even now, with his mind struggling to remember the important moments of his life, Rich retained a clear mental image of six-year-old Danny Gallegos's soccer cleats left in the sand on the day of his abduction; or the aluminum shavings found in the bloody footprint next to the body of twenty-two-year-old Charlotte Evans; or the mutilated corpse of forty-year-old Presbyterian minister Tobias Stephens, bent in the middle so his nose touched his toes, left in a Dumpster in Watts.

Hayden wrote the word "evidence" on a divider tab and slipped it into the binder. He placed a call to the LAPD crime lab and the receptionist patched him through to Scooter, the only lab tech worth a damn, in Hayden's opinion.

"Got everything I sent up from West L.A.?" Hayden asked.

"Hairbrush, blood samples, carpet fiber, soil sample. No weapons or shell casings?"

Scooter was a relaxed, unhurried twenty-two-year-old slacker just recently graduated with a degree in chemistry from UC Santa Barbara. The crime lab was a stop on the road to greater things, which to Scooter meant climbing the seven tallest mountains in the world. That's what Hayden liked about him—Scooter answered to no one. He arrived late to work and left early, but no one would fire him because he was meticulous and dependable and he didn't ask for much in return, except the occasional odd object from a crime scene, something expendable, something unimportant, something he could add to his collection and say to his friends, "Look, a half opened roll of Certs taken from Robert Blake's car when they found his wife's body," with a dried spatter of blood to emphasize the point.

"No weapons or casings," Hayden answered. "Match the girl's blood type to the blood on the brush. Check the carpet fibers against the clothes when they come back from the coroner. And let me know about that soil sample."

"It'll cost you," Scooter countered.

"I'll see what I can dig up," Hayden promised before disconnecting the line.

There was movement from across the divide. Det. Dave Thorton and his partner Nick Price had been watching him since he entered. They left their home base at Homicide II and crossed to Hayden's desk where they took up residence. The two detectives were the perfect prime-time casting error. Thorton was black, tall and slender, soft-spoken, filled with insight. He grew up in a family of veterinarians and had spent three years studying veterinary medicine. But his best friend in high school grew up in a family of cops, and the sexy allure of crime-fighting won out over any altruistic feelings Thorton had for the welfare of dogs and cats.

Hayden couldn't stand the annoying way Thorton stood over his desk with his arms folded, nodding his head lightly while repeating, "Uh-huh, hmm, yeah," as though he suspected every comment Hayden made to be an alibi for some unspoken misdemeanor he had committed. Thorton usually knew the way the wind was blowing before the breeze kicked in. His most important observations came as subtext, and the smart investigator knew to listen closely. His partner, Nick, a Napoleonic redneck, was not one of the smart ones.

"Got your suspect, Glass?" Nick roared.

"Sorry?" Hayden feigned deafness.

"The councilman homicide."

"A councilman's been killed?"

"You know what I mean."

Hayden found it shocking that Nick had been partnered with anyone, let alone someone of Thorton's stature. Nick was shaped like a .45-caliber slug and sported a military-style buzz cut. He was abrupt and pompous and he looked directly into the neck of whomever he addressed.

"He meant," Thorton inserted, "is there cause for motive?"

Thorton with the damage control. Their technique was time-tested, but Hayden wasn't one of their suspects to be baited, and he wasn't about to be bullied.

"I just came from the scene, guys. Nothing's set in stone," Hayden said casually as he opened the *Los Angeles Times* and thumbed through the sports section.

Nick's ears turned red and his head vibrated like a just-struck tuning fork. Thorton placed his hand on Nick's shoulder to placate him while Hayden checked the NCAA ratings.

"You know the word on the street," Thorton said calmly. "He had a lot of enemies, Councilman Jackson."

Hayden waited.

"We're giving you a lead, here," Nick spat, jingling keys in his pocket obsessively.

"It's my case, fellas," Hayden said, resting his feet on his desktop. "No poaching."

"Just helping a brother out," Thorton quipped, while steam rose off the ends of Nick's spiked hair.

"Twenty-Second Street, right?" Hayden speculated, not looking up from his paper. Twenty-Second was the toughest street gang in the councilman's district. They were the ones with the most to lose if the councilman's proposed Anti-Gang Initiative passed City Council.

"We got a snitch," Thorton teased. "Says the soldiers think the C's lost his nerve."

The "C" was Carlos Navidad, the Twenty-Second Street boss. He was only twenty years old but just as ruthless as any OG. He was a thinker, though, and not prone to losing his head.

Hayden finally lowered the newspaper, folded it twice, and tossed it onto his desk. "You're saying, what, a power struggle? Someone hit the niece to push Carlos's hand?" he asked.

"Hey, you're the golden boy. We just got what we got," retorted Nick, dropping a folded notepaper with the phone number of their snitch onto Hayden's desk.

"Glass!"

They looked up to see Lieutenant Garcia waving Hayden into his office. Hayden picked up the lead and left his desk.

The lieutenant was just getting off a call when Hayden took his seat.

"Shit, Hayden, that was the mayor's office. They want a press conference on this councilman thing."

The lieutenant was wiry and nervous and, at thirty-two years of age, too young to be managing the top detective table in the city. Hayden didn't think he'd done enough street time to gain the respect of the twenty- and thirty-year vets. But Garcia followed procedure and jumped when the captain called, and that seemed to be enough.

"The city's calling you direct on this?" Hayden asked, incredulous. A call from City Hall should go to the captain first and trickle down to the lieutenant. He was hoping the mayor's office didn't have *his* cell phone number. "It's premature."

"Forsythe wants a written assessment tomorrow morning," Garcia said anxiously. He raised a shaky hand to his forehead.

So this is how it goes, Hayden thought. He had worked some of the most brutal homicides in the city yet none had involved a politician or movie star. And Captain Forsythe had never asked him to write a report before the facts were in.

"I'll give him what I can."

"You check out that lead from Thorton and Price?" the lieutenant asked.

Hayden glanced at the paper still folded in the palm of his hand. This was beginning to feel like the first month into a new relationship when she said, "Wouldn't you feel more comfortable in the *blue* shirt?"

Then, without giving him time to respond, "What does your gut tell you, Glass?"

Finally, Hayden thought. It was usually the first question they asked. Hayden had always been given free rein to do as he pleased. He wasn't used to the second-guessing. Maybe it was the pressure of politics, maybe it was the fact that Rich wasn't at his side. Rich the mentor. Rich the buffer. Together he and Rich were like a team of ten. Was Hayden alone perceived as less than enough?

"I'll bring my thoughts to the captain in the morning," Hayden said, turning to leave.

He didn't want to tell the lieutenant that the crime had nothing to do with the councilman. Still, there was nothing he could point at to support his conviction. It was his gut talking, which the lieutenant had asked for but didn't really want to hear. What Garcia wanted was for Hayden to parrot his theory that the young college student was murdered in retaliation for the actions of her uncle. Hayden hadn't risen to the rank of Detective D3 by rearranging the facts of a case to satisfy politicians, and he wasn't about to start now.

He unfolded the notepaper as he returned to his desk. Might as well start by eliminating their lead. Before he could pick up the phone he heard the lieutenant's voice from the office door.

"Glass, got a call-out!"

Hayden looked at the call-out board. His name was chalked in at the top.

"Coral Reef Motel in Hollywood, on Western, just south of—"

"I know it!" Hayden called back as he dashed from the squad room.

3

The Coral Reef Motel was one of ten or so dilapidated, Holly-wood sex motels that rented rooms by the hour. It was located in a particularly decrepit part of town where hookers and drug dealers still ruled the night. The area had not been through the gentrification that characterized the more popular tourist traps of Hollywood Boulevard, where the Chinese Theater sat in its glory opposite the Disney-renovated El Capitan. There was simply no reason to visit the Coral Reef except to engage in some sort of illicit behavior or to arrest someone who was en-gaged in some sort of illicit behavior.

Hayden recognized the motel immediately. He had been there twice and not once on official police business. The two-story motel sat like a dirty old heroin addict nodding slowly, as if recognizing Hayden from a hazy night they'd shared long ago. The second-story windows had yellowing shades pulled half-mast like drugged-out eyes squinting at the streetlamps. He remembered the set of concrete stairs he had climbed once, years ago, trailing behind the eighteen-year-old prostitute he'd seen hanging around the parking lot, pretending to be waiting on a friend. She had looked innocent enough and whatever story she told kept the heat from pulling her off the street. But any john passing could've seen she was gold, and most would risk being sighted by Vice if they thought they had a shot at her. Once marked by Vice, a john should disappear for the night or move to a different cruising area in another part of town. Or better yet, hit that strip club or massage parlor on the way home. Like superheroes they thought they could pick up a pro right under a vice cop's nose. They phased out of the real world and channeled into the numb vibe of cruising.

Hayden parked his car, got out, and ducked under the yellow crime scene tape. A patrol officer caught his sleeve. Hayden flashed his badge.

"This way, Detective."

The hotel room was dark even with all the lights on. It was humid with the smell of recent death. Cops sullenly viewed the body of a once attractive twenty-year-old blonde whose hair was now a deep dark red with the blood from her wounds, and what looked like pink gelatin peeking through concave divots in her skull—caused no doubt by the discarded tire iron left at the scene. She was naked, her body twisted by angry hands. All ten toes clipped off clean.

Charlie was there, leaning against an oily wall. His rust-colored hair was damp, and he ran his fingers through it for the umpteenth time. He was always running his fingers through his hair, and Hayden suspected that it was a self-conscious attempt to brush away the ubiquitous smell of death that clung to his scalp.

He didn't acknowledge Hayden, his eyes apparently fixed on a blank television screen across the room. Hayden followed his gaze, saw what held him so rapt. Two clear plastic cups filled with ten little toes.

Hayden pulled his notepad to sketch the room. Sketch the body. The sharp angles of her face. Her form tugged and twisted. He wished he had charcoals to capture the anguish of the image. Like the drawings done by prisoners at Dachau and Auschwitz. He finished, acknowledged the rendering. Her figure seemed to reach off the page.

He took a breath and plugged into the channel that blew through his soul. He turned a slow silent circle, absorbing the room. As a kid he could disappear into a room, become the room itself and also a device set to record the room, capturing the sight, scent, and tone of things around him.

It was an escape, this trick of disappearing into things outside himself. His therapist—the woman he had agreed to see in an effort to save his marriage—told him that his parents had been vacant, nonentities in his life. He had been forced to reach outside the family for connection— a connection to things not there. Or to things not seen, as Hayden would describe it. Maybe it was nothing, really, but the act of sitting quietly still for hours at a time.

He felt the colors of the room pulsating. Red, yellow, pale green, deep dark lavender, blue-black bruises punctuating the shadows. He saw images of rose shears clipping the beady toes from their stems and knew them definitively to be rose shears before forensics could confirm it. He knew the toes were clipped post-mortem; the tire iron was purchased new for the killing; the killer had never been to this hotel before. These were all things Hayden could pick up in the first glance. The thin layer of oil that glistened on the tire iron was factory applied and would have disappeared after nominal use. The toe-ends had been scissor cut with a large, dull blade, leaving sharp, jagged bones. The lack of blood at her feet meant that her heart had stopped pumping before the killer started cutting. And a half dozen bloody footprints led to the bathroom door, where the killer sought his escape before remembering that the exit was behind him. From these observations Hayden guessed that the killer didn't know his victim. It looked like the guy wanted to make a kill and the girl on the floor fit a certain criteria in his head.

As he circled he felt a vague sense of familiarity with the crime scene. He wondered if it was the relationship of the body to the sofa that drew some comparison. Or the shape of the room, or the positioning of the furniture.

He passed and nearly toppled Charlie. Hayden couldn't help but regret seeing him. He had convinced himself that he would see the other coroner again, the girl from the West L.A. double homicide. He couldn't let it go, and he blamed Charlie for having taken her place.

"Missed you this morning. Thought you'd gone comatose," Hayden half-joked.

"And you give a shit? Did you even try the hospital?"

Charlie busting his balls.

He was a brittle diabetic and occasionally neglected the strict insulin schedule he was required to keep. More than once Hayden had to restrain Charlie in the middle of a sports bar, forcing sugar packets through Charlie's clenched teeth.

The two met as freshmen in college. In those days Charlie was thin with bright red hair and white freckled skin. He was an Alabama transplant and still held the hint of that slow Southern accent, though he had long since dropped the gentlemanly "sir" and "ma'am" from his conversations. He had been a real joker back in school. Hayden remembered the Halloween Ball hosted by the regents of the university, where Charlie arrived dressed in a giant papier mâché penis he'd been secretly constructing to honor the event. In those days Charlie was nimble and spry, like some trickster god in Native American mythology. But his years with the dead made him morose, and it showed in his weight and the diabetes and the fact that he was alone, he had no mate, and that, perhaps, was the worst of it.

Hayden placed a hand on his friend's shoulder. Charlie stiffened momentarily, then relaxed as he exhaled.

"They dust for prints?" Hayden asked gently.

"Yeah."

"ID guys take their pics?"

"Uh-huh."

Hayden surveyed the crime scene. "Everyone's just waiting on you, then."

Charlie nodded, peeled himself slowly from the wall. He retrieved his equipment and stretcher from the doorway and went to the body.

Hayden watched the door sway from the release of Charlie's stretcher. He sketched the door in proportion to the rest of the room then noticed something on the page that stopped him short. For some reason he had drawn the room number in thick, bold lettering. Exaggerated. He looked at the door in front of him—the letters were a thin Helvetica. Room 203.

He shuffled through the pages of his notebook, found the sketches he made from the West L.A. murders. The apartment number on the door, drawn in proportion to the rest of the room. It was hard to make out, but there it was. Room 203.

4

Hayden sat stuffed in a hard wooden chair opposite the desk where Capt. Jimmy Forsythe read the police reports. Hayden held a white mug sporting a DEA logo filled three-quarters with burnt black coffee in one hand, and in the other a Krispy Kreme chocolate glazed doughnut planted on him by Reggie, the captain's Number Two, who weighed in at 314 pounds and was happy to share the load. The pastry held the imprint of Hayden's grip.

He chewed his bottom lip while he waited. His eyes scanned the museum of Captain Forsythe's life laid out in framed photographs and newspaper clippings on the office walls. The captain was an exhibition parachutist. The photograph to the right above his desk showed him and two partners in a three-man teardrop formation with red, blue, and yellow canopies opened above their heads. The wall to Hayden's left featured a half dozen photographs of Forsythe with his diving team over familiar sites like Dodger Stadium, Fenway Park, and the Eiffel Tower.

This was what Forsythe did on his time off, to *relax*, he told Hayden once. The captain was the closest thing Hayden had ever come to seeing a superhero in person. At fifty, Forsythe was tan with pure white hair and a body of solid muscle. He reminded Hayden of Doc Savage, a character his father used to read to him from old paperback novels when he was a kid. Forsythe had many of the same attributes as Savage—he was wise, tough, honest, and capable of detecting all forms of bullshit. With Hayden in the room, Forsythe's bullshit meter was on high alert.

After what seemed like hours, the captain dropped the reports on his desk and gave Hayden a penetrating look. Hayden shifted uncomfortably.

"It's a coincidence," Forsythe announced, and immediately turned his attention to what looked like a personal calendar or address book. Hayden cleared his throat. "I don't think so, sir," he countered.

The captain smirked in a way that reminded Hayden of his ex-wife; it was the look she gave him when she thought he believed his own crap. Hayden knew the captain would never view a crime scene the way he did. In the West L.A. apartment and the Coral Reef Motel, Hayden breathed the air the killer exhaled. There was a scent of sameness in the two. He looked beneath the surface of observable events, in a way the captain could never conceive.

"Where's the councilman connection?" Forsythe prodded.

"It's not about the councilman."

The captain sighed, folded his hands on his desk. He stared again into Hayden's eyes. Hayden tasted blood on his tongue, felt the pain in his lip from where his teeth went in.

"You gotta give me something here. Media Relation's holding back the press, but they want to know we're close. They want details."

"We're not close. We don't have any details."

"Hayden, I told them that we put our best man on it, but they want *every* man on it."

Hayden wondered if the captain was trying to get him to give up the West L.A. case. But Hayden wasn't about to let Thorton and Price parade a bunch of gangbangers in front the cameras just to satisfy City Hall.

"You taking me off the case, Captain?"

"I need you to focus on West L.A. Drop the other one if you have to. Jackson's had his gang initiative in committee for months, it's about to go to the Council. We've had intel that the Twenty-Second Street Gang had something to say, well, now they've said it. Any investigator worth his salt would've had Carlos and his compadres in here for questioning before the mayor's office could even *think* to dig up Lieutenant Garcia's cell phone number. It's embarrassing that we haven't produced a single suspect from the dozens of leads we've got. Don't complicate an uncomplicated case."

The case did appear simple. Motive was already established. The timing of the event met everyone's expectations. A first-year detective could connect the dots. The problem was that it was too simple.

Hayden's silence validated the captain's concern.

"You should be contacting the councilman personally," he continued. "His associates, political opponents, anyone who has an axe to grind. You thought about a partner yet?"

The captain leaned back in his chair. It tilted with his weight and he looked for a moment like a big, burly ten-year-old in a carnival ride, about to be lifted high into the air and then dropped like a lead ball to a surprisingly safe landing on the ground.

"Rich will be at his desk in a month," Hayden assured him, although his voice cracked when he said it.

Forsythe raised an eyebrow.

"Christ, Hayden. Who told you that? Rich? His wife? I'd show you his department medical file if the ACLU wouldn't crawl over my ass about it. He's plateaued, is what it says. Confirmed by two different specialists."

This was news to Hayden. It was Rich's family doctor he had talked with, two months earlier. At that time he had predicted three months to a full recovery. Hayden had held to the time frame despite the fact that

Rich didn't seem to be improving at all. Maybe that was why Hayden hadn't managed the nerve to visit Rich in the past month and a half.

"The guys at City Hall don't want to hear 'no suspects,' they don't want to hear that the best we got is a matching room number," Forsythe continued. "I got the name of a guy out of Hollywood, your old stomping ground. A detective two years, looking to advance. Blaire Eddington—"

Hayden squirmed in his seat. "Eddington's sloppy, Captain. Shoddy police work when he was on patrol, he's worse as an investigator. Leans on his lieutenant—they're buddies, the lieutenant covers his back."

"You need a partner, Hayden."

"I need a profiler."

This stopped the captain in his tracks. Rich had always been there to buffer these confrontations and without him around it got a little tense at the station. But the captain had continued to let Hayden run his investigations without interference and Hayden continued to bring in the collars and close the cases. It seemed to Hayden that things would be different this time around.

"Getting enough sleep, Hayden?"

"Just during my shift."

The captain smiled. Hayden figured he'd won a point for wit.

"All right, then," Forsythe relented. "You've got a room number. M.O. is from another planet. If you separate the West L.A. scene from the councilman you've got a dead guy in the car and a dead girl, raped, upstairs. Looks like a love triangle gone wrong. This Coral Reef guy's M.O. is completely different. He's a psycho or a fetish creep. You'll find him in the sex offender database. Other than the fact that two of the victims are female, there's not a single similarity between the two."

"There's the room number."

Stalemate. Hayden felt in his gut the connection. *Room 203.* If Hayden focused on the forensic evidence he would have to treat the two cases separately. But his feelings told him there was something more. The image of the room number on the door appeared wherever he looked. On the ATM pad at the Bank of America. In the bar code on the box of Wheaties in his kitchen. In the keypad on the captain's desk phone.

The captain seemed to study him for a long time. Forsythe reached for his phone and just when it seemed he would dial "2-0-3," he punched "2-5" and Officer Reggie Langston answered with a curt, "Yup?"

"Reggie, bring in that thing we talked about."

Hayden's coffee, cold now, tasted bitter from the slow, long burn of precinct neglect and his doughnut was a mush of sticky bread between his fingers. He relaxed in his seat while the captain dispensed with other business. He forgot the pastry and it dropped from his hand. He dove quickly to retrieve it too late, spilling coffee on a floor recarpeted months earlier to address the stains of coffee decades past. The captain leaned back instinctively as Hayden lunged forward to pluck the two remaining Kleenex tissues from the box on his desk. The tissues dissolved uselessly in a pool of brown liquid side-stepped by Reggie, who continued on his way to the captain's desk to drop a manila file.

"Just . . . leave it, on the floor, Hayden. Reggie'll take care of it."

Reggie acknowledged the comment with a grunt as he closed the office door.

"You know Abbey Reed?" Forsythe continued, flipping through the file.

The name didn't ring a bell.

"Investigator with the L.A. Coroner's Office," the captain prodded.

Hayden winced.

"We've got a complaint. Just a verbal, but we have to write it up. Said you made comments inappropriate for an officer of the law."

"Yeah, I think it was the crime scene that spooked her. She seemed new to the game, probably her first double homicide," Hayden said, attempting a save.

"She's been twelve years with the coroner."

Hayden shifted in his seat. Tapped the tip of his shoe against the soggy mound of Kleenex on the ground.

"Didn't we get a similar complaint," the captain continued, "I don't know, a year ago, maybe? I remember there was a gal at the DA's office."

Hayden went numb. He didn't want the department looking over his shoulder. Not for *this*.

"Do I have to worry about you, Detective?"

"Jesus, Captain, I think I smiled, she got the wrong idea. You can't fucking smile at a girl these days, all the harassment suits . . ." His voice trailed off. He tried to think of something he could add to his defense.

The captain nodded, closing the file and dropping it somewhere out of sight on his desk. "Just be careful, that's not the kind of publicity we're looking for. How're you doing, anyway? Got that alimony situated?"

Hayden couldn't think to respond. The guys at RHD assumed his marriage collapsed from its own weight, as most department marriages did. Only two of his professional associates knew the truth. It probably came from a good place, his captain's concerns, but it felt like an assault. A year and a half since Nicky left. The alimony was settled a long time ago.

A moment passed while the captain waited for a response. Hayden's eyes drifted back to the wall of photographs. Forsythe followed his gaze.

"You ought to join me sometime," he said, his mood more relaxed. "Thirty-five bucks, I'll take you on your first jump out at Elsinor. Tethered, y'know, not much can go wrong. Well, I did know a girl once, on a tethered jump, fell from three thousand feet and her canopy tangled up. She should've cut away . . ."

Forsythe seemed lost for a moment. He wasn't in the room. Then he snapped back, turned to Hayden.

"It had nothing to do with experience. She'd done about a hundred-eighty drops . . . but all it takes is one. She should've had a partner."

Hayden sat with that for a moment, his eyes on his shoes.

"All right. I got to be someplace, ten minutes," Forsythe announced, packing files from his desk into a sleek, leather briefcase. "Do what needs to be done on the councilman case. Work with your lieutenant, update him every few hours until the heat burns off. And you'll have to live without a profiler; I can't justify the expense."

It was what Hayden expected. Others would have to die before a connection was made. He was tired and ready now for sleep, and the thought carried him out of Robbery-Homicide and Parker Center and into his Jeep, where he passed out for twenty minutes before the luncheonette on wheels blasted its call to arms and turned the parking lot into an Arab bazaar. Food seemed like a good idea, but it burned when the hot sauce in his burrito seeped into the tender white folds of the newly formed canker sore in his lip. And yet he'd rather feel pain than nothing, and the thought reminded him that he hadn't been to a meeting in a very long time.

5

"hank you. It wasn't easy. This time around."

The Serenity Prayer stood in raised letters off the little plastic chip in his hand. *God, please give me the serenity to accept the things I cannot change, the courage to change the things I can, and the wisdom to know the difference.*

"It's my third ninety-day chip in the past year and a half."

Sixteen men in the room, five of them sitting in tiny blue plastic kindergarten chairs. The Monday night meeting in Venice at the Unity Presbyterian Church. Hayden was anxious. There was no instant detox button he could press to relieve the stress of witnessing violent death. The meetings offered his only route to serenity.

The room itself was cheerful and childlike. A corkboard displayed drawings in colorful crayon of Noah's Ark, the Three Kings, Baby Jesus in the manger, Jesus ascending to heaven. A little terrarium in the corner housed what at first Hayden thought was a collection of dirty brown sticks—a strange thing to see out of the corner of his eye every week, but it seemed to make sense. Sticks as pets didn't die or sneak out of the tank and they required no maintenance or love. The perfect relationship. Sticks as plants required no watering or sunlight. It seemed clear to Hayden that the children who visited this room during the day were learning valuable lessons about how to avoid the responsibilities of a committed relationship.

It was only after spending one night a week for three months in this room that Hayden noticed the sticks were moving, and that they were in fact stick *bugs*, which he thought existed only as fiction in some volume of mythology he had studied back in college. So the sticks did in fact live and were capable of being loved and required attention and maintenance, and the church kids who spent the day with them were probably not addicts. They were young, though, and their time would come.

If it weren't for churches there would be no place for meetings like this. And because the meetings were held in churches, Hayden initially thought it was about religion. He thought God or Jesus Christ would be forced down his throat. But he discovered that it had nothing to do with a particular religion or a particular god. Addicts talked about *Higher Power*. Higher Power could be God or Jesus Christ or Buddha or Allah or Krishna or all or none of these. The problem with Hayden and all the addicts he came to meet was that their addiction wanted to *be* their Higher Power. God took a backseat to crack cocaine. To alcohol. To gambling. To sex. The program demanded that first an addict admit he had been unsuccessful in stopping his addiction—that he was powerless to control it. Then he humbly accepted that only God, or a true Higher Power, could change him.

Hayden was later shocked to learn that there were atheists in the program. To them, the Higher Power was simply a power "greater than ourselves," meaning the addict and *anyone else who would listen*. To the atheist or agnostic, the Higher Power equaled the addict plus someone else. The someone else made him accountable. The someone else listened to his story, to his secret world, and told him if his behavior was sane or not. That's what a sponsor did, helped the addict dance through the famous Twelve Steps toward a life of peace and serenity in a world without the consequences of addiction. In the meetings the group was the Higher Power. The group strived for sobriety and abstinence and the individual couldn't help but follow. And each day was a new day for the addict. Each day that the addict didn't act out was a new day of sobriety. And thus, *one day at a time . . .*

The room was unnaturally quiet. Maybe they were surprised that Hayden had made it this far. He was usually the guy striving for thirty days, the guy who couldn't tackle his own moral inventory to begin work on the Fourth Step.

Hayden held the little plastic chip up to the light, recited the Serenity Prayer silently to himself once again. "It feels good to hold this," he said finally. "To be able to put it in my pocket, take it home with me tonight. Now I can obsess on getting my six-month chip."

There was a laugh or two from the group, although most were serious. Sobriety was a serious thing, he knew. Ninety days was a hard time coming. They said it was the first year that tested you. After that it got easier, so long as you kept up the program, kept going to meetings. *Progress not perfection . . .*

"I wish I could say I've been the perfect addict in recovery," Hayden said, feeling self-conscious now. A bug under a microscope. "That I've been doing the steps every day, or reading, or journaling. Or praying. Praying's tough, it doesn't feel natural to me. The job makes it tough . . . I see women on the street and I just white-knuckle it, take a deep breath, try to stay on track. I've had some slips. But, God willing and with the help of the program, those days are over. My inner circle is picking up prostitutes, going to massage parlors, strip clubs, sex outside of a committed relationship, one-night stands. My middle circle is cruising, looking at pornography, flirting in Internet chat rooms, hanging out at bars and nightclubs in Hollywood, hanging around malls and cafés looking for that connection, that look in some girl's eyes that says come on, let's go. My position on the force . . . it isn't good for my middle circle. Covering my beat, working Sunset Boulevard, looks a lot like cruising."

Hayden looked up at the ceiling for a moment, aware of the impact of the things he said.

"Sorry," he continued, "I didn't mean to mention street names."

A cardinal rule. The last thing you wanted to do at a meeting was give an addict instructions on how or where to act out. It was no big secret there was a lot of action on Sunset Boulevard. But you didn't want to give the newcomer any ideas he hadn't already considered. And you were careful how you described the things that turned you on. Didn't get explicit about your fantasies or about the details of your sexual encounters. The things you said and how you said them could trigger another member and start his own obsessive spiral into fantasy, and that could lead to acting out. If you described the perfect encounter with the perfect prostitute, you'd find yourself reliving the excitement of the moment and reactivating the addict inside you. When this happened, any member of the meeting could simply raise his hand and it was understood that your words had been a trigger. The group watched out for its members.

Hayden exhaled deep, moist. "I'm tired of this fucking thing. I want to be normal. I guess I've never been normal, right? I mean, that's what defines us. It's hard for me to think that I've got to live with this the rest of my life. And, since my divorce, it's hard to tell anymore what constitutes acting out. If I meet someone and sleep with her that night, what, I have to start my time again? My sponsor says yes. I have a hard time with that one. And I don't want to come to these meetings, but I know I feel better afterwards. Always. If anything's got me through this past ninety days it's you guys. Your stories, the wisdom that comes from this room. Seeing you struggle with me, watching you get your six-month, nine-month, year chips. Does it get easier? Will there come a day when I can feel pain and rely on some inner strength or Higher Power, instead of the girl out there somewhere, on the street or in the bar? When will this Higher Power thing kick in?"

The timer beeped, letting Hayden know that he had sixty seconds left to speak.

"Well, I know you want to know how I did it. I don't know. I wish I had something to contribute, something to help others who are struggling. Maybe something clicked, finally, and this is the first ninety days of the rest of my life. It wasn't anything conscious, although I've been told that it should be. It should be conscious. I'm just going to keep riding it. It feels good these days. *I* feel good. Thanks for letting me share."

Momentary, fervent applause, which followed anyone with the courage to share. Hayden leaned back, relieved that his share was over and embarrassed that he didn't have more to give. He kicked himself for not planning ahead. The ninety days' share wasn't supposed to be about him, it was supposed to be about *him* helping *others* find their own paths to lasting sobriety. Hayden wondered if he would ever be more than a selfish prick.

David, who was leading the meeting that night, spoke next. "Congratulations, Hayden. Is there anyone here with six months sobriety? Nine months? Do we have any birthdays tonight? Any multiples of a year? Okay, whoever wants to share will have two minutes on the clock, then after the timer you'll have another minute. Who would like to start?"

Carl raised his hand. Carl was forty-four, with a runner's physique and a face weighed with worry. "Carl, recovering sex addict."

"Hello, Carl," responded the room.

"I don't know about everyone else, but I just can't go on with the meeting like nothing happened here. I don't feel safe in the room."

The men shifted in their chairs. Eyes darted over to Hayden. Hayden felt the room's chemistry change in an instant. A strange tingling began in his feet, rising with painful subtlety.

David tried to refocus the meeting. "Carl, there will be no cross talk here. If you wish to share you have three minutes."

No cross talk meant that you didn't address another member directly, you didn't confront him or ask him to explain himself or challenge him. No cross talk meant that, for a handful of minutes, each member was free to speak without interruption. It meant that what they had to say was important and would not be judged. It sent the message that this was a place to let their secrets into the light of day, because a secret kept was a dark and dangerous thing. Secrets begot secrets begot shameful actions begot a downward spiral into isolation and compulsive, destructive behavior. Hayden knew self-destruction. He knew it in some H.U.D. home in South Central copping a blow job from a hooker while her eight-month-old watched through the bars of his crib, little wet cheeks and sad eyes. Hayden knew shame.

"Come on," Carl continued. "There's a fucking elephant in this room. We discussed this, I thought someone was supposed to talk to him."

Hayden felt the tingling in his arms.

"What's going on?" Hayden quietly asked of no one in particular. His voice shaking. David studied his own sandals. Hayden searched their faces. Most avoided his eyes. Hayden had never felt in any setting, social or business, the kind of warmth, acceptance, and safety that he had felt in this room. Before he'd been identified as a sex addict he didn't even know it was possible to have this kind of intimacy with another human being. Intimacy began with one thing—safety. If a person felt safe to tell the honest truth, he would tell the honest truth. There was nothing to lose and everything to gain. But the normal, day-to-day world didn't allow it. You couldn't tell your boss that you'd been picking up prostitutes between business calls and expect him to nod and pat you on the back and say, "Progress, not perfection." At the very least he'd draw his wife closer the next time he joined you for dinner. People judged people, and when a person had it in his power to do so, someone might choose to fuck you over as a consequence of your honesty. There were precious few places where Hayden felt safe with his honesty, where he grew more intimate with others by the release of his secrets.

So the fact that someone didn't feel safe in this meeting meant a great deal to the group. The fact that more than one member had the same concern, and that the feeling was strong enough to discuss it in public, was downright grave.

"Hayden, we had a business meeting a few weeks ago, after our regular meeting," David soft-shoed. "Some of the members have very strong feelings about what you do for a living. Many of us . . . don't feel safe in the room anymore. I can think of five guys who left in the past year, since you came."

The tingling had reached Hayden's head. He recognized the feeling now as anger. The meetings weren't supposed to be like this. He couldn't believe this was David talking. David, the old sage of the group, who had just celebrated his eighth year of sobriety over a particularly cruel obsession with forcing sharp objects into his anus. His acting out resulted in a half dozen trips to the emergency room, and he'd been pronounced dead twice. David said nothing out of turn. He stuck to the rules and he stuck to the program because he knew it worked. The program kept addicts off the street, kept David out of the ER. David was a prime example of how the program could improve lives, keep families together, create happier homes and healthier children.

Hayden also knew what had started this. A month earlier he was asked to supervise a Trick Task Force in Hollywood. He had spent an afternoon training the team on tactics, and on a Tuesday night at the corner of Hollywood and Wilcox he stood outside Rico's Tacos and watched as two policewomen dressed as prostitutes lured johns into conversation. If the john said the magic words, if he discussed money in exchange for sexual services, the decoys would step away from his car and signal the undercover vehicles nearby. Hayden stepped in after every bust to critique the way it went down. Carl was one of the johns picked up that night. When Hayden saw that they'd netted one of his "brothers," he arranged to have Carl released with a warning, and no one was the wiser.

Hayden stared Carl down. "Is this about what happened that night, Carl? 'Cause if it is you've got a hell of a way of showing appreciation."

David cleared his throat. "Carl discussed the incident at a meeting, Hayden. We haven't seen you in a month."

Hayden kept his eyes on Carl. "If I hadn't intervened that night he wouldn't have been at the meeting. He would've been in jail. I know you haven't disclosed to your wife about your addiction, Carl. I know if you had gone to jail you would've come unglued."

"Maybe you know too much, then," Carl shot back, too nervous to hold Hayden's stare.

"What do you mean by that?"

"Maybe you set me up to get caught that night."

"Maybe you shouldn't have been out there picking up hookers. Maybe you should've been at a meeting or on the phone with your sponsor—"

Steve, twenty years old, clean-cut, lanky and anxious, raised his hand. "Steve, sex addict."

"Hi, Steve," responded the room.

"How do we know he's really an addict? He never makes any calls, he doesn't attend Fellowship, he's never had a service position in the meeting, he just kind of comes and goes—"

Hayden's face was turning red, his scalp was burning hot. He was doing his best to stay centered, focused.

Another brother jumped into the fray. "Tim, recovering sex addict."

"Hello, Tim."

"There's no requirements here. No one is forced to take a service position or make calls or have a sponsor. The room is here so that Hayden has a safe place to go—"

"Don't *I* deserve a safe place?" Carl asked.

"What's not safe about this room?" Hayden shouted suddenly. His hand was forming a fist around the chip he had earned moments before.

"You were a fucking *vice* cop!" Carl exclaimed.

"This is an open meeting for sharing only," David interjected. "If you want to propose a business meeting to discuss this—"

"This is how you know I'm a fucking addict!" Hayden announced, holding his ninety-day chip in a shaking hand for everyone to see. There was rage in his voice. "And fuck the business meeting. Whatever needs to be said can be said here and now."

Carl, who Hayden had guessed spent hours before the meeting cruising Sepulveda Boulevard, and hours before that thumbing through pornography at the local arcade, slipping tokens into the mechanized video screening room, where cum from his ejaculation mixed with the cum already on the floor and on the bench where he sat . . . Carl was up to the challenge.

"We feel you should find a different meeting," Carl said.

Hayden felt himself floating away. It had taken almost a year to trust the group, to know that what was said in the room really was confidential and that word of his addiction wouldn't somehow leak back to the precinct or to his captain. It was the first time in his life Hayden had started to feel comfortable in his own skin, had felt accepted for who he was. Or so he thought.

"*I* was at this meeting before *you*, Carl," Hayden seethed.

"I'm not alone here." Carl looked around the room. "We had a meeting, Hayden. Guys who have been here longer than both of us."

Hayden stared at the ceiling. Green and red streamers were looped in sections, Christmas décor long forgotten with the advent of warm weather and the onrush of new holidays. Attached by a string to a streamer was a piece of white construction paper with a Crayola drawing of the baby Jesus in the manger, the cows huddled offering whatever warmth they could give.

"This is my *home* meeting," Hayden whispered under his breath.

David cleared his throat, speaking softly. "It's not something I ever thought I'd have to consider, Hayden. The only people I've asked to leave were sexual predators, people who were using the meeting to try and hook up. There's plenty of other meetings, I'll get you a schedule. It's probably a better idea, for you, not to reveal your profession to the next group. I don't feel comfortable with this, because I know you're a brother in need. If there's another way, a way we haven't considered—"

Hayden shot out of his seat.

"Don't soil yourself, David. I can handle my own shit." He pulled a wrinkled five-spot from his pocket, handed it to Ben, the treasurer. "I never skimp on the Seventh Tradition, like half you guys. I support what keeps me sane."

There was a dull vacuum in the room as he left. No one spoke for a full minute before the shrill beeping of the timer cut through the air.

"Does anyone know his sponsor?" David asked.

"I think Sol, from Tuesday nights," someone suggested.

"Would you give him a call, Ben?"

6

Hayden made it to La Brea and Santa Monica Boulevard when his cell phone rang for the third time. He looked down to see his sponsor's number on the display. He hit the "ignore" button again, then shut the phone off. He took a right onto Santa Monica Boulevard without thinking, then cursed himself. There were already transvestites on the street waving him down and he wanted to get to Highland and drive north to avoid them. Santa Monica Boulevard was fag territory, and no matter how damn convincing one of those girls might appear, they were guys and they were always going to be guys. It made Hayden's skin crawl, the thought of it. His feelings were fueled in part by the fact that he had once picked up a girl, received a hand job, and dropped her off before he realized that the girl was a guy. He'd tucked that experience far back in the deep shameful part of his compartmentalized mind. *It didn't happen to me,* he thought.

He relaxed when he reached Highland and made his turn. The street corner trannies disappeared in the distance, replaced by warm, empty shadows in the night leading north to Fountain Avenue and then up, towards Sunset Boulevard. Sunset was the motherland of Hayden's addict. When his addiction would wrest control of his life, that was where it took him.

Sunset Boulevard, Hollywood Boulevard, Santa Monica Boulevard, Sepulveda Boulevard, Lincoln Boulevard, Long Beach Boulevard. Streets that knifed through entire cities. Streets like dirty brown rivers with soft, inviting quicksand banks. A step in the water left dark oily residue like liquid tobacco that came off slow, leaving hives in its wake. The current unforgiving and relentless in its crusade to sink a man.

The sounds outside his window hummed a familiar lullaby. The street stroked his head, coddled him, and whispered damp nothings in his ear. *Sunset Boulevard.* It stank of urine and sweat and old, dusty hotel rooms that rented by the hour. For a brief second he considered a sharp turn to the right on La Brea to bring him back to the 101, out of harm's way. He could call his sponsor, spend an hour talking about the things that were bringing him to this low, the things that were taking him close to the edge. In the morning he could celebrate his ninety-first day of sobriety, grateful to God that he hadn't acted out the night before.

But a glint of blond hair in the shadows, in the dark of the night, emerged. He found himself at curbside, parked, the engine purring, the passenger side window down. Her hand extended, reaching for the door, Smiling as she sat down. "You're not a cop, are you?"

He did not know where he was when he awoke. His head throbbed. The thump of his heart pushed the pulse in his wrist, pushed the pulsating drum beneath the numbness in his skull. There were voices nearby mumbling, bitching. A man, cursing out a woman. He felt a tug at his pants, which seemed to be pulled down to his ankles. Someone had put a soft, warm, wet washcloth on his forehead. The floor was a tight, knotted Berber carpet and it felt hard and coarse against his naked ass. He reached down, struggling to pull up his pants. The carpet felt like the grime of a thousand years and a thousand tricks and it would never be clean even if it were ripped up and torn out and replaced. The ooze and slime would creep up from the floorboards and again contaminate the carpet, walls, bedding, towels. A male voice behind him, "Sixty bucks is all this jack's got?"

"He gave me fifty," a woman said calmly, and she took a hit from a small, broken glass crack pipe.

Liar, Hayden thought. He gave her a hundred, plus he paid for the room. The night had already cost him two hundred bucks.

"Jesus, Darla! You fucking picked up a cop! You stupid fucking whore!" The pimp was rifling through Hayden's wallet and had come upon the badge. Hayden heard the sound of her face slapped, hard; the crack pipe knocked from her fingertips; the tinny sound as it ricocheted off the wall. She leapt spontaneously from the bed to retrieve it, catching her knee on the side of Hayden's head in the process.

"You lost my rock!" Her fingernails scratched the carpet; the sound was like earthmovers on a hillside.

Bad move, Hayden thought. He usually kept the badge hidden in his glove compartment. But a month ago he made a big deal out of putting it back in his wallet, in a gesture meant to say, "I'm more cop than addict." Tonight, he was mostly addict.

Hayden took the washcloth from his forehead. It was sticky and dense. This wasn't water. Pulled himself to his feet, wobbled, reached out to grab the pimp's arm for support. The pimp turned away fast and Hayden teetered until his heels and toes managed a tricky balance that propelled him forward toward the bathroom. He closed the door behind him and locked it, flipped the light switch. He heard the muffled, anxious whispers of the pimp, the loud, slumped silence of the blonde who was draped over an empty crack pipe and an unmade bed.

"Fuckin' Darla, how can you be so fucking stupid? I don't know what we gonna do now, we half killed him already with that fucking bottle, don't know if we should just finish the job or ditch him here right now. This is priority one fucked up. Bitch, participate in this conversation, goddammit. I can't think through this thing without you, honey. Come on, come on, baby, think this out for us . . ."

Hayden examined the cut in his head. Clean laceration. A lot of blood, but that was what happens with head wounds. He was more concerned about a concussion. He looked like shit in the mirror. He held a clean, dry towel tight to his head. The bleeding slowed. He was lucky—the wound was under his hair. People might not notice. He wondered how he would make it out of this one. The pimp could have a gun.

He searched the bathroom for anything he could use as a weapon. Toilet roll dowel, shower mat . . . towel bar. He wrestled the bar from the wall; the aluminum bent easy. It wouldn't be much more than a visual deterrent. He turned the knob and threw the door open, swinging the towel bar from side to side. No flying bullets. He peeked around the corner, saw the empty hotel room, the tousled bedsheets, the open door. The pimp and the hooker did the right thing. They would've been fucked if they killed a cop.

He saw his wallet on the floor. The sixty bucks was gone and so was his badge. He lost his balance, gripped the doorframe, his chest pounding now.

The pressure pounded in his head. Suddenly aware of his bladder, he went limping to the toilet but didn't make it. He held onto the sink, holding the weight of his body as the pressure released and his pants grew warm and wet. He saw his jagged reflection in the cracked mirror and turned away.

He returned to the bedroom. Searched the floor, chairs, and bed. Under a pillow was a small stationery pad from the Twenty Palms Hotel. Penciled in a drug-induced drawl, the name "Darla," and an address on Crenshaw Boulevard. He crumpled the note and tossed it behind the bed. Found his car keys on an old cushioned lounge chair covered in broken glass and the spray of his own blood. Pocketing the keys, he took a step towards the door, glanced around the room, turned to the door, then back around again, and stopped. He moved to the bed and fished behind the bedboard with his fingers, reaching then finding the crumpled note and Darla's address. He shoved it in his pocket and left the room.

He tiptoed along the hotel's second-story cement walkway and proceeded down the stairs. The hotel's night manager, a thirty-something

East Indian in a pressed white cotton shirt, ascended at the same time. Hayden felt the man's eyes pass over him and he imagined what was seen—a disoriented man with his pants sagging under the weight of fresh piss, his hair matted with blood and broken glass, his hand holding a soaked, crimson towel to his head. Their eyes met for a moment and Hayden cringed at the look he saw in the other man's face. It wasn't a look of fear or hatred or sympathy. It was a look of pity.

7

"You should be dead, Hayden."

It was twelve hours since the assault and he felt dead. Even doubled up on Motrin and Tylenol, the throbbing continued. They sat in a Starbucks in Sherman Oaks. Hayden wanted to meet him in the Starbucks on Sunset and La Brea, and Sol responded with a dial tone. Hayden wore dark sunglasses, avoided looking directly at his sponsor. Sol spooned a Vente Caramel Macchiato Whatever, while Hayden took it straight up. Sol was balding, forties, a family man with three kids, all boys, all within two years of each other. He was an anesthesiologist and could probably write a prescription for the thing to relieve whatever was going on in Hayden's head.

"In your professional opinion," Hayden asked, "do you think it's a concussion?"

Sol touched the wound on Hayden's head with practiced hands. He brushed Hayden's hair over the wound paternally.

"Do you know who you can thank for your life?" he asked.

Hayden thought a moment. "I didn't get his name. I like to think of him fondly as Darla's Pimp."

"You have God to thank for your life."

Hayden winced. "Oh, yeah, I should've thought of that."

"You never think of that. Is there room for God in your life, Hayden?"

"I've left the door open."

"You think it's funny, but that door will save you someday." Sol was earnest. He had gentle eyes that saw through Hayden's bullshit. He was a tall, slender man, some would say gaunt. His neck seemed unnaturally long, with a very pronounced Adam's apple. Hayden worried that Sol wasn't getting enough sleep, that maybe he was trying to be Super Dad ever since his wife found out about the addiction almost three years ago. Sol worked at the hospital six days a week and spent most of his off time doing family "catch-up"—attending soccer games, karate tournaments, saxophone recitals, and Cub Scout campouts. The cracks in between were spent sponsoring addicts like Hayden.

"You should've answered your phone," Sol continued.

"I . . . couldn't."

"You were powerless, you were out of control. You could've said one thing—'God, I'm powerless to stop this. Please, help me answer that phone.'"

"I suppose I could've said that."

Sol always had the right answer. Hayden thought it must have something to do with the literature he read—the Twelve Step bibles, the Big Book, and the books on sexual addiction by Patrick Cairnes. There were always new pamphlets coming out, or books pushing daily affirmations on how to live a burdenless, addiction-free life. Hayden preferred to read books by men consumed by their addictions—Henry Miller, Jack London, Edgar Allan Poe, Charles Bukowski. They seemed to be having a pretty good time.

"How do you feel this morning?" Sol asked, sensing that Hayden was drifting.

"A million bucks."

"You feel some shame, don't you?"

"Yeah. I don't think I *came*, you know. Do you have to start your time over if you don't come?"

Sol gave him a look, then put his hand out, palm up.

"Ah, I told you too much." He reached in his pocket, retrieved Darla's address, dropped it in his sponsor's hand.

"Now, don't you go doing anything I wouldn't do." Hayden smiled.

Sol tore the paper apart, put the shreds in his pocket. Hayden laughed to himself sadly. They both knew the lengths an addict might go to get his fix. If Sol had merely thrown away the shredded note then Hayden might be digging through the Starbucks trash bin an hour from now to retrieve it.

"Are you enjoying your first twelve hours of sobriety?" Sol asked, a subtle, wicked smile on his face.

Hayden was surprised that his sponsor's sarcasm hurt as much as it did. It had been a hard-fought ninety days and Hayden was unwilling to accept that he was back at day one. And Sol's comment reminded him that every addict had a cruel streak. Hayden tried to remember Sol's particular affliction. Oh yeah, he thought, masturbation. Excessive masturbation to Internet pornography. Whoop-di-doo. With a loving wife at his side, helping him through the program and his therapy. They had actually gotten *closer* from his addiction, from his disclosure. Sol said they *connected* now. That was the Holy Grail of recovery, to reach the point where you could connect with your spouse or your friends or any human being. Hayden felt it would be so much easier to connect with one of those stick bugs. People were more likely to crawl in and bite you from the inside.

Hayden was taught that the way most addicts lived their lives, the way some of them still did, was labeled "disconnected." Sol liked to call him "The Disconnected Detective." After Hayden's wife learned they were disconnected and probably were never meant to be connected, she packed her things and walked away. Long nights followed endless hours of cruising the streets, catching glances at tables across cafés, looking for the glance from this woman or that, the eyes reflecting his stare, the hint of a smile, *the hit he felt*, all in an attempt to find a connection. Not with a wife or child or friends. Not with a Higher Power. With something out there, outside of himself. It was all about *connection*.

"So what am I going to do about this?" Hayden asked.

"What do you think you should do about it?"

Hayden thought back to his repertoire of program tools. Sol looked up from his drink as if waiting to see what Hayden had learned from his sponsorship.

"Inventory. Journaling. Step work," Hayden said assuredly.

Sol nodded, satisfied. He slurped the rest of his designer coffee with a straw.

"You know what happened, right, Sol?"

"Yeah," he said sympathetically. "I guess you're going to have to find another meeting."

Hayden appeared lost in thought, his gaze leveling off into the distance over Sol's shoulder. He knew Sol was right. Hayden could wallow in self-pity or he could move forward with his life.

"Stop looking at her. Three-second rule," Sol reprimanded gently as he gathered his things to go.

Hayden didn't even realize he was staring. But, yes, a girl stood at the counter waiting for her Tall Americano, and her hips and buttocks looked pure and fit for her height. There was a nervous tightness about her lips that came from a woman held under the microscope of an addict's stare, and Hayden realized that he was the addict. It made him sick to his stomach, sick of what he was, of how he appeared before his sponsor.

Hayden stood up, grabbed his car keys. "You're right," he admitted. "I gotta get out of here."

8

Hayden left Sol and returned to the West L.A. crime scene alone. He studied the carport roof to see if the techs missed the 9 mm slug that would have been lodged there if the shooting occurred where the car had been parked. He found nothing, and assumed that the shooting happened elsewhere. There was a chance then that someone in another vehicle had witnessed it, or that someone parked at a stoplight had glanced over to see the immobile passenger with a trail of blood trickling from the hole in his head. Hayden might get a witness yet.

His cell phone rang and he picked up.

"Your West L.A. girl was AB positive and the guy in the car was O neg." It was Scooter calling from the lab. "There was no other blood at the scene."

"Any fibers?" Hayden asked.

"What we found on her clothes matched the fibers in her apartment. No semen or saliva, no foreign skin under the nails."

"How about my soil sample?" That was the only forensic anomaly Hayden had uncovered.

"It's rich in nutrients. It could've come from anywhere; off someone's shoe, or maybe someone knocked over a potted plant."

"Where did it originate?"

"Who knows? I'd say Northern or Central California. But this stuff gets shipped to local nurseries everywhere."

"Thanks, Scoot, keep me in the know."

"Any somethin'-somethin' for me, Detective?"

Hayden poked around the carport, thinking.

"How about the registration tag off the Camry?"

"Boring. I'd rather have a cranial fragment."

"You know I can't get you anything organic. Hazmat would have my ass."

"Yeah, yeah," Scooter said, and disconnected the line.

Hayden left the Camry and walked up to the empty apartment. He crossed under the crime scene tape and let himself in. He examined every cabinet and bookshelf for a hint of anything he might have missed. Nothing. As he left he looked up to see the number on the door, 203. Nothing but this.

He retreated to his Redondo Beach apartment where he promptly fell asleep, in his clothes, on the sofa. He woke to the sound of his fax machine beeping. It was Charlie's report arriving from the coroner's office.

A few faxes were already in the tray. The blood spatter report for West L.A., trajectory specs on the 9 mm that took out the driver, a complete copy of the thirty-six sets of fingerprints lifted from the party. The last fax was a handwritten list of Twenty-Second Street gang members with their cell phone numbers, thoughtfully provided by Thorton and Price. Lieutenant Garcia's official stamp in the bottom right corner marked his approval. Hayden felt expectation rising from the page.

He pulled the folded notebook paper from his pocket. "Gordo"

Sanchez. The snitch with the lead on the "vendetta killing" of Council-man Jackson's niece. Maybe the lead was a couple of innocent guys he wanted off the street, a vendetta move of his own. Of course, none of these guys were wholly innocent. Any one of them could be locked up for any number of crimes. West L.A. Division had been pushing for a reason to take down the Twenty-Second. Now they had their chance.

On the phone Gordo seemed hesitant, as if he were contemplating the wisdom of his move now that things were set in motion. Hayden sched-uled the interview for later that afternoon at the squad room. Just stan-dard procedure, Hayden assured Gordo, though on his next call Hayden booked five hours with Sergeant Anthony Hempel, the RHD polygraph examiner. Hayden decided to bring in Gordo and five other gangbangers for questioning and he hoped to poly at least three out of the group. Hempel was the best they had, and the only examiner Hayden ever used. A good examiner didn't just circle peaks and valleys on a page, he con-sulted with the investigators and prepared questions meant to tug the suspect from his comfort zone to a realm of uncertainty where his body might betray him.

Hayden's own experience on the other side of the polygraph needle came as an intimate disclosure to his now ex-wife, Nicky, with Sergeant Hempel as a necessary witness. It was a pivotal moment, the culmination of all that had gone wrong in his life.

On the surface the source of his pain seemed less than extraordinary. Hayden's father, Peter, a religious man by nature, spoke often of the sanc-tity of marriage, yet in the private hidden hours of his day went carousing the neighborhood for lonely housewives, friends of Hayden's mother. As a preteen Hayden endured the quiet rumors of his father, an eighteen-year-old girl, and her abortion. All this before he even knew what sex *was*. Sex and dishonesty and infidelity were a constant, unnamed tension in the Glass home.

He hated his father for never seeking help, for not having made amends to him and his mother before that errant bullet from a drive-by shooter pierced his car windshield, punctured his skull, and sent him full speed into a freeway dividing wall.

Hayden's gift for investigation began with his father's death. He spent his teenage years following the long cold trail of an investigation that was eventually abandoned by the LAPD. He continued where the police left off and, at nineteen, he tracked his father's killer to the city, neighborhood, and house in which he lived. It was a turbulent, angry time for Hayden and his temper ran high. He remembered beating the shit out of the man who killed his father. He remembered little else.

He confessed the encounter to his mother and found that she didn't really seem to care. Her life began the day his father died and she was surprised to learn that her son held such a long-simmering vengeance. With casual detachment she suggested he follow his interest with a formal education in the criminal justice system. It was the first thing he'd ever heard her say that made sense. He did his homework and found that San Jose State offered a cheap, first-rate criminal justice major. He enrolled the following semester.

In college he met and corrupted the young and studious Charlie Dawson, who at eighteen knew he would end up in forensic medicine. Hayden introduced Charlie to the world of the fraternity, the endless beer keg, the natural and man-made hallucinogens. Hayden's tutelage added another year to the pursuit of Charlie's degree, which, for a while, made Hayden a forbidden topic of discussion at Dawson family Christmas dinners.

After the drudgery of four years in college, Hayden launched himself into three years of personal drifting, or what he liked to call his graduate course in the Sexual Psychology of Women in America. He spent the last of his student loan money on bus tickets and room and board for youth hostels and roadside motels.

He loved the allure and intrigue of first sight. The challenge of turning a casual glance into a night-long affair. In those few years he met nearly eighty girls and slept with most of them. He had no idea he was forming a pattern. He would have laughed if someone told him it was an addiction.

And he fell for the towns as he fell for the women. He fell for Kalispel, Montana, and its dark black nights and stars so close they seemed to rest on his eyelids. Kalispel girls with white freckled skin meeting in beer pubs with their girlfriends. With microbreweries serving silky amber ale that swept his senses. The girls were fun and the lovemaking was hard on the ground in the cool night air with pine needles crawling and biting their exposed skin.

Annapolis, Maryland, on Christmas Eve, the cold air pumping through his lungs and nostrils mixed with smoke from a tightly-wound Cohiba. Little Main Street antique shops aglow with holiday chaser lights and the warm, chummy burst of noise from restaurants filled with family and friends, laughter and rising anecdotes punctuating the quiet, empty street with the opening and closing of doors. Standing at the docks to watch and hear the moored yachts bobbing, their wooden torsos nudging one another for comfort. Annapolis girls from the Naval Academy dancing by high on eggnog, feeling Hayden's need, responding. Hayden waking in a dorm room, showering in the girls' locker room, amid giggles and glances.

Tulsa, Oklahoma, on a humid summer Earth Day Festival in the downtown promenade. Pseudo, neo-hippies in beads and East Indian ponchos and hip-hugger blue jeans and sandals, cannabis rolled and passed from hand to hand, protesting Iraq, while amplified, echoing activists reverberated. Tulsa girls aged eighteen, nineteen, coming on to Hayden thinking him a marauder for the traveling he'd done, for the passion with which he condemned the world, and they loved as a group in the park, in the sunset and fireflies.

Chicago, Illinois, on the mishmash of Navy Pier, the architectural obelisks like Art Deco cornstalks planted on all sides of the snaking river, the river pouring green on St. Patrick's Day, viewing it all from the rotating height of the carousel with giddy Chicago girls alive and humming electric, touching his arm and elbow and looking into his eyes with gazes slipping. A light alcohol mist spraying from their lips as they stared into his earlobes searching again for the eyes with which to connect. Taxicab to Rush Street and a jazz club where a trio of black musicians slammed jazz harder than Hayden had ever heard; sax, upright bass and drums, never heard such wide fat sounds like a Jackson Pollock painting, pushing the love in the air and sending Hayden back with the slightly chubby, big-titted redhead to the hostel, where international drunks snored through the banging, creaking bunk-bed sex.

Nashville, Tennessee, where music honky-tonked with a lifeforce that threatened to shatter pub windows. Where cowboy arms grabbed him by the elbow and pulled him into smoky Michelob and Jim Beam dance floors with Conway Twitty sound-alikes and backup bands filled with young studio musicians wise to every form of music known to man. A heavy jazz dependency swinging the country upbeat like a fusion known only to Nashville, better, unexpected, more sincere than anything he'd heard in New Orleans. Hayden hooking up with a Nashville black chick, line-dancing, Ozark Mountain music pushing fiddles, harmonica, washboard, vocals, spinning the two arm-in-arm, walking into early morning streets echoing the sharp clap of her black cowboy boots to match the slender black legs and blue jean miniskirt. Then to her apartment where they made love to Dizzy Gillespie, and when they were done he nestled in a feather pillow and she stood lonely and sad to turn off the music and play "Body and Soul" herself on an upright piano. She kissed him and asked him to leave. He was on a Greyhound to New York City while he tried to remember if he had asked for her name.

Ultimately, eventually, he found his way back to Los Angeles in a wastepaper apartment in Van Nuys with a tattooed stripper unconscious beside him while the television ran episodes of *Psychic Detectives* as a New Year's Day marathon when Hayden suddenly remembered he had an interest in police work.

A little investigative calisthenics and he managed to locate Charlie, who was also in L.A., getting his doctorate in medicine at U.S.C. Charlie pulled some strings and Hayden found himself in the LAPD academy and on the fast track to first in his class.

He had met Nicole at a hometown fair in Venice Beach. He was manning the department's community outreach table when she approached the donation jar and turned, distracted, dropping the dollar on his knee; their hands touched. They spent the next thirteen days together, in between work and full weekends, never having sex, a perfect if obsessive courtship and an engagement by month's end. Six months later they were married.

What made Nicky and Hayden the perfect match was that neither wanted anything to do with the other. Neither would get close enough to risk getting hurt. She had his mother's talent for manipulation, and Hayden *hated* to be manipulated. Losing each battle was emasculating and he gradually came to the semi-conscious understanding that he *deserved* better, that he was *entitled* to more. And just about the time when he was settling on this notion he picked up a prostitute on Sunset Boulevard and, though he had every intention of making the bust, her hand came down on his crotch and the rest was history.

For the next nine years, he remained submissive in his relationships— with Nicky, with the academy, with the force, with his captain—and he received his entitlement in twenty-minute vignettes where twenty-dollar bills bought him perceived control of his life. It bought power and what, for that moment, seemed like a real connection with another human being. Hayden, like most addicts, mistook the physical transaction for a connection of body and mind, when in fact all he was doing was paying for sex. He did get one thing from the prostitutes that he didn't get from Nicky: the final word.

A touch, a smile, an orgasm. Infidelity. Have your cake and eat it, too. So why, for nine years, could he not face himself in the mirror? Why couldn't he keep an erection when he was with his own wife? Viagra at age thirty. Embarrassing.

And then one day Nicole came home to tell him that her doctor suspected that her yeast infection was actually an STD. He tripped over himself with lies and alibis and ultimately he came through to admit that he had visited a massage parlor for a hand job. He was sorry and he begged forgiveness. She was cold and quiet and distant. They went to their respective doctors for testing and it was determined that it was a yeast infection after all.

But inconsistencies in his story plagued her. She needled him for information, playing one response against another, pointing out the deviations, the lies he had used to hide the depth of his infidelity. And it began to spill out. One encounter followed another. A run-on list of prostitutes, strip clubs, and massage parlors. He wouldn't know until later, but this had been his First Step, the full disclosure of his addictive behavior to another individual. His confession grew manic in its immediacy. He felt an exhilarating need to cleanse his soul.

She told him to leave and never return. He was certain the marriage was over, but two days later she asked him to come back. Her face bloated from crying, she had questions and she wanted details. He continued, cautiously, conscious of the tenuous line they were walking. Again she stopped him and sent him away. This time for a week. Then she called again. They continued that way for two months. When there wasn't anything more to say they stood before one another as strangers. Neither had truly known nor cared to know the other. And when the decision might easily have been divorce, Nicky suggested therapy. It was a wonderful and amazing second chance for Hayden. He charged into marriage counseling and individual therapy and within a week he was in the program.

The addiction was tough and it had him beat. He learned that it was supposed to have him beat. It was essential that he come to that conclusion—"We admitted that we were powerless over addictive sexual behavior"—and then relieve the burden onto someone else—"Made a decision to turn our will and our lives over to the care of God as we understood Him." After Hayden started working the steps, going to meetings, seeing a therapist, having a sponsor, he saw his life begin to blossom. The program made him define his addiction as inner, middle, and outer circle behaviors. And as he learned to focus his sexual energy on Nicky, his erectile dysfunction vanished. She became the focal point of his passion and they experienced a sexual renaissance like neither one had ever known. The best of it climaxed in the moment he heard her proclaim, "I finally have you whole." He had always been two people. Sterile and gentle and boring with Nicky; dark and controlling and soiled with prostitutes. Finally he had married the two halves, and Hayden felt complete, and Nicky knew it.

But his change hadn't come fast enough, for her. As she would always try to control the things around her, Nicky tried to control Hayden's recovery. She monitored his actions, his SAA meeting schedule, his step work. His right to masturbate was rescinded. She demanded strict adherence to his recovery on her terms and required an inventory of his very thoughts. He grew resentful of her paranoia and suspicion. He worked his steps and was sober in his actions, but not in the lust in his mind, where the images of women and sex and promiscuous encounters seeped through cracks in an armor fissured by feelings of guilt and self-loathing and shame. It made him nervous before Nicky-the-parole-officer, who demanded absolute rigorous honesty and in the pain of her own recovery from his neglect and *dis*honesty, she experienced sudden unannounced flashes of "telepathy" where she became suddenly certain that Hayden was lying to her. His desperate protestations sounded like admissions of guilt to her ears until he finally called out, "What do I need to do to prove I'm not lying?" and she responded with what she had wanted all along: "A lie-detector test."

At the time it seemed like a good idea. Hayden was willing to do almost anything to keep his marriage intact. He had been honest with her and he was sure the test would prove him right. In fact, however, it proved to be the beginning of the end.

9

Hayden arrived at Robbery-Homicide to find stacks of crime scene photographs on his desk. Councilman Pete Jackson's niece in a soggy patch of blood, her dark skin even darker in contrast. *Her name was Lori.* The young black male in the Camry, front passenger seat. Entrance wound at the back of his skull. Exit wound just above the left eye. *His name was Devon.* The girl at the Coral Reef. Blond hair darkened to black with blood and brain matter. Close-ups of the toeless feet. Close-ups of the toes in cups. *She had a name. Someone would know her name.*

There were coroner photographs of all three bodies, but still no preliminary notes on the Coral Reef body. It more than pissed him off. He hit the speed-dial for Charlie's cell phone.

"Purple Penis Mausoleum," Charlie answered, knowing it was Hayden by caller ID.

"Where's my notes on Coral Reef, Charlie?" Hayden growled.

"Not mine. You gotta check with Abbey Reed."

"Abbey Reed? What the fuck . . . why Abbey Reed?" It was a name Hayden hadn't expected to hear again.

"She's assisting Dickerman on this one."

"Yeah, but . . . she's not an ME, she's an investigator."

"She splits her time as a forensic tech. Dickerman doesn't do preliminary notes. If you want them you gotta get them from Abbey."

"Dammit, Charlie, can't *you* get them? You've got seniority, right?"

"Technically, yes. But she answers to a different ME on this one. What have you got against Abbey Reed anyway?" And in the split-second that followed, Charlie had him figured. "Christ, you didn't hit on Abbey, did you?" Hayden heard laughter in his voice.

"Just let it go, Charlie." Hayden didn't want to end up in the L.A. Coroner's soap opera mill.

"I'll talk to her, Hayden. But leave her alone, okay? She's going through a tough separation right now."

The comment surprised him. He hadn't even considered whether Abbey was married or not. It didn't help to know that she was available.

"Get me those prelims, Charlie."

Hayden hung up just as Lieutenant Garcia's hand came down on his shoulder.

"Your six murderous fucks are in the waiting room. Wanna split 'em up with Thorton and Price?"

Thorton and Price, Hayden observed, were busying themselves at their desks, pretending not to eavesdrop on his conversation.

"I'll take them one at a time," Hayden said, grabbing a notepad from his desk.

Gordo Sanchez, Thorton and Price's "snitch," refused the polygraph, which meant he had something to hide. Hayden suspected that Gordo's lead on the West L.A. murder was a dud. For the benefit of Thorton and Price, Lieutenant Garcia, Captain Forsythe, and the mayor's office, Hayden also interviewed the six other members of the Twenty-Second Street gang, including Carlos "The C" Navidad himself, whom he also polygraphed. Carlos was open and honest and, despite Hempel's attempts to trap him in a lie, he produced a truthful reading.

Hayden found it hard to watch the polygraphs. There remained an awkward feeling between himself and Hempel, stemming from the one time Hayden asked him to do some work on the side.

He had known Anthony Hempel almost seven years before he contacted the man on Nicky's behalf. Hempel had been with the Hollywood Division going on twenty-three years and had administered nearly four thousand polygraph tests in that time. Hayden had witnessed the tests before, and despite its effectiveness as a tool for interrogation, he had trouble buying into the claim that it could divine truth or lie from the meat of human flesh. It seemed absurd. He couldn't fathom how heart rate, blood pressure, and pulse equaled fact or fiction. So Hayden agreed to take the test on the principle that it was a marital accommodation, something that meant a lot to Nicky and little, if anything, to him.

Nicky prepared forty questions that ran like a long slow assault on Hayden's burgeoning morality. When Anthony arrived at their home, at *Hayden's home*, to wire his fingers and strap his chest and monitor his heart and blood and lungs, they discovered that forty questions wouldn't work, the test was designed for five or six at the most. Nicky's inquisition would have to be boiled down to the broadest run-on sentences deliverable in seven-second intervals.

Before the test, Anthony helped define and refine the questions so that "Have you picked up a hooker since you began recovery/have you entered a strip club since you began recovery/have you had sensual massages since you began recovery" simply became "Have you engaged in any inner circle behavior since you disclosed to Nicky?" In this way all combinations were boiled down to a question that could be tested against a control, such as, "Is your birthday in June?"

When the questions were determined Nicky was sent to the bedroom—*her* bedroom, which had once been *their* bedroom—to wait out the results. As a preliminary test, and as a way to calibrate the machine to the unique pitch of Hayden's circulatory system, Anthony presented him with a choice of ten cards and instructions to memorize one card and place it back in the deck. Anthony told him to lie when he read Hayden's card. "Was it the eight of spades?" "No." "Was it the Jack of clubs?" "No." "Was it the two of hearts?" "No." And so on. After a moment of analysis, Anthony announced with confidence, "It was the Jack of clubs." He spread the sheets out and traced the lines with his finger. "See, when I asked you about the Jack of clubs your heart rate increased and your blood pressure plummeted." In that second, Hayden's opinion of the process changed and he was instantly gripped by fear, not because he knew the machine could detect a lie, but because he felt the machine would read his anxiety as deception.

The test began. Controlled breathing. Hayden tried to remain calm. He pictured himself as a cork bobbing in the water, floating, without direction, going where the ocean would take it. The rubber tubing felt uncomfortable around his chest and stomach. Metal nipples were clamped to his fingertips; he could feel the pulse throbbing in each digit. A blood pressure monitor inflated around his right arm, stabilizing it, stiffening as if by rigor mortis. It felt to Hayden like a cruel violation of his home, of his privacy. It must have been what Nicky felt when Hayden had disclosed to her.

The questions began. "Is it Wednesday?" "Yes." "Do you like chocolate?" "Yes." "Have you engaged in any inner circle behavior since you disclosed to Nicky?" "No." "Is your birthday in June?" "Yes." "Have you been with prostitutes less than fifty times since you've been with Nicky?"

Hayden felt his blood pressure drop, his heart rate accelerate. His body numbed up and tingled and he knew at once that he would be called *liar* by the machine. He asked himself if it had been fewer than fifty times. He and Nicky had agreed on fifty because it seemed like such an extraordinary number. How could anyone have been with prostitutes more than fifty times? But in that moment, with the needles dredging his soul, he was not certain. If he sat down to remember the times, the moments that came and went, the doors that opened to dimly lit hotel rooms or roach-infested apartments or cars along busy side streets . . . he didn't know if it would amount to less than fifty.

"No," he responded, unsure. And it was *no*, because he did his inventory and he wasn't counting strip clubs or massage parlors, only whores he'd picked up on the streets. But the girls at the massage parlors were whores, as well. Under fifty even *with* them, he concluded, not entirely sure.

"Have you seen the play *Evita*?" "No." Hayden knew it was too late, that he'd blown it. He could feel his heart like inconsistent dynamite blasts pushing blood through the broken dams of capillaries and veins drawn tight to the meat, and his breath shallow and short and his head warm and wet. He was sure he'd blown it.

The questions over now, they rested, turning off the machine. Hayden was a spent cartridge, leaning against his straps. "We'll rest for a couple minutes, then start again from the beginning." Hayden imagined the end of his marriage, the battle for alimony, and the hemorrhage of funds. Then it was time to begin again and he didn't feel he could do it. He felt so very alone with the machine poking and prodding and listening for the slightest flicker of doubt.

Hayden didn't want to be alone and he leaned in for help—maybe he asked for help—and there it was in the form of the Third Step. He was willing to release his will to the comfort and care of God. And with that thought came a desperate lunge at that spiritual door, *Yes, yes! God, if you are there, be with me now! Please, help me. I need you.* And Hayden felt the flow of something . . . *spirit?* . . . envelop him. He imagined his hand taken by that spirit, his hand held by God. And then there was another unfamiliar presence—his father. His right hand held by God and his left held by his dead father.

And in that state he was preserved. He was not alone. The questions came and went and his responses came and went and there was no sense of agony about it. He was in a bubble of warm down pillows, or the feathers themselves, floating around him as if in space, a microgravity sphere lifting the pristine white feathers to circle and nuzzle and gently hold the weight of his weakened soul, his newborn conscience, cushioned in the soft spot of God's belly.

There was another rest and then a third and final probe. By now he was in that sphere and floating and Anthony was a far-off hum of words, his own responses a far-off rumble in the back of his throat, and before he knew it the machine was off and the blood pressure sleeve deflated and the sphere punctured. The spirit that had filled it leaked out quick and the feeling came back to Hayden's hands and fingertips, and he could feel his breath and his lungs inhaling and he slumped in his chair, exhausted.

"You can relax, Hayden. It's over. Go bring Nicky out."

He removed the little Kaiser-hats from his fingertips, unstrapped the blood pressure sleeve, slid from his chair. He found Nicky watching *The Little Mermaid* on DVD. She paused the film and followed him back through the hallway and into the living room, where Anthony shuffled accordion pages and circled peaks and valleys with a red pen. Nicky sensed failure in the room and was hardening for battle.

"Good news, Nicky. He's on the straight and narrow. Anything in the range of plus three to plus five shows a truthful response. He scored in the plus twelve. It doesn't get much better than that."

Hayden was as surprised as she. "I felt this huge anxiety attack in your first set of questions."

"It wasn't as big as you think. And it settled in the second and third. Your body responses were consistent through the course of the test. If you didn't have a conscience, you'd read like a reptile. You had a solid, truthful reading."

Hayden's relief was dampened by his energy drained, and the growing resentment over the fact that he agreed to take this test, that he had agreed to *always* take the test any time Nicky saw fit. He suspected that Nicky's relief was tempered by the knowledge of the things he had done. The polygraph test proved only that he told the truth about all the lies he had told.

They held hands as Anthony packed and accepted their three-hundred-fifty-dollar personal check awkwardly. "Of course I'll keep this confidential, Hayden." He excused himself as the couple held tight, perhaps aware that the moment would never be as intimate again.

Things improved through the next six months. They got used to the idea that Hayden was an addict. And he continued on the path they had set for him—twelve steps, sponsor, therapy. She kept the pressure on, never letting him forget that he was the bad guy. If the Volvo's battery went out, it was Hayden's fault. If the trash collectors went on strike, it was Hayden. If the dog died from old age then Hayden accepted responsibility. He let her have this anger, this rage, because it was owed her. But his resentment grew and he became quiet and disconnected, and her telepathy kicked in and she demanded another polygraph test. It was scheduled two weeks out and Nicky was certain that Hayden had lied and cheated and made a fool of her again and she was determined to keep her self-respect *this* time.

He nervously bit his nails and the inside of his lip and found himself sitting for long stretches in the parking lots of strip clubs, staring at his fingers, gripped white against the steering wheel, listening vacantly to the chatter on his police scanner. And cruising again—middle circle stuff—on the Boulevards. Pretending to police the streets. Looking. Lost in the bubble of not acting out. Not calling his sponsor, because this was before he met Sol. His first sponsor was too volatile and young and incapable of mentoring another, especially an addict who was, incidentally, a cop. So Hayden first made feeble calls and was given feeble service. Then he made calls during hours when he knew he'd get his sponsor's machine, and he left feeble messages and received no feedback or service. Pretty soon he was alone again.

As the days closed in and the test loomed closer, Nicky's biting comments came one on top of the other and Hayden felt his will collapse. With keys in his hand he stepped from his Jeep and walked across the parking lot and into TJ's Gentleman's Club for the first time in eleven months. It was really just for a peek and then he'd walk out, he didn't even have any cash, it would be a quick nothing and he deserved it after all that he'd done for Nicky. And it was that easy. His favorite seat and a borrowed C-note turned to ones that lay on the damp-sticky beer counter under his fingers, and he looked up to see that Natalia still danced there.

She remembered him, and danced for him alone it seemed, her eyes always on his, the addict's perfect fix, her naked, firm, fit twenty-year-old tanned body looking tall on the stage although she was only 5'2". She appeared four inches taller in the tan leather lace-up snow-bunny boots that she wore to counter her absolute nakedness, naked even to the hairless cleft between her legs. More ones dropped, and then he found tens, and then he remembered the ATM machine and there were twenties, and Natalia was in his lap moving forward and back against his stiffening cock and he wished he had worn dark silky pants instead of the corduroy, which was still better than the stiffness of blue jeans. She was the last girl he had been with before disclosure and recovery and here she was with her fingers slipping behind her ass and finding his cock through his pants and squeezing and it was *over*, he came, and he was suddenly fully aware that his sobriety was gone. It was gone the moment he walked through the door.

Hayden left the club carrying the weight of his shame. He called home to leave a message on the machine, but Nicky picked up and she knew before he breathed a word. The silence on the line sealed their fate.

"I'll call Anthony and cancel for tomorrow," she offered.

"Yeah."

"You'll need a place to stay."

"Okay."

Silence.

"Nicky, I—"

Dial tone.

That was over a year ago and he never had more than ninety days sobriety since. It didn't seem to matter that much, there wasn't anyone in his life to cheat on anymore. Now he cheated on himself, and his sponsor, and his God.

Hayden jumped when he heard the sharp knocking on the two-way mirror that separated and concealed Hayden from the polygraph room. The room was empty now and Sergeant Hempel was letting him know that no further suspects had been scheduled for testing. Hayden knocked twice to let Hempel know that he was free to go for the night.

Hayden moved into one of the witness interview rooms where he proceeded with the first of two separate interviews he had scheduled with attendees from Lori Jackson's party. The first, Jessica Theis, was Lori's childhood best friend. She still held a grudge over the fact that Lori had stolen her boyfriend three years earlier. So there was motive, however slight. The grudge had turned to searing guilt after she was informed that her best friend and ex-boyfriend were brutally murdered the week before. She could not think of anyone at the party who might have stayed late or returned even later to carry out the deed.

The second was Devon's younger brother Todd, who revealed a long-standing crush on Lori. But he was a good kid and he cherished his brother. Hayden didn't consider him a suspect, but he had hoped the curious sixteen-year-old might have been hovering on the sidelines when the killer approached his brother. No chance. An older cousin had shuttled him home around 1 A.M.

It frustrated Hayden that the two crime scenes lent no credible leads. No witnesses, no suspicious fingerprints, no DNA through semen or saliva. The *only* thing that felt visceral was the matching room numbers, and Hayden had to admit they were looking more like a coincidence than a connection.

He never had a case go so cold so quick, and now he had two in a row. He was tempted to hand the West L.A. case over to Thorton and Price and let them fry in the limelight. But he had never dropped a case and the fact that he was being encouraged to do so made him even more determined to keep it. He needed a new perspective. He needed the help of someone he hadn't turned to in a long time.

10

Rich lived in a two-story, four-bedroom home in Northridge. It seemed like a ghost house now with his four kids grown and gone, with the blades of grass in his front lawn frayed brown under the heat of another San Fernando Valley summer. Rich used to do the landscaping himself, but the stroke left him with nothing to do now but convalesce.

Hayden rang the doorbell and an intercom crackled on the stucco wall just above his shoulder. He didn't remember an intercom before. What he heard was mostly static and a stuttering of syllables that sounded like, *"C-c-c-c-ha-g!"*

"Hello?" Hayden called. "That you, Rich?"

"H-hayyyden! G-get . . . your asssss . . . in h-here!"

Rich didn't sound any better than he had almost two months before, when Hayden had last visited. At that time there was the promise that acupuncture might restore his motor skills. Hayden was stunned to find Rich still in bed in the stuffy upstairs guest room, oxygen tubes dripping from his nose.

"Where's Judy?" Hayden asked, cranking open the windows and hitting the switch to the overhead ceiling fan.

"Her . . . sh-sh-she's . . . put h-her mother in . . . in a h-home."

Hayden remembered. Judy's mother was in her nineties and they had just placed her in a retirement home when Rich had his stroke.

Hayden sat on the chair beside Rich's bed. They stared at each other for a time. He could see in Rich's expression an acknowledgment that the change was permanent. The left side of his mouth and the skin of his cheek hung in concentric folds, lazy, looking to rest in the hammock of his neck. It dragged down the left lower eyelid a bit, exposing the round redness of the eyeball. The eyes had gone gray, but Hayden remembered them cobalt blue, when Rich was the quintessential *Dragnet*-era detective.

Hayden had learned so much from him. Rich was the type who gave of himself. He gave through training and mentorship and guidance. He gave to the point where one would wonder whether Rich might ever exhaust his reserve for giving, and then he gave some more. Everyone was surprised that Hayden and Rich had gotten along so well, considering Hayden had the reputation for being such a taker. Hayden always pushed the envelope of what he could get from the department. He wanted computers that worked. He wanted an answering service so the detectives wouldn't have to be their own receptionists. He wanted a profiler. He took what he could get when he could get it.

Rich stared at Hayden expectantly, with warmth, like a father whose son had returned from war. Hayden was suddenly aware of the time he had spent away from Rich. They had been together when it struck. Hayden with his feet up on his desk, eating a Pink's chili cheese dog, laughing, rattling on about something, it might have been the Dodgers against the Marlins. It was four o'clock and the squad room was nearly empty, only the lieutenant and a few detectives at their desks. Rich was shuffling through the cold cases, picking a file, fidgeting with the top pages, replacing the file, picking up another file, repeating the process. He prioritized one above another, reprioritized another above that. He seemed perplexed. The stroke occurred in one silent instant.

Hayden had stayed at Rich's side for the next questionable forty-eight hours. He returned before his shift every day for two weeks thereafter. During that time he filled Rich in on the developments of their cases as well as current events and internal LAPD gossip. Rich was most interested in his cold case files. He made Hayden promise that the files would not be returned to storage. Hayden assured him that they would remain on Rich's desk, awaiting his return. To this Rich made no comment.

Now Hayden looked at the man and knew he would never work again. He took Rich's hand. The fingers stiff, the forearms like dry forest branches. Rich tried to speak, but Hayden asked him to listen.

Hayden described the West L.A. crime scene. He walked Rich through the apartment, as he had walked through the apartment four days before. He summarized the various reports, the list of evidence. He described the Coral Reef crime scene and again detailed the evidence and summarized the reports. He shared the crime scene photos and the sketches he had made. Rich seemed moved by the drawings that, in a strange way, were more disturbing than the photos themselves. Through it all, Rich listened attentively, nodding, trying as he always had to read past Hayden's enthusiasm and focus on the facts of each case.

"And the number on the hotel room door," Hayden concluded at last, "was two-oh-three. The same as the apartment number in West L.A."

Rich appeared to be processing the significance of Hayden's words.

"Wh-wh-what else h-have you got?"

"That's it. That's what there is."

"I-I-I . . ."

Hayden held on to his patience. This was impossible. He couldn't imagine how Rich could live with this. Hayden would have stopped speaking altogether if it had happened to him. Maybe put a bullet in his brain.

"I . . . seen th-th-this on TV. N-news. What a-about c-c-council . . . man?"

Hayden stood up, exhausted. "I don't know anymore. I was hoping . . . I was hoping you could help."

Rich seemed to turn inward. "I-I . . . d-don't s-see it . . ."

Hayden leaned his head against a wall. For a long time he said nothing. He breathed, feeling his belly expand against his belt. He had never been aware of his belt before, through his belly. He was aware that the room smelled. That the open windows and the ceiling fan didn't help. Not in the San Fernando Valley. Not in July.

He went to Rich's side and touched his shoulder. Rich reached up and squeezed his hand.

"T-t-time for . . . a n-n-new . . . p-partner," Rich managed.

11

It was 7:05 P.M. Hayden drove up and down Long Beach Boulevard looking for the Zion Temple Church of God. He never understood why it was so hard to find a new SAA meeting. Or why someone would pick a place just off Long Beach Boulevard, one of the most traveled cruising strips in the Southland. He remembered a Discovery Channel special he saw about prostitution in Long Beach. He swore he recognized his own car crossing the background in one of the shots.

He needed the meeting tonight. His visit with Rich scared the hell out of him. He couldn't imagine what Rich had done to deserve this. Rich had been everything to everyone all his life. He had commendations for bravery, for going beyond the call of duty—awarded but never displayed. He supported a wife and sent all four kids to college. He paid up his mortgage and was set to retire in less than eight years. All that planning, while God watched, laughing.

On Hayden's sixth time passing West Willow he saw the little side street that curled behind McDonald's and led to a steeple that peeked through the tree line. He took a hard right and found the parking lot.

Hayden burst in, ten minutes late. Three of the twenty guys nearly fell from their seats. With an entrance like that he figured they had him pegged for a cop. But instead of resistance he met friendship as chairs were pushed aside and an empty seat sprouted from the floor. The speaker finished his lead and the meeting turned back to the secretary.

The secretary was a squat little man in his forties with round spectacles and a few strands of hair brushed over a very large scalp. Hayden could easily see him tucked into the back of an adult bookstore flipping through the latest issue of *Barely Legal*.

"I'm Alex and I'm your sex-addicted secretary."

"Hello, Alex," responded everyone in the room.

"Would the latecomer please identify himself?" Alex continued.

Hayden cleared his throat. "Hi, I'm Hayden and I'm a sex addict."

"Hello, Hayden," the group replied.

"Are you new to SAA, Hayden?"

"No. I'm new to this meeting. I've been sober ninety . . . I've been sober two days."

"Welcome, Hayden. Keep coming back."

Hayden nodded, wondering if, once they got to know him, they would really want him coming back.

12

The Cohiba in his hand burned warm and smooth in the crisp night air outside Charlie's Silverlake duplex. Charlie smoked Punch, a trendy cigar that, to Hayden, didn't quite make the grade when it came to consistent draw and aroma. Hayden's pockets were a hundred bucks lighter after a full night of poker with the Odd Bunch—Charlie's gang of morticians, morgue assistants, and grave-diggers. They had all gone, leaving smells and stains in an otherwise flavorless home.

Hayden went there as soon as his meeting ended. Charlie's voice mail message said that Abbey had faxed preliminary notes on the Coral Reef crime scene *to him*. When Hayden called back he heard the poker game in the background and decided to make a night of it.

The two sat quietly in the creaking night acknowledging the thunder of distant jetliners and the hollow chirping of nearby frogs. Hayden reviewed Abbey's notes, reading and rereading each meticulous detail. A possum stared at them through the darkness, his nose twitching to the tempo of his heart. Hayden put the notes down and leaned back in the stiff wicker chair. He looked into the orange-red ember of the cigar in his hand. It seemed a cushioned bed of burgundy ash—warm, comforting, enticing. He could feel endorphins released, without the shame that came from cruising.

"Pretty fucking thorough, huh?" Charlie said while exhaling a long plume of smoke.

"Did you not give her my home fax number?" Hayden asked, regarding her weaknesses above her strengths.

"I gave her your fax number," he said.

"So, she has a problem with authority?"

"Nope. She told me she has a problem with assholes." Charlie didn't try hard to hide his smile when he said it.

Well. That would have to be addressed at a later date. When all was said and done her notes had been worth the wait. Not that it revealed the magic clue that would solve the case, but it did provide Hayden with the kind of well-researched forensic assessment he required from the coroner's office.

"Ran into Nicky a couple weeks ago," Charlie announced.

"Where the fuck would that have been?" It caught Hayden off guard. Hearing her name still caused an ache in his chest.

"In the hospital."

The comment stopped Hayden like a baton to the head. He hadn't even thought to ask Charlie about his health when they ran into each other at the Coral Reef.

"How many days were you in?"

Charlie shifted in his seat, tapped ash onto the ground. Hayden saw the tender embers float away. He wanted to snatch them up quickly, join them with his own.

"Four this time. I was out cold when they found me."

"A tough stretch?" Hayden asked, concerned.

Charlie shrugged uneasily. "The fucking nurse shifts," he mumbled.

Hayden waited for him to continue.

"Third day I was there, middle of the night, some nurse reads my chart wrong, quadruples my insulin. I started tacking and she panicked. She put nitro under my tongue, my blood pressure took a dive, and I flat-lined. They had to paddle me back. A fucking nightmare."

Hayden stared past the tree line, into the mist of a foggy, starless night.

"I'm sorry," Hayden said finally. Sorry for more than what had happened with the nurse. Sorry for being too self-absorbed to even know Charlie was sick.

"Yeah." Charlie took a long puff from his cigar.

"You made it out in the end," Hayden said encouragingly. Charlie sighed and took a pull from the Corona in his hand.

"How'd she look?" Hayden inquired after a moment. Charlie stared ahead, considering the question.

"Oh, you know," he said finally. "Nicky always looks good."

Hayden nodded. Nicky never looked anything but stellar.

"Did she . . . say anything?" Hayden pressed.

Charlie rolled his eyes. "You mean, about *you*? When she was visiting *me* in the hospital? Let's see, I think she said 'Good to see you, Charlie. How ya doing? Hope you're not allergic to the flowers. Am I the first to stop by?'"

"Okay already, Jesus. I brought you cigars, didn't I?" Hayden countered defensively. "Fuckin' Cubans and you won't even light one."

"I have a hard time accepting gifts from a police evidence bag."

"Suit yourself," Hayden said through a long swirling puff. "Just leaves more for me."

The possum shifted its weight to a back leg and took a timid step forward. He waddled like a water balloon on sticks, disappeared behind the ivy. They sat in silence for a while. An owl launched off a nearby tree, dropping a shower of dust off its enormous wings.

"I assume you're still a sex addict," Charlie asked. It was more a statement than a question.

"That's what they tell me."

"They giving you something for that?"

"Just chips. When I earn them. If I do a year I get a cake."

The silence was interrupted for a moment by the rat-a-tat of automatic gunfire coming from Korea Town a few miles away.

"What's on your mind?" Charlie tested.

Charlie had known Hayden long enough now. Read his expressions if not his mind.

"I don't know. You always see the endgame," Hayden said.

"And that means . . . ?"

"We're all just slabs of meat."

Hayden took a long drag on his cigar, watched the slow burn as the embers went from bright orange to red then black. A light breeze carried ashes into the night. Charlie stared at him quizzically. At that moment the evening erupted in sound as both their cell phones chimed urgently with text messages.

13

An apartment this time, just off Melrose and Fairfax. Female, in her seventies. Hayden ducked under the crime scene tape and an officer grabbed his arm.

"Detective Glass, Downtown," Hayden said.

"Need to see your badge, Detective."

Hayden reached into his pocket and produced his wallet, then remembered. "Yeah, that's a problem, see—"

"Can't let you in, sorry."

"Hayden, what's the hold-up?" It was Homicide Detective Reese Philips, waving him in. He was Hollywood Division, they'd worked together for years. "He's good, Officer, let him through."

He followed Philips past a group of uniformed officers. Philips still had a bit of the cowboy swagger from his years with the Mounted Unit.

He used to chase suspects on horseback through all the streets Hayden cruised.

"Where's your badge?" Philips asked.

"Went AWOL."

"Better find it before your captain gets wind. I hear he's hot about your councilman case."

Hayden sighed, shaking his head.

The first thing he did before stepping into the apartment was look at the room number on the door. *Twelve.*

Charlie appeared behind him wheeling a gurney. He pushed past Hayden and entered the crime scene. Hayden hesitated, listened to the buzz of Melrose down the street. Clubs, restaurants, cafés, trendy boutiques.

He stepped into the apartment to see Mrs. Palistrano, face nailed to her kitchen table by a knitting needle jammed through the back of her neck. She was thin, maybe seventy-five years old, but with full breasts that poked out from a bra that had been cut by a serrated knife. She was otherwise dressed in a paisley skirt from an era Hayden didn't recognize. Two bloody finger markings could be seen on the side of her right breast—smudges made undoubtedly by the printless tips of latex gloves.

Hayden surveyed the room. Nothing appeared disturbed or out of place. The crime seemed random. The air was stale. She lived alone and didn't get out much. She was trusting, maybe even opened the door for her killer. Maybe she was expecting Meals On Wheels.

Hayden spun in a slow circle, taking it in. Old photos of an old man. Grown children who lived somewhere cold, maybe Minnesota. A two-year-old grandchild of indeterminate sex. More knitting needles. Sweaters, scarves, and a comforter made and unfinished by hand. Fresh fruit in a bowl; she shopped at the farmer's market. Two TVs, one old and one new. The new Panasonic probably sent by the children to ease the guilt of leaving her alone. Maybe they'd half-heartedly asked her to join them in their Midwest home where she could dawdle all day and watch the grandchild evolve. But she was stubborn and brave and she wasn't about to leave the city where she had lived for forty years. And maybe there was the fear that if she wasn't reminded of her memories every day, in everyday sights and smells, she would start the slow process of losing them to the venomous advance of age.

There had been a cat once but all that was left were the stains of body oils and a light, pungent smell of fur lost in the folds of sofas and leather armchairs. Knickknacks from a life lived long. Drawers were unopened—the killer had rifled through nothing except the clothes she was wearing. The prints, bloody, seemed to indicate that the fondling occurred after death, or at least while she was still struggling for life.

Hayden breathed the stale, damp air and it felt and smelled familiar. There was something about this scene that reminded him of the others. He couldn't isolate the connection—it was just a gut feeling. If the room numbers had been the same then Hayden would have known for sure.

Hayden ran the similarities in his head. The two women of the previous killings had been stripped naked and raped. Mrs. Palistrano, a woman in her seventies, had been fondled by hands soaked in her own blood. It was the brutality of the thing that begged comparison. If this were the same killer he might have avoided detection if he had only resisted touching the old woman's breast. But it seemed he couldn't help himself.

Hayden wondered if the killer *wanted* the connection to be made. If this was the same killer, a serial killer, he would yearn notoriety. But if that were the case he would have made the connection more obvious. Instead, there was a different MO at every scene; a black college student, a blond prostitute, a lonely old grandmother. Hayden suspected he was witnessing the killer's first sloppy moves, before experience and confidence defined him.

Hayden's thoughts were premature, he knew. He sounded like a criminology student desperate to connect three random homicides and earn a passing grade. All he had was a hunch. A hunch backed by years of experience in the field and an addict's perspective on the mind-set of the sexual predator.

God, he hated that affiliation—the sex addict and the sexual predator. In the world of sexual addiction there were three levels. Level One was the addict whose actions hurt no one but himself. His crimes were victimless, even accepted by modern society. Yet society evolves, for better or worse. One generation's deviant is the next generation's innovator.

When Hayden was a kid the deviant was the thirteen-year-old boy who snuck a silent, black-and-white, Super 8 porno film into the boys' locker room. Who would have guessed that, years later, pornography would be sold at the neighborhood DVD store and that middle-aged housewives would pick them up when they stopped by to return the overdue Disney film? At what point does the healthy couple who swings and practices S&M in the privacy of their own home cross the line from normal sexual behavior to sexual addiction? Hayden knew a radio DJ who was terribly abused by her husband, sexually humiliated in front of his friends, forced to endure gang rapes and cigarette burns. Yet on her radio show she recorded a public service announcement for a hotline for abused women. It didn't occur to her that she might fit the profile.

It usually took a crisis before people were forced to review their actions from the outside and discover that they had an addiction. Hayden spent nine years of his marriage picking up prostitutes, getting blow jobs at massage parlors, and feeling up girls at the strip clubs, yet he never once thought of himself as a "sex addict." It was his marriage counselor who announced the shocking news. A Level One sex addict might be a chronic masturbator, someone who stayed on-line all day or night, masturbating ten, twenty times in a row to Internet porn sites; or he might have driven himself into bankruptcy spending his family's savings at strip clubs and massage parlors. Hayden was Level One.

Level Two sex addicts were the voyeurs, peeping toms, flashers. They left victims behind, but no physical harm was done. The Level Threes were the real fuckers, and Hayden did everything he could to put them away. Rapists, child molesters, murderers. Level Three sex addicts gave all the other sex addicts a bad name. And they were all lumped together in the meetings. Hayden might be sitting next to a child molester and never know it. He would hear an addict's share, listen to the pain and struggle, and never know that the man had left his nine-year-old daughter at home in a corner harboring suicidal dreams and shaking, unable to cry or call out for help.

What made it more confusing was that Hayden did in fact feel the predator's struggle, his pain, his wound. Regardless of how their addictions presented, the addicts' pain came from the same place. Most, as kids, discovered that love was conditional and they were made to feel abandoned and accused and dirty and ashamed for the things they thought and did. Some, like the predators, experienced physical and mental torture at the hands of the very people responsible for their protection. Hayden both despised and empathized with the predator. It was a swirl of emotion—he didn't understand the counterpoint of compassion and contempt or how the two could possibly exist at the same time in the same place, the way a streak of light existed as both particle and wave.

A photographic flash brought him back to the present. The ID guys were taking their pics before passing the body over to Charlie. Hayden looked again at the finger markings left on the victim's breast. The killer knew this would be a shocker. It was a "fuck you" to the detectives. And yet something told Hayden that it wasn't premeditated. More like a compulsion that became a message in afterthought.

Hayden pulled out his sketchbook and a broken pencil. He felt his pocket for the rubbery eraser that was usually wedged in the seam. He rescued it, holding it comfortably between thumb and forefinger while he worked the sketch. Mrs. Palistrano emerged on the page with thin, angular arms that accentuated the bones and her saucer-shaped shoulder blades. With long blue veins stretched on her forearms like yarn on a loom, ending at the tips of knotted fingers that gripped the table in some useless attempt to push her head free from the needle that held it.

The image stark and lonely, in his sketchbook.

Charlie worked diligently beside him. None of the hesitation remained from the last murder scene. He didn't seem phased by the bloody spike in Mrs. Palistrano's neck and instead set his sights on the challenge of moving her body without dislodging it, maintaining the structural integrity of the wound for further examination at the coroner's office. They had their moods, the people who tended to crime scenes. Times when the walls were up and no amount of violent disregard for life could offend them. Then there were times when the shell of a human being left at the scene seemed a pointed mile marker on the road of one's own life, leading to the lonely, inevitable end awaiting everyone, even the crime scene investigator.

Hayden paced the room, stopped at the windows overlooking Melrose

Avenue where he saw hip, young Angelenos ducking for cover from an unexpected rainstorm, landing under psychedelic awnings and pink neon lights. Summer heat produced strange weather at times, even rain. Droplets pelted the glass before him, assaulting the image of himself peering back.

Charlie looked up from his work, a gloved finger steadying the tip of the upright needle imbedded in the table and Mrs. Palistrano's neck. They shared a conspiratorial smile at the absurdity of their situation.

Hayden finished the sketch and flipped through his drawings of the previous crime scenes. He stopped when he saw something scribbled hurriedly between the margins of one of the pages. In his handwriting, Darla's address transcribed from the note she had left for him. The note that Sol had subsequently destroyed.

Hayden felt a rush of excitement at the discovery. He had no recollection of having done this. He marveled at the nature of his addiction, its duplicity, its ability to evolve, to mutate, to learn what it needed to do to survive. Tonight, his addiction was calling the shots.

14

The apartment complex he was looking for was just off S. La Cienega in the Crenshaw district. La Cienega was a cruising street but the girls were tough and scarred and tanklike. The street was better known for the massage parlors that capped the ends of its mini-malls. He felt anxious as he passed Randy's Donuts, with the knowledge that Serene Touch Massage, his favorite massage parlor in the city, was only a few blocks away. He gripped the steering wheel hard as he drove. He passed another stoplight and a half block later it came into sight. Serene Touch sat in an innocuous white stucco building that shared its walls with a pet grooming service. The sign on the building read "Asian Acupressure"—the sure mark of a brothel. Hayden had never encountered a legit licensed masseuse advertising "acupressure." If the sign wasn't enough to tip the passing john, then the gated buzz-in entrance and the armed guard was.

Hayden was eight months sober from massage parlors; a particularly impressive accomplishment considering that the addict in him *loved* massage parlors. Picking girls off the street was risky. Every time he let a girl in his car he risked discovery by fellow Vice officers. He risked his reputation, his street clout, his job. Then there were the risks that every john knew—an angry pimp's gun in your face, an angry girl's gun or knife in your face, an angry cop's gun in your face. And there was herpes, AIDS, gonorrhea, syphilis, hepatitis. Although Hayden liked to think he had been safe, he knew he had accepted unacceptable risks that could have been passed on to his wife. Could have, but for the grace of God, had not.

So he played the game that a pro in a massage parlor was safer than a pro on the street. And like the hazy high that came from cruising the Boulevard, the massage parlor had its own realm of narcotic anticipation. He remembered the last time he visited Serene Touch. He had treasured the drive that brought him there, as if somehow he knew he would never allow himself the pleasure again. There was excitement even in the traffic he encountered, the obstacles placed in his path. The thrill of pulling into the parking lot, turning off his cell phone and pager. Buzzing in and landing on the musky sofa next to three men in business suits, all avoiding the shame in the others' eyes, pretending to laugh at reruns of *Gilligan's Island* spinning a seemingly endless loop on a black-and-white television set.

The roly-poly host, with acne and yellow teeth, emerged from a particleboard door to call out "Next!" and the closest businessman stood, attempting nonchalance, folding a newspaper under his arm, following his host into a network of dim hallways.

The next businessman moved a seat closer, and the next, as well, and Hayden again. And a buzzer rang and the dim-witted guard rose with a thousand keys jingling on his belt as he unlocked two sets of iron security gates to admit yet another client.

Finally it was his turn to follow Roly-poly into the hallway. By then he was boiling over with anticipation. It was like being a kid again, stepping into that roller coaster, feeling the bar come down, the intractable movement of cars up the hill.

"Been here before?"

Hayden had long since abandoned the defeated sigh that came with his response, instead letting out a practiced, "Yes."

"Who do you know?"

"Kathy, Tammy, Sara, Beth, Kim, Kimberly, Donna, Trish."

That shut the guy up until they reached the room.

"Hour or half hour?"

"Half hour."

"Okay, that'll be five thousand pennies, ha-ha."

Hayden dropped a fifty to the house.

Before slipping into the shadows, Roly-poly shot his parting comment, "Make yourself comfortable, *he'll* be right with you, ha-ha."

"Ha-ha."

Finally he was alone. Tingling with anticipation, more exciting than the massage itself, because in that five to ten minutes anything could happen. Who would walk through that door? Someone he knew, someone he'd had before, or a new face, a stranger? She would be Korean, that he knew. There were only Korean girls in this place. But always beautiful. Aged eighteen to twenty-six, firm, thin, petite, tight stomachs, tight asses, long straight black hair, natural breasts, altered breasts, it didn't matter.

He preferred complete strangers, playing a game in his head that the girl was a legitimate masseuse and through the course of the massage found herself drawn to him beyond control.

He stripped naked in the small room, glancing around at the sparse, proplike furniture and the massage table that stood like a tomb in the center, with a fresh sheet of wax paper pulled across it to suggest sanitation.

He circled the room, enjoying the rush of being naked in a public place, in a place outside his home. Then he lay down on his stomach, head angled towards the door, to wait.

The minutes stretched on. He wondered if there were hidden cameras, if he had stepped into a sting operation and his associates in Vice were watching, whispering, "Is that Detective Glass? Should we contact IA?" Or maybe the brothel owners were recording porn to sell overseas. Or maybe the scene was being recorded to prevent the girls from pleading to their johns for help or relating stories of forced sexual slavery.

The longer he waited the more he tried to focus on the door and the prize that would follow. And then, finally, a soft knock and a softer "Hello," and she was someone he'd never met and she was beautiful, wearing a light summer dress accentuating her cleavage and long, toned legs. She placed a small white towel over his ass. The girls were far more cautious than the johns. For all she knew, Hayden might be a cop.

"Have you been here before?" she asked in hesitant pidgin English.

"Many times."

"I've never seen you."

"I've never seen *you*."

"Who do you know here?"

"Kathy, Tammy, Sara, Beth, Kim, Kimberly, Donna, Trish."

"Oh."

"What's your name?"

"Katrina."

"And Katrina."

He rested his head on the table and let her rub his shoulders, neck, and back. They knew how to massage here. Most were as good as any legit licensed masseuse. And they brought a touch of the Orient with them. He had had women walk on his back, delicately kneading his muscles with their toes and the balls of their feet. He had had his neck cracked with chiropractic skill. Hayden imagined a school somewhere, or a madam or a slave mistress, who taught these women the Kama Sutra basics. Hayden had girls insist they put his socks and shoes on then tie his laces before he left the room. It was this kind of attention to detail that made a john a regular and kept him tipping high. Hayden typically dropped a C-note to the girl for a half hour of service.

Her hands found his calves and thighs, and Hayden's addict took over. He had practiced a way to arch his back so that his genitals lifted from the table and lightly touched her fingertips. It was ambiguous enough to deny as a ploy, yet as he repeated the action it became obvious that he was there for more than a shoulder rub. Her hands opened, reaching under to touch him, hesitantly, testing. It was the most exciting moment of the encounter, his fantasy fulfilled, the innocent massage student overcome by his magnetism.

At this point they knew the score and she slipped off her dress, letting it fall to the ground in a gentle puff. She as naked as he, with firm tight breasts and nipples rising hard and a manicured tuft of dark black hair between her legs.

He began his massage parlor addiction with simple hand jobs, just as he had when he first let a girl in his car. The massage table seemed a safer place and the hand jobs progressed to blow jobs, and it soon became his preferred way of acting out. This was before he knew it as "acting out." It was simply called cheating. Or, as his wife would later call it, adultery.

He never allowed a pro to put him in her mouth without a condom, and the girls were deft at slipping a rubber in their mouths and sliding it onto his penis with their lips and teeth. He wondered if that slick little move didn't defeat the purpose.

He only had intercourse once outside his marriage, with a massage parlor girl who let him slip in from behind as she stood over the table. She encouraged him to watch in the mirror and he did, until he imagined Korean gangsters watching from an adjoining room, laughing, critiquing his technique while adjusting the tracking on sophisticated digital recorders.

Eight months ago and it all seemed like yesterday. Eight months was an eternity.

Hayden blinked and found that he had been sitting for a quarter hour in the parking lot of Serene Touch, his eyes fixed on the gated entrance. The security camera above the door was trained on his Crown Vic, its little red light blinking frantically. His behavior had probably initiated a meltdown inside the building. He didn't remember pulling into the parking lot. He didn't remember turning off his pager and cell phone. It was the kind of blackout that often followed his addictive behavior, where time and place were held captive to the addict inside.

Hayden put the car in gear and drove up to Slauson Avenue and, after a mile or so, turned north onto Crenshaw Boulevard.

The apartment complex was set against a row of identical buildings constructed in the seventies—gray concrete blocks, all squares with very few windows. Barbed wire fencing and barred doors. Best to keep her locked away, he thought. A white girl in this neighborhood was a target for the local street gangs. Palm trees and birds-of-paradise did their best to dress the place, but California flora didn't fool the natives. Even the worst 'hoods in Compton and Watts bore the stamp of California landscaping, built during an era when the wide streets and large homes housed wealthy and middle-class Angelenos.

He found an empty parking space in the carport beside her apartment. He took the stairs two at a time. He could convince himself that he was there to pick up his badge, but his addict knew better. He didn't know why, but he was dying to see her.

The door opened slowly on his third knock, stopping when the chain went taut. She appeared pleased and not at all surprised to see him. She smiled at him through the crack in the door, looking bright, young, mischievous. She ushered him in and locked the door behind them. She was barefoot with pasty white legs that rose to the brim of a black pleated miniskirt, standing braless in a white shirt that exposed her belly. As she turned to face him he noticed the dark, inviting full moons of her areolas and the small lift of each nipple. She stood with her legs slightly crossed in front, set against a backdrop of dirty dishes.

The place smelled like a drug den and Darla seemed too young and too fragile to be living so disparate a life. Her hair blond to the shoulders and unwashed for the day. The look she gave him was both inviting and pathetic and Hayden felt compelled to grab her and run. He wanted to whisk her from this neighborhood, and into a salon where she might be fed and exercised and detoxed and bathed and massaged and pedicured and pampered, then educated and enrolled in a university where she could study to be a nurse and live long enough to forget her first twenty-two years as a drug addict and whore. Yet there was another part of him brewing, too. It wanted to squeeze and tug her tits and pull her head to his cock and fuck her and leave her to dwell in this mess of her own making; fuck it, he couldn't save everyone, not even himself.

"You're a detective, right?"

She enjoyed the upper hand, when she had the something that someone else wanted. With Hayden she had more than just the badge, she had his addiction and with that she had *him*.

"Where's the fuckhead?" he asked, not so politely. "I don't think I can take another bottle to the head."

Her smile was curious now. "Did you bring your gun?"

He shook his head.

"The fuckhead's out," she said. "Why do you pick up whores, cop?"

The question caught him off guard. He couldn't find an answer.

"Does that make you uncomfortable?" she continued. "I *am* a whore."

"I've never heard a girl say it. I usually just say girl, or date, or pro."

"I'm not ashamed of what I do. How 'bout you?" Said smugly.

She played with her hair in her fingers. She *was* cute; she looked better than most girls on the street.

"I thought you guys took an oath or something. Uphold the law."

"Some do it better than others."

"And you judge us . . . whores, people on the street. There was this guy I used to date, he was a cop, came around every few months then stopped. He was *something*. Mean, though. This was before Dewey. I don't think Dewey would've done anything to him anyway, not to a cop."

"Who's Dewey?"

"The guy that hit you."

She walked over to a decorative wood cabinet by the wall, found a bottle of perfumed lotion, rubbed it into her hands and arms.

"Danny Gallegos. You know him? Said he was going to marry me, can you believe that?"

The name stung Hayden. Danny Gallegos was a young officer working Central Division, spent six months in Hayden's Vice unit before a stint in Narcotics.

"He was killed over a year ago," Hayden whispered.

Darla was quiet for a moment, rubbing small circles of lotion into her hands.

"That's all right, I guess. I thought he left, you know. That he was embarrassed of me."

He didn't tell her that Danny had a wife and young boy. That Danny would never take a whore off the street to be his wife just as Hayden, even broken and divorced, would never make that promise except in the heat of passion, and only to keep a girl on a string for the next time his addict needed a fix. That's probably why Danny had been mean to her—he was ashamed.

"Where's my badge?" he demanded.

"You'll get your badge."

She found a glass pipe on the cabinet, picked up a lighter and a nickel rock of crack cocaine.

He watched her bring the pipe to her lips. She inhaled long; her shoulders dropped and the stress in her body evaporated and when she opened her eyes they were on fire.

"Want a hit, Detective?"

"No thanks."

"You're a stiff one."

She looked him over. "Very stiff," she continued, lifting the pipe to her lips.

She danced playfully around him, humming a song that must have been popular. She placed the pipe on the cabinet and peeled her shirt clean over her head.

"I wasn't always a whore. I was a dancer. I danced Cheetahs in Vegas. Spearmint Rhino. I made five hundred bucks a night. I was the *fucking-A bomb*."

With her shirt off he could see her ribs and for the first time was aware of how thin she was. She dropped her skirt and was naked except for a lavender lace thong that cupped the softness of her cunt. She fingered the straps, ready to draw them down, but she must have seen the look of sadness in his face, which flashed for a moment then was gone. She seemed wounded, suddenly.

She was weak and starving and addicted. He looked past her sex to the concave stomach, sullen cheeks, eyes dark and red, sinewy legs. Her movements held the weight of permanent depression and he knew if there wasn't sudden drastic intervention she would be dead in six months. She would be dead, and he would go to the street to pick up another whore to fuck to forget the one that had died.

She turned from him, embarrassed. Picked up his badge from the cabinet. It was in plain sight all along. Gentle steps toward him, the badge held as an offering.

"There was sixty bucks, too," he reminded her.

"Sorry," she consoled him. Her hand lingered on his wrist, her fingernails lightly brushing the hairs along the back of his arm. "You could take it in trade."

He felt the tingling between his legs, like circulation returning after a leg or arm has fallen asleep. The addict nudged awake. He grabbed her wrist. It was all bone; he could snap it without even twisting. He drew her hand close, placed her fingers in his mouth. His tongue feeling the skin between each finger, tasting cocaine residue. She looked into his eyes, wanting him in a way that was more than a hooker wanting a john.

Program jargon tugged at his soul.

God, please take me out of here, I cannot control this.

God, please be at my side now and instruct me.

God, please take care of this poor child and help her find her way.

He took one step back, still holding her wrist. Another step and he pushed her hand away and found the door behind him. His eyes remained downcast, staring at her feet. His hand behind him fumbled with the lock, then fumbled with the chain. She took a step toward him. He continued to run the affirmations in his head. She reached out. He threw the door open and ran.

He sat in the front seat of his Crown Vic in Darla's carport. He sat there for five minutes before he noticed the kids all around him. Laughing. It wasn't until he turned the ignition that he saw the word on the hood of his car. He stepped out for a better view.

Spray-painted in large gray block letters on the navy blue hood was Hayden described in a word: WHOREFUCKER.

15

Building #1102. The Los Angeles Coroner's Office. There were sixty thousand deaths in Los Angeles County every year, and roughly one-third of them were under the jurisdiction of the L.A. Coroner. After subtracting natural deaths and accidents, the facility ended up with about nine thousand bodies annually. There were around three hundred bodies in the place on any given day.

Hayden had come to the coroner's office after first stopping by his apartment to pick up his Jeep. The last thing he wanted was the chief coroner investigator asking why "whorefucker" was spray-painted on the hood of Hayden's Crown Vic.

He took the elevator to the basement then stepped into the Control Area where Dottie checked in bodies for processing. She smiled when he waved, but her mind was elsewhere. He watched her go back to measuring the sleeping baby on the metal cart beside her. Only the baby wasn't sleeping. Hayden stepped back and away, averting his eyes.

He walked through a hallway crowded with bodies on gurneys. One body had just arrived, wrapped in clear plastic, with the hospital's ER equipment sandwiched inside. Next, a woman under a sheet, her head exposed. In her twenties, Hispanic, with the high cheekbones and long forehead of an Aztec princess. Cause of death wasn't apparent and Hayden wasn't about to peek under the sheet to find out. The body beside her was the one causing all the stink. It had "marbled," turning a pukish, bloated green. Maggots fed on the side of the dead man's face.

A Stryker saw buzzed from one of the three large autopsy rooms. Hayden peeked through a window to see a forensic tech zip off the top portion of a cadaver's skull. Off someone's loved one.

The rooms were large enough to perform five simultaneous autopsies, side-by-side. The examiners did fifteen to thirty a day. Hayden saw Charlie finishing up at one of the tables. A technician assisted him, and Hayden winced when he realized that it was the same man who had assisted Abbey Reed at the West L.A. crime scene. Charlie assigned him cleanup duties and the tech tackled them with vigilance, as though the corpse was in mortal danger and might live or die by the quality of his care. Charlie peeled himself from the scene, rolling his eyes, leaving the tech with a half dozen stainless steel instruments to sterilize and a lot of mopping up to do. He motioned for Hayden to join him in an X-ray room.

"Your apprentice?" Hayden inquired when Charlie had closed the door to the X-ray room behind them.

"Investigator looking to be a forensic tech."

"He'll never make it."

Charlie unlocked a long, metal drawer and began thumbing through the acetate. "You think?"

"Yeah, too fucking serious. Can't you chill him out?"

"If I can't, nobody can."

Charlie pulled a half dozen X-rays, seemed to hesitate, staring down at the name "Abbey Reed" handwritten in dark ink on the film.

Hayden peeked at the X-rays. "Whatcha got for me?"

"I shouldn't be doing this," Charlie groaned. Hayden looked down to see what concerned him.

"Oh. Spare me the conscience."

"It's Abbey's work. I shouldn't present her results."

"You read her report, right? I couldn't make *sense* of it. I needed a walk-through. I came on her day off." Hayden smiled coyly. "Don't worry about it."

"Well, now that you put it that way." Charlie threw up the first set of X-rays, hit the lights. "This is the West L.A. crime scene."

"Any semen?"

Charlie shook his head.

"Prints on the body?"

"Smudges. Nothing discernible."

"Smudges from a glove or bare hands?"

"Might be latex gloves."

"And the male?"

"Bullet through the brain, died instantly. Close range—he wasn't moved there. I think it was a love triangle. A crime of passion."

"Residue on the girl?"

"No."

Charlie posted the film of the other murder victims: the Coral Reef hooker and Mrs. Palistrano.

"He washed his hands," Hayden pondered. "Or changed gloves. So why do you think it was a love triangle?"

"I feel it. In my gut. It sticks in my claw."

"Sticks in your *claw*, Charlie? Like you're a fucking bird of prey? How about 'sticks in your *craw*'? Why do you say things you don't know what they mean?"

"Claw makes sense."

"No, don't argue the point. Stay on course. Jesus. And leave the gut feelings to me. I think he wanted us to *think* it was a triangle. I think it was calculated."

"How's that?"

"So we wouldn't tie it to the pro at the Coral Reef."

"But if your room number thing is true then he *would* want us to tie it to the Coral Reef."

"Maybe he wants to throw the police off course. Maybe he wants to tell us something and hide something at the same time."

"Hmm . . ." Charlie considered.

"Yeah. It's complicated."

"Shit, Hayden, killers aren't that smart. Sometimes they're just perverts."

"Not this one."

"Your door number thing didn't stick, y'know."

"There'll be something else."

"They'll be cold cases soon."

"Not if I can help it."

"And you're sure the first two are tied to the old lady?"

Hayden drummed his fingers on the film of Lori's body, her rib cage scraped by the knife inserted seven times. The film of Devon's skull with its 9 mm entry and exit wounds. He studied the film from the girl at the Coral Reef. The bones of her feet, without toes. More knife wounds. He studied Mrs. Palistrano's film—a circle the diameter of a knitting needle between two vertebrae in her neck.

"They're connected, Charlie. We gotta look deeper."

16

Sol called and asked him to meet for an early dinner at Rocco's
Pizza. He had been concerned about Hayden's sobriety ever since
he was kicked out of his home meeting. Sol insisted that they meet
face-to-face at least once a week until Hayden settled into a new SAA
routine.

Hayden thumbed his GPS system, searching for Rocco's, which was
located somewhere in the Sherman Oaks/Encino/Studio City/Ventura
Boulevard megalopolis. Ventura Boulevard stretched on through countless
miles, from one end of the very long Valley to the other, trailing off somewhere into the North Hollywood environs where Burbank became Glen-
dale and ultimately Pasadena. Hayden didn't really know where it ended
because all roads that skirted Hollywood tended to lead him to Sunset
Boulevard. Ventura Boulevard was the only boulevard Hayden knew that

didn't draw prostitutes. It just wasn't done on Ventura Boulevard. And there was no goddamn reason why. Perhaps all that was affluent and artsy-fartsy about the Valley collected along the banks of this boulevard like so much sludge and waste and even the whores couldn't stand it.

Hayden had spent the previous hour and a half addressing the issue of his Crown Vic "problem." He bought two Brillo pads, bleach, and a quart of lye, which he used to remove the graffiti. He then applied a thin layer of gray Bondo to the surface of the hood.

Sol was already at the restaurant when he arrived. They greeted each other warmly, but there was clearly a little tension at the table. Hayden sensed a lecture coming. They ordered quickly and chitchatted until the food arrived. Hayden talked more than usual, trying to fill the silence. When the food arrived, they sat for a moment, wondering when the real discussion would begin.

Hayden watched Sol nibble the edges of his eggplant Parmesan sandwich. He refused to eat like a man and it took every bit of Hayden's self-control to keep from driving the foot-long sandwich down the length of Sol's throat. Hayden had "everything pizza," his own personal concoction, something like an everything bagel but in pizza form.

Sol finally jumped in. "Chrissakes, Hayden, can't you just be present in a room? You should do some meditating."

"You seem a little touchy yourself," Hayden observed. "Maybe there's something going on. Maybe you should do a Fourth Step on it."

"I'll work my steps with my own sponsor. You seem to be having trouble getting thirty days."

"Yeah, well, I had ninety a couple weeks ago."

"You can't rest on your laurels."

"Apparently not."

Hayden shook a half-inch layer of crushed chili peppers over his pizza. Sol watched, grimacing. He reached into his pocket and pulled out a small baggy containing seven of the little white pills he used to control his acid reflux. He downed a couple using the room-temperature Evian he had ordered while waiting for Hayden to arrive.

"You need to work your first three steps again," he said, peeling excess cheese off the eggplant.

"I'm tired of them. I want to begin my fourth again," Hayden insisted.

"You're not ready."

"Says who?"

"Your sponsor."

Hayden called the waiter over, ordered a Moretti. Sol gave him a look. Hayden didn't care.

"Who gives you the fucking right." Hayden said it like a statement.

"You did."

"I mean, what makes you such an authority?"

"Why are you being defensive?"

"Why are you argumentative?"

"You want to do your Fourth Step?"

"Yes."

"Good. Do the first three and then you'll be ready."

"I've done the first three."

"Three times. Why are you so willful?"

"I'm not willful. I'm . . . argumentative."

"You're willful. Why won't you open a door to God?"

"Because . . ."

"You did. Once. You embraced God and your dead father and He was there for you."

"It was a moment of weakness."

Sol gave him a long, steady look. Hayden knew checkmate when he saw it. The beer came and Hayden drank straight from the bottle.

"You need more moments of weakness, Hayden. You need hours of weakness. Days. Years. You can't do this alone."

Sol always knew how to cut through the bullshit.

"You've been in your middle circle," Sol observed.

"Does it show?"

"You've been cruising."

"I sat in the parking lot of my old massage parlor today, for twenty minutes."

"You didn't call me."

Hayden tasted blood on his tongue, where his teeth went in.

"You going to your new meeting?" Sol queried.

110

"Yesterday. I'm thinking of going again tonight."

"Keep thinking. You should do more than one meeting a week, you know."

"Yeah, everyone wants a cop at the local Twelve Step."

Sol's phone rang. Hayden was used to it. Sol's phone was a live wire. If it wasn't the hospital, it was his wife or his kids or some sex-addicted brother in need.

Sol looked at the number, apologized. "I've got to take this. New-comer."

Newcomer was someone new to the program. Probably still in crisis mode, Hayden thought. The guy must have just found out that a brother-hood of like-minded psychos existed. He wouldn't consider himself one of the flock yet, but he probably yearned to be part of a fellowship of men. To assist a newcomer or to be a sponsor was the pinnacle of fulfill-ing one's service commitment, since the early days of AA. Sol sponsored three brothers. Hayden had never been a sponsor. He was too . . . willful.

"No, no trouble at all," Sol told his sponsee on the phone. He pulled a rumpled meeting schedule from his wallet. "I'm glad you came Sunday. It's probably a good idea to hit a meeting every day for a while. It's like pushing a reset button on the way you live your life. You've been on au-topilot, we all were. You start by being present, by feeling your feet on the ground. By listening to the wisdom in the rooms. I know a great meet-ing in Venice, and a spot just recently opened—"

The last statement was made with a wink to Hayden, who whispered a stern "Fuck you" in reply.

Sol read from the schedule. "Unity Presbyterian at 5301 Lincoln Boule-vard in Venice. Room 203. Need the phone number?"

It felt like a Louisville Slugger against Hayden's jaw. He blacked out for the length of time it took to blink. His pupils must have shuttered by a de-gree or two because the restaurant went ultraviolet.

Room 203? This was his old meeting, his *home* meeting, before he started attending his *new* meeting in Long Beach. He had attended the old meeting, off and on, for two years. He knew everything about the room ex-cept the room number. He must have known it at one time, as a newcomer. But once you're in the meeting, you're in the meeting. You go up the stairs or around the corner or up the ramp or whatever, but you are drawn to the room by the faces of friends and fellow junkies. Hayden *knew* the number, in the back of his mind, hovering in his periphery, rising to the surface of the dark cold waters of his subconscious mind.

His home meeting, room 203. The West L.A. murder, room 203. The Coral Reef murder, room 203. Mrs. Palistrano's murder . . . *room twelve*.

Sol continued his conversation on the phone, with warm paternal chuckles and sage comments. He held the cell phone to his ear with one hand while folding the schedule with his other. He slipped it back into his wallet; his hands did this by rote, he had done it so many times, this man-full-of-service.

Hayden grabbed the wallet from his sponsor's hand. He tore the schedule from its gut and unfolded it, hands shaking, bits of the schedule ripping and coming off in his fingers. Sol whispered "Hey!" as Hayden searched, searched, finding it . . . Long Beach, Zion Temple Church of God, off Long Beach Boulevard . . . *room twelve*.

17

*F*uck *fuck fuck fuck fuck fuck fuck* . . .

Hayden couldn't remember leaving the restaurant. Only images—his Moretti tipping over as he shot up from the seat; the crumpled twenty-dollar bill he threw down to cover the tab; Sol's expression, confused, concerned, the cell phone still at his ear; the angry look from the waitress who he elbowed on his way out; the cloth napkin still tucked in his pants as he drove away. His cell phone was ringing already—Sol. He switched it off.

He drove semiconscious, shifting gears, checking the rearview, punching gas and clutch, letting his Jeep take him where it would. He was on the 405 going south.

I am the evidence connecting these crimes.

He wondered if that was his ego talking. Everything revolved around him, of course. There were two things constant with every addict: they had low self-esteem and they were the center of the universe. Hayden remembered the saying that drew a familiar laugh from every addict who heard it—*I am the piece of shit the world revolves around.*

His addict was itching. He was off the freeway. Long Beach Boulevard. Seedy fucking streets.

He saw a girl on the Boulevard—a real mess. He drove on. He felt himself slipping into the bubble. Drug addicts, gangbangers, Vice cops. Yellow light. Red.

Someone's watching me. There's no other answer. This isn't right. This isn't fair. I can't go to the captain with this.

A dyed blonde appeared up ahead. Plump, but that was okay. At least she was eating, he thought. Maybe she was healthy. The crack whores could have AIDS. Anyone could have AIDS.

God, she's cute. Nineteen? A runaway?

There were guys cruising all around him. The car ahead got there first and took her off the street. Hayden pounded the steering wheel with his fists—he could be out all night and not see a girl like that again. He threw a U-turn, passed an alley, peered in. Thought he saw something, but it was nothing, a homeless something or other . . .

He took a side street into a commercial driveway, slammed his foot on the brake. There were lights on poles and designated parking spots. A church in front of him. He had arrived at his Thursday evening meeting. It was 7 P.M.

He sat staring at his dashboard, engine on. Others walked from parked cars to the meeting. To room *twelve.*

One or two looked his way. It must have seemed odd, Hayden sitting alone in his car with the engine running, the soft amber light from the dashboard illuminating the sweat on his forehead.

He knew he had been wrong about the killer. This was no amateur. The killer must have known that Hayden was on call the night of each murder. He knew that Robbery-Homicide would respond.

Paranoia set in. He didn't want the killer to know that he knew. He would have to play it cool, stay in control. Work the cases like nothing had changed. A guy like this would be watching him, looking for a connection. Hayden wasn't about to give him the satisfaction.

He stepped up to the room and stood in the doorway. The men were in their seats, fourteen of them. They seemed fixed on their own problems. Eager to share, to confess their actions of the past week, to recount their gradual victory over addiction. This ninety minutes was the only thing holding their lives together.

Hayden tried to think of all the things he had confessed in meetings past. The killer knew what Hayden did for a living. He knew that Hayden fucked the whores he was supposed to arrest. He knew that Hayden broke the laws he swore to uphold.

"Welcome to the Thursday night meeting of Sex Addicts Anonymous. Will all those who want to rid themselves of compulsive sexual behavior please raise their hands?"

Hayden looked around the room, trying to determine if he had seen any of these faces before. He saw a guy in the back, he thought from the Brentwood meeting. Hayden had only been to the Brentwood meeting twice.

They all looked familiar. None of them looked familiar. One guy looked like the teller at his bank. Looked like the guy, but wasn't him. The guy leading the meeting had a smirk on his face. Hayden wondered what that was all about. They turned toward him, their hands still in the air. He felt his own hand begin to rise. He nodded quietly and took a seat in the room where he belonged.

18

He didn't sleep that night. He tried, but when he settled into bed the sweat came. The ceiling fan wobbled and clicked with each turn. He opened the window, which brought the noise of the ocean. He had a decision to make.

It was bigger than him. This thing he had stepped into. This thing that had stepped into him. If *he* was the connection to all of these murders then he was morally obligated to disclose to his captain. So far nobody in his professional life, except Charlie and Sergeant Hempel, knew of Hayden's addiction. To reveal the connection would be to reveal his addiction. Not just to the department, but to the city, the nation. The mayor and city council would want an explanation. There would be press conferences. CNN. Hayden couldn't face that kind of scrutiny. The picking and prying apart of his life. The media dissecting him. His shameful actions held up as an example. His life a cautionary tale. He would lose more than his job, he would lose his credibility, his dignity.

But his sacrifice would be small, in comparison. To the four people who had died. To the others who might follow.

Something inside him argued that to disclose would be foolish. It wasn't as if Thorton and Price would suddenly solve the case if they had this information. They had proved themselves shortsighted by accepting the Twenty-Second Street Gang as a patsy. The voice inside Hayden said to leave it alone, let fate take its course. Hayden was the one who could actually *do* something with the information, after all. If Hayden spoke up he would be taken off the case—*the one person capable of solving the case would be banned from the case.*

Something inside his head whispered in his ear.

Come on, now. Don't be a quitter. Keep this to yourself.

But lives were at stake. It wasn't right to put his life above others.

Your life must be preserved to save *the lives of others. You must stay on the case. You're the best shot they've got.*

Hayden knew the voice. It was a voice he sometimes trusted, sometimes feared. He had learned, through his meetings, to ignore it. It was the voice of his addict.

As dawn broke Hayden continued to stew over his dilemma. Before Hayden's divorce, the therapist had asked Hayden and Nicky to make a list. All the reasons to stay in the marriage on one side, all the reasons to separate on the other. Hayden's reasons to stay roughly equaled the reasons to go. Nicky's reasons settled the question.

Hayden made a list now. Hide the connection or disclose it? End his career or watch others die at his expense? The list spoke clearly enough—he would speak to his captain. Hayden's career was expendable while innocent lives were not. With that decision came some peace. It would all be over soon. No more hiding. No looking over his shoulder for Internal Affairs. He could disappear. He thought of Kalispel. Montana seemed like the perfect place to start over.

He rose from a fitful two-hour sleep and cooked himself a three-egg omelet with fresh asparagus, avocados, onions, and bacon. He brewed coffee, drank it black. He found the *L.A. Times* outside his apartment door and read it quietly and comfortably at his kitchen table.

He called the precinct but Captain Forsythe was out. Hayden made the appointment with Reggie, who assured him that the captain would arrive in an hour. With the appointment scheduled, the last of Hayden's tension dissolved. He felt in control, which should have been the first sign that something was off. He knew from his meetings that control was an illusion. This would have been a good time for him to call his sponsor.

At the station Hayden sat in the same seat where he had asked Captain Forsythe for the help of a profiler. The same seat where the captain had asked about his behavior with Abbey Reed. Now the captain would have his answer. He would think back to the reports that were made in the past, to the offhand remarks about Hayden's character and his actions around women. Of course, it would all make sense now. He was a sex addict.

Hayden checked his watch. The captain should have been there by now. The starch in Hayden's collar burned a circle around his neck. His hairline sweated. The welt on his head throbbed, agitated by the heat in the room. He noticed damp, red pixilation on his fingertips from the fresh blood that came off his scalp.

He turned around when he heard footsteps, but it was just Reggie peeking in. Reggie flashed him a thumbs-up and an open palm—*five minutes*. Hayden nodded. He reran the speech again in his head.

"So what's up?" the captain would ask. It's the West L.A. murder, Hayden would say. And the Coral Reef. And Mrs. Palistrano from Melrose.

"Focus on West L.A.," the captain would insist, then, seeming concerned, "What's the deal, Hayden?" Hayden would disclose. Tell of his addiction, the meetings, *the room numbers*. The captain would understand. And that would be the end of it.

Hayden took a fall. From a stationary seat, onto the floor. His lungs collapsed. He grasped his throat, scissor-kicking the carpet. He came face-to-face with the wad of damp Kleenex he had used on the coffee spill days before.

Air escaped in high-pitched gasps, but nothing came in. He felt pain in his chest and his neck and the back of his head. Was this a heart attack?

He didn't think so. It was more than physical. There was anger in it. There was addict in it.

He pulled himself up, fumbled with the door, unintentionally locking himself in. He turned the knob again and there was pressure from the other side. As he pulled back, the door was pushed forward and suddenly Captain Forsythe was in the doorway. Hayden ran past him into the bullpen where the detectives milled about their desks. Reggie raised an eyebrow as Hayden flew by. Hayden made it to the elevators, then down, then out.

He sat on the curb outside Parker Center, holding his knees to his chest. The ground vibrated and Hayden realized that the earthquake had come from inside of him. His legs and hands shook with adrenaline. It seemed an exclamation point, this tremor. An exclamation point that followed the statement delivered by the voice in his head, *"The day you disclose is the day that you die!"*

19

Hayden found his way to the L.A. County Coroner's Office. He had left Parker Center in a daze, struggling with the stick shift on his Jeep as he drove. He'd planned to go home, but the coroner's was closer. And Charlie was there. He felt that he needed to be around Charlie.

He sat alone in the Crypt. Not exactly alone: there were two hundred twenty bodies on the racks around him. Wrapped in clear plastic. Tied with rope. Thin, stiff feet with overgrown toenails. Young, old, male, female. Murders, suicides. Teenage boys who lost the struggle fighting society and their homosexuality, loveless women who razored themselves for revenge, gangbangers carrying bullets in their bellies. Death by fire, suffocation, asphyxiation, drowning, freezing, starvation.

Here Hayden found a renewed sense of purpose. These folks didn't make it but they might have if Hayden had been on the scene. It was too much weight on his shoulders, his therapist once said, as Hayden was a man and God was God. Why would Hayden want this responsibility? It was the same responsibility he had accepted for the loss of his father, although he had been just a boy when it happened.

Hayden felt that things might have been different if he had been in the car that day with his father. He wondered if he would have seen the shooter. If he would have grabbed the wheel from his father's hands. Or, if he had screamed, would his father have hit the brakes, allowing the bullet to pass before them and into the concrete divider beyond? As a youth he studied the trajectory of that slug, how it entered from the passenger-side window and caught his father at a 35-degree angle, arcing up. If Hayden had been in the passenger seat his father might have survived.

The double doors opened and Charlie came in, pushing a body on a gurney. Hayden was nursing his Starbucks, watching through the hive of bodies that hid him from Charlie's view. Charlie stared at the naked woman on his cart, his eyes bloodshot tired. His experienced fingers massaged the tendons in the woman's neck then proceeded along the sides of her face. He opened her mouth, maneuvered her tongue from side to side. His fingers continued along her cheeks, nostrils, eyes. Opened her eyelids and pushed the dead round spheres in and around, studying the pixilation of blood vessels that would reveal the secret of her death. Ocular petichia. Did this eighteen-year-old die from strangulation or was her brain predestined to stroke out early, leaving her beautiful for eternity?

Hayden knew that Charlie would figure it out. In the morning he would remove her brain. He would be able to tell immediately if there had been a hemorrhage or stroke from the blood in the cavity when he opened the skull. If blood didn't exist, Charlie would have to clip the gelatinous organ from her spine and place it in a formalin solution for a month in order to have something firm enough to dissect. Only then would the boyfriend who was under surveillance be left alone to mourn her passing. That, or maybe Hayden would be brought in to arrest him for her murder. It was all up to Charlie.

"Don't know how you can do this fucking job, night after night."

Charlie nearly pissed himself hearing Hayden's voice behind the bodies.

"You are a fucking psycho case," he managed after finding his breath.

"Hey, I've got a normal job," Hayden replied.

"I'm here because I'm working. Why are you here?"

Good question. Hayden felt he belonged in this room, at least as much as Charlie.

He noticed the Stryker saw in Charlie's hand. "You're not going to deface her *now* are you?"

Charlie ran the saw absently. It produced a clean, shrill sound. "Not now. They're never really the same after I open."

"They're never really the same when they arrive."

Charlie nodded. He seemed to stare past the body. Hayden wondered if Charlie ever regretted his decision to become a medical examiner. It was probably just a hop, skip, and jump from peeling the face off a cadaver to performing the latest plastic surgery on Hollywood's aging starlets. Providing, of course, that he could keep his previous place of employment off the record.

"I've found the connection, Charlie."

"Hm?"

"My killer. My serial killer."

Charlie put the saw on an empty space in the shelves. The place where the body on his gurney would go. He pulled a Sharpie from his pocket and wrote the cadaver's name on a small placard to be placed at the front of the shelf.

"Really," he said. "I thought everything came up zero."

"Naw. He's a tricky son of a bitch. He's going to make me fight for it."

"Time you fought for *something*."

Hayden took that with a grain of salt. "I'm going to have to work closely with you on this one," he said.

"You in trouble?"

Charlie had always been there for him. When Nicky kicked Hayden out of the house it was Charlie who put him up. Extra room and a cot. Silverlake frogs chirping and the sounds of gunshots in the night.

"I'm working on it," Hayden said in response to Charlie's question. He considered telling Charlie everything. All that he couldn't tell Captain Forsythe or his sponsor or anyone else. What good would it do? It would only make him complicit, forcing him to choose between his loyalty to Hayden and his legal obligation to alert the authorities. Why force a dilemma?

Hayden chose to remain silent. If all went according to plan, a plan he had begun to devise since leaving Captain Forsythe's office, Hayden would have his man behind bars without anyone ever knowing what truly connected these crimes.

Hayden walked from the Crypt, leaving his empty Starbucks cup on the gurney next to long thin pasty sexy lifeless legs.

20

Hayden sat in the waiting room of the investigation firm in West-wood. Impressive building, small office. You needed an *address* in this town. Everything was image, façade. This little office rubbed elbows with a talent agency, a modeling firm, Oliver Stone's accountants, three celebrity attorneys, and twelve psychotherapists.

He held a bag under his arm labeled "Police Evidence" with a chain-of-custody adhesive sticker attached. Written with indelible ink on the sticker were the names of the officers on the scene, the forensics investigators, the evidence storage custodian, and Hayden.

He thumbed through the *Sports Illustrated* swimsuit edition in the waiting room of Kennedy Reynard and Associates, Field Investigations. The subscription was in the name of Raul Guiterrez, a client or potential client who didn't know better than to leave evidence of his visit in the form of a mailing label with his name and home address. But, if he had been in this office he was probably in the position of chasing, not running.

Kennedy Reynard seemed like the right profiler for the job. Hayden had spent Friday afternoon downtown reviewing the two local cases she had been assigned—one for the LAPD two years before when she was still with the FBI, and one last year for the Burbank Police Department. The Burbank job was a simple one-hour phone consultation. The investigator on the case had been tracking a series of bank robberies and needed to narrow the field of suspects. Ms. Reynard's work confirmed the detective's suspicions and the suspect that fit her profile was subsequently arrested and confessed to the crime.

The LAPD case was more elaborate. It involved an LAPD/FBI task force targeting the killer of five homeless men in downtown Los Angeles. Two FBI profilers were employed, and Reynard was the junior. But the files clearly read that she was the more capable of the two. It was her momentum that carried the operation. The eight-month investigation led to a produce trucker who lived in Arizona and fit the FBI profile to a tee. It wasn't long after the arrest that the senior FBI agent received a commendation and Reynard left the Bureau to open a private firm in L.A.

Profiling was one of Hayden and Rich's points of contention. It was tricky—more intuition than science—and viewed by veteran cops with the same admiration they reserved for psychic divination or amateur witchcraft. Rich saw facts as sacrosanct, and he could cite a dozen cases where speculation or innuendo carried a weak case through trial to conviction, only to be overturned years later after DNA testing. Hayden agreed to a point, but he also recognized the value of profiling as a tool to help the investigator narrow his suspect pool. Profiling would never replace traditional investigative technique. Hayden had attended a couple FBI lectures on profiling and was impressed with the accuracy of what ultimately amounted to well-educated guesswork.

It seemed that killers and rapists fell into very specific types of sociological groups defined by the ways they chose to kill and rape. If a man knocked a girl unconscious before raping her, it placed him in a different category from the man who kept her conscious while torturing her. If a man covered a victim's face after murdering her, it placed him in a different category from the man who left her in full public view. Hayden learned that these little details were gold to the profiler, who determined if the killer knew the victim, if he lived close by or far away, if he drove a Ford or Toyota. The process would seem absurd if the results didn't so consistently prove true. But the profile was only as good as the profiler.

Hayden had required that his profiler meet certain criteria. He wanted someone with FBI experience, because the FBI hired the best of the best. He wanted a private investigator—someone who wasn't affiliated with any agency. He didn't want the LAPD or FBI or any other organization monitoring his investigation. And he wanted someone familiar with the LAPD and its procedures, yet with limited departmental experience, someone who wouldn't be recognized at a crime scene investigation.

But Kennedy Reynard was a woman. Hayden knew how to handle men. He knew when to be a colleague, when to show authority, when to intimidate. With women he knew only how to intimidate. He didn't know how to have a professional relationship with a woman unless the woman was, well, a "professional" woman.

The waiting room door opened and Kennedy Reynard appeared. Younger than he had imagined, thirty-three at most. Five foot four with a head full of natural red hair. Nagel-like features with stylish horn-rimmed glasses that reminded him of a schoolgirl stripper he met once in New Orleans. She was dressed business-smart in a beige silk pantsuit that clung with static to her calves and thighs. A camisole draped like liquid cotton over firm, high breasts. She wasn't a knockout but there was a natural careless beauty that bled through, that seemed to vibrate in the air around and beyond her. When the vibration reached him, which was almost immediately, it caused him to stand with such purpose that he nearly knocked her backwards. He extended his hand.

"Ms. Reynard, Detective Glass."

She led him through a short cramped hallway and into an office the exact shape and nearly the same size as the little metal desk and two chairs that occupied it. Certificates on the wall. Diplomas. FBI acknowledgments. The desk a sparse utilitarian workspace. No photographs. A handful of manila folders and case studies. And the three files that he had sent to her by courier, each labeled with the addresses of the murders that occurred in West L.A., Hollywood, and on Melrose.

She seemed secure and confident—and something more. Behind her eyes was a great black question like an ink pad just opened. Waiting for someone's touch. To feel the absorbency of her skin yet leave no mark. To come away with traces of her essence, to be left as fingerprints on things touched thereafter. It seemed as though she was used to being touched but not felt.

Hayden was definitely attracted to her, but he didn't feel the pulse of anxiety that came from staring at a woman through the prism of his addiction. It seemed more like kinship. He respected the way she had carved out a career for herself. She was working outside the system and succeeding. Although Hayden bitched and complained through the years, he never had the courage to go it alone, afraid he would fail without the force of the LAPD behind him. Afraid he'd lose access, authority, control.

He gestured to the reports on her desk.

"We've uncovered new evidence that definitively links each one of the scenes," he said, reaching into the evidence bag and producing three sets of magazines. Each set was secured in its own folder and marked with the address of its corresponding crime. "I didn't tag these at the first or second locations, but at the old lady's house they stood out like a sore thumb."

He unwrapped each set. *Hustler* magazines. From the West L.A. crime scene, dated March, April, and May 1976; from the Coral Reef Motel, dated June, July, and August 1976; from the Melrose murder scene, dated September, October, and November 1976.

"The first set was on a coffee table with *Newsweek*, *Ebony*, *People* magazine. Seemed out of place, but there was a live-in boyfriend . . . I completely missed them at the Coral Reef Motel. Tucked under the Gideon Bible. Found the last set at the old lady's home in a pantry alongside *Reader's Digest*, *TV Guide*, and *Knitting World Magazine*. Which sent me back to the earlier crime scenes where I found the matching sets. No prints, of course. None of the occupants at any of the crime scenes touched these magazines."

Until now she had remained respectfully silent. "You said the department couldn't link the crimes . . ."

"Yes. *Before* the magazines. Our official position is that they don't exist. We think the killer is watching and we don't want to tip our hand. We need help on this one. I'm not going to wait six months for the LAPD crime lab to produce results. We need help from the private sector, from someone connected without being connected, understand?"

She swallowed, nodding. He felt a cold pleasure in reeling her in. He knew it didn't seem quite fair, but he had to win this one.

"I need an expert who can fly below the radar," he continued.

"They're letting you run with this?"

"I'm Downtown, Robbery-Homicide."

He knew she understood what that meant. Hayden was the elite of the elite and the fact that he was on the case meant that the LAPD trusted his decisions. Even if that meant hiring an outsider to fill in the gaps. *That was what he wanted her to think.*

"I'll need to see everything," she said. "Coroner's reports, prints, crime scene photos—"

"How do you bill?"

"Sorry?"

"For your services."

"It's automatic, I've got a PDF file I send to LAPD accounting."

"When I said below the radar, I meant it. The bills will come to me and I'll submit them through the channels."

She took a moment to read him, to feel his pulse with her mind. He imagined a set of polygraph needles buried in her chest, quietly scratching off hills and valleys to match his heart rate and blood pressure.

"You want to be the next Serpico, Detective Glass? Ego is a slippery thing in a serial homicide."

Reeling her in . . .

"I'm aware of the pitfalls, Ms. Reynard. All communication goes through me alone. Any notes you keep will be under lock and key. Any unnecessary communications will be shredded. Your associates don't need to know what you're working on."

He wondered if she was game. He couldn't afford to blow this. The next good profiler was a hundred miles behind her in experience.

"I need to know that you're with me on this," he pushed.

Her hand absently reached for her appointment book then retreated. He could tell she didn't trust him. She must've sensed that his offer hid an agenda that she couldn't comfortably ignore. He wondered how flexible her ethics were. Where was her moral compass? Would she accept him at his word, for the thrill of the case? He could imagine her internal debate—all that talent wasted on infidelity surveillance and insurance fraud. Hayden was offering her a return to the big league, the chance to pursue an active case, *a serial killer* . . .

"When can we visit the crime scenes?" she asked.

He smiled, shook her hand, and felt in it the enthusiasm she must have felt as an FBI cadet ten years before.

21

Planting the *Hustlers* required little forethought. He had acquired them from a distributor of antiquated books and magazines in downtown L.A. Paid cash, covered his tracks. Hayden needed a competent profiler and now he had one. Technically he hadn't tampered with evidence because the *Hustlers* had never been admitted into evidence. They had never appeared at any of the crime scenes. No one but Hayden and Kennedy knew they existed.

It was not that he lacked a code of ethics, but that the code was his own and it was malleable. He justified all questions of honesty and protocol with one simple fact: it would ultimately bring justice for the victims. He never professed to be a saint and in his world the end *did* justify the means. This killer, this sexual predator, was playing by a skewed set of rules and if Hayden was to catch him he would need a skewed set of his own—certainly one with better teeth than what the LAPD had to offer.

Hayden and Kennedy agreed to begin at the West L.A. crime scene. She arrived dressed casually in a running suit, glistening from a two-mile jog through the UCLA campus near her apartment. Her long red hair was pulled back in a ponytail and her glasses had been replaced with contacts.

She was like an arrow released from a hunting bow onto the crime scene. Her eyes darted from ceiling to floor to countertop to table, and she seemed to see things where things simply weren't. Where Hayden closed his eyes to absorb, Kennedy opened hers to scrutinize.

He answered her questions—"Over here, with her legs on the sofa and her back on the floor" and "Her fingernails picked clean postmortem; the killer knew the value of forensic evidence." The killer's apparent craftiness sent a visible chill that registered as goosebumps on Kennedy's neck. He imagined them spreading across her chest and along the backs of her arms. Was her reaction one of fear or excitement? Kennedy was either devoid of emotion or simply just *tight*, wound like a rusted coil that matched the color of her hair.

Her interest kept returning to the magazines.

"Where were they found?" she asked.

Hayden pointed to a stack of magazines on the table by the sofa.

"And at the Coral Reef Motel," she continued, "you said they were under a Bible in the bed stand?"

Hayden nodded. She looked at him quizzically.

"*Under* the Bible, right?"

"Yes," he stated, now thinking how small a Bible was compared to a magazine. He realized that he might not have thought this out clearly enough.

"And nobody noticed a set of pornographic magazines stacked under that Bible," she said a bit reproachfully, almost to herself.

"Yeah . . . well, it's just not something I was thinking of looking for." He was beginning to feel like a fool.

"What were you thinking of looking for in a murder investigation,

Detective Glass?" She said this calmly, while staring at bloodstains on the carpet. He knew she was testing him. It pissed him off that he had put himself in this position.

"The magazines were turned over, under the Bible," he said firmly. "I didn't think a magazine, *any* magazine, would be relevant in a murder investigation, Ms. Reynard. When I found them at Mrs. Palistrano's I knew to look back at the earlier scenes." He figured this would put an end to it.

She nodded quietly, but he could tell he had lost a point on her scorecard. She studied the mess of beer bottles and other trash left on the kitchen countertop.

"I didn't see footprint analysis in the report," she said.

"Too many feet at the party," he said. "The best I could get was the soil sample." He took a seat on the edge of a black leather chair.

"So the magazines at the hotel were stacked upside-down?" she queried nonchalantly, peeking through the kitchen window to view the carport below.

"Yes."

"Is that how they were stacked at this and the other crime scene?"

Hayden tried to think of an appropriate response. Christ, this woman could get into a guy's head.

"They were just stacked, like I said. One on top of the other." He wasn't being sarcastic, just trying to get her to drop the subject.

Kennedy nodded her head, the picture of patience. She walked slowly across the living room to observe the scene from the doorway.

"I'm just saying," she pressed, "were they stacked in such a way as to draw attention to themselves, or were they buried like a clue waiting to be uncovered?"

"For Christ's sake," he mumbled, frustrated. "They were *hidden*, that's why I didn't notice them at first!"

Kennedy took slow steps around the perimeter of the room, scanning for trace evidence on the walls. "If the killer had wanted the magazines found, then why had he buried them at two of the crime scenes?"

Hayden sighed heavily, looking up to the heavens. "Maybe . . . maybe the killer knew that the detective would be the same, that he would piece it together somehow," he proposed.

She raised an eyebrow at the suggestion. "How would he know that each of these crimes would attract the same homicide detective? That's virtually impossible to predict."

"I guess he'd have to know my schedule. He'd have to know when I'm on call and when I'm off duty."

She stopped her movement around the room and stood directly before him.

"But that means he would be targeting *you*, Detective. That he would want *you* as the primary investigator."

Hayden didn't like where this was going.

She spoke to herself now, running the logic through her mind. "It doesn't make sense . . . unless he knows you personally, and this is some kind of vendetta . . ."

Hayden stood up, wiping sweat from his forehead with the back of his hand. He went to the only window in the room and tried to raise it, but it was painted shut.

"Listen," he said, turning back to face her, "the connection is the magazines, that's obviously how he wanted the crimes to be seen, as a series of events—"

"Right. So it has nothing to do with you personally. It could've been any investigator on the scene. It's just a coincidence that you happened to be on call and the senior investigator available at the time of each crime."

She was just stating the facts, but the coincidence did seem a bit far-fetched.

"I'm on call a lot. And maybe there's other cases out there I didn't investigate but are part of the series—"

"That would make sense if the magazines didn't represent a complete sequence. But your magazines complete three quarters of a year in 1976. There's only room for a crime before or after your appearance at the crime scene, not in the middle. Has there been anything since Mrs. Palistrano, anything that might be connected?"

He turned toward her, choosing his words carefully. "I think we need to move on from the magazines. You're making too much of them. They prove that the crimes are connected and that's all."

She seemed taken aback by his stance. But he was just getting started. He didn't want anyone backseat driving his investigations.

"What I need from you is a description of this fucker. That's your job. I need to know his habits, I need to know where he lives, where he hangs out, where he likes to take a shit. Earn your paycheck and get me something I can use."

It stopped her questions cold. She withdrew, moving to the front door. He stepped out of her way, embarrassed for reasons he couldn't quite understand.

"Look," he began, "I think we got started on the wrong foot here—"

"You needn't worry about being targeted, Detective. If he really thought you could solve this case he wouldn't have left the magazines in the first place."

And on that note she left the scene of the crime.

22

The next day they met at the Coral Reef Motel. She was dressed more professionally than the day before, wearing her signature silk camisole and straight, tan slacks that ended on a pair of beige leather pumps. She carried a sleek, black leather bag over her shoulder. Conservative, but alluring. Hayden had slipped into one of his finer suits this morning, a blue-gray Armani that he usually saved for weddings and funerals.

The first thing Kennedy did was walk to the end table by the bed and open the drawer. Hayden chewed his lip nervously while she stared at the Gideon Bible. She nodded as if answering some question in her mind, then closed the drawer and walked to the center of the room. Hayden leaned against a wall, relieved.

She went right to work, pulling the police report and crime scene photographs from the leather bag. She was most interested in things Hayden had not considered.

"Did you review the autopsy report on this girl, what's her name?"

"Jane Doe," he answered. "Of course I did."

"You know her last meal?"

Hayden took a moment to visualize the report. "Linguini with clam sauce."

"Okay. This girl was a crack whore. You don't find linguini with clam sauce at Taco Bell."

"Good point."

"The killer took her to dinner. He wooed her."

That caught his attention. "Could we tell what restaurant—"

"No. That would be psychic. This is sociological. You wanted to know his character, didn't you?"

"He would take her out to dinner because . . . ?"

"It's a power play."

"Go on."

"She's a whore. He could take her out and fuck her for fifty bucks. But he feeds her. Takes her to a nice restaurant. He's in control, he's keeping her alive. He likes control."

It was shocking to hear her curse. It didn't seem to fit the image she projected. He imagined that she'd picked it up working late with the guys at the Bureau, when she was alone with them, and she would either become the object of sexual tension or simply "one of the guys."

She traveled the room like a pinball. He sat back and watched. No wonder she left the Bureau. They couldn't keep up with her. They probably did all they could to push her out.

She slowed as she passed the TV. Wavered for a moment.

He chimed in, "Toes were to the left, by the remote."

She placed her hand on the counter where the victim's toes had been showcased in two plastic cups. Kennedy was a tall girl but seemed to stand taller, with a slight sway in her back, her chin reaching into the air, her eyes closed in concentration. It felt like he was witnessing a private moment between women, between Kennedy and the deceased.

A silver ankle bracelet slid from under the cuff of her pant leg, settled at the joint above her heel. The sight of it stimulated him. It was the same sensation he felt when he saw a tattoo etched into the small of a woman's back. There was an unspoken mystique about jewelry and its placement on the female form. What was conservative and acceptable existed on the fingers, earlobes, and wrists, and around the sinuous softness of a woman's neck. But jewelry on toes or ankles suggested something naughty. Tattoos and rings in noses and objects set in tongues or labial folds signified contempt for society, and they tended to shake Hayden to his core. The ankle bracelet showed there was more to Kennedy than he knew.

Sensing his stare she dropped back to the flat of her heel and resumed her walk-through. She stood above the empty space that once held the form of the victim's body.

"The body was in rigor mortis when you arrived?"

"Yes."

"You found her at five A.M. Coroner placed time of death four hours prior, and her last meal an hour and a half before that. Check a five-mile radius for restaurants that are open till midnight. Narrow it down to the ones that serve linguini with clam sauce. Probably fewer than ten. Interview the waitstaff from the night of the murder. Our guy had to draw attention. There would've been an uncomfortable vibe, a feeling. Maybe someone can give us a description."

Fuck, I hired the right profiler, Hayden thought.

"I'm on it. But I think he's invisible. I think he blends in like the guy you sat next to in your tenth-grade science class. We're never going to get an ID."

"I didn't take you for a naysayer, Detective."

"I know what I've seen. Guys like this, like the BTK killer, you look right at them and you don't see them."

"I was on the BTK case. We all had a hand in it. We profiled him down to the type of toothpaste he used."

"Yeah? So why'd it take fifteen years to bring him in?"

"Sloppy investigators. Local police didn't want our help. The leads got cold, then colder."

She was good. He was paying her out of his savings and so far she was worth every cent. But he couldn't have her peering into too many corners.

They would work well together as long as he managed to stay one step ahead. He wanted her undivided attention until she delivered that profile, then he'd cut her loose to forget she ever met him.

"When do I see the next crime scene?" she asked.

"I've got us in at noon."

She took another long look around the hotel room. "Okay. I'll see you at noon."

Before she slipped away she turned to him, smiling. "Five foot four, rectangular glasses—tortoiseshell—plaid shirts and suspenders, a hundred thirty pounds. Breath like onions."

Hayden found his memo pad, began writing. "Hold it . . . give me a second . . . is this our guy?"

"Nope. He's Keith Oxley, the guy who sat next to me in tenth-grade science. Works on the floor of the New York Stock Exchange now." And with that she was out the door.

23

Hayden found himself cruising Sunset Boulevard on his way to Mrs. Palistrano's house. Not much to see at 11 A.M. The best time to cruise was four to six, the evening rush. Hookers knew there'd be a line of cars heading home. Potential clients. Angry from the stress of an eight-hour day. With an easy hour to bury in the lie of heavy traffic, hiding lost time from the wife and kids in a familiar story of road construction and traffic delays. Hand job was a twenty-minute detour, unless you met Officer Cynthia Prava and ended up losing six hours at the precinct getting booked and printed. Then you better have a *really* good excuse or get set to call the divorce lawyer and lose the house.

The minute his front wheels hit Sunset, his cell phone rang.

"What?" he growled.

"Did you lose caller ID?" It was Sol.

"No, no, hey, *sponsor*, how are you?"

"Haven't heard from you in a few days, where are you?"

"I'm not currently with a hooker, if that's what you're asking."

"You cruising?"

"Goddammit, Sol, do you have a tail on me?"

"No, Hayden, I just get a feeling. Which boulevard?"

Hayden took a hard right onto Formosa Avenue, an innocent-looking residential side street.

"I'm working, Sol. I'm on . . . Formosa Avenue."

There was a second of silence, then a soft beeping through the line.

"Is that MapQuest, Sol?"

"Formosa butts right up against Sunset, from what I can tell."

"You know, I have an hour to kill, I'm here two minutes on my way to something else—"

"Don't bullshit a bullshitter."

"What's it to you? Really? I'm not going to pick anyone up, I'm just on my old beat."

He passed a hot one, twenty-two, kinky red hair, miniskirt. He rubbernecked, almost hit the Buick in front of him, considered throwing a U-turn too late. A line of johns behind him tracking her.

"Middle circle, Hayden. You're supposed to call me *before* you start cruising. When were you going to call me?"

Another call was ringing through. Hayden recognized it—Lieutenant Garcia.

"Police business, gotta go." He released the line and picked up the next. "This is Glass."

"We've got something in Century City, where are you?"

Hayden felt something rumble inside of him. His stomach contracted uneasily. "I can be there in twenty minutes."

"You okay? Captain was concerned about you."

Hayden hadn't seen or talked to Forsythe since he ran from his office. He still couldn't believe how close he had come to disclosing. "I'm good, Lieutenant. Let him know I was sick, all right?"

"Better haul ass, Scientific Division's already on the scene."

Hayden called Kennedy and got her voice mail. Left word that he would call back later to reschedule their meeting at Mrs. Palistrano's house.

He proceeded to Century City, hoping this wasn't his guy.

24

It was a modeling agency on the twentieth floor of a high-rise. Hayden paced the large reception area where the bodies had been found. He had his sketchpad out and ready, but he couldn't find the strength to begin. The agency was chic, with ultra-modern furnishings and large, glassed-in offices and conference rooms branching off reception. Irregularly shaped walls of mirrors were interspersed throughout the space and the resulting design gave the impression that the room stretched on for miles.

The receptionist had been the intended target. Her bloodied, naked body had been stuffed into a round, plastic trash container, the kind used by janitors. She had been bent forward and dropped ass-first into the container, with her face peering above its rim, through the space between her two feet.

Hayden received her driver's license, employment record, and work schedule from the sergeant on scene. The license identified her as Rhonda Stapleton. Born in Knoxville, Tennessee, in 1986.

She had been murdered the night before, having stayed late doing catch-up, while the janitorial service worked alongside her. A Honduran woman in her mid-thirties had been vacuuming and a thin Asian man in his fifties was collecting the trash. There was a small 9 mm hole under the man's chin and an open cavity just above his eyebrows. The impact spatter stretched twelve feet from the top of his skull, spraying a fine, red mist across the length of an Art Deco mirror. The Honduran woman had been bludgeoned, strangled, and stabbed in the neck repeatedly.

Rhonda was blond with almost-model looks. Would've been the hottest girl in the room at any place other than an L.A. modeling agency. She must have watched the whole thing go down, Hayden thought. He figured the killer had saved her for last.

Hayden crossed back to the entrance, checked the front door. Suite number ten. He had recently picked up another meeting at a church in Lynwood. Room number ten. Hayden slammed his fist against the number on the wooden door. The hollow thud reverberated through the reception area, causing the nearby crime scene technicians to jump.

The killer had him under a microscope. Hayden wondered how he got his information, if he had been attending the meetings or simply watching Hayden from the sidelines. He wondered if the killer had a partner, tag-teaming Hayden's activities. Hayden had never felt so helpless, so angry, so ready to do violence. If he could get his hands on this fucker, for even a moment . . . He hadn't been this angry since the day his father was killed.

He felt responsible. He was part of this now. It had been his choice to keep Forsythe in the dark and now three more people were dead. It was as if Hayden had become the killer's unwilling accomplice.

The mood in the reception area was somber. The Scientific Investigation Division and the uniformed officers worked quietly, side-by-side. Everyone sensed the terror that lingered in the air, and Hayden imagined each of them replaying the dramatic sequence of events as seen through *her* eyes, as she waited her turn. Hayden stood over her twisted form in the trash container. "I'm sorry," he whispered. *You don't know me but I brought this to you.*

She'd been a receptionist at the agency five months. She had lived in a little rent-controlled apartment in Santa Monica. It didn't surprise Hayden—most recent migrants tried to get as close to the Pacific Ocean as humanly possible. And Santa Monica was hip, definitely the place to be seen by enterprising young film producers. Rhonda probably sent scores of e-mails to old high school friends about life in L.A., the never-ending summer, the miles of beach, the friendly people.

Hayden felt that Los Angeles bore an undeserved reputation for being a city of selfish opportunists. The people who lived here knew better. It was a city of immigrants, and most residents remembered those first few months of displacement in a new country, a new state, a new city. Angelenos carried this memory with them and, when they weren't bitching about traffic, heat waves, mudslides, forest fires, earthquakes, or riots, they were generally kind to the newcomers, recalling that they were once newcomers themselves.

Hayden stood above her and closed his eyes. The room evaporated as he plugged into the scene. He imagined what she must have experienced, sitting still at her desk, hearing the "pop" and watching the janitor fall to the ground. The surreal spray of blood against the mirrors. Then the cleaning woman's valiant struggle. She had fought hard, the violence evident in every bruise and abrasion left behind. The life had been beaten out of her, before Rhonda's eyes. Hayden imagined Rhonda immobile from shock, her fingers resting just inches from a letter opener and a pair of scissors. The killer might have expected to see shock, but not the complete evaporation of soul, as though her life had already passed. He must have felt very powerful, Hayden thought.

There were marks around Rhonda's neck consistent with death by strangulation, and that was probably how the coroner would call it. But Rhonda had suffered before that. Her body was a landscape of thin, bloody channels carved into her skin by what appeared to have been a box cutter blade. Hayden imagined that after dispatching the cleaning crew the killer approached Rhonda, pulled her from her chair, and casually removed the clothes from her body. Then his blade touched down to kiss Rhonda's right shoulder.

She must have felt its cold metallic bite as it angled up sharply to slide across the top of her shoulder and up the base of her neck, along the trapezoid's curve. It hadn't been a kill-cut, just a bloodletting. But she would have known, then, that it was over.

Afterwards, the killer dragged the trash container to her side, lifted her up high and dropped her in. In one last act of defiance, he took a pinky finger. A quick, clean cut. Somewhere, Hayden imagined, there would be a collection of fingers with brightly colored fingernails.

"You gonna raise the dead or can I get in here and do my job?"

Hayden opened his eyes to bright fluorescent lights. It was Abbey Reed. There was a little aggression in her voice, enough to say, "Don't fuck with me, mister." Maybe it was the knowledge that *she* knew that *he* knew that she had made a complaint with his captain. Maybe it was the secret they shared, that his attention bothered her enough to make her lodge a complaint, that his actions disturbed the order of her life, *that what he did mattered*.

And the incongruity of those thoughts left him feeling cold. Rhonda's cloudy eyes peered out from her place in the trash container, witnessing the scene. Perhaps she recognized in Hayden's behavior something familiar, something dangerous. Perhaps she knew that Hayden was responsible.

He stepped back and welcomed Abbey into the crime scene with a wave of his hand. He let her win this one.

He proceeded to sketch the scene, although he found it difficult to move the pencil in his hand. Hard to draw a naked woman bent in half in a trashcan.

He needed to give this killer a name. Not "killer" or "bad guy" or "that fucker." Hayden needed something personal, something that would stick. He recalled the strange period of time just after the September 11 attacks, those first weeks, those two or three months when America didn't know how to label the event. The country was in shock and the media and his neighbors and his colleagues referred to it simply as "the attack," "the Twin Towers," or *"that day"* when "it" happened. It could not be objectively processed because everyone was still inside it. Ultimately the world settled on "September 11th," which morphed into "911," the national emergency phone number grafted onto the date code, then at last it joined the collective unconscious as "Nine-eleven," which was the same as "911" without the acknowledgment of fear evoked by a 911 emergency call.

Hayden needed to fit his anger to a name. A hard, tough, fucked-up name to identify this fucker until the day Kennedy came up with the guy's birth name and street address. Hayden met an addict once who used the name "Rufus" to label the addiction itself. When he was having a particularly difficult morning he would say, "Rufus was trying to take control of my life today," or "I was heading to the movie theater and Rufus took me down Lincoln Boulevard." Rufus looked for opportunities to act out. He was the addiction inside, fixed to every addict like some grotesque Siamese twin. Rufus was the voice inside Hayden's head, the voice that talked him out of disclosing to his captain. Rufus was a crafty piece of shit. Hayden would call this killer Rufus.

From where he stood, Hayden could sense that Rufus was evolving, getting bolder. He had taken Rhonda's pinky finger as a trophy. Maybe he was losing his patience with Hayden. That was fine by Hayden—impatient killers made mistakes. He hoped Rufus would get so bold as to get sloppy. Hayden would be right there to take him down.

The easy evidence was missing, but there was a lot of carnage here and even the most thorough killer couldn't keep every ball in the air all the time. Although Rufus left bloody footprints on the carpet, Hayden suspected it to be a ruse. Rufus had probably worn shoes two sizes too large, or one size too small. The treads were sharp—as if they were brand new or had been in a closet for a while, waiting.

He would have to wait for forensics to see if Rufus left any skin under Rhonda's nails. He doubted it. She hadn't made a scratch, except maybe with the missing pinky finger. Maybe Kennedy could dig something up from the autopsy report.

Hayden had just finished sketching the scene when Captain Forsythe called his cell phone.

"Yes, sir?" Hayden answered.

"You're at that Century City fiasco?"

"Yes."

"How long you been there?"

"Not long."

"I need you here. I'm sending someone else to the scene."

Hayden was disappointed. "I got the call out, Captain."

"Don't worry, it's still your case. He'll just cover for you."

"Who are you sending?"

"Listen, there's been a development. I need you here right away. Can you be here in twenty minutes?"

"I can do that, Captain."

Hayden disconnected the line. He didn't know what was up but it had to be big. He checked in with the sergeant on the scene and let him know to expect another detective from Homicide Special.

He made for the exit, throwing a casual glance at a mirrored wall on the way out. Abbey was watching him go. Her look caught his, and then she turned back to the crime scene quickly. It gave him a nervous, strangely excited feeling.

It was easier when she ignored him.

25

P lease take a seat, Hayden."

Hayden followed the captain's request, nodding to Detectives Thorton and Price as he sat beside them at the conference room table. He didn't know what they had up their sleeves, but he did know that they were wasting his time.

Captain Forsythe took a seat at the head of the table.

"The detectives here brought in the collar on the councilman case," Forsythe announced.

Hayden was dumbfounded. It made about as much sense as if he had said, "The detectives here will be feeding your testicles to the crocodile under the table." Hayden faced his two colleagues, waiting for an explanation. Thorton looked away, but Price stood his ground.

"Two members of the Twenty-Second Street Gang, an OG and a new recruit," Price barked with excitement.

Hayden folded his arms. They read his doubt.

"We've got a taped confession, Hayden," Thorton said.

"The detectives tailed them for a week," Forsythe interjected. "These are the guys."

Hayden suddenly couldn't contain his anger. The frustration had been building for days and this last bit of bullshit tipped the scales. He lunged from his chair, his outstretched hands finding Nick's stiff shirt collar. Thorton grabbed Hayden's wrists, but it was Forsythe's swift, powerful backhand that broke the hold, knocking Hayden back into his seat.

"Keep your cool, Glass," Forsythe said, taking control of the room.

"You're a fucking psycho," Nick said to Hayden, adjusting his Mervyn's non-wrinkle, pinstripe suit. Hayden massaged the welt on his chest from where Forsythe's hand made contact.

"The fuck you guys doing with my case?" Hayden snapped.

Price looked straight ahead, a smile snaking across his lips. Thorton almost spoke, but gestured toward the captain instead.

Forsythe monitored Hayden for a moment before speaking. Hayden stared back with expectation.

"I told you we needed help on this," Forsythe said at last. "I put them on and they got the job done."

"This is bullshit. It's my job. *My job!*" Hayden thundered.

"Were you even working the case?" Thorton asked. "It took us half a day to find these guys and a week to bring them in."

"We would've brought 'em in sooner, except the captain wanted to give you your shot," Nick revealed.

"My shot at making a big fucking mistake, that's a shot I don't need," Hayden said, staring at the conference room table, shaking his head.

"You haven't done shit since you brought Gordo and the others in for questioning," Nick said, brushing lint off his slacks. "We came in and did what needed doing."

Hayden wanted to knock that self-assured smile off Price's face. He decided instead to fuck with their heads.

"Your informant's lying," Hayden stated. *"You've got the wrong guys."*

Nick just nodded, still smiling. But Hayden sensed that his comment hit a chord. And then it occurred to him.

"You didn't poly these guys."

Nick blinked. His lower lip twitched a half-hair. Hayden knew that was it.

"No time to poly," the captain confirmed. "Mayor wants a press conference and we're on in twenty."

It threw Hayden for another loop. This was unprecedented. "How the fuck am I supposed to face the press when I haven't interviewed the suspects?"

The room grew quiet. Thorton stared at his thumbs. The captain's look was firm. Nick stared straight at Hayden, however, with an expression that said, "Figure it out, shithead." Hayden averted his eyes. He had figured it out.

The captain picked up the slack. "Don't make this more difficult than it already is."

Hayden addressed Forsythe. "I want to interview them."

"You can view the tape," Forsythe answered.

Thorton wouldn't look Hayden in the eye.

"If Rich were here you wouldn't pull this shit," Hayden said quietly.

"If Rich were here I wouldn't have to," Forsythe countered, standing up, signaling that the meeting was over.

Hayden took the hit. It was a low blow but a long time coming. They all left the room before he did.

Hayden found the tape in the witness interview room next to LAPD Media Relations. Through the walls he heard the press conference from the seven TVs set on seven different channels. It ran on all the local affiliates as well as CNN and MSNBC. Rufus would be watching. Rufus would wonder why Hayden wasn't there.

The confession was exactly what Hayden feared. The details the suspects got right were taken verbatim from LAPD press releases, and the details they got wrong were summarily ignored. Their move was a grab for street clout by an OG and his fourteen-year-old nephew. At age thirty the OG was already out of touch. He was most likely trying to mobilize a faction of Twenty-Second Street gangbangers, but needed a defining event for his reintroduction. Copping to the murder of Councilman Jackson's niece would give him the credibility he needed and cost him nothing. Maybe a short stretch in County for a minor parole violation, then a quick release as the case against the two fell apart. They knew the charges wouldn't stick because they knew they didn't do the crime. They'd receive a slap on the wrist for interfering with an ongoing police investigation and be set loose to resume their civil war on the streets.

Hayden wondered if there was anything he could have done to prevent this. Then he thought, no, probably not. Things had been set into motion and they were going to take their own course.

God, please give me the serenity to accept the things I cannot change, the courage to change the things I can, and the wisdom to know the difference . . .

There were a thousand everyday reasons to repeat the Serenity Prayer. Hayden would have to accept things as they were. He couldn't control this. He could not have predicted this. He could not have stopped this.

God's will be done.

He popped the tape out and walked it back through Media Relations. LAPD Media staff watched the press conference on the many TV screens. Councilman Jackson held a handkerchief to his eyes, crying, emotional, wrapped in the warm half-embrace of the mayor's arm. The mayor spoke with conviction: ". . . due to the tireless efforts of Detectives Dave Thorton and Nick Price, and of Captain Forsythe of the LAPD Robbery-Homicide team . . ."

Hayden continued on his way to the Robbery-Homicide Division. He dropped the tape onto Thorton's desk. The detectives in Homicide I and II were standing, sitting, or leaning on chairs amid desks pulled in a circle around a damaged TV set someone brought from home ages ago so the guys could watch ballgames in between suspect interviews. Today they watched the press conference on CNN.

Hayden left the station, feeling everyone's eyes on his back.

26

"Didn't you have any say in the investigation?" she asked.

Hayden stirred Sweet'N Lows into his coffee. His mind was elsewhere. They sat by the window in his favorite Starbucks, at the corner of Sunset and La Brea. Their seats looked out onto the street where hustlers and dealers and hookers passed by. The location made him feel closer to where he needed to be. Closer to the darkness, closer to the anger. Closer to Rufus.

"These guys," she continued. "They are so clearly not the right guys. You don't need to be a profiler to see that. They might fit the case for West L.A., but they sure as shit don't match the others."

He avoided looking at Kennedy's face. He stared at her legs. At her breasts. It was how he responded when he was anxious, when he felt weak, overwhelmed, when his addict stepped out. She was obviously aware of the attention, of its inappropriateness, but she remained cool. He'd never met a girl like her, one who could hold her own under the stare of an addict.

"Why did they separate West L.A. from the others?" she asked.

"It's kind of political." He winced at his own response. It sounded like a blow-off line and he half expected her to hammer him for details.

"Well, it's kind of politically risky to arrest suspects while sitting on evidence that connects one crime to at least two others," she said, folding her arms across her chest.

Hayden shifted in his seat while she waited for his response.

"Do they think the *Hustler*s were planted?" she continued. She was beginning to take on the tone of an FBI interrogator.

"I don't know what they think. They took me off the case."

She studied his poker face apprehensively. "Maybe I should meet with your captain—"

"You get the reports I sent on the modeling agency?" he asked quickly, an edge in his voice. He had given her too much room to maneuver and it was time to clamp down.

She seemed jolted by the deflection. His stare remained fixed on hers. She was first to turn away, stabbing at the foam in her cappuccino with a plastic spoon.

"This agency murder," she said, proceeding slowly, "it was different from the others. Why do you think he's our guy?"

"He's our guy."

"You found *Hustler*s at the scene?"

"No magazines at this location. He's evolving."

She looked up from her drink. "There's something else. You're not sharing."

He felt a slight twitch in his cheek. He looked past her and out the window, where an MTA bus screeched to a halt across the street, discharging students, winos, and fast-food servers. Hayden considered her comment. *Sharing.* Funny she should use that word. Sharing was what got him into this mess. Sharing his First Step with the group, sharing the inventory of his personal fuck-ups from the beginning of his life to the present. There was a lot of shit revealed. They all listened, and through their brotherhood his shame began to evaporate. One bastard listened too well.

"It's our guy," he continued. "Do you have *anything* new for me or not?"

"I should have been at the scene," she said, holding on to her anger.

"I told you, you're under the radar." He shuffled Sweet'N Lows like miniature cards between his fingers.

"You've tied my goddamn hands," she complained.

"I've given you crime scene photos, autopsy reports, toxicology—"

"I want to be there when *you're* there—"

"Sorry."

"What are you hiding, Detective?"

He tossed the Sweet'N Lows onto the table and spoke to her directly.

"This is my investigation. Downtown trusts me. I don't trust them. I run my investigation the way I run it and they leave me alone." He raised his eyebrows as if to say, *"These are the rules—live by them or get out."*

"I sent you preliminary notes from the coroner on Century City," he continued. "What did it say about her stomach contents?"

She took in a quick breath and let it out slowly. She spoke quietly through gritted teeth. "There was nothing of note in her stomach. Chicken McNuggets. Nothing that ties her to the earlier victims."

"I need your profile."

"I don't have it. I've got some ideas but—"

"Give me your ideas, then."

He leaned back in his chair, gesturing for her to proceed. She tapped her fingernails on the armrest of her seat. She looked him in the eye and spoke with conviction.

"He's black, white, or Asian, aged twenty-four, thirty-five, or fifty-six, studied history, medicine, or architecture, and weighs one hundred forty-five pounds."

"You're clueless about everything, but you *know* he weighs one hundred forty-five pounds?"

"The weight matches the depth of the depression left in the carpet from his footprints."

"You got this and you didn't visit the crime scene?"

"Imagine what I could find if I'd been there. Have you visited the restaurants near the Coral Reef?"

"No, I . . . There hasn't been . . ." He felt the ingrained guilt a detective feels when he doesn't cover every lead he's got. This was why detectives had partners.

"It's okay, I covered it," she said smugly. "La Bruscetta, Corleone's, Sunset Grill, Spago—"

His back straightened. "You went to these restaurants?"

"—interviewed the waitstaff, busboys—"

"This is not why I hired you."

"So you get a little extra for your buck. I'm an investigator, I'm not going to split hairs—"

"Goddammit, I hired you to do a profile, nothing else. You understand? And I needed that profile *yesterday*. Before he fucking killed three more people."

In an instant it all hit him: the blood on his hands, the impossible position he was in, the three people who had been alive just yesterday. He almost cried, but held back. She sensed it and her eyes softened. But he wasn't about to take any pity.

"I don't want you meddling in anything else," he said sternly, avoiding her eyes.

She glared at him like a scolded child. He imagined that her superiors at the Bureau had seen this face once too often. She looked into her cup, spooned excess foam off the top of her cappuccino.

"Fucking baristas," she cursed under her breath.

Hayden grabbed her wrist, looked into her eyes. "You understand? Stick to the paperwork."

She pulled her wrist back with a snap, knocking her cup over and onto the table. The foam caught most of the cappuccino while the rest trickled off the table and onto Hayden's lap. She released a Mona Lisa smile. "I understand the rules, Detective."

What a cocky little bitch, he thought, wiping his pants. Spirit, was what Rich called it. He remembered that Rich described him as "spirited" when he was first pitched to the captain about joining the RHD. Hayden recalled that it had something to do with his contempt for authority and his know-it-all attitude. "And that's why he's right for our team," Rich had insisted. So maybe Kennedy was right for the team, too. If he could keep her from running the show.

"Get me that profile," he said, standing to leave.

27

The Moreton Bay Fig Tree stood like a giant angel on the church grounds. It was planted in 1875 after its journey from Australia to the docks of San Pedro. Its owner placed it beside his home, and when the property was sold to the church the tree seemed to grow larger and stronger overnight. The parishioners saw it as a symbol of their love rooted in Christ, with its branches like the arms of disciples reaching toward the heavens. Its limbs spanned one hundred twenty-four feet east to west and it rose to a height of four stories. The leaves together formed an enormous, oval-shaped canopy spanning the entire north end of the property. But Hayden was taken more with its roots. Rising like the Sierra Nevada Mountains they emerged high from the trunk and arced down into a series of hills and valleys, which disappeared under the park benches that framed the tree in a lopsided octagon. Before meetings the addicts circled the tree, their glances grazing the root system's Celtic knot. They walked silently, nodding occasionally to the brothers they passed.

The tree was an enigma to Hayden. He remembered stepping from the insular world of his meetings, leaving the hour and a half introspection of his addictive life to stand before this giant, humble, world witness. The tree seemed to wait on his exit with an expectant, "So, what have we learned tonight?" attitude, while Hayden stared up at its magnificent green and brown plume. Then, as if avoiding the question, he would turn his gaze to the tree's magnificent roots. His daily struggle with sexual sobriety seemed insignificant in the presence of the fig tree. Why should it care what went on in his life? The tree reminded him that he would be dead someday and the world would continue on as though there had never been a Hayden Glass. And yet, there seemed to be a sentience in this tree, and the magical beatitude it emanated suggested that it cared. Hayden didn't know if the other addicts felt the same, but from the way they circled the tree before meetings, the way they tripped over roots without thinking, he suspected that many of them did.

Hayden sat in the cab of his Jeep, watching through the binoculars in his hands. He recognized Pete, a regular, wearing long blue beach shorts and rubber Zorries. He circled the tree, passing Barry, a slim, athletic type wearing brightly colored Lycra bicycle gear. Hayden focused the binoculars on the meeting room entrance where another eight members gathered. A small sign on the door, barely noticeable, read "203."

He circled names on an old SAA phone list each time he recognized a member. He turned his attention to the cars pulling into the parking lot and copied license plate numbers into the margins of his list.

It was 7:05 P.M. He counted seventeen members. He knew ten of them. The rest were either new members or guys who came irregularly. More would trickle in over the next twenty minutes.

There were a few members Hayden didn't see. David, who usually ran the meeting. David, the old sage, the brother with eight years under his belt. And Carl, the fucker Hayden had saved from the sting operation in

Hollywood a few months before. The brother who got Hayden expelled. To Hayden's recollection, Carl never missed a meeting. He wondered where Carl might have gone tonight. He wondered if Carl was capable of committing murder.

28

Hayden sorted documents on his desk at the station. Crime scene photos and coroner reports spilled to the floor. He had only completed one murder book—the one for West L.A.—and Thorton and Price were making a play for it. "It's your case, now. Make your own god-damn murder book," Hayden snapped at them. They complained when Hayden wouldn't just hand it over, said he refused to be a team player. But Hayden knew the West L.A. case was connected to the others. It was all one case in his mind and he wasn't about to give away any of his research tools.

He dialed the crime lab, unfolding the phone list and his notes from the meeting the night before. He waited while the receptionist transferred him through.

"What up, boss?" Scooter said in his slow, personal elocution. Hayden was impressed that Scooter never appeared rushed. He couldn't imagine that kind of self-confidence. He hoped that someday he would find such serenity. Then again, Scooter didn't have a crazed killer watching his every move.

"I need you to run plates for me, half an hour, max."

"Excuse me, Detective, but my business card says 'Bench Tech.' As far as I can tell I was promoted from Data Entry two years ago."

"If I trusted someone in Data Entry I would've called someone in Data Entry."

"I kinda have a full load here."

"You understand life and death, Scooter?"

"Let's see . . . I think we covered that when I studied existentialism at Rutgers."

"Good, 'cause we're talking life and death here. And that college degree you've got makes you qualified to run my plates. I'm faxing the list now. I need names, addresses, priors."

"Does this take precedence over the stuff your partner sent in?"

"Rich? What's he got you doing?"

"Not Rich, some other guy. Initials are L.W. From a case in Century City, the paperwork says it's yours."

Hayden remembered that Forsythe sent someone from RHD to finish up at the scene. He looked around the bullpen, at the empty seats and the seats that were filled. He couldn't think of single a detective with the initials L.W.

"Yeah, that's my case. Not my partner, though, probably just a fill-in. I need this ASAP."

There was a sigh on the other end. Hayden imagined Scooter counting the hours in his day. "How about that souvenir, Detective?"

Hayden gritted his teeth. This kid wasn't going to stop until Hayden produced a severed finger from the next grizzly crime scene.

"Run the plates, Scoot. I'm sure I'll find *something* you can put in your petri dish before this case is closed."

Hayden hung up, wrote Scooter's name on the SAA phone list, and faxed it through to the LAPD Crime Lab. He returned to his desk and continued his work on the three-ring binders he had started for the other crime scenes. He three-hole-punched forensic reports and crime scene photographs and placed them behind dividers in the appropriate sections. He stopped when he saw photographs of the receptionist. *Rhonda.* Folded forward with her nose against her toes, peeking up from the top of the large, plastic trash container.

He stared at the photo for a long time before hole-punching it and placing it in the modeling agency binder. He pulled his sketches of the scene and taped the 4×4 sketch pad squares onto an 8½ × 11-inch piece of construction paper. His rendering had her staring straight ahead, with dead-open eyes, her expression something in between expectation and contempt. Demanding justice or assigning guilt?

He compared his sketch to the crime scene photograph. The drawing was more personal. Dramatic license allowed for an emotion that was felt in the room but didn't translate through the camera lens. Yet the difference was greater than that. It was simple, but hard to place. Hayden closed his eyes for a full ten seconds then opened them to view the two images side-by-side.

There it was. In his rush at the scene, Hayden had sketched the round, plastic trash can as square and metal, like a commercial trash *bin*. The kind seen in alleys outside apartment buildings. It was incongruous, but he knew he had seen this before.

He looked past his desk to the dusty mess of Rich's desk, and the clean stack of cold case files in its center. He rolled his wobbly chair over and picked them up. It was the third file from the top. Forty-year-old Tobias Stephens, found in Watts, naked, his body mutilated. A Presbyterian minister. Left in a Dumpster eighteen years ago. Bent in the middle, with his nose touching his toes.

Similar, but dissimilar, Hayden reflected. There was a big difference between a forty-year-old black man from Watts and a twenty-two-year-old white female from Tennessee. It had to be coincidence. He remembered the way Rich talked endlessly about these cases. To everyone he knew, to anyone who would listen.

Rufus seemed to know so much about Hayden. Things that could only be gleaned from the confessions Hayden had made in his meetings. But how close *was* Rufus? Could he have known this, too? Could he have known that Hayden's partner had resurrected this ancient cold case?

Hayden opened Rich's file. The crime scene photos were gruesome. The man's body was a mess of cuts, welts, and abrasions. But mostly cuts. *Like Rhonda.* Hayden read through the autopsy report. The cause of death was asphyxiation. Some type of ligature had been tightened around the man's neck before the mutilation. It left markings around his skin. The ligature was never found.

This was eighteen years ago. It could have been Rufus's first. Maybe Rufus wanted Hayden to make this connection. First the room numbers and now this. It appeared that Rufus had a story to tell. Hayden finally had a foothold, but he'd need more than that if he was going to catch this guy. He'd need help from a friend.

29

There was worry in Judy's eyes when she let him in. "I'm glad you stopped by."

"How is he?" Hayden asked.

She took his arm as they walked up the stairs to the guest bedroom where Rich had taken up residence.

"The same," she replied. "I sometimes think that if we could get him to the station, you know, just to help out, or maybe to offer advice to the new recruits . . ."

"Yeah," Hayden pretended to agree, although he knew that a position like that would be the death of Rich. He could just see the cocky Academy graduates looking for street action, forced to sit for training and policy review with an old stroke victim the LAPD didn't have the heart to let go.

They reached the door to Rich's room, but Judy wouldn't release Hayden's hand.

"See, what he needs," she continued, "is to move on to the next level. Just something, some reason to get up in the morning, like we all have. I think that's why he's not improving, and *you* know the things he's done for the department. The incredible debt that we both know he's owed. He's too proud for his own good sometimes, he would never himself . . . but you, after all, could talk to his captain, you talk to him every day. It wouldn't be so hard for you to slip in a conversation . . . you know how much it would mean to Rich, and to me. Then the kids wouldn't have to see him like this. He's been like a father to you, more than anyone, Hayden. I'm not saying you owe him, of course, he would never even think . . . don't, *please* don't say I said that, but he did fight for you, and you wouldn't be where you are if he hadn't picked you . . ."

There was a subtle tug-of-war going on between Hayden and Judy for the ownership of his hand. He had never seen this side of Judy, never knew it existed. Hayden had attended a few Thanksgiving and Christmas dinners with them and Judy had always presented herself as the perfect host. She seemed comfortable managing the background events in Rich's life, allowing Rich and his career to take center stage. Hayden respected their marriage and the roles they had established for themselves.

Nicky joined him at one of the dinners but had come away feeling disgusted with the *Father Knows Best* mind-set that held sway in their household. Most of their stories revolved around Rich and the LAPD, and anything Judy brought up for discussion suffered Rich's didactic, conservative analysis before being put to bed with patronizing finality. It drove Nicky crazy that Hayden listened in awe to Rich's stories, never challenging Rich's politics or moral righteousness, even though she knew that Hayden's own views differed considerably. Hayden didn't completely kowtow to Rich's opinions, in fact he could be quite divergent in their discussions about investigative procedure and police tactics. But something about being with Rich and his family during the holidays gave Hayden a feeling of great comfort and he didn't want to be anything less than perfectly agreeable.

Hayden grew up an only child in a broken home and dinners with

Rich and Judy were his only opportunity to witness filial support and unconditional love. He could sit for hours watching the subtle interplay of one sibling against the other, chuckling at the biting, loving parental advice ignored by all. It was like sitting inside a foreign film about a Greek, Italian, or Danish family. And Hayden envied Rich's children the most, because they had been taught the difference between right and wrong, and they had grown up with a man of principle to serve as a model. Of course all of Rich's children went on to enjoy successful careers. They were satellites of Rich.

Hayden finally snapped his hand from Judy's grip and latched on to the doorknob.

"Of course, I'll do what I can," he proffered quickly, then stepped through the door and closed it firmly behind him.

He heard Judy's flustered breathing from behind the door, followed by her slow, defeated steps down the stairwell. Hayden turned around to find Rich sitting in a rocking chair at the far corner of the room, his head poking out an open window, with a lit cigarette stuck between his lips. He turned when he saw Hayden and the two shared a smile.

They had been sitting in Rich's room for almost an hour. Hayden did his best to decipher the slow-motion staccato of words Rich spat like a misfiring machine gun.

The heat was unbearable. Ceiling fans pushed hot air and blew paperwork from the cold case file onto the floor.

From Rich, Hayden was ultimately able to glean the following information: that the Tobias Stephens case initially garnered a lot of attention at the LAPD due to the sheer violence involved. The brutality seemed to indicate that the killer knew the victim. But there were also elements suggesting that the murder was a crime of opportunity. The killer had slipped through a locked sliding glass door into what appeared to be an empty house. He might have intended to rob the place. He had approached the victim from behind and used some type of chain to strangle and kill the man. Then, in what appeared to be an absolute frenzy, the killer mutilated the body. Nothing was stolen from the home. The victim had forty-five dollars in his wallet, which was found in his torn clothes on the kitchen floor. His naked, bent body was discovered the next day in a Dumpster outside of a Vons grocery store in Watts.

The case went cold quickly and LAPD resources were redirected to other cases that could be closed immediately. Rich couldn't remember how he ended up with the file. It might have been passed down from the original detective, who had moved on to more solid cases. It might have been passed up from the coroner's office. It hadn't come from the victim's sister, who had been interviewed during the initial investigation. Rich spent a half hour interviewing her when he reopened the case. Rich's notes in the file stated that the sister could not name anyone who might have had a grudge against Tobias. He had been a very active member of the church and a Big Brother to two at-risk teenage boys before becoming a minister. It took some digging, but Rich had eventually learned that Tobias lived a darker past before finding God. He had been a gangbanger, in and out of prison on minor drug and burglary charges, until about age thirty.

"So, this was a retaliation killing? A rival gangbanger who held a ten-year grudge?" Hayden asked.

"Wh-who kn-kn-knows?" Rich breathed, tiring now. "H-he . . . shouldn't . . . have g-got-ten away . . . with th-this . . ."

Hayden agreed. He shouldn't have. And he wouldn't get away with it again, if Hayden had any say in the matter. Hayden suspected now, more than ever, that this was his Rufus.

He may have spent another hour picking Rich's brain if he hadn't received the urgent call from Lieutenant Garcia.

"Glass, where are you?"

"I'm in consultation with an expert." He heard Rich gargle incoherently beside him. "Rich says hi," Hayden added.

"I got a major scene in Mar Vista. If you can't get there in ten minutes I'm calling Deeter. But, this one, Hayden . . . I'd rather send someone with your experience."

There was something in Garcia's voice that Hayden hadn't heard before. It sounded like fear. Hayden checked his watch. Northridge to Mar Vista at rush hour was at least thirty minutes.

"I'll be there," he said, and bolted for his car.

30

Ten squad cars on the street, twelve officers manning the police line. Must have been a quiet night in Mar Vista. Hayden flashed his badge, though there were plenty officers present who knew him. It felt good to have the badge back and he felt compelled to let others know that he was on the right side of the law.

It was a row of bungalow-type apartments that had once been a private hotel for Hollywood day players back when Culver Studios was RKO and films like *Gone with the Wind* required large, available casts housed close by. The units were individually rented and had fallen into disrepair. Winos, crack and meth addicts, and lower-tier drug dealers lived here now. And hookers.

He checked the door on the way in and was relieved—apartment 3B. No connection here.

The door pulled open as he reached for it and his forward momentum stalled as he stumbled into Detective Dan Hicks, a twenty-year veteran from the West L.A. Division. Hicks said nothing but grabbed Hayden's forearm and squeezed gently with a message firm enough to express something that rarely showed in these circles—horror. His eyes flashed a warning: *This is one that will haunt you.*

Hayden took a second to breathe before proceeding. Hicks patted his shoulder, pushed him gently forward and into the room.

The white, crumbling walls had become a theater of cruelty, an exhibition of atrocity fit for a viewing by Pol Pot. The room was anger incarnate. Two women had been obliterated. Shotgun blasts began the event and a butcher's knife ended it.

The walls were dripping mostly with the bits and pieces of what #4 shot took when blasted through flesh and bone. Brain matter, bone splinters, chunks of muscle tissue, bits of fingernail, a mosaic of nerve patterns like macabre snowflakes, strands of hair. Blood dripped and trailed over lamp shades and wooden chairs.

The furniture had been pushed to the sides, leaving an empty space in the center of the apartment where three bodies lay. A naked man on his back, his face covered by the bottom half of a naked woman, her crotch over his mouth and her legs up above his head like long rabbit ears. Her belly rested just under his chin, spilling the contents of her severed abdomen onto his neck and chest. She had been cut straight across and it was evident that the upper portion of her body was what hung and dripped from the walls and furniture. The lower half of another woman's body lay on top of the naked man's lap. Her black legs, wearing tall red leather hooker boots, rested on top of the man's own legs. The contents of her severed belly spilled out onto the man's groin. The upper portion of her body had been concussion-blasted into the walls with shotgun pellets, mixing with the remains of the other woman in a landscape of textured pointillism.

Everyone in the room was staring silently at this scene. A few uniformed officers. A couple detectives from Robbery-Homicide. A couple Pacific Division homicide detectives. A forensics team. Captain Forsythe. No one moved. All were alone in their thoughts.

Hayden wished now that he'd gone into another line of work. Or had stayed in the Hollywood Division, Vice Squad. Or moved to a homicide division in some small town, like Annapolis or Tulsa or Taos, New Mexico.

Forsythe stepped up beside him, his eyes downcast. "You're lead on this, but we're all going to take a piece."

"Yeah," Hayden agreed.

A patrol officer stepped between the two, whispered, "Detective Glass?"

"Yeah."

"Officer Trujillo. Apartment's rented out to Molly Behrens. She works the streets with her roommate, Pam Gables. Pam's black, Molly's white. We think the bodies are theirs."

"What about the man?"

"No ID. Probably a john."

The captain cleared his throat. "Listen, Hayden, I'll be at the station. When you're through here I want you to join me."

"All right."

The room lit up from the camera flash of an LAPD crime scene photographer. Captain Forsythe squeezed Hayden's shoulder, then left the apartment.

Hayden took a step closer, careful to clear the photographer's frame. This *would* haunt him. It was an image with no place in his psyche. There was no frame of reference to ground him in this moment. The longer he stared at the crime scene the more it seemed like the set of some senseless play, a Halloween theater-in-the-round. He stepped forward, then back, then walked around in a small circle, keeping his eyes on the images before him. He weaved a bit, balance eluding him. His senses were numb. There was behind his eyes a feeling of sponginess, like a wall that absorbed the viewed images while deflecting their substance, if substance existed at all. What was substance, anyway, he wondered. The mind's attempt to make sense of the things placed before his eyes? Did a rock make sense? A tree? There was a low frequency hum in his forehead. He shook his head, trying to knock these absurd thoughts from his mind. His head felt like dull, dark emptiness, with a metallic taste settling into the back of his throat.

His sketch pad was in his hand but he couldn't remember pulling it from his pocket. He almost dropped it. His pencil jotted down notes. He tried to sketch the scene but the lead in his pencil continued to break. The tongues of both women had been pulled outward, and each tongue was pierced with a ring. Hayden noticed a ring on the man's wedding finger, as well. There was a strange shape to it that he'd seen before. He stepped closer and realized that it was formed of Hebrew letters—a common wedding ring worn by Jewish men. *Ahnee l'dodee v'dodee lee—I am to my beloved as my beloved is to me.* He had learned this from Sol on their first meeting as sponsor and sponsee. Sol had one of these rings, and Hayden had used the ring as an icebreaker to delay the discussion of his addiction. He had learned that the ring was new to Sol, that it represented a renewed commitment to his wife after his disclosure and membership in SAA. It represented a new life, a life free from acting out.

Hayden made note of the ring in his pad.

The photographer signaled that he was done. He called for the coroner to bag the bodies.

There was a heaviness in Hayden's skull, weighing down his neck and shoulders and tightening the muscles around his spine. He looked up from his notebook at the male victim's body, with the spattering of female body parts seemingly placed to hide his identity. Hayden was drawn toward him. He reached forward to push the woman's torso aside.

"Please, Detective, that's my job."

Hayden turned to see the coroner investigator he had seen at Charlie's side in the autopsy room and at Abbey's side the day of the West L.A. murders. The man positioned a plastic bag in line with the woman's feet then slipped it over her toes, pulling it up and across her torso.

"Charlie come along?" Hayden asked.

"No," he said as he scooped entrails back into the open cavity of the woman's abdomen. "Abbey's out front. Threw up on her coveralls." He finished wrapping the woman's torso and leaned forward to lift it onto a gurney.

"Can you give me a hand, Detective?" He held out a pair of latex gloves. "I'd wait for Abbey, but I think she's had it for the night."

Hayden nodded. One of the gloves stuck stiff to the man's gloved fingers by the blood that had dried there. It released with a slow, taut snap that echoed in the room. Hayden put the gloves on and grabbed the female's rigid legs through the plastic. On the count of three they lifted and pulled the torso up and onto the waiting gurney.

Hayden stood frozen, his shoulders bent forward, his gaze caught on the image of the man now revealed.

"Detective?" the investigator asked, concerned.

Hayden thought he had heard someone calling, but it was his own name repeated in his head, pronounced in the soft cadence of someone who knew him well, someone who cared.

Hayden. Hayden?

The victim on the floor, his throat cut, his neck a deep, floppy crevice of blood and cartilage. His face marred by knife wounds across his cheeks and forehead. His tongue pulled forward, pierced through the center with a corkscrew, securing his tongue to the roof of his mouth.

But his eyes seemed alive as Hayden stared into them, as they stared back at Hayden.

Hayden, they seemed to be saying, *what have you done?*

The dead man on the floor was Sol.

31

Hayden was dry-heaving in the lavender outside the bungalow. Patrol officers and homicide detectives snuck glances. Their looks revealed their shock. *What the hell is in there? It must be bad if Glass can't handle it.*

At that moment Hayden didn't care about his reputation. He felt stucco bite into his hand. He slipped in his vomit, wiped his mouth with his shirtsleeve.

An engine turned over. He glanced sideways to see Abbey Reed putting her Ford Explorer into gear. He felt his keys in his pocket and staggered to his Jeep.

———

A moment later he looked up. It had only been a moment. He couldn't remember how he got here and he didn't know where he was. He was parked in a residential neighborhood. Abbey's Ford Explorer was parked in front of him. There was a modest house with a small, well-tended flower garden. On the side, but within view of the street, there was a slightly open window through which the sound of falling water could be heard. It sounded of familiar midnight showers in the loneliness of an empty house.

Hayden could see reflected in the light of the shower a flash of dark hair and hands working a coarse sponge into a forearm stained with the blood of a crime scene.

Her skin soft and white in the pool of light, obscured as it was in the hot steam from the open window. The syncopated patter of water droplets on tile. It was a vision and a sound that captivated him. It was a moment that softened the lines of their rough lives, a moment in their loneliness, shared.

Then a short loud burst of sound at his side, almost inside his head. A sound more familiar than the lonely patter of water in a shower. Loud enough to uproot the flowers in her garden. A squad car siren.

Hayden squinted into the blinding light of a patrolman's flashlight, recognized the silhouette of a police car and the synchronic red then white then blue patches of light above.

"Detective Glass?"

"Yes?"

"You responded to the call?"

"The call."

"Peeping Tom. In the neighborhood—"

"Yeah. False alarm."

The officer held for a moment, his flashlight burning circles in Hayden's pupils.

"Oh, sorry." The light went off and Hayden counted a dozen hot blue spots in its place. "Then I'll call it in, false alarm. Have a good night, Detective Glass."

Hayden nodded. He felt a vibration against his leg, his cell phone. His eyes adjusted, saw the return number in between blue dots. Captain Forsythe.

Hayden turned the ignition, took one last look at the window.

The steam was gone now and the light in the shower illuminated Abbey's face as she stared at him through the darkness of the night. Her hair was matted wet against her scalp, her eyes penetrating, staring into his. She didn't appear to share his sense of connection. She appeared, instead, alarmed.

32

He was in the RHD conference room with Captain Forsythe and Detective Lawrence Wallace. Hayden remembered that Larry had been at the West L.A. murder of Councilman Jackson's niece. It had been his case, before RHD took jurisdiction. The captain was talking and he seemed angry. He ended suddenly and stared at Hayden with expectation.

"What?" Hayden asked.

"Have you heard a thing I've said?"

"I shouldn't have left the crime scene."

"For Christ's sake, Hayden!" The captain sighed. He motioned to Detective Wallace. "You know Larry. We bumped him up to Homicide Special last week, he's the guy I sent to your model agency. He's your new partner."

"What . . . ?"

"I'm looking forward to it, Hayden," Larry acknowledged, leaning in to shake his hand. Hayden pulled away. Wallace's hand retracted slowly. He glanced at the captain, who motioned for him to proceed.

Hayden wasn't sure if he shouldn't just walk out of the meeting. With his seniority and his years at RHD he expected to be consulted, or at least given the opportunity to review from a list of top candidates. He folded his hands over his chest, deciding to give Wallace his shot.

Wallace turned to the notepad in his hands.

"We got positive ID on the women," he began. "Both live there, known prostitutes and drug dealers. Male vic's still a John Doe. We think he's a regular, his night with the girls. Wrong place, wrong time. Probably an angry pimp—"

"He wasn't killed there," Hayden stated flatly.

Forsythe seemed almost embarrassed. In a hushed voice, "What are you saying? Do you know what you're talking about?"

Wallace looked from one to the other, trying to gauge the dynamics of their relationship.

"He was brought to the scene," Hayden finished.

Wallace flipped through a sheaf of notes in a manila folder.

"I received some notes from the coroner investigator, it doesn't mention anything about the body being moved—"

"The investigator left her assistant in charge of the scene. Talk to Charlie Dawson at coroner's, ask him to examine the body. He'll verify time of death and confirm that the man wasn't killed there."

Hayden sighed. He couldn't understand why these guys weren't getting it. He wished everyone would just leave him alone to do his job.

"So our John Doe was the intended victim?" Wallace asked, prodding.

"You'll find your John Doe in tonight's Missing Persons report. Get me the list and I'll filter through it."

Forsythe almost chuckled. "This guy was killed today. The odds that he's been reported missing—"

"He wasn't killed today, his body was placed there today. The body was over thirty hours old."

Hayden waited for them to acknowledge this, through the hesitant sound of shuffling papers.

"He was wearing a wedding ring," Hayden continued. "Someone is waiting for him to come home. This is a guy, he doesn't miss dinner."

Hayden stood up too fast, felt a dull rush of blood to his head. It seemed to level off and settle in the back of his skull, in the spongy base of his brain. He walked to the door. "Get me the Missings list. I'll notify next of kin."

33

ayden sat in his Crown Vic outside Sol's house. It was two o'clock in the morning. The kitchen light was on and he could see Penny's shadow as she paced the floor. Making coffee, pouring coffee, crossing to the refrigerator, pouring cream, sitting, standing, crossing to the stove.

He sat for a very long time in the car. It was a quiet, residential neighborhood in West Hills. Near parks and hiking trails. AYSO would be starting up again soon and Sol's boys would be busy. Then baseball season. It would be too much for Penny.

She rushed to the front door as she heard his approach.

"Penny?" he said, not knowing what else to say. She stared at him through the screen door.

"I'm Hayden." He thought she would know him, would have heard his name mentioned as Sol's sponsee. Then it occurred to him that perhaps Sol hadn't told her about him, that he had kept the lives of his sponsees private. He cleared his throat and took on an official tone. "Detective Hayden Gla—"

"I know who you are, Hayden," she interrupted in a weary tone. Her stare made him feel like a naughty boy, like someone who deserved to receive a look of contempt. He shifted from one foot to the other, slipping his hands deep into his pockets.

"Can I come in? It would be better if we were sitting down."

The screen door remained closed between them.

"What's the matter?" she asked, suddenly concerned. "Where's Sol?" She looked over his shoulder towards his car. He started to mumble something unintelligible. He looked into her face and realized he couldn't do this.

He stepped away, leaving her at the door. He sat down on the curb by the driveway. She stared at him from the door. He held his head in his hands. A basketball hoop was set up in the cul-de-sac, the ball sitting under a nearby bush.

He stood quickly and returned to the front door. Penny's grip remained on the handle.

"Sol's been killed, Penny."

She hadn't expected this. She stumbled. He reached for the door but she flipped the latch, locking it. His hand dropped to his side.

"I don't understand," she managed. He saw a familiar barrier materialize. The *look*. Her psyche watching the movie unfold from a seat in the back of the theater.

"He's been killed, Penny."

"There's been an accident? Is he all right?" She stared through him.

"Can I come in?"

"No . . . the boys are asleep."

Another moment.

"I'm . . . sorry. I shouldn't have come."

"He was robbed?"

"You're not going to want to read the newspapers or watch the news. If reporters try to contact you . . . I would take the boys to your place in

Big Bear. Keep them out of school. Have a phone on, so the police can call. The newspapers will say . . . terrible things. But Sol was a victim. This had nothing to do with his addiction."

Her look changed when he said this. She seemed to focus more directly on Hayden, although her expression remained confused.

"Why would it have to do with his addiction?" she asked.

What am I doing here? he thought. *I should have left this to Wallace. I'm making things worse.*

He turned and walked quietly, respectfully, away from her.

"He's not like you," she said to his back. Her voice rose with anger. "He's not like the rest of you. You should all just leave him alone now, okay?"

Her accusations echoed in the numbness of his head. As he started his car he saw her return to the kitchen and to the preparation of coffee, and to the pacing, and to waiting, for word from Sol.

34

Alcohol didn't help the dull pressure in his head. Still, he consumed shot after shot of what Chelsea poured from her private stash behind the bar. When the pressures of life overwhelmed him, Hayden always turned to his addiction. It was true of every addict. They had no mechanism for coping with the stressors in their lives. The gamblers gambled, the alcoholics drank, the dopers doped, the sex addicts cruised. A drink to Hayden wasn't much more than a drink. A lap dance was a different story altogether. Because the club was fully nude, the bar only served soft drinks, for seven dollars a glass, with a two drink minimum. But Chelsea knew Hayden from back in the day, and as soon as she saw him she felt that he needed a drink. The clubs took care of their top clientele, especially sex-addicted Vice cops.

He hadn't seen Chelsea in three years and the extra time got her a new set of tits and a nose job. Unfortunately, she couldn't fix the lazy left eye with its pupil floating like a Frisbee in water, spending most of its time in a corner facing the tip of her nose.

He slammed another shot and before he knew it he was in a chair with two topless strippers in g-strings giving him lap dances. The stage seemed to materialize from nothing before his eyes and he was staring down at the pulsating vulva of Shelly, another favorite from his acting out days, as it hovered like a curious street lamp above Hayden's face.

He felt dizzy from the motions of grinding asses and knees into his crotch. His hands found their thighs and the sides of their breasts and a little more. The slow-motion gyration was intoxicating. Swirling colors and flashing lights, the musky smells of perfume mixed with the sweat of the dance and his testosterone brewing, and the loud, pounding, thunderclap music.

He pulled himself free of the girls, pulled five twenties from his pocket, and threw them in the air before desperately running for the door.

In a moment he was back in the Crown Vic. The car seemed to drive itself, leading him from Orange County's Beach Boulevard to the 91 West to the 405 North to Slauson Avenue and into Crenshaw.

Hayden found himself driving through a neighborhood that seemed vaguely familiar. Birds-of-paradise stretched along both sides of the street, hiding chain-link fences and cinderblock walls. He parked in a familiar carport. He walked a familiar set of concrete stairs. He approached a familiar door. He raised his fist to knock but the door opened and Darla was there, surprised but not put out. She wore a man's white sleeveless undershirt that showed her nipples dark hard and red and a pair of short silver silk running shorts that split up the side, revealing the youthful shape of her ass.

He fell into her arms and they dropped to the carpet where he tore off her shirt while she unbuckled his belt and removed his pants. He grabbed her tits hard and she pulled his hair, causing a pain that barely registered through the booze and depression. He pulled off her shorts and dug into her with his lips, his teeth, his tongue. She stroked his cock in her hands as he worked his tongue into the slight dip between the folds, feeling the hair moisten, tasting the sweet familiar bitterness in his mouth. She was squeezing him hard with nails that bit and he saw her reaching for a condom, but the pain of her grip caused a tremor and a surge and all at once he was coming. She quickly pulled away, but not before catching most of it on her arm and belly and some of it between her thighs.

"Fuck, fuck!" She crawled to the kitchen, grabbing a hand towel and a container of Lysol Wipes, which she promptly opened and shoved between her legs. When she was satisfied she dried herself with the dish towel and threw it back on the rack near the sink.

"Well, there," he said, "looks like you got it just in time."

He pulled up his pants, drew out two hundred dollars in twenties and placed them on the coffee table.

"I'm lucky your boy was out."

"He'll be home any minute."

He found his car keys, checked to confirm that his wallet, ID, and badge were still with him. She smiled at his caution.

"Then I better be gone."

He leaned over to stroke her hair. It was smooth and soft and a little oily from not being washed in a day or two.

"Are you going to be able to get out of this?" he asked softly.

"Are you?" There was a hint of sarcasm in her voice, but her concern was genuine.

"I think . . . there will be an end," he contemplated. "The great thing about finding each day worse than the last is that there will eventually be a bottom. And then things will get better."

It sounded like program talk, he thought. Maybe he was getting something out of the meetings after all.

"What if you reach bottom and that becomes your life?" She stared, earnestly. She must've thought that he really had the answer.

He held her chin in his palm. "I left two hundred on the table. If I left another three hundred would you walk away from here tonight, catch a bus to someplace where the roads are made of dirt, a place without these boulevards . . . ?"

"I could do that with two hundred." She smiled that old hooker's smile.

"Will you?"

"I will," she assured him.

She walked slowly back to her cabinet—sashayed, really. As if she knew he was looking at her ass.

"Every night," she continued, "when I go to sleep, I take the two hundred and I go. In the morning I wake up and I remember"—she reached for her crack pipe and lighter on the counter, lit a bowl, inhaled—"and I go out and earn another two hundred bucks."

Her head fell back and her body wavered. All the tension seemed to rise off of her with the smoke. She steadied herself against the kitchen counter, and slowly descended to the floor.

Hayden considered lifting her from the ground and helping her off to bed. She took another hit and he watched her persona slide away. She became the smile of a Cheshire cat. He left her on the kitchen floor, naked, the smoke enveloping her.

Outside he found his car again and took a seat. Before he could turn the key in the ignition he recognized the familiar smell—spray paint.

He left the driver's seat and stood out in front of his Crown Vic to read the message left in the Bondo on the hood of his car: "Whorefucker Returns."

35

Charlie slapped a pair of latex gloves on his hands. He hit the light switch to reveal Hayden sitting on a stool by the door.

"Fuck! You fucking motherfucker!"

"Relax," Hayden breathed.

"You know, someday you're going to catch this guy and his defense attorney is going to ask what you were doing alone at the coroner's office the morning *this* victim's body arrived."

Charlie turned on an overhead fluorescent, revealing a sheet-covered body on a seven-foot gurney. He opened drawers, pulled out the tools of his trade—forceps, knives, saws, ladles, devices for crushing things, devices for collecting things. He shot a look at Hayden.

"You smell like, what, really bad perfume, bad pussy, bad booze—"

"There's no such thing as bad booze."

"Have you had any sleep at all, I mean, in the past week?"

Hayden felt tears in his eyes. He turned so that Charlie wouldn't see.

"What's going on?"

"I've been . . ." Hayden's voice cracked.

Charlie waited. Hayden felt the tense indecision, sensed Charlie's desire to console him. He stepped back, pulled his emotions in check. There had been a time when Charlie was all there was for him. Hayden's de facto sponsor, before there was Sol. Charlie didn't know the lingo and he didn't know the steps. But he listened, and that had been enough.

"You didn't see this crime scene, did you, Charlie?"

"I saw photographs."

"You should've been there. Why weren't you there?"

"A homicide every twelve hours in L.A. County. And only one Charlie."

Hayden pulled the sheet off the body before them. "Do you know who this is?" he asked.

"They told me John Doe."

"This is Sol, Charlie."

It didn't ring a bell. Hayden stared at Charlie a long time.

"Your sponsor . . . you're telling me it's your sponsor?"

Hayden gazed at the body on the table. What was left wasn't Sol. It was something from a movie set. It couldn't be real. There was no Sol here. The corkscrew embedded in the roof of his mouth forced an unreal expression. If only it were a Halloween prank.

"He did this. The guy I've been after," Hayden said somberly.

"Who? The *serial killer*? Is that what you're saying?"

Hayden nodded.

"What the hell have you two gotten into?"

"It's about me, Charlie. Sol just stepped into the crosshairs."

Charlie closed the drawer of tools and wandered away. He paced around the empty autopsy tables, looking lost.

"Is this someone you put away, someone on parole?"

"I don't have a clue, Charlie. A clue is what I fucking *need*. I'm depending on you."

Charlie ran both hands nervously through his short hair. His eyes narrowed and his forehead wrinkled in the middle. Hayden could sense that he was asking too much of him.

"This is why you had Abbey taken off the case," he said finally.

"She left her assistant in charge, the guy couldn't even tell the body had been moved. I need *you* on the case. You understand."

Charlie understood.

"I need carpet fibers," Hayden continued. "Rope fibers, dog hair, human hair, saliva, semen, duct tape adhesive . . . I want every fiber you find matched with every fiber from every scene I've worked these past two weeks. I want you to search Sol's body until we come up with the killer's home address."

Hayden flipped the sheet back over Sol's face and started for the door.

"I know the cause of death," Charlie announced abruptly. Hayden turned back to him. Charlie walked back to the evidence bag at the foot of the gurney and reached in. He pulled out a chain necklace with a silver cross attached. He pulled back the sheet to reveal markings on Sol's neck.

"You see the bruising here?" he continued. "It's consistent with the links on this necklace. And here is where the cross dug in, just below the trachea."

"*This* is what killed him?" Hayden remarked in disbelief.

"He died from asphyxiation. There are marks on his fingertips consistent with the links, as well, from where he tried to pull it loose. Everything else, the knife wounds, *everything*, was done postmortem. You know where I found this?"

Hayden shook his head slowly.

"In his shoe," Charlie revealed.

This was too much. Sol was Jewish; he didn't wear a cross. As far as Hayden knew, Sol didn't even own a cross. This meant the necklace had been brought to the scene for the purpose of strangling him. The killer must have stuffed the necklace in Sol's shoe because he knew that the first person to find it would be the coroner. And the second would be Hayden. Everything else must have been a diversion, to keep the police from knowing that Sol was the killer's target. It was as though Rufus were whispering directly into Hayden's ear.

The realization turned his stomach. It forced nausea into his gut like nothing he'd felt before. He closed his eyes and ran his fingers over his temples. He tried to relax, tried to distract himself. He noticed a strange vibration in the room and realized that he was humming.

"Go home, Hayden. Get some sleep." Charlie appeared frightened by what he saw in Hayden's eyes.

"Yeah," Hayden replied. He bumped into gurneys on his way to the door. He felt his hand resting on the heavy, metal doorknob. Hayden turned back to Charlie, with something important to say, but he couldn't remember what.

36

What's going on, Detective?"

Hayden opened his eyes; he'd drifted off to sleep. He and Kennedy shared a table outside by the docks, near boats creaking in the gentle rising and falling bay water. It was a warm summer night at the Marina Del Rey Cheesecake Factory.

She wore a dark pleated skirt that settled just below the knee. He was quiet, alternating his glance between the hypnotic dance of the boats and her legs beside the red bougainvillea. Her green silk top hung loose across her breasts, leaving her small, rounded shoulders bare. She wore jade earrings and a necklace to match.

He thought about her question. What was going on was that he hadn't really slept. It was Saturday now, fourteen days since the murder of Councilman Jackson's niece. Hayden had left Charlie's side and spent most of the night scrubbing the hood of his Crown Vic with lye and bleach to remove the words "Whorefucker Returns" from his life one more time. He'd added another few coats of Bondo to cover the mess.

He couldn't seem to concentrate on any one thing for more than two minutes at a time. He had spent the morning MapQuesting the homes of his SAA meeting members from the list Scooter had faxed to him. He had too much to do and no idea where to begin. He saw images from the crime scenes circling endlessly in his mind: *Rhonda in a trash can, she's bent in the middle, Tobias Stephens in a Dumpster, he's bent in the middle, Sol's body mangled on the floor, my father's cross stuffed in a shoe. My father's cross?*

He had meant Sol's cross, or the cross that was used to kill him. Hayden had forgotten all about his *father's* cross. Forgot until this moment that his father used to wear one, under his shirt, rarely seen.

He became aware that Kennedy was staring at him and had been for some time.

"Things . . . have gotten complicated," he finally replied.

He hadn't told her about Sol. But he figured she must have heard; it was all over the news.

She reached across the table for a fork and the outdoor lighting silhouetted her breasts against the silk. Hayden could see so slightly the rise of her nipple, upturned on a soft bed of areola, nestled atop the slim, firm cushion of her breast. Silhouetted for only a second but leaving a lasting impression on his mind.

"Is there something I can do?" she asked, doe-eyed.

"Why don't you tell me what you have."

"Well, I've got an incomplete profile. I was waiting to visit Mrs. Palistrano's house and the modeling agency—"

"It's not going to happen, you'll have to work from the photos and reports."

She pursed her lips. It was a look less of anger than defeat, as if she was deciding how hard to fight for this. He waited patiently, stacking little plastic creamers one on top of another.

"I think he's thirty to forty years old," she began.

He dropped his hand slowly beside the creamers and turned to give her his full attention.

"White. Been to college. He's traveled a little. Awkward with women. He had or has an estranged relationship with his mother. His father's not around—probably passed on in his formative years. There's a lot of rage directed at women; maybe he blames his mother for his father's absence. He's in a tense line of work and he works odd hours. His job requires painstaking attention to detail. He drives an official vehicle for his job, but slips into something innocuous when he trolls. He has pride in his work and feels undervalued. Both in his 'real' job, and in what he considers his 'real work'—the carnage he leaves behind at a crime scene. He's seeking recognition. He flips from overconfident egoist to sad, insecure sap. The people who work with him think he's quiet, calm, dependable. They wouldn't think him capable of the crimes he's committed. No one knows him well. No close ties. He's delusional, imagines he's admired but he's really a loner. He's searching for someone to connect with—a friend, a partner, a father—someone to impress and someone to validate him."

He rocked slowly back and forth as if hypnotized by her words. He knew that it was all speculation, but it felt right. It felt close. And hearing it, *it hurt.* She described half the people he had met since he read his First Step at his home group meeting.

"Detective?"

"Go on," he nodded.

"The murders have more in common than just the magazines," she continued.

"What do you mean?"

"You're right about the scenes being staged. He's performing."

Hayden leaned back in his seat, watched the masts of sailboats cross the horizon.

"You've been on this investigation longer than I have, Detective. Who's his audience?"

The lonely quiet of the evening was disturbed by the barking of a sea lion across the water. Hayden stood, his knee catching the table and sending his tower of creamers to the floor.

"FedEx the profile to my attention tomorrow. I'll settle your bill by the end of the day."

He walked away without looking back.

37

His father is driving Hayden's Crown Vic, smiling, drumming his fingers to Mussorgsky's Pictures at an Exhibition. Glancing at fourteen-year-old Hayden in the passenger seat, ruffling the boy's hair, whispering, "Whorefucker," as if it were a term of endearment. Hayden's smile dropping as his father's chin explodes and a slow-motion Mai Tai umbrella mushrooms out, followed by a gusher of blood that takes his jaw and half his face with it. Nineteen-year-old Hayden ducking as the blood passes his ear, splattering pieces of his father around him. Hayden covers his eyes. A hand towel falls to the floor. He is in the bathroom at the Coral Reef Motel, nursing the bloody cut on his head. He hears Darla's scream through the door. He opens the door and finds himself in Tobias Stephens's kitchen. Tobias writhes on the floor, tugging at giant, rusted, interlocking chain links of the size that hold a ship's anchor, *around his neck. He looks into Hayden's eyes. "Could you have loosened this?" Hayden reaches down to try and falls into a dark hole, landing with a loud echoing slap against industrial metal. Maggots scatter and crawl through his hair and over his cheeks and eyes. He leaps back and the light behind him illuminates Tobias's face, smiling or maybe laughing or maybe it's just the maggots. Hayden pulls himself up and over and falls from the edge of the Dumpster and onto the pavement next to an unknown grocery store. Winos and hookers scatter. Darla stands naked on blue, prosthetic legs. Her smile turns to fear as she looks up and behind Hayden and a shadow passes. Hayden turns to see a caped antihero launch from the Dumpster and hover momentarily like a tarantula inflated, before descending onto Hayden's head and neck with claws and fangs protracted . . .*

Hayden sprang from bed, his heart and head thumping. Sheets sticky with sweat. Connected to its charger, his cell phone beeped. He played the message—Lawrence Wallace.

"Yo, Hayden, I know you don't like it, but we're a team, all right? Let's put a little time in together. Meet me at five o'clock at the pub in Hollywood, you know the one. See you there."

Hayden dropped the phone, went to the medicine cabinet for Motrin, swallowed twice the recommended dosage. His head hummed room tone. He stripped, stepped into a cold shower that was warm by the time he stepped out.

He parked in a deserted alley next to a rusted Dumpster beside a building that had been a Vons grocery store. A negative image of the name remained from where the sign had been removed. Hayden looked at the crime scene photograph from the cold case file. The Dumpster had been repainted and rusted over again since the day of the murder.

He flipped pages in his Thomas Guide, matching it to the street address from the crime report in his lap. His car with its damaged hood fit neatly into the streets of Watts, but the Crown Vic was LAPD's first choice for undercover OPs and Hayden didn't think he had anyone fooled.

He found the house and knocked on the front door with his badge in hand. A woman and her three children answered. A two-year-old balanced on the woman's hip stared at Hayden and then at the shiny silver badge. Hayden explained that the LAPD had reopened an old, unsolved case. The woman said she had heard of it. But it happened before her husband bought the house, she said. Years before. She said her husband was at work and would Hayden mind coming back another time? It was a matter of some urgency, Hayden told her. She let him in warily. He found the kitchen. Things were different from the photograph; the woman told him they'd remodeled a bit. Hayden walked to the spot where the murder had occurred and pulled out a coroner's photo of Tobias's body. The kids stood on tippy-toe to get a glimpse, but Hayden bent the photograph away from their curious eyes.

He channeled into the crime scene vibe and the air became suddenly heavy around him. The murder was eighteen years old and he still felt pain in the room. He noticed a thin blade depression in the wall at the floor. He leaned in close, measured its size against the length of his finger. In his mind he saw Tobias's body striking the floor, then a kitchen knife forced through his abdomen, sliding through and sticking into this spot on the wall.

He saw the sliding glass door mentioned in the crime report and took steps toward it, measuring the distance with his feet. *One, two, three, four, five, six . . . there.* He jiggled the locked door but it stood its ground. He pulled a credit card from his wallet, slid it swiftly behind the lock and yanked the closest section toward him. The door slid open. The kids of the house were impressed. The woman of the house was shaken. It was time for him to go.

He drove past angry neighborhoods with garbage on the lawns and laundry hanging on the line and residents in night robes smoking cigarettes on dining room chairs placed in the grass, their eyes watching his every move. Crack-thin mothers taut like isolated muscles. Their eyes on *him*, as if *he* were the guilty one.

He passed the Burger King five blocks away, where Tobias had worked as a night manager after he hung up his life of crime. Then the church where, later, Tobias had his small ministry. Hayden wondered why in hell this guy, this minister, was so important to Rufus. He also worried whether Tobias was important at all. Hayden might have established this convenient connection between Rufus and Tobias in an effort to demonstrate some semblance of control over the investigation. He hoped the connection was real, because he had little else to go on.

He passed the Wilshire exit and realized that he was on the 405 North. He hadn't planned this, but he suddenly knew where he was headed.

Hayden entered to find Rich lying in bed with his head tilted back on a pillow. His mouth was open and he wheezed as he slept. His covers were thrown off and Hayden saw that he wore an adult diaper along with his T-shirt and socks. Hayden crept quietly toward him and pulled the sheet up to Rich's chest. He took a seat in a chair beside the bed and cleared his throat.

Rich smacked his lips and rolled to the side. His eyes blinked, then widened slowly as he recognized his old partner. A smile crossed his lips.

"Hey, k-kid. Y-you . . . good?" Rich asked.

His voice was dry. Hayden noticed a pitcher of water on the end table. He poured a glass and handed it to him.

"I'm okay," he answered.

"L-look . . . like p-piss," Rich laughed.

"Look who's talking," Hayden countered.

"Got . . . g-got partner?"

"Yeah, Larry Wallace out of West L.A. He's good as any, I suppose."

Hayden watched the slow sickening movement of Rich's Adam's apple under translucent skin. He leaned in close.

"I know there's more on this Tobias Stephens case," Hayden whispered.

His menacing tone surprised Rich. "Wh-what?"

"You spent ten years on this case. You're saying that all you learned is that he used to hang with the Crips? That's bullshit, Rich."

"Wh-wh-what h-have you f-f-found?"

Hayden stood up and paced the room. The heat was stifling. He found the switch to the ceiling fan and clicked through every setting.

"Well, Rich, I've found that the guy who killed him is fucking killing people all over this city."

Hayden abandoned the fan and moved to a window, forcing it open. The outside heat came blasting in. He slammed the window shut.

"He fucking killed someone very close to me, Rich. And now I'm . . . *responsible*. I'm the only one who's going to stop him and I've got *nothing* to work with. You've given me *nothing*."

Rich's eyes were wide with shock. The side of his mouth that was not paralyzed began to quiver. Hayden noticed a small air-conditioning unit built into the wall and lunged at it. He pressed the "on" button, but nothing happened. He slammed his fist into the control panel.

"And there's every indication that he's going to kill again, and again, and the only thing I've got to work with is your bullshit cold case and . . ." Hayden slammed his fist into the control panel again. "For Christ's sake, Rich, how can you stand it? Why doesn't Judy call a fucking air-conditioning repairman? No wonder you can't get out of bed, you're fucking melting away!"

Hayden rubbed his sweaty temples with his thumbs and forefingers. Rich inched back against the headboard. Hayden walked to his side with sudden purpose, then stopped, noticing the pitcher of lukewarm water by Rich's bed. He stuck his hands into it, cupping the water and lifting it up and over his face. He let the water fall onto his forehead, shoulders, and chest. Rich recoiled. Hayden pounced, grabbing Rich by the shoulders.

"What haven't you told me?"

"I d-d-don't kn-know . . ."

"What was special about *this* case? This one guy, out of hundreds of thousands in this whole fucking city. Why would you give a shit about this one guy?"

"I-I-I . . . f-f-for Ch-christ's sake . . . !"

Hayden shook him like a Magic Eight Ball, hoping the answer would surface and Hayden would finally know how to proceed.

"Hayden!" It was Judy standing in the doorway. She was trembling and she held the doorframe for support. But she stood her ground.

A terrible stench enveloped the room. Hayden let Rich's shoulders drop back to the mattress. He watched the bedsheet change from white to brown as Rich's diaper overflowed. Rich turned to face the wall.

"Get out," Judy said from behind Hayden. She was seething. The room was silent except for the creaking ceiling fan and the sound of Hayden's hesitant footsteps against the wood floor as he backed away from the bed. He hid his face as he slipped past Judy, raced down the stairs and jumped into his car.

38

There weren't many traditional Irish pubs in Los Angeles. Not like Chicago, where neighborhood history went back five generations. In Chicago, the polished redwood, oak, and cedar bar tops were stained with the oils and sweat of hands and forearms, glossed by the buff of a million bar towels, shone by the nightly Windex, polished with the blood and alcohol of its patrons. The bartender wasn't an actor, the bartender was the owner, and he wasn't looking for a better job. In Chicago the bartender was a leader among men, the focal point of his community. His bar was his home, his ship to steer.

Most authentic pubs in L.A. ended up in one of the few local guides advertising "well-kept secrets in the City of Angels." They enjoyed a small but faithful following for years until the day some Hollywood asshole walked in with a friend he knew from college. They had a beer, threw darts, met women, yelled shamelessly across the bar like howler monkeys. The next day they returned. One put their drinks on his expense account, phoned another with instructions to bring two more the next night. Word spread and the bar made *L.A. Weekly's* "Pick of the Week." The locals were driven out and Hollywood moved in. The "new find" bustled with business for five, six, eight months. Before long you needed to know the doorman to get in. It didn't just *make* the scene, it *was* the scene. And then something indiscernible occurred and the fervor was gone. The crowd grew stale and the B-list executives stayed on until even they, ultimately, got the hint. If the pub hadn't been sold by then or if the owner hadn't lost faith in humanity, the old neighborhood crowd found its way back. But it was never quite the same.

O'Donovan's on Sunset and Greene was one of the few that ran below the radar, despite its high-profile location in the center of Hollywood. It was located in a transit patch between the Strip and the Cinerama Dome, with an assortment of all-night Thai restaurants, head shops, strip clubs, and one-hour hotels in between. The dicey neighborhood saved it from the pretenders.

Hayden sat at the long oak bar with his whiskey up and a dozen crime scene photos in a stack. Detective Wallace entered squinting, leaving sunlight in gaps around the front door.

"Hayden . . . what've you got there?"

"A Dewar's for my friend, Paul," Hayden called without looking up.

"On the rocks, with a twist," Wallace told the barkeep. "What're you drinking?" he asked Hayden.

"Lagavulin, up," Hayden responded.

"Ooooh," Wallace cooed mockingly.

He dropped a FedEx package on top of Hayden's photos. "Arrived yesterday, return receipt. I signed for you."

It was Kennedy's profile and invoice. Hayden tucked the package under a stack of files on the stool beside him.

"From some private investigation firm," Wallace continued.

"Unsolicited crap," Hayden snapped. "Fucking P.I.s hover over everything we do. You'll see."

The bartender placed Wallace's Dewar's on the bar.

Wallace dropped a shoulder bag on the bar top, retrieved a thick binder.

"I've started our murder book on that whack job next to Culver Studios."

"I didn't tell you to do that," Hayden admonished.

"Just getting us organized."

"There is no 'us,' Larry. Organize *yourself*."

Wallace put the book down on the bar. He turned in his seat to face Hayden head-on. "All right," he said. "I've been waiting to get into Homicide Special my entire career. I'm five years older than you, we went to the Academy at the same time, and you still got into RHD seven years ahead of me—"

"I can't believe you resent me for this. Let it go, Larry."

"I did let it go, Hayden. A long time ago. I got different priorities since my little boy and girl were born. It ain't all about the force. So I don't really give a fuck that I got here ten years later than I planned. And I don't care if they brought me in 'cause they thought you needed baby-sitting. All I know is I'm here and I'm gonna stay here, whether you're with me or not. Forsythe don't know me 'cept by reputation, so I gotta prove myself. You won't be taking me down. Are we understood?"

He stirred his Dewar's and took a plug.

Hayden remained silent, sifting through crime scene photos. "I didn't tell you to make the murder book," he said at last.

"Well, Captain did." Wallace looked away, his eyes peering into the shadows of the bar.

"Can't believe they won't let us smoke here. Remember, back in the day?"

Hayden wrote notes into his sketch pad, ignoring him.

Wallace sighed. "What you got against me anyhow?"

"It's bigger than you, Larry. You're not ready for this. This isn't divisional bullshit, Crips versus Bloods. I got a John Wayne Gacy on my hands."

"Yeah, Captain told me you think this is all one guy. I don't see it, but I'll back you." He took another long pull on the whiskey.

Hayden shook his head. "Thanks, partner. For backing me." The sarcasm was not wasted on Wallace.

Hayden gathered his photos, folders, and the package from Kennedy.

"Do what you think you need to do," Hayden continued. "Leave me out of it."

"Why do you want to carry this alone? He's one guy, right? You've got RHD. You've got the whole police force. You've got the FBI. The marshals. Sheriff's department. Psychics, profilers, bounty hunters, snitches. The whole justice system is on our side. He's just *one guy*."

"I work alone."

Hayden was almost out the door when Larry countered, "You got God, too, you know."

It stopped Hayden in his tracks. "What the fuck does that mean, Larry?"

"I'm just saying," Larry said, "a guy like this, there ain't hope. God is definitely not on his side. Whatever you think of yourself, if there's room for God you've got an edge on this bastard."

Hayden rolled this over in his thoughts for a moment. It was the kind of wisdom he would have expected to hear from Sol. He couldn't imagine what prompted it to come from Larry's lips.

Hayden figured he'd resume his search for God after Rufus was dead. He let the door slam behind him as he left.

Rush hour was a bitch in Hollywood and Hayden chose to avoid the freeway free-for-all by skirting traffic through side streets across the oasis of Beverly Hills. It was a nice retreat from the flash of Hollywood, where crosswalks burst from a swelling display of eccentric human behavior. The characters inhabiting the streets of Hollywood lived desperate reality-show lives in full view of the passing producers and studio executives who had the wherewithal to cast them in the real thing. Sometimes Hayden simply needed a break from the circus.

Sunset Boulevard west of the Strip was Beverly Hills, and the road snaked in luscious green curves like a country drive through Ohio's Amish hillsides. It was a slow and peaceful tour passing great mansions that peeked over tall walls hiding palatial estates. Driving by was as close as Hayden would ever get to living a life of luxury.

Beverly Hills became Brentwood and he turned south on Bundy to Olympic, where he figured he'd ease on over to Lincoln Boulevard and continue with a forty-minute drive into the South Bay. But a half mile later he drove past a building he hadn't seen in five years, though he paid rent on it monthly. He took a U-turn at the next light and pulled into the driveway of a large, commercial building. A long black electronic gate held him at bay. He stared at the numbered keypad that sat atop an imposing metal pole jutting out from the ground. He concentrated. *Nine-five-five-one.* He punched in the code and the gate opened.

Hayden parked in a spot next to Building A. His footsteps echoed off plywood walls in cavernous empty hallways. He walked the maze by rote, his fingertips brushing the doors as he passed.

Unit A29. A combination lock. He stared at it. He stared through it. He touched the dial. Spin right . . . thirty-two. Spin left twice . . . six. Spin right . . . fifteen. The lock opened.

He stared at his history in boxes. It smelled of musty cardboard. "High School," "First Apartment," "Grade School," "Mom." He pulled the box marked "Mom." He sat on the floor looking through old photographs and jewelry and ribbons, her journal and letters and a ten-year-old death certificate. When he had reached the bottom he pushed the empty box aside and uncovered another box, marked "Dad."

He peeled back duct tape. The first thing was a newspaper clipping dating back twenty-three years: "Cerritos Man Killed in Drive-By." He reread the article. "LAPD is actively searching leads. Anyone with information on this crime is encouraged to contact the police . . ."

Hayden dug through old crumpled papers, notes his father had written on sales slips from his various jobs. Nothing significant, just words that his father wrote. An old watch rusted from the one time they surfed together in Malibu. His father had insisted the watch was waterproof until the day he had to admit that it told the correct time only twice a day. That was his father's humor. That was as good as it got.

Other things. A penny collection. Each slot with a date, going back to 1909. His father's favorite pen—a poor man's Mont Blanc. Some jewelry. A turquoise "pinky" ring that never seemed in style. The hood ornament from the E-type Jag he owned before it was repossessed. A puca shell bracelet. A "Nixon for President" button. A jewelry box hidden under a wad of newspapers. He opened the box. His father's cross, on a chain. Hayden felt it in his hand, the cold metal growing warm with contact. He slipped it over his head, felt its weight against his chest. He tucked it under his shirt.

39

When Hayden was younger he rated girls one to ten and he never pursued any that didn't qualify as an eight or above. Now, at thirty-eight, Hayden understood that youth itself was beauty and that any girl aged eighteen to twenty-five earned an automatic eight or above. He admired youth as a quality all its own.

Sitting in his apartment in Redondo Beach he did the best he could to ignore the international fashion show of women in bikinis and thongs that passed outside his bay windows as he poured over Kennedy's profile. It was a distraction he could live with.

Kennedy's profile was good, but incomplete. What it revealed was that the scenes were staged, and that Hayden had a very calculating killer on his hands. The things it said about the killer's character might be the things Rufus wanted them to know. If Hayden shared the details of Sol's murder with Kennedy the two might be able to use the information to lure Rufus into a trap. Hayden remembered one case where a profile was used to anticipate the killer's response to false reports delivered through the media. The reports were used to bait the killer into contacting the victim's younger sister, and ultimately into a trap. If Hayden and Kennedy worked together they might be able to devise such a plan.

But this wouldn't happen. He could barely afford the four-thousand-dollar check he would cut for the work she had done. And he didn't want her involved any more than she already was. The profile as it stood would have to suffice.

The report was fifteen pages, typed. The general description ran a few pages, segueing to an analysis of each crime scene. Hayden highlighted the notable factors. The killer lived or worked within the city of Los Angeles. He knew the city well and was comfortable operating within it. He might have a getaway someplace out of town, where he kept trophies and souvenirs from his victims. He would consider this a safe place where the chance of his discovery was remote. He was able to fade into the background or, when required, appear charming or outgoing. He was a master manipulator, and as a manipulator he could change form to meet the needs of his environment. He had an enormous ego. He was lonely and his actions appeared to be an attempt to communicate or share his unique point of view with others, or with another unique individual such as himself. While his killings were clearly staged, they were not ritualistic.

One paragraph stood out above the rest:

The actions themselves aren't what gets him off, it's the presentation of the material that excites him. He is performing for someone. If you can find that someone and gain his or her trust, you might be able to lure the killer into the open.

Well, that person had been found, he thought. Hayden could feel him closing in. He wondered if the spray paint on his car was Rufus. Maybe Darla's pimp? Or one of the neighborhood kids; they all must know the local whores. But Rufus was near, circling, always in the periphery.

Hayden stared through the windows, beyond the heated sand to the horizon where the ocean met the sky. He was thankful that his father had moved them to the ocean instead of the plains or the mountains or the desert. The ocean had always been there for Hayden. It reminded him that there were things in this world greater than himself.

Standing by the windows he felt a strange sensation. Was it Rufus?

Hayden turned to see. Down a bit, to the left, not thirty yards away, on the esplanade below . . . Abbey Reed.

He let her in and she seemed to saunter as a panther, ferocious, seeing him and the room all at once, seeing into the crevices of darkened corners in a glance. She was stronger than he expected, her sinewy muscled arms pumped, dressed in a man's sleeveless T-shirt and sweats. She was braless, and under the thin white cotton shirt Hayden could see the firm details of her breasts. She pointed her finger like the barrel of a gun in his face.

"What does it feel like, Glass? To be watched in your own home. How does it make *you* feel?"

Hayden replied without thinking, "Excited."

She took this in. "You fucking pulled me off a case," she accused him.

"I didn't pull you off a case, I put someone better on."

"Fuck you, you don't know what I'm capable of."

He drew closer. "What are you capable of?"

He touched her shoulder. She pulled back. He sensed fear in the anger.

"You stay away from me or I'll get a restraining order. I'll get Internal Affairs on your ass if I see you outside my house again."

There was a steam that rose from her body that only he could see. He grabbed her shoulders, drew her to him, kissed her hard on the mouth, knowing intuitively that she would collapse in his arms, that her posturing was prelude to passion, that she wanted to be taken.

She struggled as he encircled her. He pinned her arms until the resistance became subdued calm. Her mouth relaxed and accepted his tongue and he felt her hands moving gently up his leg. Then sudden pain as her knee found his groin. She followed it with her hand and she held his testicles tight, squeezing and jerking down like a reverse dumbbell curl. He pounded her forearm with his fist to loosen her hold, leaving him a few short seconds of relief before she sucker-punched his jaw. She followed with a quick left-right-right combination that dropped him. He remained on the ground writhing, rocking, nursing a bloody nose.

She shook her sore wrist and turned for the door, then came back again and landed a field goal punt into his kidney. He kept his gaze at her feet, attempting to focus on something other than her face. He was bloated with shame and wouldn't dare meet her eyes.

"I've had enough of men like you. And God help you if you ever pull me off a case again."

He heard the door slam as she left. Hayden rolled around on the floor, waiting for the fiery, pulsating pain in his groin to subside. He pushed himself to his knees and wiped a long trail of blood from his chin. He raised his head and caught sight of the world beneath him, through the big bay window in his apartment. The perpetual movement of pedestrians had stopped and small groups of walkers, skaters, bicyclists, and joggers stood looking up at him, some with fingers pointed, some laughing, some in shock from the show of violence and blood. Hayden reached forward and grabbed a pull-string, which dropped a wall of blinds across the face of the window from ceiling to floor. A twist of his fingers and the blinds became a wall that shut off the world.

40

Long Beach Boulevard. He was in his Jeep this time. Driving stick shift wasn't easy with an ice-filled Ziploc baggie balanced against his cheek. Hayden looked for the blur of headlights in pockets that branched off the Boulevard. Cars hovered around the last known sighting of the evening's prostitutes.

Hayden noted the activity but stayed clear of the crowds. The women were dropped off close but not directly in the lights. No john wanted a line of hungry sex addicts waiting to pick his leftovers. When business was done the john only wanted out. Hayden knew a guy once who pushed a crippled pro from his car onto a dirt road in the Hollywood hills because he couldn't face the shame of having picked up a crippled whore in the first place. He'd wiped clean from his conscience the fact that she would have to limp a quarter mile in the dirt to find Mulholland Drive, then hitch a ride back to Sunset Boulevard to finish her night.

Hayden's head pulsed from the beating he took. His left eye hung black and blue, his cheek was split, his nose trailed blood. His back hurt and his ribs creaked.

He wondered if this was bottom, but figured it wasn't since he was out cruising a connection. He hadn't intended to work the street, he had only wanted to run. He wanted time to think, forgetting that the street offered the opposite. Street time was time dropped from his living world. It was a no-man's land blurred around the edges and softened by leather seats and shock absorbers. He circled the Boulevards and rocked slowly with the nurturing movement of his Jeep. It allowed him to blur out the scene in his apartment with Abbey. Blur out the torture of Sol, the staging of bodies like Lincoln Logs. The street shock-absorbed it. He could do this all night long; the two-mile cruise from Broadway to 17th Street along Long Beach Boulevard. Eyes trained ahead and out, with peripheral vision sampling every shadowy sidewalk tramp.

He hesitated when he saw red leather shorts served tight, with long dyed blond hair streaked black and lowered to her waist. A little chunky but young and healthy with tits round and full under a button-down shirt tied above the belly. He slowed and immediately three cars were behind him, slowing, too. There were too many johns tonight and Hayden was first in line so he had to act fast. He pulled alongside and pushed the passenger door open.

"Hey, what's up?" she said as she sat down beside him. "Holy fucking shit! What happened to *you*?"

"Close the door, it's hot out there."

"You ain't a cop, are you?"

"Hardly," he answered.

She closed the door and he drove from the curb. He took to the Boulevard, making consecutive turns on side streets until he lost the johns behind him.

"What you got in mind, honey?"

"Where's a good place to park?" he asked.

She pointed out a series of streets, led him to a parking garage where an attendant stood beside a mobile barricade.

"Underground parking?"

"Paco keeps watch. You tip him a five. It's private property, the cops can't get you."

He stared at her admiringly. "You've got this whole thing figured out, don't you?"

"Come on, time's money-honey. What you got in mind?"

Paco moved the barricade, waiting on Hayden.

His silence disturbed her. "Let me help you out," she prompted. "Fifty for a blow job, eighty for sixty-nine, a hundred for straight sex, and anything else is negotiable."

"How long have you been out here?"

"What? I don't know, a couple hours—"

"I mean how long have you been hooking?"

"Dude, we gonna do this or not? Don't get psycho on me."

"Do you . . . have a name?"

"Okay, listen, you can just let me off here. I'll take twenty for the fucking break in my stride, though."

She opened the car door, stayed safely clear of the car with just her head in the window and her arm outstretched for the money. Hayden reached for his wallet. A wave of nausea surged in his gut. His head felt like the steel hull of a steamship. His hand on his wallet was shaking. He looked at her open hand, filled with expectation. He gripped the gear shift instead and flew into reverse as she pulled clear. She flipped him off in the rearview mirror, cursing him to hell.

41

My name's Hayden, and I'm a sex addict. I've been gratefully sober for one day, although I . . . I nearly assaulted a woman today. I had a sponsor, but . . . I had a sponsor . . .

"I never thought I needed something, I mean, the meetings. A higher power. I just have always prided myself on being strong, or tough enough. Who am I, you know, that *my* problems, compared to people who *really* . . . that God should give His time, for *me*, right? My dad . . . taught me to take responsibility for what I do . . . did . . . but he *believed* in God. He had that comfort. I'm trying . . . to make this work. I *want to* believe. If you saw the shit I see, what I see people do to each other. What parents do to their children, to their *babies*. People who put knives into their children, I've seen this, for *no reason* . . . how could there *be* a reason? There's no sense in it. And this is *God's design*? And there's Rwanda and

Cambodia and Darfur and Serbia and . . . and Germany . . . Do any of you really believe in a just God? I'm sorry, I can't be spoon-fed, it has to come from . . .

"And I've *been* sinking, I mean, really sinking . . . I could *use* this . . . God. I don't know where to turn, or who to call . . . it's this, and I've got this pulsing thing going on now, for a few days . . . a drumming, *inside* my head. It's this *weight*, and I can't really *think* anymore. It's just not there. Not that I can trust, at least, you know, to get me from point A to point B. Or even figuratively. It's like the neurons are firing, but into a *sponge* with a . . . thud . . . and I really can't call anyone, there's *no one* to call. I don't have someone who would really understand what I'm going through . . . no one I can ask for *service*. No, 'Hello, I've just seen a baby hopped up on crack cocaine and his parents ran his arm through a, because they, they said, oh, I didn't know it would *hurt* him.' Who do I call for *that*? Who wants it? Should I . . . pick a name off my phone list? Anyone here interested? The sponsor I *had*, for your information, is dead. His throat was cut and a corkscrew was shoved into . . . through the roof of his mouth and . . . *Next*? Who wants to be *my* sponsor? And I can't defend that . . . and *you* can't save me. None of you can *save* me. Only God, right? So why is it *my* job . . . to find *Him*? He knows where I am. I could use His help. So is it any wonder my sponsor told me that I'm not ready for the Fourth Step? That I have to do Step Three again, and maybe again even, because I can't fake Step Three, you can't fake *'Came to believe . . .'*"

Right at Hayden's last words a newcomer stepped into the room, which was a tremendous relief to the other members, who were more than a little freaked out by Hayden's speech.

It wasn't uncommon for a brother to walk in ten minutes late. It wasn't even an interruption, really. The group would wait until the speaker finished his share before asking the newcomer his name. It was less common, however, to see women at SAA meetings, although Hayden occasionally saw one or two. He never attended the Love and Sex Addicts groups, where meetings were generally split fifty-fifty. Love and Sex Addicts emphasized the addiction to the relationship itself, and it was no secret that the psychology of a relationship was a more appealing motivator to women than to men. Almost all the women at Love and Sex Addicts Anonymous were addicted to romance novels. They were looking for a connection, too.

So it sent a charge through the room anytime a woman walked into an SAA meeting. But when the woman was young and attractive, the charge was a jolt. When that woman was Kennedy Reynard, it was a different story altogether.

She wore an oversized man's corduroy jacket and a Nike baseball cap. Her hair was tucked in, but what spilled out was a luscious red halo that drew every eye. There was nothing she could do to hide her natural beauty. Her eyes were downcast as she shuffled meekly in, taking the seat offered by an appreciative group member who would've given his six-month chip to have her sit on his lap. But there was respect and some sobriety in the room and after an initial three seconds of longing, the eyes turned back to their own hands or feet or books.

After a moment, their eyes returned to Hayden, except for hers. Uncomfortable shuffling in the wooden chairs. Hayden imagined the sound of sweaty palms. Their eyes urged him on—none could stand the silent vacuum filled with the presence of gentle pheromones.

"Um . . . the Third Step . . . I remember . . ."

The sound of his voice tickled her senses. She looked up slowly. Into his face. His eyes.

His eyes, bloodshot, watering as he looked back. His face beaten. His head cocked to the side.

In her face he saw her surprise. But it was the surprise of an investigator undercover, stumbling upon another investigator undercover, marveling at the coincidence. How had they both determined, independently, their best chance of finding this killer lay in the front line trenches? She must have been impressed with his ability to transform into a creature of sympathy, a struggling sexual addict, in his attempt to draw out the killer they pursued.

"My sponsor . . . he was the one who explained it to me. How he . . . how it breaks down. The Third Step."

He hesitated, swallowed, then continued, his eyes focused squarely on Kennedy.

"Came to believe that a power greater than ourselves could restore us to sanity. Came . . . came to . . . came to believe."

He uncapped an Arrowhead bottle by his feet and took a long drink.

"First . . . we came," Hayden continued. "To the meeting. The first meeting. We didn't want to but we did. And in the meeting things made sense. And we 'came to.' We were suddenly aware that we had something, an addiction. That all the terrible moments we experienced, all the humiliating things we'd done, that it had a name. And others shared this disease. Then, ultimately, we 'came to believe.' To believe that there was a way out. That there was help. That something out there was bigger than any of us alone. Came to believe that a power greater than ourselves could restore us to sanity."

As he spoke he saw in Kennedy's eyes the growing realization that this was not an act. It started as a question, a subtle arch in her brow at his earnestness, at the focused peering of his eyes into hers. Then the turn like a switch and her understanding of the meaning of his words. That he *wasn't* undercover. That this was his life, his confession. He wasn't stepping into a foreign world; he was at home.

The very slight smile that had graced her lips, the smile that expressed her knowledge of their scheme, fell. Disappointment took its place. It would have been so easy if he had played along, squinted his eyes in a semi-wink that told her she had matched him at his game. A "touché" nod of the head. But he was tired of the charade. The meetings stood above the lies of everyday life. Even if the killer sat in this room it would be hard for Hayden to lie to the group. He had hoped to find the murderer in a meeting, hoped that he would be able to see that much deception in the face and movements of someone so clearly off the path. Plenty of brothers couldn't get a sober day, but the fact that they were trying was evident in every move they made. And out of all the faces there might be one man capable of killing others. Hayden hoped that his instincts were sharp enough to vet him out.

He was tired of lying to the people he knew. And here was Kennedy doing her best to work the scene, hooked by the intrigue of the investigation, doing all the right things, and she had stumbled into something she could not have prepared for. Her disappointment turned to anger. She felt betrayed, he knew. And then in her eyes he saw the most alarming thing of all—fear.

"My sponsor was going to walk me through the Fourth Step. Because I need help. I can't even begin to inventory the number of people I've hurt through my addiction. What does an apology sound like? I guess I can start with one, ask forgiveness from the first person I see, and then maybe the rest will follow."

His eyes remained on Kennedy. She wilted under the completeness of his stare.

"I'll close my share with that," he finished, "and open the door to someone who needs us tonight. We have a newcomer."

The eyes turned to Kennedy and she was suddenly on the spot. She shivered, looked away.

"Can you tell us your name and identify yourself?" Hayden asked.

She lifted her chin to face him.

"My name is Kennedy. I'm a sex addict." She said it flatly, like something rehearsed.

"Welcome, Kennedy. Keep coming back."

And she saw in that moment the truth in his face, and in her eyes the fear of him vanished.

42

The meeting continued with Kennedy listening but not participating. They didn't look at each other again. When the members stood to recite the Serenity Prayer, the words came back to Hayden, but went unspoken by Kennedy. Hayden slipped out when the group broke up, leaving her to fend off the literature steward who overwhelmed her with a selection of SAA-approved leaflets.

Outside Hayden found his Jeep, dropped his keys, bent down to retrieve them, and saw Kennedy's running shoes peeking out from the church doorway. He fell into his seat and took off, just as Kennedy reached her car.

———

He drove on autopilot, feeling like his life was collapsing. He would need to be more careful in the future. Censor his words. He couldn't allow himself to show such personal weakness at his meetings, not when Rufus might be watching. Sol would have said that he needed more moments of weakness. But Hayden couldn't afford even one.

He pulled into a parking lot and looked up at the sign on the building before him. If he had only stayed at the meeting. He might have joined the others at the deli where they gathered for fellowship. It was a time set aside for members to get to know one another, to talk and to be human together. A time for service. If he had stayed he might have found his next sponsor. But he would have had to face Kennedy. And now she knew his secret. He wished he had never met Kennedy Reynard.

Hayden left his Jeep and walked into TJ's Gentleman's Club.

The club was rocking. Juniper was at the pole, with full, natural breasts and close-cropped pubic hair in the shape of a heart.

"What do you say, Hayden?" she coaxed. Hayden smiled.

He tucked himself into a small loveseat in the V.I.P. room. The lighting was low, but he could see Juniper's body perfectly as she stood unfastening the light blue teddy she'd stepped into after her dance.

The music began. Green Day's "Boulevard of Broken Dreams." Apropos. And graciously slow.

The teddy fell. She wore a lavender lace thong and nothing else. Her ass slid down his chest and landed snugly in his lap. She moved in synchronization with the music. He closed his eyes, his body moving with hers. He touched her thighs, traveled her hips. She let him.

His hands crept up along her ribs and his fingers found the underside of her breasts. Her nipples appeared between his fingers, disappeared again as his fingers tightened around them.

She turned to face him, letting her breasts dangle over his lips. She deftly lowered a knee into his lap, raised it to her shin and ankle and foot, keeping the pressure on his groin. He moaned softly with the music's crescendo and the steady movement of her leg against his cock. He threw his head back as he ejaculated, his body convulsing then slowly growing still.

Juniper stood up and off him, reaching for her clothes. Hayden sat slumped for a moment then opened his eyes. He saw Kennedy, across the room, watching him. He shot up in his seat. She wore the same androgynous clothes he saw at the meeting but the cap was now off and her hair flamed across her shoulders. Hayden fished fifty dollars from his pocket and handed it to Juniper. But his eyes were on Kennedy, until, ashamed, he looked away.

He snuck around Juniper and slipped into the men's room, passing too close to Kennedy in the process. He kept his head low, but heard her small voice as he passed, "Detective. Detective Glass."

In the men's room he untucked his shirt and tried to cover the fresh stain on his pants. His shirt barely covered half of it. He took paper towels from the dispenser and ran them under warm water, which he spread liberally onto his slacks. The stain appeared even larger. He flung the paper towels at his reflection in the mirror. Graffiti stared back at him. He finally pulled his shirt down as far as it would go and left the men's room.

He held his breath, making a beeline for the back exit. He felt the safety of the Jeep's door in his hand, and then her voice exploded in his ear.

"Hayden, goddammit!"

He jumped back. She wedged herself between Hayden and the Jeep.

"Maybe we should, um . . ." he mumbled. He saw a Taco Bell across the parking lot and went for it. She sighed, slowly following him inside. He was already tucked in a corner booth when she stepped through the door. She dropped onto the hard plastic seat across from him.

"So . . . this isn't an act, I take it."

He shook his head. She studied him for a moment.

"Is it a court-ordered thing? You're not a child molester, are you?"

"Jesus, Kennedy, no."

"Did you . . . are you a rapist or something?"

Hayden sighed, looking down at his hands. "You have no idea what you're talking about. I'm not a rapist. I'm a normal guy."

219

"You're a sex addict."

"You don't know what that means." He couldn't look her in the eye. He spoke softly, humiliated. "I'm like anyone who has an addiction. Like a gambler. More like an alcoholic. I've never hurt anyone. I don't victimize anyone. Except myself, maybe. I pick up prostitutes, I go to strip clubs. I have a problem with that."

She brushed her hair out of her eyes. "I know guys that go to strip clubs. Or to prostitutes, even. They don't call themselves addicts."

He looked up from his hands and stared into her face earnestly. "Yeah, well. Maybe they should. If they spend all their money doing it. If they can't stop it even if it ruins their marriage. If they hide it like it's a different life—a different person living it—then they *should* call themselves addicts." He was spent. He was beat.

"What's going on with you?" She was sincere now.

"I'm having a hard time holding things together." He looked away, peering out the window at the blue and pink neon sign advertising TJ's Gentleman's Club.

She reached for his hand, held it. He felt his body recoil from the shock of it. The shock of a real, human touch. He held on.

43

He fumbled with the keys to his apartment. The latch gave and he pushed the door open, gently guiding Kennedy into the darkened room. He hit a wall switch, which produced a sudden glaring light that in an instant illuminated the stark, modern aesthetic. He toggled the dimmer to lower the light. In that quick flash he knew that Kennedy saw the overturned coffee table and broken whicker chair. Remnants of Hayden's encounter with Abbey. He guided her through the living room and into his bedroom.

He turned on a small table lamp, and pulled rumpled clothes off the bed and stuffed them into a bulging closet. He saw her observing the room, his *lair*, with the same calculated look he had witnessed on her face when she had studied the West L.A. and Coral Reef crime scenes. He followed her glance to see the books lining his shelves. Hume, Locke,

221

John Stewart Mill, Charles Dickens, Hemmingway, Steinbeck, Kerouac, Jack London, Henry Miller. And the ample supply of magazines spilling off the bed tables and onto the floor—*Newsweek*, *Scientific American*, *National Geographic*, *Architectural Digest*, *Playboy*, *Penthouse*, *Hustler*. He dropped the bed covers over the magazines with a smooth, seemingly careless tug.

She wandered the room, staring at his sketches, taped haphazardly to the walls. Crime scene drawings, sketches in charcoal and ink and pastels. Stark black-and-whites that tore through the paper with a violence magnified by diminishing perspective. Every sketch placed at eye level, as though Hayden had torn them from his sketchbook and slammed them directly onto the wall in front of him.

Except for the clutter, the room was stylish, with lush white carpeting and unique modern furniture. Boutique pieces purchased from the design centers on Melrose Avenue and Rodeo Drive, and the exclusive shops on Santa Monica's Montana Avenue. The themes were mostly black and white, with his bed dressed in shades of gray. The walls above his bookshelves were lined with prints by Matisse, Picasso, and Monet. One of Monet's *Haystacks* took a central position above his bed. The place seemed a combination of Sharper Image and Frank Lloyd Wright.

She watched him press a button on a CD player in the wall and the rolling sounds of John Coltrane seeped through hidden speakers. She found the button, turned it off.

"I don't like jazz," she said, to his disappointment. He pulled open a drawer to reveal a dozen other options—Beethoven, Handel, Dvorjak, Debussy, Brahms, Mussorgsky, the Rolling Stones, the Who, Beatles, Chili Peppers . . .

She touched his hand. "No music," she whispered.

He touched her hand back. Reached up to her hair, ran his fingers through the long, thick waves.

"I've seen you safely home, then. Maybe it's time for me to leave," she suggested, moving slightly away.

"I've been dying to touch your hair."

She let him. "I should go." She stayed.

He leaned in and kissed her neck. His hand fell between her legs and he squeezed the warmth he found there. The suddenness surprised her and she pulled back.

"No," she insisted gently.

Her rejection shook him. What was he doing? She wasn't some whore he had found on the street. "I'm sorry, I'm sorry . . . just go."

She walked to the bedroom door. He pulled off his shoes, avoiding her stare. Looking for immediate distraction, he went to his bookshelf. He picked out a collection of poetry by T.S. Eliot. He opened to "The Love Song of J. Alfred Prufrock," then felt her hands gently pushing his chest back toward the bed. The book fell to the floor.

He reclined, but she pulled him forward. He thought she wanted him to stand but as he did, she pushed his shoulders down and maneuvered him into a sitting position on the edge of the bed.

She stood before him, seeming to make a decision.

She unbuttoned and lowered her slacks cautiously. He reached out but she pushed his hands away. She unbuttoned her shirt to the bottom, but left it on, her bare breasts half exposed.

Hayden's hands lifted again, and again she gently brushed them aside. Her legs were creamy white and the whole package reminded Hayden of strawberry shortcake. The red hair, the white sugar-scented skin, liberally sprinkled with freckles.

She sat on his lap, her back to his chest. She grinded against him, the way she'd seen Juniper do it. Maybe it was the height or the angle of the bed, but she couldn't keep the motion. She resisted his help, bent upon seducing him on her own. There was an art to this and it wasn't something they taught the cadets at Quantico.

He reached into her shirt to find the small, firm breasts. He drew her nipples out, felt them rise. His other hand worked beneath her, unbuckling his belt and pulling down his pants. He placed his hard penis in her hand. It felt warm, a little sticky and damp. She must have realized that he had come in the strip club, with Juniper on top of him. She tried to pull her hand away but he held her. She squeezed and tugged him as he played with her nipples, pinching and rubbing in gentle circles.

He pushed her off and grabbed her hair, placed the palm of his hand against the back of her head, forcing her mouth toward his penis. She pulled back involuntarily and he pressed harder. He was in her mouth before she knew it. She pulled off her shirt, bare-chested now, and he felt her breasts slap against his thighs. She grabbed him by the shaft, ready to put him inside her. She wanted him now. And suddenly there was pressure at the back of her throat and she pulled back and off. He grabbed her hand and pressed it hard on his cock as he finished, his cum spraying into her hair and across his stomach. She hadn't even started and it was over.

He reached down and found her shirt, which he used to wipe the cum from his belly. He tossed it to the ground and pulled her onto his chest. He held her in his arms.

He felt comfortable, satiated. His breathing slowed as he began drifting off to sleep. She lay quietly in his arms, but he sensed that she was unsatisfied, even angry. Her skin felt hot. She tugged at a blanket for cover.

She had been naïve. Maybe she thought she would have been better than the stripper. Maybe she thought they would make love. He figured that when he awoke she would be gone.

She was curled at his side with her head nestled on his chest when the phone woke them. Somehow in the night they had managed to pull sheets and blankets across their bodies and snuggle into the feather pillows. She was wearing only her panties.

The time on the clock on the nightstand read 4:30 A.M.

Hayden held the receiver to his ear. He fidgeted with the cross on the chain around his neck, grunting "Uh-huh" and "Got it" with a final "On my way" before hanging up. He dropped the receiver and looked at her.

"Hey," he whispered.

"Hey."

"Christ, you're gorgeous."

She didn't say anything.

"You can stay, I'll be back in a few hours," he said.

He started off the bed.

"What happened?" she asked.

"A homicide. My partner's at the scene."

"I didn't know you had a partner." She sat up. "It's connected to the others?"

He was already in the bathroom turning on the shower.

"They seem to think so," he lied.

"I'm going along."

He stepped out of the bathroom and saw her stabbing a mound of wrinkled clothes on the floor with her bare foot. She grimaced upon seeing her shirt caked with dried cum. Hayden watched as she went to his closet and began rummaging.

"You are *not* going," he snapped. She ignored him. She found a clean pair of gym sweats and a button-down shirt, which she pulled off a hanger. She walked back to his bed to get dressed. He threw his hands in the air and returned to the bathroom where he pulled off his jockeys and stepped into the shower. The water warmed his face and he stood quietly meditating while the stress ran like little rivers off his body.

There was an instant breath of cold air from the curtain pushed aside, then the colder feeling of metal against his cheek. He didn't need to open his eyes to know that it was the barrel of his Glock. But he did, just the same.

"I want to know what the fuck is going on," Kennedy demanded.

His limbs trembled involuntarily as he felt the metal slipping across his wet cheekbone, as he watched the large, unfocused image of Kennedy's wet finger slipping over the trigger. He knew the Glock was calibrated for a light touch and he hoped that Kennedy's finger was that much lighter.

In her other hand he saw one of the *Hustler* magazines from the floor beside his bed. He saw the problem immediately. The girl on the cover sat in a chair with her legs spread wide. She had pubic hair that covered half an acre, and long, thin, straight hair with bangs, and a headband. The date on the issue was December 12, 1976.

"You've got me at a disadvantage," he managed after a pause.

She butted the barrel into his temple, sounding a dull *whap* that produced an instant welt. He stumbled.

"Jesus!" he exclaimed.

She pressed the gun to his forehead. "If you killed those people I have no problem putting a bullet in your head right now."

He raised a shaky hand defensively. "I did not kill anyone. I'm fucked up, but I'm not a killer."

"Under the right circumstances a person can do anything. Like at this moment I could kill you without a second thought, if I was certain you were the guy."

"I'm not the guy," he insisted.

"Why did you bring me into this?"

"I needed a profiler."

"You've been playing me. You've been holding back. I think you killed these people."

Hayden reached up and turned off the shower. "I swear I didn't—"

"Sit on the floor," she barked. "Hands on your head."

He did as he was told. Her expression hardened.

"You fit the profile," she said at last.

"What?"

"I should have seen it."

"I didn't kill these people. Just . . . take a step back. Think about this for a moment. Why would I have approached you, why would I have hired you? Just think about it."

She did, the gun still held to his head. He could imagine every crime scene running through her mind. Every piece of evidence examined. After a moment she seemed to relax a bit. She looked him in the eye, searching for truth.

"Tell me about the *Hustler*s," she said.

"I had to prove to you that the scenes were connected. That we were after a serial killer."

"Then there were no *Hustler*s at any of the crime scenes."

"No."

"You've completely altered my profile."

"Your profile is good."

"Why did you fabricate evidence?"

He took a moment before answering. He was afraid to speak of it, as if the telling would make it true. Until now it had remained in his mind only. Keeping things secret meant they didn't exist.

"*I'm* the only thing that connects these crimes," he admitted finally.

"That's not true. There's plenty to connect the crimes," she insisted.

"Once you've determined that the crimes are connected, yes. Very subtle things. If you read each police report back-to-back you'd see that the path the killer's knife takes across each victim has the same upward arc. That all the knife wounds were made by a right-handed suspect. But you wouldn't notice it if you weren't already certain the killer was the same. Would you have put the crimes together if I hadn't introduced the magazines?"

She understood.

"How are you connected?" she asked.

"He's targeted me. He's watching me. *I'm his audience.*"

He could see her processing, putting it together.

"You don't manufacture evidence," she said. "You've contaminated the crime scene, you've compromised the cases."

"I've only compromised the profile, which nobody knows exists. Nobody knows about them but you."

"So I'm expendable."

"You're expendable," he agreed.

"Providing that you get enough from the profile to help you catch this guy."

His silence must have confirmed her thoughts.

"Then you'll have to trust me. With everything. You have to tell me everything you know. This guy is playing you and you're going to need some help."

His head sunk into his chest. He knew she was right. And he felt, deep inside, that he needed her. He couldn't do this alone anymore. Sol would have told him to let go of his will, that now would be a good time to ask for help.

"All right," he uttered finally. "I'll tell you everything. But it stays between us. The killer knows how to play the system, and if we stick with the system he's got us. We play this on *my* terms."

She took a moment to think it over. "You don't intend to see him in court," she realized.

"You understand, it's a moral decision."

"It's personal."

"Yes, it should be. If I gave each of his victims the opportunity to pull the trigger, most of them would. If I gave their family and friends, husbands and wives the opportunity, they would. You yourself told me that if you were sure I was the killer you'd put a bullet in my head right now."

His words were having an impact. He could see it in her eyes.

She placed his gun on the edge of the sink and went for the door.

"I'm going to the crime scene," she announced. "I'm part of this now."

44

In his Crown Vic on the way to the crime scene, he told her everything. How the room numbers matched the rooms of his meetings.
How he'd been kicked out of his home group for being a cop. How he'd
told endless groups of strangers about his addictive behavior. How the last
victim, the one most cruelly murdered, was his sponsor. It was liberating,
talking to her, finally talking to someone. It felt like disclosure without the
fallout.

"You didn't tell me that the last scene was part of this. That the vic was
your sponsor," she said, disappointed.

He wondered if things would be different if he had been honest from
the start.

"The only connection at the modeling agency was the suite number?"
she asked.

"There's more. When he folded the girl and put her in the trash. I believe he was referencing another murder, nineteen years ago. A cold case. I think it might have been his first."

"Why would he tip you off to that?"

Hayden gave her a look. "I don't know. Maybe my profiler can figure it out."

She appeared ready to meet the challenge.

"I want everything you've got on that cold case," she affirmed, and turned to view a row of jacaranda trees outside the window. Although it was late in the season, many of the trees were still in bloom. They sprouted like giant, lavender broccoli tips across the city.

Hayden took the La Cienega exit off the 405, following the directions he'd been given for the crime scene.

"He's bringing it closer to home," she said. "He doesn't think you're paying attention."

"Oh, he's got my attention."

"It's not enough. He wants something specific."

Hayden grew quiet as the streets became familiar. He passed the giant plaster "O" of Randy's Donuts. Then Serene Touch Massage. A right on Slauson Avenue, then north on Crenshaw Boulevard. Rows of palm trees and birds-of-paradise. Concrete apartments.

He drove through a police barricade, flashing his badge. Detective Wallace was conferring with the divisional homicide unit outside the apartment. He looked up when he saw Hayden take a parking space by the curb. He intercepted Hayden as he stepped away from the car.

"A local pro got hit," Wallace said. "Wouldn't have left Southwest Division if it weren't execution-style. Plus, well, you'll see."

Hayden walked past him toward the stairs. He glanced at the carport where the taggers had twice hit his Crown Vic. The spot was empty. Wallace followed Hayden up the stairs, his limp growing more pronounced with each step. He turned when he realized that Kennedy was following him.

"Who's this?" Wallace asked.

She moved ahead quickly to shake his hand.

"Kennedy Reynard, P.I."

Larry gave her the once-over, saw the loose-fitting man's shirt and sweat pants. He turned to Hayden. "Is this for real?"

"It's for real. Let her pass."

"No, no, no—" Wallace objected, shaking his head.

"She's with me, Larry. She's ex-FBI, let her in."

Hayden wanted to get up those stairs and into that room to discover that Darla *wasn't* the pro Larry was talking about. He wanted to see it with his own eyes.

Wallace backed off, hands in the air. "Jesus, Hayden. I didn't know we needed help from the Fucking Bureau of Investigations."

Kennedy gritted her teeth as she pushed past him to join Hayden upstairs.

Hayden stopped in the doorway and stared past the boxlike living room to the kitchen beyond. Darla sat on the kitchen floor with her body propped up against the dishwasher in the same position he had left her in the day before.

Hayden immediately saw the thing that Larry didn't have words for, the thing that caused Pacific Division to bump this crime scene up to RHD. Written across her chest in blood was the word that Hayden had come to know too well—WHOREFUCKER.

He lost his equilibrium and Kennedy reached out to steady him.

Wallace squeezed past them into the crime scene. He walked over to two uniformed patrolmen standing a respectful distance from the body. Hayden figured they were the first responders.

Hayden took out his notepad, yet seemed unable to begin. Darla was naked, but unlike the other victims, there was no dismemberment, no cutting of the skin, no taking of fingers or toes. In fact, she seemed relaxed, and if it weren't for the bullet hole in the center of her forehead, it would seem as though she were waiting for her lover to arrive. Hayden noted that her eyes were open, with her head positioned to look up slightly to catch the eye of someone walking through the door. Someone roughly the same size and height as Hayden Glass.

He should have expected this. He should have staked out Darla's apartment. It frightened him that Rufus was coming on this strong, that he could be so bold, so taunting. He covered his tracks well and Hayden felt Rufus would kill indefinitely if he couldn't find a way to draw the bastard out.

Charlie was already at the scene, crouching just outside the police photographer's frame. He stood up when he saw Hayden and Kennedy enter. He approached them, his eyes trained on the beautiful woman at Hayden's side.

"Sickening, the things we see," he said, his hand outstretched toward Kennedy. "I'm Charlie, from Coroner's." She took it and he winced unexpectedly from her grip.

"Kennedy Reynard, P.I.," she said, her attention focused on the crime scene. She turned back to Hayden. "If you don't mind, I'm going to get a closer look," she said.

Hayden nodded and she left his side.

Charlie glanced at Hayden and raised an eyebrow almost imperceptibly.

"I don't want to hear it," Hayden said, surprised that his tone came off as harsh as it did. But he didn't feel like apologizing. Trivial banter, always viewed as inappropriate by people on the outside, seemed inappropriate to Hayden now.

They watched Kennedy kneel down and stare into Darla's eyes. Wallace watched her, too, from across the room. He pulled a notebook from his pocket and walked up to join Hayden.

"We got one suspect," he began, flipping through the dozens of notes he'd already written. "Dewey Cleveland. Her pimp or boyfriend or both. Can't find him, he's not answering his cell."

"I wouldn't be surprised if you find him in a Dumpster," Hayden said.

"You don't think he did her?"

"He's small-fry, check his sheet."

Wallace seemed confused. "I don't understand. You know this guy?"

"Picked him up when I was in Vice," Hayden lied. Wallace stared at him quietly until Hayden averted his eyes. Hayden could feel those polygraph needles working away. It was going to be a long, rough ride if Larry didn't buy his crap.

"Okay," Wallace said, letting Hayden slide. Charlie leaned into Hayden, his eyes on Wallace. "Who is this guy?" he whispered.

"My partner," Hayden said with obvious disdain.

"I thought you didn't have a partner."

Wallace glanced up from his notebook.

Hayden growled to himself. Charlie looked him over again.

"You okay, bud?"

"Where's my evidence, Charlie?" he said pointedly. Charlie got down to business. He fumbled for the clipboard where he had written his preliminary notes.

"She fought back pretty hard. We've got skin tissue under the nails and I think I can lift a print or two off one of her thighs."

So she had been a fighter, after all. Hayden saw the blood trail in the living room from where she had been shot in the head. It arced across the sofa and produced a red halo on the wall behind Darla's perfume cabinet. Rufus must have dragged her body to the kitchen then stripped her down and staged her in the position she was in now. Whatever tables or chairs they had upended in their struggle had been carefully set back in place. Rufus wanted to control the visual impression of every crime he committed.

"I don't want anyone else touching her," Hayden told Charlie. He placed his hand on Charlie's shoulder. "Only you," he said with a stern look. Charlie held his stare and nodded slowly.

"You might watch your girl there," Wallace said. "She's stepping all over the scene."

Hayden's expression changed ever so slightly. Charlie caught it and they both shared a subtle smile. Charlie knew how Hayden felt about partners. Great partnerships were rare in the department and, as far as Hayden was concerned, the best one ended when Rich had his stroke.

Hayden and Charlie stepped away from Wallace simultaneously—Charlie to set up his equipment and Hayden to join Kennedy beside Darla's body. Wallace sighed, looking very much like the new kid on the block.

Hayden took slow, deliberate steps around Darla's body. She was stiff and lifeless now, when just the day before she had seemed vibrant and self-assured. Her jaw hung slack, exposing her teeth, yellowed from the poisons that vapored off the smoke of rock cocaine. He couldn't get the thought out of his head that he had *just* been with her. It was *his* tracks that had led Rufus to her door. The bullet that took her life might as well have come from the gun he owned.

Kennedy was examining evidence on the cabinet where blood and bits of brain mixed with perfume bottles, drug paraphernalia, and trash from fast-food restaurants. He stepped up behind her.

"You notice the staging?" she asked without turning.

"Yeah."

"You think it's your guy?"

"It's him," he said.

There was a hint of perfume in Kennedy's hair and Hayden could detect its subtle fragrance over the stench of cheap scents that were spilled over Darla's cabinet.

"I gotta get out of here," he said suddenly.

"What?"

"Larry can finish up. I've seen enough."

She looked into his face and seemed to understand that it was killing him to stay.

"Let's work on that profile," she said. He nodded and she followed him out the door.

He escorted her down the stairs to the Crown Vic and found himself opening the passenger-side door for her. He couldn't remember the last time he had done that.

Wallace raced down the stairs awkwardly, approaching Hayden just as he was settling into the driver's seat. "Where you going?"

"To the station, then the coroner, most likely. You can handle this—just make sure you door-knock the neighbors. Someone should've heard the struggle, the gunshot. And find her calendar or appointment book. See if she scheduled a date for last night." He wasn't saying anything Wallace didn't already know. Hayden wanted to keep him busy canvassing the scene, making murder books, doing follow-up calls. Anything to keep Wallace out of his hair.

Wallace nodded. "You'll be reachable?"

Hayden sighed, annoyed. "Yes, I'm reachable. I got a cell phone, just like you."

Wallace seemed stung by the comment. Hayden turned the engine over and started backing away. Wallace rapped his knuckles on the car's hood, which was still an unfinished gray Bondo from Hayden's fix-it-yourself bodywork.

"I thought you were taking this thing to Automotive."

"I filled out the forms. Waiting on a replacement car," Hayden said through his window as he toggled it closed. Wallace kept his eyes on Hayden's car as it passed through the police line and continued south on Crenshaw Boulevard.

45

Hayden adjusted the dial on the thermostat in Kennedy's office. The big buildings in Westwood wouldn't let you open a window to catch the ocean breeze. Instead, everyone suffered through the same recycled, recirculated air. He loosened his tie, unbuttoned the top button of his shirt and walked past Kennedy, who vigorously punched words into her computer keyboard.

Hayden walked back to where he had spread a dozen crime scene photos on the floor. He had stacked one small office chair on top of the other, to eke out another two square feet of usable space. Kennedy's associates were in, working from their own tiny offices down the hall. Hayden occasionally heard their voices as they made phone calls or engaged in conversation with each other.

"Give yourself a raise," he told Kennedy. "Rent a bigger office."

"I'll get there," she said.

Hayden had the photos spread in an arc, starting with the West L.A. murders and ending with Darla on the floor of her apartment. Kennedy sifted through the data Scooter had assembled on Hayden's SAA list. She pulled member employment histories off LexisNexis.

Hayden stared at the photographs, looking for a pattern.

"What do you got?" she inquired.

"Nothing. Do me a favor, look at the whole thing. Like it was one moving picture."

She peered at the collage, moved from side to side, looking for the best angle. Finally, she pushed her computer aside and crawled onto the desk to look directly down at the images, her hair gently touching his arm.

"He's a fucking artist," she announced at last.

"What do you mean?"

"Not in the sense of beauty, but in the sense of craft, discipline. The thing that stands out is what's missing."

"What's missing?"

"Do you know theater terms?"

The closest he had come to actually studying theater was the two months in college when he slept through all the female cast members of *Chicago*. He shook his head.

"There's this thing in theater," she continued. "The fourth wall. It's the invisible wall that we assume exists when we watch a play. When you see a set on stage you only see the back wall and two side walls. The fourth wall is the perspective of the audience. The audience stares *through* the fourth wall to observe the actors."

She made a sweeping gesture over the photographs with her hand.

"These images," she continued, "the staging, it's like we're looking through the fourth wall. Each new scene brings his audience closer."

Hayden was beginning to feel like an unwilling actor in a play Rufus was directing.

"He knows exactly how to get you to a crime scene," she went on. "He knows when you're on call. He knows which crimes are bumped up to Robbery-Homicide and which stay at Division. He's teasing you by staging scenarios that ring false—to you. He's leading other investigators down the wrong path, but he knows you'll catch the scent. In the early murders, he was testing. Mrs. Palistrano's was gruesome and sexual—he was pushing your buttons. But then he got mad, I think because you weren't responding the way he wanted. Your sponsor was the turning point. His decision to target you directly, to get your attention. The girl, she must have meant something to you."

"She did."

Kennedy was quiet for a moment.

Hayden stared at the photos. He didn't know how to play Kennedy. He didn't want her to follow in Darla's footsteps. Everyone he knew, everyone he touched, seemed to become a target for Rufus. He wasn't sure how he felt about Kennedy, but he knew he didn't want to see her get hurt.

"What?" she asked, smiling at the concerned look on his face.

He was embarrassed that his feelings for her were so obvious.

"I'm just . . . wondering about . . . the wisdom of having you work this case anymore," he admitted, not looking her in the eye.

She responded with a little laugh that turned into a snort. She touched her nose quickly to make sure it was dry. Hayden smiled.

"Come on now," she said, wiping her nose on her sleeve. "You think I could end up like Darla or Sol?"

He shrugged. It was *exactly* what he thought.

"Was Sol or Darla trained in counterterrorism tactics at the FBI?" she asked in a light, patronizing manner.

Hayden smiled again. Of course, he had already considered the facts. Kennedy really couldn't be compared to any of the victims.

"Do you really think that someone could get the jump on me?" she asked. "I carry a nine millimeter Beretta. I can disarm just about any *armed* felon with my bare hands. I think you need to start seeing me as a real partner, as someone who's got your back. I expect you to be there to cover me, and I want you to feel confident that I'm capable of covering you. Not only capable, but the best choice there is."

She studied his reaction to make sure that he got it, that he truly believed what she said. He felt he could trust her, but he wasn't convinced that she could take Rufus if she faced him alone. And Hayden didn't want to be the one responsible for getting her into that position. He decided that he wouldn't let it happen. If things got too hot, he'd find a way to shake her off the case.

It appeared she mistook his faraway look for one of acceptance.

"Check this out." She smiled, pivoting on her desk to face her computer monitor.

"I've got the schedules of every SAA meeting you've attended in the past two years. You've indicated that these four had a regular attendance of more than twenty."

"Yeah."

"And this was your home group, the one you attended most often."

He nodded.

"The one you were kicked out of."

"That's where I did my First Step, where I talked about all the hookers I've picked up, all the addictive things I've done in my life. He would've heard everything."

"How many people were in that meeting?"

Hayden counted in his head.

"Twenty, maybe twenty-five."

"Our killer has never been in that meeting. You know everyone there, you know their stories, you'd spot someone new, even if he came only once or twice. Did you ever disclose in a bigger meeting?"

He thought hard. "Once more. At an intergroup meeting in L.A., there had to be seventy people there."

"Intergroup?"

"All the different meetings, the home meetings, get together for an intergroup meeting once a month to exchange ideas, listen to speakers, collect money to help addicts in need. They encourage people to speak, to reach as many members as possible."

"That was probably it. It was arbitrary. It could've been anyone, but he chose you. You caught his eye—a cop working both sides of the street. Maybe he's jealous, or maybe he wants to teach you a lesson. At some point it became an obsession."

"What about this old murder, the guy in Watts?" he asked.

"I'm not sure it's him. You think, what, because he folded this girl and put her in a trash can?"

"Yes. That and the way he mangled the guy's body. It's too much of a coincidence. Who knows how long this fucker's been watching me. Scrutinizing me. I think he wants me to know his history, how it all started."

"I don't get that sense. I haven't seen anything here that leads me to believe it's the same killer."

"I don't know. It feels planted to me." He seemed to be trying to convince himself. There was so little to go on; he needed *something* to match up.

Her hand touched his knee. "That case," she continued gently, "has been cold eighteen years. I'm just saying, it's a stretch."

It was all a stretch, but he had to put pieces together somehow. If Rufus would only come to a meeting, Hayden was sure he could spot him. He imagined himself at a meeting, seeing something in a look. He saw himself lunging, the Glock rising in his hand. The group members parting like a cloud of gnats. The look of shock in Rufus's eyes as he realized, and then Hayden's hand shoving the Glock into his mouth, knocking his front teeth backwards, three full shots of lead blasting out, sending the teeth through the holes where the chunks of brain flew out, the teeth like little stilettos stuck in the acoustic tiles of the church walls.

"What are you doing?" she asked calmly. He looked down to see his hands gripped tight around her thighs. He let go.

"What was going through your mind?" she asked.

His hands were shaking. It scared him to think that he hadn't been aware of his actions.

"I want to kill this fucker," he said quietly.

He shoved his hands into his pockets and turned away from her. He didn't like the way his anger seemed to flare, how it surprised him with its sudden presence.

She seemed more curious than concerned. "Have you ever hurt a woman?" she asked calmly.

"I told you, no. Never."

She grabbed his hands, placed them back onto her thighs. "Why do you do it, with the prostitutes?"

"Don't ask me that."

This was beginning to feel like a therapy session, except that Kennedy was pulling his hands up along the inside of her skirt. The tips of his fingers found the soft mound between her legs. Her panties were soft, malleable, suddenly warm, suddenly wet.

"What do you say to them?" she whispered.

Her hand reached down along his waist, settled between his legs. It felt like the moment a hooker touched him in a car—that first touch that let him know he was going to score. He pulled away. He felt the crime scene photographs crackle under his shoes.

"I don't want to do this," he said.

"You see a girl on the street. How do you know she's a whore?" she persisted.

She pulled him back slowly. He let her. He felt her hands between his legs again. The tension in his body dissolved. He felt the surface of his skin tingle as the bubble emerged around him.

"You just do," he said, relenting.

"What do you say?" She removed his tie. She unbuttoned his shirt.

"'Are you dating?' I . . . I ask them if they're dating." He sounded like a little boy.

She pulled his shirt off completely. "You ever ask a girl who wasn't a whore?"

His head balanced against hers as she began unbuckling his belt. "Yes. Once."

"Did you fuck her?"

Hayden spoke in a monotone. "No. She smiled at me. At a 7-Eleven. I asked her if she was dating and I saw the look on her face. Like she couldn't believe I would be asking her this—she couldn't believe what she was hearing. She said, 'What? What are you asking me?' And I stuttered. I just kept repeating the word 'date.'"

His voice was passionless. Like he was reading facts off a police report.

"What did she say to that?" She had removed his belt and was working on his pants.

"November tenth. She told me the date. She thought I was retarded, that I was asking her what the date was."

She pulled his pants down to his knees. He leaned forward, his hands removing her shirt, cupping her soft breasts. "Does this turn you on?" she asked.

"Yes."

"More than them?"

"Different."

"Are you rough with them?"

"Sometimes."

She was massaging his penis through his underwear. His body leaned into hers, but he remained submissive, unwilling to play along.

"Do it to me. The way you do it to them."

"You're not like that."

"You don't even know me."

"They're . . . fucking whores. You're not like that." She was making him angry. She wasn't listening.

"I could be anything, you don't know."

"You've got class. You're . . . clean."

"I'm clean?"

"They're dirty."

"Are they dirty? Or is it you?"

He always felt dirty when he was with them. The whole act was dirty, disgraceful, shameful.

"Fuck me the way you fuck them," she whispered.

"Don't talk that way. Just . . . be quiet, let it happen."

She was pulling down his jockeys. He pulled off her skirt. He leaned toward the door to lock it.

"Don't," she whispered.

He turned back to her. He couldn't figure her out. She was acting out and didn't know it.

He was having trouble getting hard. She noticed. She tried to force it.

"Not so hard," he said.

He didn't want to think of her this way.

He pulled away, closed his eyes, pressed the palm of his hand to his forehead. There was that hard, dull pressure that circled his head like a lead cowboy hat. She reached out and drew him back. He tried not to think of her as a colleague. He tried to think of her as a whore.

He grabbed her thighs hard. He saw her skin turn white where his fingers dug in. He felt his cock stiffening. His eyes remained closed as he bent over her, biting her nipples with his teeth. Her breathing grew deep and husky. She pulled him into her, enveloped him, sank her fingernails into his shoulders and back. He pushed hard and she pushed back, thrusting quickly, tightening around him.

His cell phone rang. He didn't hear it, he was already coming. He collapsed on top of her. She lay there on the desk, her legs spread in the air, half wrapped around his waist. She was still in the moment. Waiting for something.

He lifted himself off, pulled up his pants. The office was quiet. His cum drained from between her legs. Her hand found a box of Kleenex tissues. She wiped, pulled her shirt over her breasts, found her panties and skirt discarded on the floor.

"God, it's all about you," she said at last.

He heard the shame in her voice. The shame of acting out. It must've been a new feeling for her.

"What did you expect?" he said.

"I don't know, I thought I'd be different."

In the meetings he was told that an addict could spot an addict. That an addict sent out a certain kind of signal and other addicts responded. It was true like that in crime, too. A pickpocket saw every other pickpocket in a crowd. The junkie knew another junkie with a look. Sex addicts sought each other out. Kennedy was drawn to him because she recognized herself in him.

"I'm sorry," he said.

"Don't be sorry."

"It's shameful."

"Yes, it is," she agreed.

"Fuck you, it didn't have to be that way."

"So why was it?"

He buttoned up his shirt and tucked it into his pants. "Don't try to be what you aren't."

"How do you know what I am?"

"I know that you aren't a whore. Whores end up as crack addicts. Whores end up with AIDS. Picked off by disease, overdosed, or strangled, murdered, throats slit, left in a Dumpster by the Boulevard. You're not a whore."

She turned away from him to put on her clothes. He fastened his belt and found his tie. He stepped off the crime scene photographs, which were bent and crumpled under his feet. He knelt down to pick them up.

His phone beeped, and he remembered that there had been a call. He dialed his voice mail and put the phone to his ear.

It was Charlie.

"Hayden, I think I need some help—"

The line disconnected.

Hayden found Charlie's number in his phone and pressed send. He got Charlie's voice mail. He hung up and tried again. Same result.

He looked at the collage of crime scene photos like dirty, black-and-white snow shoveled onto his feet. He saw the bodies piled up, the dark, impossibly black blood on every page. Hayden looked up and into Kennedy's eyes.

"We gotta go."

46

It was a quiet trip, with Kennedy staring straight ahead, avoiding his gaze. Hayden called Charlie twice with no response. Still, Charlie rarely heard his phone when he was working. He fell into a state of quiet, controlled meditation, like a man playing chess or a kid with autism assembling a thousand-piece puzzle. More like disassembling a puzzle, as he removed intestines, heart, liver, kidneys, stomach, lungs, brains. Carefully cutting and weighing the contents of the human jigsaw.

Hayden double-parked in front of the coroner's office and walked quickly from his car. Kennedy hustled to keep pace. Hayden nodded to Dottie when they entered the control area. She was checking in a dehydrated, waiflike John Doe who appeared to have passed from AIDS. Hayden had pulled corpses like that from abandoned, downtown warehouses when he worked patrol years before. No fluid left in the body; the techs would have to inject chemicals into the man's fingertips to obtain readable prints. Kennedy hurried to keep up as they rounded a corner and pushed through a set of double doors into Autopsy Room One.

Darla's body lay naked on a metal gurney under a single glaring light. The room sparkled and her body on the gurney glowed like an overexposed photograph. Except for the word "whorefucker" drawn in blood across her chest, she was as clean as the room she occupied.

"Charlie?" Hayden called.

He walked out and stepped into Autopsy Room Two. Kennedy trailed behind him. An examiner stood holding a Stryker saw above a body. Flesh and bone dust sprayed onto his face mask. He looked up when they entered.

"Restricted area," he said, pointing to a sign on the wall.

Hayden nodded, stepped back into the hallway. Kennedy doubled back, following him. He walked into Autopsy Room Three, empty save for two bodies on gurneys. He returned to Autopsy One, where Darla's body remained on its gurney, taunting him. He went to the hallway again, reentered Autopsy Two. Kennedy followed like a puppy, bumping into his heels each time he reversed direction.

"Hey? You know Charlie?"

The examiner looked up from his work again. "Who's asking?"

Hayden flashed his badge.

"He was here earlier. I think he left."

Hayden plowed into Kennedy as he backed out of the room. She followed him into Autopsy One. She had had enough.

"What's going on?" she asked.

He walked slowly to Darla. Her body had been cleaned, but no incisions made. He figured Charlie would have been far into the procedure by now. It wasn't like Charlie to leave before his work was done.

Hayden tried Charlie's cell again and it rang through to voice mail. He hung up and tried again. This time there was a click on the line.

"Charlie?"

The line was open but he couldn't tell if anyone had picked up. Then it died. Hayden checked his phone's reception—no bars. Reception was terrible in the catacombs of the coroner's office.

He became acutely aware of the room as his perceptions went from casual observer to crime scene investigator.

"What is it?" Kennedy asked.

He was too much in his head to respond. He saw signs, subtle, of something more than the clean white stainless steel room. On the floor, a drop of blood. Three more steps, a drop of blood. At the door frame, a palm print, and a tiny chip of wood dug out from the frame, as if by a fingernail intentionally trying to leave a mark. It would have left a thin, painful splinter. It wasn't something anyone would want to do unless it was absolutely necessary. Unless Charlie knew that Hayden would see it.

Hayden began a quick shuffle from the room, which turned into a jog, which turned into a sprint. Kennedy seemed shocked by his sudden departure. She trailed behind, left to negotiate the halls, stairwell, and entryway by herself.

Hayden landed on the car seat and stabbed his key in the ignition just as Kennedy pulled open the passenger door and fell into the seat beside him.

She looked at him expectantly.

He returned a look of sheer panic as he gunned the engine and sped through the parking lot.

Charlie's house appeared quiet as Hayden's car approached. The afternoon cicadas had not yet began to hum, but the crows were loud and a solitary hawk circled high above the trees, belching a crisp predatory call.

Hayden pulled his Glock. Kennedy, alarmed, produced a sleek chrome Beretta from her purse. He watched her check the mag, handling the piece expertly.

"Maybe you should stay in the—" he began. She cut him off with a look.

They stepped from the car and approached the house.

"Charlie?" he called. "You in there?"

He tried the door; it was unlocked.

"Okay, Charlie? We're coming in."

Kennedy covered him as he opened the door. She followed him as he stepped inside.

The living room was clear. They continued into the kitchen. Nothing. Hayden peeked into the bathroom, then Charlie's bedroom. Kennedy slipped back through the living room to check the rest of the house. Hayden checked Charlie's bedroom closet, then under the bed. He walked back to the living room, pressing the speed dial number on his cell phone. He heard Kennedy's voice from another part of the house.

"Hayden."

Just then he heard the tinny sound of music from another room. The Doors, "This is the end, my only friend, the end." The ring tone to Charlie's cell phone.

The hairs on his back and arms rose.

"Hayden . . ." Kennedy's voice again.

He sprinted through the living room, barreling into a balsa wood coffee table that split in his path, taking a bite from his shins in the process.

He entered Charlie's study. It was a warm faux-oak room with a cherry wood desk, wood floors, and a bay window with a view of the trees beyond. In the padded leather chair sat Charlie, slumped to the side, his face puffed out and blue.

Hayden leapt over the desk and put two fingers to Charlie's neck. His fingers rose imperceptibly with the pulse. He pulled Charlie out of the chair and dropped him to the floor.

"Call nine-one-one! Tell them to bring insulin!" It had been years since he had administered CPR. He was well into it by the time Kennedy reached the dispatcher.

The ambulance arrived ten minutes later. Hayden knew they would get a quick response when Kennedy mentioned Charlie's name. Most everyone knew Charlie and no one wanted to be reading about him in the obits.

Hayden passed the CPR baton to the paramedics. One sank a hypodermic needle into Charlie's arm. They worked on him for fifteen minutes while Hayden and Kennedy watched from the doorway. Hayden overheard familiar comments: "That fuckin' Charlie. He survives this, he better get on the treadmill," and "The guy doesn't regulate his food intake. You ever see the crap he shovels in?" and "I went through all the cabinets, couldn't find a single vial of insulin."

A few minutes later Charlie was breathing on his own and the color in his cheeks had returned. Kennedy came up behind Hayden and gave him a tender squeeze on the arm. He reached back and touched her fingertips with his own. The gesture seemed to give his body permission to relax. His shoulders dropped and the tension in his neck dissolved.

The senior medic slipped an IV into Charlie's arm while another prepped a gurney for transport to the hospital.

Charlie's eyes fluttered, then opened. He watched the activity in the room with a sense of dawning realization. "Now, hold on just one second. What the hell's going on?" he said, slurring his words.

The paramedics continued their work, ignoring him. Two of them packed up the heavier equipment and carried it from the room. "Welcome back, Charlie," the lead medic said.

Charlie deftly pulled out the IV and held his finger to the wound in his arm to staunch the bleeding. The medic grappled with him for the needle, but it landed on the ground next to Charlie's feet.

The two medics who had left the room came rushing in when they heard the fracas. It took all three to restrain Charlie and force him back into his chair.

Hayden and Kennedy watched wide-eyed from the sidelines. Hayden's lips curled in an amused smile.

"You're going to the hospital, Charlie," the lead medic insisted, fixing another IV.

"I am *not going to the hospital*!" Charlie countered.

Hayden leaned casually against the wall with his hands in his pockets. "Charlie," he said, "grow the fuck up."

Charlie glared back at him. "I'm not doing it, Hayden. All I need is a stock of insulin. I've had worse episodes than this, you know."

"Worse than *this*? You were *blue* when we got here!" Hayden laughed.

"Yeah, well, like the last time I was in the hospital," he said defensively. His eyes were wide with fear. "You remember what I told you about the *last time*."

Hayden remembered. The midnight nurse and the overdose, the nitro, the defibrillator.

"I don't need this fucking IV!" Charlie shouted, pushing the medic's hand away. The medic stepped aside, perplexed by Charlie's behavior.

"He going to be all right if he stays?" Hayden asked.

The medic reviewed the notes they had made after reviving him. "His vitals are good. If his blood pressure holds he'll be fine." He folded the notes. "But he's out of insulin. We're liable—it's our job to bring him in."

Charlie held his chair firmly. "They've got insulin on them," he said, staring at Hayden expectantly.

Hayden sighed, turning to the medic.

"You've got insulin?" he asked, his voice suddenly sharp with authority.

The medic looked up, catching the shift in Hayden's tone. He stepped back, toward the other two paramedics.

"For emergencies," the medic said, trying to gauge Hayden's purpose.

"Thank you for everything you've done, guys. You can leave your insulin with Charlie before you go," Hayden said matter-of-factly. Kennedy looked from Hayden to the paramedics. She appeared to be enjoying the turn of events.

The medic turned to Charlie.

"Charlie . . . ?" He smiled awkwardly, waiting for someone to acknowledge the joke. Charlie did not return the smile.

"The only ones riding back in that ambulance are you and your boys here," Hayden said.

The medic looked to his colleagues for support. They averted their eyes. One began packing up the gurney.

The insulin they left on the kitchen table seemed enough to harvest a brand new pancreas, or so Hayden figured. The medic made Charlie sign, in triplicate, four separate releases clearing the paramedics of any liability that could be attributed to their visit. Charlie breathed a relieved sigh when he watched the ambulance speed away from his house.

Hayden guided him toward a large, padded recliner with a view of the TV set. Kennedy approached with a cold glass of water. Charlie drank half the glass and settled into the chair. After a moment, he cocked his head to the side and regarded Kennedy as if viewing her for the very first time.

"You seem like a nice young lady," he acknowledged. "What are you doing with this schmuck?"

"You're welcome," Hayden said.

"We're just working a case together," Kennedy lied. Charlie gave her a look that said he knew better.

"I guess you got my message, then," Charlie said, addressing Hayden.

"You could've told me you were at home. You were practically dead when we got here."

Charlie shrugged. It was his "sorry" and "thank you" in one gesture.

"So what the fuck happened?" Hayden asked.

"Didn't know I was low. I guess I blanked out, knocked my head on the counter. Came to with a bloody nose. I thought I had insulin at home."

"You came all the way back, you didn't even have it."

Charlie shrugged again. Kennedy kneeled down beside him, took his hand.

"Are you going to be all right?" she asked. He smiled at her.

"I like her eyes," he said.

"You scared the shit out of me," Hayden growled. "You know I got this fucker out there killing people. Dammit, Charlie."

"I'm sorry. I'll get another examiner on that body right away."

"I'm not talking about that. I thought he had gone after you. I thought it was going to be *your* body on the gurney."

There was a quiet moment as each imagined the scene Rufus might have left behind with Charlie's body.

Charlie noticed the mess that had once been his balsa wood coffee table, left splintered on the floor. "Jesus, fuckin' paramedics trashed my coffee table."

Kennedy looked at Hayden expectantly.

"Yeah, fuckin' shame," Hayden agreed, dodging the blame. Kennedy shot Hayden another look. He ignored her.

Charlie smiled, watching their interplay.

"Christ, Hayden, you look worse than me. Bags under your eyes, weird bumps and bruises all over your face and hands."

Hayden rolled his eyes.

"You know," Charlie continued, "you guys could take a little time off. A couple days out of the city. I got a friend has a place in Idyllwild, just a few hours out."

The room was quiet again. Kennedy seemed to appreciate the gesture. Hayden picked up the cable channel guide that sat in the ruins of the coffee table. He started pacing the room, flipping through the guide with growing interest.

"HBO's playing *Tightrope* in forty minutes. You ever see *Tightrope*, Charlie?"

Charlie reclined in his chair, popping up the leg rest. "Of course I've seen it. But *Unforgiven*, that's the one, *that's* Eastwood. How about *Ten to Midnight*? You ever see that one?"

"Bronson, right? I haven't seen it in years. That was a top-notch cop film."

"So, you boys are going to start talking old Charles Bronson movies. Bunch of crap, if you ask me."

The guys looked her over. Hayden turned a page in the guide. "Oh, here's one for you, Charlie. *You've Got Mail.* Starts in three minutes."

"I don't know," Charlie commiserated. "All those scenes of rejection and misunderstanding. For most of the story you don't even know if they're going to get together in the end."

Kennedy mumbled a few obscenities under her breath while the men laughed at her expense. She didn't have to prove she was one of the boys— she carried a gun.

Hayden pulled up a chair beside Charlie. He grew serious. "I need what's on that body, Charlie. I need an autopsy."

"I'll get you the best person for the job," Charlie promised.

Hayden squeezed Charlie's shoulder, thanking him with his eyes.

47

Hayden waited in Autopsy Two. Darla's body was still on the gurney, but someone had put a sheet over her, leaving just her face exposed.

He knew this would be the way he would eventually see her. But he didn't think he would be responsible for putting her here. He wondered if things would be different if he had forced her from that apartment. Driven her to the train station, put a wad of cash in her hand, sent her to someplace like Colorado Springs. Or Fort Collins. A small town with a good school where she could study to be a nurse or a paralegal. Would she have made something of herself, or would she have become the town prostitute? Would she have ended up beaten and killed and left for the coroner at the morgue in Colorado Springs?

He was beginning to feel like a sitting duck. It dawned on him how everyone he knew was a target. Charlie might have disappeared from his life, just like that. No one who knew Hayden was safe. He wondered if the oxygen in Rich's tank would be mysteriously emptied one day. Or if Nicky would get a bullet in her head some night as she perched on the shoulder of an empty road to change a flat tire. Or if Kennedy really was as safe and prepared as she thought. He figured what he ought to do, at the very least, was put a detail on Charlie.

Hayden jumped when he heard the double doors push open behind him.

"I was on vacation," he heard. "This isn't my body."

Hayden turned to see Abbey Reed donning a plastic smock and latex gloves.

"Fuck," he said under his breath. "You're my examiner?"

She approached Darla's body, pulled back the sheet. "I'm doing this for Charlie," she stated flatly, not looking at him.

Hayden felt compelled to explain everything. "There's a serial killer, out there. This is just one of his victims."

"Charlie briefed me. He's told me everything I need to know," she said dismissively.

The comment didn't make him feel any better. He wondered if Charlie told her that the man killed in Mar Vista was his sponsor. Or that Hayden was hopelessly addicted to sex. He moped around the exam room while Abbey prepped tools on her cart.

"I can take it from here, Detective," she said coolly.

He hesitated, wondering how far he could push her. "I need an examiner I can trust," he stated carefully.

"Then you've come to the wrong place," she shot back, focusing on her work. Of course *that* didn't sit right with Hayden.

He paced the room, fidgeting with autopsy tools left on the countertops.

"Please don't touch the equipment," she admonished casually. He could sense that she was enjoying the reversal of power.

He stepped up beside her respectfully. "There's a latent print, on her thigh. We noticed it at the crime scene—"

"I've got Charlie's report," she said, turning to face him. "I said I can take it from here, Detective."

He observed her determined stance. He was going to have to trust her if he hoped to get the evidence he wanted. She stared at him expectantly. It was Hayden's cue to go. He walked to the door and stopped.

"I appreciate your help on this. I'm sorry about your vacation."

It broke through her veneer. She hesitated, then looked up and gave him a nod. "What the hell, I can ride Sturgis next year."

48

Hayden picked up a sloppy joe from Max's Diner down the street from Parker Center. He had just about finished eating when Reggie called him in for a meeting with Captain Forsythe. He left the diner quickly.

When he entered the conference room he could feel the veins in his head pulsating. He wished he could cut them to relieve the pressure. This thing in his head, whatever it was, seemed to come in waves. It felt like the weight of a lead vest draped over his skull, the kind they put on someone about to get an X-ray.

Wallace was there, sitting next to Captain Forsythe.

"You know about Thorton and Price?" the captain began.

Hayden shook his head. It caused a swirling, dizzy sensation.

"They had to cut loose their suspects on the councilman case."

"No kidding," Hayden said in a monotone.

"It was a tough case, a tough call. Circumstantial. All we had was their confession, and they had their own reasons to lie to us. The DA won't take it, so it's open again."

Hayden wasn't about to say, "I told you so."

"There's something we need to talk about," Wallace interjected. He seemed nervously focused on Hayden. It made Hayden uncomfortable. He looked from Wallace to the captain and back again.

"Okay," he said apprehensively.

"We pulled some prints from that apartment on Crenshaw," Wallace said, gauging Hayden's response.

Hayden was suddenly interested. "Good. Finally."

The captain watched Hayden closely. He shared a look with Wallace, nodded for him to continue.

"The prints are yours, Hayden," Wallace said.

Hayden took this in. He felt his fingertips sweating. His mind was slipping, attempting to leave the room, the way it did when Nicky made him take the lie detector test years before.

Wallace observed every nervous twitch Hayden made.

"Did you know this girl personally?" the captain asked.

Hayden could have lied. He could have said he left the prints during the course of his investigation. But they would know. Hayden didn't make those kinds of mistakes.

"I've seen her once or twice," Hayden acknowledged.

"You've been in her apartment before," Wallace pressed. He was taking notes now.

"Yes." Hayden could see that they were concerned, that they didn't know what they had on their hands. By admitting that he'd been to the apartment he provided a reason for why his prints had been found. If he had lied they could have arrested him on suspicion of murder, since they had evidence proving he had been there. Now all they had was a detective who admitted that he visited a known prostitute. A prostitute who had subsequently been murdered.

"What about the body?" Hayden asked. "Charlie said there was a print on the body."

"We don't have the coroner's report yet," Forsythe said, watching his reactions.

Hayden stood up. "Well, we'll know more when we get the report. It looks like that body is the only evidence we've got," he said, his hand already on the doorknob. He wanted to get the hell out of the room before someone's handcuffs came off their belt.

Captain Forsythe stood up, took Hayden by the arm. Hayden froze. He had the distinct feeling that he was about to throw up.

"Your girl's outside," Forsythe said.

Hayden turned around, not understanding his meaning.

"I contacted Ms. Reynard, Hayden," Wallace explained. "We asked her to come by. We don't think you're in any condition to drive." Hayden resented the fact that Wallace was there at all. Resented the rapport that had seemed to materialize overnight between Wallace and the captain. Forsythe liked by-the-book guys, and Wallace was all that and more.

"I'm good, thanks anyway," Hayden said, pulling his arm from Forsythe's grip and reaching for the door.

"It's all been arranged, Hayden," the captain said.

"We'll get that hood of yours into Automotive," Wallace chirped, wearing a friendly smile. "It'll look brand new in a couple days."

"In the meantime you should take a day or two off." The captain's suggestion sounded a lot like a command.

Hayden looked from one to the other. He knew they were up to something, but he also knew he'd been dealt a good hand. He decided not to call them on it.

49

Hayden practically melted into the white leather seats in Kennedy's Mercedes. She reached around and buckled his seat belt before driving off.

For ten minutes they drove in silence.

"The buzzards are circling," he said at last, just as the motion of the car put him to sleep.

He heard noises around his apartment while he slept. Pots clanging. Closet doors opening and closing. The blast of a vacuum cleaner. He smelled air freshener, felt small, warm hands on his back, massaging his shoulders and neck. Soft lips touched his cheek. Wonderful smells: basil, oregano, garlic.

He awoke starving and found a plate of steaming pasta on the kitchen table. It warmed his face.

"I'm sorry, penne was all I could find," she said, emerging from the open refrigerator.

"Penny," he repeated, thinking of Sol's wife.

"I would have put vegetables in, if I'd found anything that looked like a vegetable."

He had never seen her so relaxed. Her hair looked like something out of an Impressionist painting. Hayden took a bite and became instantly involved in feeding himself. He hadn't had a decent meal in days. He noticed his apartment was clean, manicured, bright. He felt warm and protected. Kennedy was mothering him and mothering was what he needed.

His chewing slowed as he was reminded of the examination room at the coroner's office. Darla's room. Clean, manicured, bright. And he thought of Penny having to identify the mess that was Sol. He thought of Sol's kids, whose lives were unraveling. They were soccer camp kids, Cub Scouts. Now there would probably be a lifetime of therapy. Phobias, emotional attachment issues, drug or alcohol abuse to contend with. He wished he could be there for Sol's boys, the way Sol had been there for him, although he doubted that Penny would let him get close enough.

He knew there was something he could do. He could bring Sol's killer to justice. A boy whose father was murdered should live to see the murderer punished. The survivors deserved closure. Hayden could give Sol's boys that, at least.

"I can't stay," he told Kennedy. It sounded like an apology.

She ran her fingers through his hair. He leaned into her hands.

"Stay just a while," she asked.

He wanted to. There was nothing he would rather do than lean into her arms, lead her back to his bed, hold her tight and sleep, for days.

She hugged him in a way that accepted the apology, not just for this, but for all that he had done. For the way he had treated her before.

"I gotta go," he said.

"Do you mind . . . if I stay?"

He smiled. It felt good to have someone there. The apartment had grown so cold. Too much of Hayden in it. Somehow the addition of Kennedy, even for a few hours, warmed it.

He pressed his lips against hers, felt their soft cushion.

"I won't be long," he lied, and she knew it was a lie, and it was fine.

50

ayden arrived at the home of Esther Bayless. It was dusk and the warm red hue of "magic hour" colored the Santa Monica bungalows in pastels. It was a wide street, five blocks from the beach, west of Lincoln Boulevard. Esther lived in a modest, one-story stucco house with a Spanish façade.

He stepped from his Jeep when he saw her car pull into the driveway. She had to be at least sixty years old and she filled her pink and white jogging suit with bulges that seemed to roll and sway with her movements. He approached her as she started unloading groceries.

"Esther Bayless?" he asked.

She dropped her bags, turned to see the badge in Hayden's hand. "Oh my Lord," she exclaimed. "You sure made my heart jump!"

"I'm sorry, ma'am. Are you Tobias Stephens's sister?"

Something changed when he spoke her brother's name. "What's this about?"

"I'm Detective Glass with LAPD Homicide. We've reopened your brother's murder case."

She met his eyes at last. "I don't talk about this anymore. That was a long time ago. He's gone and nothing I do will bring him back."

"Mrs. Bayless, I believe the man who killed your brother is responsible for a series of recent murders. More could die if I don't find him. I'm asking for your help."

She turned from him as he spoke. Her eyes darted toward the house, then to a neighbor's driveway.

"I made my peace with this," she said. "My baby brother's gone. He didn't deserve what came to him. He done some things in his life, things he wasn't proud of. That was a long time ago. Only he and God know the extent of his sins. But he was a changed man when he went. He was with Jesus."

She grabbed four plastic grocery bags, clearly too much for her to carry at once. She pulled the bags back sharply when he reached out to help, and started for the house.

"You can leave now. I don't hold nothing against no one. Understand? It's in God's hands."

Hayden dropped his LAPD business card into one of her bags and told her to call if she thought of anything. She continued walking without looking back.

He returned to his Jeep and placed a call to Sergeant Hempel. Hempel knew a lot of the guys doing private security. Most were retired cops. If a retired cop needed extra cash in L.A., he did private security or guarded sets for the film studios. Hempel answered his cell.

"Sergeant Hempel here."

"Anthony, this is Hayden Glass. Can I ask a favor?"

"What can I do for you, Hayden?"

"I need security on a house. Twenty-four seven, for a week or two. A couple blue-and-grays."

"Two twelve-hour shifts, one guy each. It'll cost you three grand a week."

Hayden winced. Two weeks would eat up the last of his savings.

"Okay," Hayden agreed. "I need this tonight."

"I can have someone within the hour."

Dependable Hempel, Hayden thought. He gave the sergeant Charlie's full name and home address.

Another call rang through. Hayden finished with Hempel and switched lines. It was Scooter.

"Scootie-boy, what's the word?"

Scooter's voice sounded hushed and urgent. "Do you know what they've got us doing to your car?"

"Well, I'm supposed to get a new hood."

"We're doing fiber, hair, and semen analysis."

So now I'm a suspect, Hayden thought. That nauseous, helpless feeling gripped his gut again. He leaned back in his Jeep, waiting for the tremor to pass.

"Did you hear what I said, Detective?"

Hayden took deep breaths to settle his nerves. "I heard you, Scooter."

"They're not fucking around," Scooter continued. "They're doing an acid bath on the hood."

Hayden took this all in. The acid bath would reveal the message under the Bondo. And they would probably find hair samples in the passenger side of his car, a place he should never have a suspect.

"All right, Scooter. It's okay, just do your job. I haven't done anything that a few day's suspension won't cure."

He could tell by the silence that Scooter didn't seem so sure. Hayden released the line. This was not good. Wallace and the captain were turning the investigation onto one of their own. He didn't care if they weren't going to help, but he wouldn't stand for them getting in his way.

He dialed his home number as he pulled away. "Don't get up," he said. "Don't cook anything. I want to fall into your arms and sleep for at least six hours." Kennedy's response was groggy, but comforting. Let her sleep, he thought. He hadn't meant to wake her but he also didn't want her sitting up waiting for his return. The fact that she was there still, sleeping in his bed, both excited and frightened him. Unfortunately, his excitement abated and his fear won over.

While it had been his decision to check in, wasn't that exactly what she had expected? He couldn't stand checking in with anyone or being checked on by anyone. He barely knew Kennedy and there were already *expectations*. Expectation made him anxious and it drove him into the arms of his addiction. His addiction never expected anything, except total subservience.

His thoughts turned him around and he found himself driving Lincoln Boulevard, south of Venice. He should've taken Olympic to the 10 East, then south on the 405. He threw a U-turn at Washington to head north on Lincoln. He was suddenly aware that Lincoln Boulevard had once been his favorite cruising route, after Sunset. There were pockets of trouble from Pico all the way to Venice Boulevard.

It was rare to find young, attractive pros on Lincoln Boulevard. Most were overweight or sickly thin. But he remembered one. Blond, sexy, and surprisingly smart. Somehow on their short drive to a deserted side street he had learned that she loved Jane Austen, William Carlos Williams, Jack Kerouac, and William S. Burroughs. She quoted a passage from Kerouac's *Doctor Sax* while jerking him off. "'You'll never be as happy as you are now, in your quiltish innocent, book-devouring boyhood immortal night . . .'"

In four years he'd seen her on the street only twice. The second time he picked her up she was showing signs of street neglect. Acne, sallow cheeks, raccoon eyes. She was barely responsive, but performed the hand job just the same. The poetry had left her. He looked for her tonight, as he did every time he drove Lincoln. He knew he'd never see her again.

He was tired and wanted to get home. But there was activity on the Boulevard, a question on every street corner. He caught a glimpse of long, bare legs in red pumps slipping into the low bucket passenger seat of a Lotus. He saw a trail of cars on a side street where two or three girls had been. He came to the end of the stretch, Lincoln and Pico, threw a U-turn and continued south for another run. He had traversed the Pico to Washington route three times and it was getting late.

His phone rang just as he caught sight of a girl leaving an '05 Infinity.

He was the first to spot her. Her eyes tracked him as he took the closest side street and parked by the curb. He answered his phone.

"This is Glass," he said, watching the girl stroll along the boulevard and turn the corner onto his street.

"I'm scared, Detective."

It was Abbey and her tone shocked him out of his bubble.

"What's going on?" he asked, unable to mask the dread in his voice.

"There's nothing here, nothing at all," she said, her breath coming in quick bursts.

The line disconnected.

The streetwalker approached Hayden's car cautiously, checking him out. Hayden didn't even notice.

He hit redial. The number rang through to the coroner's central voice mail system. "You have reached the Los Angeles County Coroner's Office, our switchboard is now closed . . ."

He threw his Jeep into reverse and punched it, clipping the hooker with his side-view mirror and knocking her to the ground. He hit the brakes.

She was splayed out with her tight yellow miniskirt caught above her thighs and her black panties exposed.

It was just a bump. A bruised shoulder, a scraped knee. He cut a hairpin turn and sped away.

He was at the coroner's office parking lot in twenty minutes. He drew his Glock as he sprinted into the building.

He ran straight to Autopsy One. It was empty except for Darla's body on the gurney. Abbey's metal tool cart was on its side, scissors, knives, and scalpels spilled across the floor. One scalpel lay in a pool of blood by the door.

He backed into the hallway and kicked through the doors of adjacent exam rooms. All were empty except for the bodies left behind. He checked the crypt, the photo lab, the storage room. He took a set of stairs up to ground level, walked cautiously through the administration offices. Down a long hallway. As he drew closer, he caught the muffled sound of bodies colliding, then someone slammed against a wall. Glass breaking.

He kicked open the door of a darkened room and immediately saw the silhouette of two bodies. One dropped the other and leapt across the room to a window that opened into the parking lot. Hayden fired six steady shots, chasing the movement across the room. His bullets found wall and then window, everything but the suspect.

He ran to the window, heard footsteps on pavement, saw the back of a hooded figure in a jogging suit disappear down an alley. He lifted himself through the window frame, but stopped when he heard shallow breaths.

He dropped down to find Abbey on the ground with a coil of fishing wire wrapped around her neck. Her fingers were wedged between the wire and her throat, her face blue-red, her eyes bulging. Hayden found a shard of glass from the shattered window and pulled it from the frame. He used it to sever the line and free her windpipe. A deep, throaty gasp of air rushed through her lungs.

51

She was black and blue and unconscious in the hospital bed. An IV in her arm and a tube in her nose. Stab wounds from the scalpel. Her body was covered in bruises, her knuckles raw. Hayden recognized the defensive wounds on her fists, the scrapes a victim received when she fought for her life. In what she thought would be her last act of defiance, she had reached out to scratch. Hayden imagined that she had done this just for him, determined to capture a sample of the killer's DNA under her nails so that Hayden might find irrefutable evidence. Maybe she scratched his face, too, so that the killer would be easily seen in a crowd. He made certain the EMT at the scene cut and bagged her nails in the ambulance on the way to the hospital. He wasn't about to let her efforts go to waste.

———

Hayden stayed there ten hours, waiting through prep and surgery and post. A nurse came and went, checking vitals, adjusting valves on the respirator. There was internal bleeding. They were concerned about loss of oxygen to her brain. They were keeping her in a coma until the swelling went down. He was amazed by her strength, by her will to live. He lifted her hand and held it protectively in his own.

The door opened again. He expected to see the nurse, but it was Kennedy. He placed Abbey's hand down by her side.

Kennedy touched his shoulder. He reached up and held on.

"We have to go," she said.

In the hallway they walked arm in arm. It felt comfortable to Hayden, a new sensation. He couldn't remember the last time he felt this comfortable in a woman's arms. Not even with Nicky.

They turned a corner to find Detective Wallace and two uniformed officers sitting in hard metal chairs. Hayden's arm dropped from her shoulder. She stepped off to the side.

"Any news?" Hayden asked Wallace.

Wallace stood up, shaking his head. There was a stiffness to his movements that put Hayden on guard. The other officers stood, as well, taking Wallace's cue.

"I want those fingernail samples rushed through the crime lab," Hayden ordered. "You need to ride them on this, Larry. I've seen the lab stall a sample six months."

Wallace had trouble looking him in the eye. "Hayden . . . you were the only one who saw the guy."

Hayden took a deep breath. "Yeah," he said. "Just me and Abbey, I suppose."

"She's still unresponsive?"

Hayden nodded in slow confirmation.

"No one reported seeing anyone out of the ordinary," Wallace said uneasily. "You were alone when you found her?"

"Uh-huh."

"So the evidence the EMT collected under her fingernails, there's no one who can verify it was there when you arrived?"

No one said anything for a moment. Hayden felt the tension as it enveloped him, forcing his breath out in short, shallow bursts. "Cut the foreplay, Larry," he whispered.

Hayden knew Larry was doing what he thought was necessary. Following orders, following the evidence. But it was short-sighted. Larry was on the path the killer had laid out for him. He was a seasoned divisional cop, but an RHD rookie.

"I'm not arresting you," he said cautiously. "You're not a suspect. But Hayden, you *are* a person of interest."

"Thanks for the euphemism."

"I need your cuffs," Wallace said, holding out his hand. He looked Hayden in the eye. "And your gun. And your badge."

Larry's movements seemed robotic. It was an awkward situation for everyone. Hayden chose to cooperate.

Kennedy, however, was fuming. Hayden motioned for her to settle down. She kept her cool, but under protest. It was a tough turn of events, but Hayden should have known to expect it. It meant that he would *have* to produce Rufus now, if only to clear his name. Strangely, he felt at ease. He had finally lost everything, and with that came a sense of freedom.

"You can't leave L.A. County," Wallace continued, kicking into official gear. He was finding his voice. "You must remain available at all times for questioning regarding this and several other cases. You are not to continue with your investigations. You're on paid administrative leave until further notice. You understand?"

Hayden nodded, removed the mag from his gun, checked the chamber, handed it butt-first to Wallace. Next he produced his badge, then the cuffs.

Wallace handed the items to one of the officers, who placed them in a small canvas bag, which he had kept under his arm.

"I wish you could see the bigger picture, Larry. You're playing into his hands. You need to look past the cards he's dealt."

Wallace lowered his head, disappointed. "How can I see anything, with *your* hand so close to your chest?"

Fair enough, Hayden thought.

The elevator doors opened and Hayden stepped inside. Kennedy slipped in beside him. Wallace and the officers turned to face them.

"Don't play this down, Hayden," Wallace warned. "They're watching you."

Hayden looked him squarely in the eye. "If you only knew, Larry," he said, as the elevator doors closed between them.

52

She fell hard on top of him in his bed. They rolled into the pillows and back again and nearly over the side. She removed his shirt, his belt and pants. He tore off her slacks to find the complication of pantyhose. He nudged them left and right, but abandoned the effort after Kennedy's fingernails, like talons, sliced them in half. She pulled off her shirt as he worked the last nylon shred from her ankle.

They were naked in a moment, with Kennedy on top. Her fingers in his hair, pulling and scratching. Her red fiery hair dancing like a slow-motion tsunami around the contours of her face and shoulders. Sudden pain as her fingernails swooped across his cheek, drawing blood, its salty-syrup taste at the corner of his mouth. Her nails dragging like the wheels of a locomotive across his chest. The pain intense but fueling his lust as she rocked above him, and he inside her.

The nails were on his chest again but this time he grabbed her and forced her sideways on the bed. He mounted her from above, her facing him, missionary. Her face in his hands, he kissed and bit her neck. Her nails lashed out at his back. He pushed himself deep inside her.

He tugged back a length of her hair at the scalp, lifting her chin to the ceiling. Kissed her neck down to the breasts, his tongue and teeth teasing the rising nipples. He kissed her face, her lips. He felt her teeth sink into his tongue. He tightened his grip on her hair.

He opened his eyes to see her staring at him. He held her look. Their movements slowed. He released her hair. Her fingernails relaxed, would have retracted if they could. He pushed into her deep but slow, and at once there was something more than lust. There was warmth and a comfort he almost recognized, memories of long-ago moments with Nicky. Kennedy's body enveloped him. He shuddered, pushing, and she shuddered, accepting, in balance, a perfectly passionate yin and yang. Their bodies in motion together, greater than the sum of their parts. A symbiotic sensation machine.

They rode an unfamiliar landscape. Her soft cries became syncopated gasps that fueled his own voice, matching in rhythm, building in rapid succession the sensation in his loins, hips, nipples until he was no longer present.

Their climax came together, as it did in the movies. He landed on his back with her on his chest. He wrapped his arms around and pulled her closer still, sinking his face into her hair, losing himself in her aroma.

"Hayden?"

"Yeah."

He waited for her to continue.

"So this is being a sex addict?" she asked at last.

"No. This was . . . something else."

"I could get used to it."

After a long silence, Hayden whispered, "I could, too."

He woke to pounding at his door. Three loud, rushed knocks, then silence. He instinctively reached for the gun that was no longer there. The clock read 1 A.M. It took a full minute to get untangled from Kennedy's naked body. She rolled sideways, finding Hayden's replacement in a feather pillow. He reached under the bed to find the .38 Smith & Wesson he kept loaded in an ankle holster as backup. He picked it up, donned a pair of sweats, and left the bedroom. He peered through the peephole in the front door but saw nothing. He opened the door to find an empty hallway. Whoever had been there was gone. But a DayGlo orange flyer was taped to the door.

He was drinking a cup of instant coffee and dusting the flyer for prints when Kennedy joined him at the kitchen table. She was wearing the black silk kimono he had picked up in Kyoto fifteen years ago, when he was twenty-two and chasing the world. Tied loosely to reveal her white, white skin, red hair, and a flash of red nipples against the dark black silk.

"What's that?" she asked.

He tapped the flyer sideways on the kitchen table to disperse the dust. No prints. He handed it to her.

"An invitation to an art exhibit. At some place called The Slough of Despond, in downtown L.A."

"That was the knock at the door?"

He nodded. "Look at the date."

She studied the sheet. "Today?" she asked.

"Now. The place is open all night. The show began at midnight, an hour ago." Things were beginning to escalate. He felt that he would be facing Rufus soon.

"I didn't see who left it," he said.

"You think it was him?"

"Yeah. I think it was him."

He stirred his coffee absently. He watched the grinds bubble up from the bottom of the cup, churning over with the motion of his spoon.

"So he knows where you live," she said, pulling the kimono tighter around her chest.

"He knows more about me than I do."

She put her hand on his shoulder gently. "Don't ever think that," she whispered. He didn't take her hand in his, only stared into his coffee, trying to muster the courage to say what needed to be said.

"We better get going," she said, starting toward the bedroom.

He caught her arm at the wrist, waved the flyer in her face. He pointed out the message printed clearly in the upper corner—"Admit One."

"What," she said, "you think that's for you?"

"Of course. I'd be willing to bet this was the only invitation printed."

"Well, I've got your back." She smiled, referencing the conversation they had at her office before.

He knew the time was now. He couldn't keep leading her into this. "He wants me alone," he said dispassionately. He couldn't look her in the eye.

She stared at him, seemingly confused. She took a seat at the kitchen table.

"Since when does it matter what *he* wants?"

Hayden stood up from the table and poured himself another cup of coffee. He didn't offer her any.

"What's going on with you?" she asked, perturbed.

"I know what I'm doing," he said. Now he looked her in the eye. He leaned back casually against the kitchen counter, holding the cup and saucer together in one hand. He projected an image of callous indifference. It was a part he knew he could play, because it was part of who he was.

The silence seemed to last forever.

She proceeded gently, as if she were speaking to a child. "You're a good detective, Hayden. But this is a bad call. Why don't you take a moment and think it over." Said without malice. Said as a statement of fact.

"No. You see, this is where I shine. This is exactly where I rise to the occasion," he said. He took a slow sip of his coffee.

She was growing more agitated by the moment. "You're delusional. You are the last person that should go out there alone. You *are* this guy's target, you'll be playing into his hands—"

"He's not going to harm me. You said it yourself, he wants something from me. I'm his audience. You don't kill your audience."

She stood up from the table, her palm to her forehead. "Just because he assumes a relationship doesn't mean one exists. You're not assuming a relationship, are you?"

"He *wants* a relationship—"

"Doesn't mean you have to provide him with one. Know the lines, Detective. He kills people, you don't."

"I've killed people—"

"In the line of duty."

After a moment. "In the line of duty."

"Then you can't presume to know the way a real killer thinks." She paced the kitchen, searching for something to do with her hands. She found a coffee cup and poured the last of the coffee into it. It was mostly grounds.

"Fucking . . . *instant* coffee, Hayden? Jesus . . ." She poured her cup into the sink. Hayden quietly sipped from his own cup.

She turned to him suddenly. "Goddammit, Hayden, you can't see how he's played you?"

"It's the other way around. I'm playing him. It's what you guys do, the FBI, profiling."

"We do it at arm's length."

"You've set up decoys. The L.A. Transient Killer, the case you worked, it was your idea—"

"We had a task force of fifty officers! I'd be a fool to send a decoy alone!"

"This is different—"

"You can't do this alone, Hayden. Don't be a fool."

He placed his cup and saucer in the sink. There was a crisp *clank* as porcelain hit stainless steel.

He knew this was the moment. He tried to separate his emotions from the task at hand.

"I'm only going to say this once," Hayden began, his tone like a teacher admonishing a student. "You've served your purpose here."

He turned around and faced her head-on.

"Go back to philanderers and insurance fraud cases," he said pointedly. "Hang around if you want, but don't fuck with my investigation."

She pulled the robe tight around her body and quickly stepped away.

He averted his eyes. He couldn't look at her, even though his attack produced the results he had expected. He couldn't separate his feelings from his actions after all.

"Just when I think I know you—"

"Don't think you know me," he whispered. "You don't know me."

"Your pain doesn't justify your actions."

"You have no idea—"

"—doesn't justify . . . your cruelty."

It stopped him for a moment. He had never been called cruel. She walked away from him, stomping into the bedroom. He followed her. She began picking her clothes up off the floor. She balled up his kimono and tossed it to the ground. She dressed in a hurry.

"Yeah, well, fuck you, too," he said. "If you were any good you'd still be with the Bureau. What did you do to get kicked out, anyway?"

"I *left* the Bureau. I kicked *them* out."

"Couldn't take the heat."

She was fully dressed now, stuffing her bare feet into her heels.

"I couldn't take watching my partner get promoted for the work I'd done. I ran circles around half those assholes for half their pay. When chauvinism becomes incompetence, I walk."

She grabbed her purse and pushed past him on her way out of the bedroom. "And it's time for me to walk," she announced.

He followed her to the front door.

"Good luck tonight," she said. "I hope I don't read about it in the papers."

He opened the door for her. She turned and looked him in the eye. He saw compassion, and longing. "Shit," she said. "For one moment there, I thought . . ."

She seemed more disappointed than anything.

And then she was gone. The door slammed in his face. He fell forward, catching himself with a thud when his forearm hit the door. He stayed there a long while, his head in the crook of his arm. He gradually pulled away, running his fingers through his hair. His scalp was sticky with sweat.

He walked back to the kitchen and picked up the invitation. He wondered how he might prepare for this "art exhibit" at the Slough. What might give him an edge. He walked to the bedroom and kneeled down beside his dresser. He tugged at the bottom drawer. It was heavy and the wood stuck in places, but with enough wiggling he was able to pull it out. Under a layer of mismatched socks and a stack of old tax returns he found a collection of items he'd accumulated over the years. Some were things he had confiscated from criminals or informants: a stiletto with a silver inlaid handle, a solid gold nose ring once owned by the toughest narcotics dealer in Los Angeles, the lock-picking kit used by the perp who kept Robbery Special on its toes for almost eight years. There was also a collection of high-tech gadgetry Hayden had acquired from previous cases: a writing pen that doubled as a mini-USB downloadable recording device and a "bionic ear" sonar reader capable of recording sounds from a distance of one hundred yards. And the thing he was looking for—his iTrax GPS tracking device, used specifically for metropolitan areas and accurate up to five meters. It was the size of a postage stamp.

Hayden put the receiver in his pocket. He found the tracker: a miniature flat-screen monitor with a cigarette-lighter power adapter for the car.

He strapped his backup gun to his ankle and searched the floor for his shoes, finding them under the kimono Kennedy had tossed to the ground in a huff before leaving his apartment. He picked up the kimono and let the soft, black silk slip through his fingers. He promised himself that he would get her back, that he would fix it all in the end.

53

The Slough of Despond sat on the corner of Sixth and Main in downtown L.A. Few ventured into this part of town at night. There was, of course, a nearby island or two, well-managed tracts of commerce groomed for museums and monuments. The Music Center, the Mark Taper Forum, the Los Angeles Public Library, MOCA. Then there was vast, ugly urban acreage deserted by the day's banker, lawyer, and theater patrons. Skid Row was like Bruegel's *Triumph of Death*, where the homeless roamed and decayed and died. The downtrodden, the down on their luck, the permanently downtowned. For years the city made a push to clean and renovate this ancient center of civilization, but the weight of poverty tore through the sack of opportunity and gentrification failed. Minimal success emerged as a slew of artists' lofts were built from old warehouse space and sold at reasonable rates to people eager to replicate

New York City on the West Coast. The purchases came with secure underground parking, dead bolts, and alarm codes.

The artists spilled into diners and pubs, and from the fertilization of commerce there grew gritty art house venues for the showcasing of counterculture poetry, video, and fine art.

The Slough of Despond had been a biker bar in the Sixties but clashed with the Hispanic, Korean, and black communities that sprouted around it. Its history was marred by violence in the form of fistfights, knifings, and an occasional gunshot. Its current incarnation was a pub for the Gothic art crowd and a space for the introduction of local painters.

Hayden parked by a Dumpster in an alley beside the bar. He double-checked the .38 in his ankle holster before leaving the Jeep, then walked around the ancient stucco façade to a front door made of thousand-year-old oak. He pushed the heavy door and it creaked open. He stepped down and into the Slough.

His eyes adjusted to the low ambient light as he entered. There was a mood luminescence achieved through bounce-back glare from the light on the paintings that graced the walls. Eight paintings were featured in the exhibit. Eight typical Goth wannabes sat at nearby tables. No one paid attention to the art. Hayden scanned the room.

The paintings themselves fit the backdrop. The colors were mostly burgundy and brown with thick black lines to accentuate violent images. Oils on canvas. Textured strokes that lifted off the surface, capturing the memory of passion behind movement frozen in pigment and paint and time. Each image a melee of nose-to-nose brush strokes like molten metal stirred. The crest of one stroke—crimson—knifing the body of another—black. A step back revealed the larger picture. The black lines drawn between red outlined meaty forms. They spoke of human organs, internal, exposed and agitated as if by an eggbeater in the hands of a sadist.

The title of one painting—*The Water's Warm.* The "water" was a seemingly endless stew of blood and carnage. Another painting, titled *You and Me, Tweedle-Dum and Tweedle-Dee,* featured a morbid red orchid made of two opposing profiles connected at the back. The brains of each were exposed and intertwined like layered petals. Hayden was shocked to recognize his own profile as one. The other seemed oddly familiar.

The paintings were signed "Tophet." He doubted this was the killer's real name, but rather some pseudonym hinting at a personality trait he enjoyed, the way a vanity plate broadcasts a private joke to like-minded drivers.

With one hand Hayden peeled the plastic seal off the tiny GPS beacon in his pocket. He reached out to touch *Tweedle-Dum*, leaving the quarter-sized beacon behind, tucked under a hidden lip in the back of the frame, secured by its adhesive strip.

"They's a sore for sight eyes, eh?" said the bartender from the dark oak bar fifteen feet away. The bartender's Aussie enthusiasm clashed with the Slough's Gothic theme.

"You from the papers, then?" he continued.

"No." Hayden shrugged. "Just found myself on the mailing list." Hayden walked cautiously toward the bar. He felt the weight of the .38 on his ankle and he figured it would take three full seconds to pull it from his holster and dive for cover.

"Big load a'crap, if you ask me," the bartender went on, rubbing fingerprints and black lipstick off a half dozen shot glasses with quick precision. "He's what they call an artist manqué," he went on.

"Manqué?"

"Frustrated. 'Cause he ain't got the talent. Hitler was an artist manqué, you know. Rejected from the Vienna Academy, before he turned to politics."

Hayden took a seat at the bar.

"What you drinking, mate? You can't be hanging here without a tumbler or a beer or we toss you out with the homeless."

Hayden looked at the selection on the wall. "Dewar's on the rocks. This your place?" He kept his eye on the man, watched his hands disappear under the bar to find whiskey and ice. Hayden drummed his fingertips nervously on his knees.

"I'm just a field hand. Owner shows up around noon," the Aussie said, pouring Hayden's drink.

"What do you know about the guy who made these paintings?" Hayden asked.

"Just what I see on the wall. And it's bullshit."

"You haven't met him?"

"Nope. Heard he dropped five hundred on my boss to show his stuff, then missed the ad deadlines. You're the only one I've seen that ain't a regular."

"Hey." A soft voice behind Hayden's shoulder. Her sudden presence surprised him.

"Hey, luv. The usual?" the Aussie said, already pouring her drink.

She took the stool next to Hayden, shot him a well-rehearsed smile. "I'm Tina."

Hayden nodded and turned back to his drink. He felt the vibe that came with her presence. He didn't want the distraction.

"You got a name, honey?" she prodded.

"Hayden," he said, then, feeling her eyes on his back, turned around to face her.

Her smile was vibrant. She was maybe twenty-three, her blond hair in a bob, accentuating the roundness of her face. There was youth in her cheeks, a healthy plumpness lost in the angular faces of older, physically mature women. She had freckles high on her nose that dropped like milk chocolate sprinkles to either side. She wore her long-sleeved pink blouse tight to showcase the curvature of her breasts. Her skirt was a short, classy suede, with white stockings underneath. She exuded a vulnerable tough-ness that Hayden knew by heart—she was a prostitute.

"I haven't seen you here before," she prompted.

"He's here for the artwork," the Aussie warned, wiping the bar.

"I think it's disgusting," she stated flatly, picking up her drink. She reached over to the condiment tray and lifted a fat Maraschino cherry. "I can't wait till they take it away."

"You meet the artist?" Hayden asked, trying to sound nonchalant. He looked from her to the bartender and back again. He expected that one or both of them knew more than they let on.

"Nope," she answered. She noticed the Dewar's fixed firmly in his hand. "You ought to put a twist in there." She reached around him, her breasts brushing against his shoulder. She produced a slice of lime from behind the counter.

"I'm not a twist kind of guy."

"What kind of guy are you, then?" she said in a singsong.

"Tina," Aussie reprimanded. "He hasn't even bought his drink, you're gonna drive him off."

"I'll buy his drink, then," she offered.

"You gonna pay his tip?"

"Oh, I'll take care of your tip," she flirted, fingering the lime as she brought it toward Hayden's drink.

Hayden caught her hand out of reflex as it hovered above his glass.

"Really, I like my whiskey straight." Even as he pushed her hand away he felt excitement in her touch. His voice cracked when he spoke, and he could tell that his rejection lacked conviction. She held his stare until he looked away. He leaned back on the barstool to get some distance between them. She smiled playfully.

"I learned a little something for guys like you," she said, "who like their whiskey straight. You want a hint of adventure. Just a dab on your tongue. Afraid to go all the way, afraid maybe you won't like the taste. You just need someone to draw you out. You get a good taste, before long it's all you want."

She took the juicy lime in her hand and squeezed it onto her full lips, producing a glossy, wet sheen. She leaned toward him again, brought her lips to his, lightly, enough to wet them, enough to let the scent of lime linger in his nostrils. Her scent with the lime was like a crisp morning walk in a grove of fruit trees. She pulled away slowly.

"Now have your whiskey. Just put your lips to it, sip."

Hayden brought the tumbler to his lips. She was right. It livened the whiskey by a hair. It left him wanting more whiskey, more lime, more lips.

"I thought so," she smiled, dropping down from the barstool. "Later, Brad."

The bartender nodded, his hands ever busy behind the bar. "Take care, luv."

Hayden returned to his drink.

Tina gave him a nudge. "Well?" she flirted.

"Hm?"

"You can bring your drink along," she said demurely, turning again and walking with a sway that dared pursuit. Hayden stood, reached into his pockets.

"Don't worry, mate, the lady's got it," Aussie said, winking.

Hayden turned to see her slowly disappear up a set of stairs. He glanced around the bar. He wondered if she would lead him to Rufus, if this would be their meeting at last. He didn't know if it was his instinct for the investigation or simply his addict that told him to follow the girl. He guessed it really didn't matter which.

He left the bar, walked past the paintings, through the cluster of patrons, to the bottom of the stairs. Her figure disappeared at the top as she walked through a door, letting it swing shut behind her.

He entered to find a makeshift office with a sofa bed against a wall. There was an old wooden desk with the clutter of bills and paperwork. A comfortable Persian throw rug sat on the wood floor with an array of decorative pillows tossed casually about. This was the space designated for Tina to do her work.

Hayden took a seat in the wheeled wooden chair at the desk, sipping his whiskey. He observed his surroundings carefully, his internal radar scanning the room for signs of mischief.

She patted the pillows beside her, motioning for him to join her.

"I'm good," he said, smiling thinly.

"You're a cautious one," she said.

"I never kiss on the first date."

"Oops, too late," she smiled. "What else don't you do on the first date?"

"What don't you have in mind?"

She unbuttoned her sleeves, unbuttoned her blouse. He could see the hint of a white lace bra. She pulled the blouse away. Hayden choked on the whiskey when he saw her skin exposed.

She enjoyed seeing the shock on his face. "Not exactly what you expected," she said.

She unlatched her bra. He raised his hand to object, but couldn't find the words. The bra came down, revealing what should have been healthy young breasts.

He drank more whiskey. Observed her arms, chest, stomach, shoulders, and back as she moved. Her body was covered in scars. Most were old, years old. Others were in various stages of healing. Some wounds were fresh, sticky with coagulating blood, shiny from ointments and balms. There were scars on top of scars. The breasts which he anticipated as smooth and young were sacks of brutalized flesh. Her body was a canvas torn and restitched, as grotesque as the artwork she hated on the walls downstairs.

She reached under a pillow and produced a metal box about the size of a small fishing tackle. She popped the lid to reveal a selection of knives with intricately carved handles, packs of razor blades, and lethal devices he didn't recognize, but whose purpose he could guess.

She chose a set of brass knuckles that featured a sleek, stainless steel blade. It looked like it came straight from the back pages of *Soldier of Fortune* magazine. The blade was jagged like a shark's tooth.

"There are over two dozen ways to inflict a pain so penetrating that the euphoria it produces is better than the best orgasm you've ever had. It's an art, but it's also a science."

Recited from memory, as if she had just returned from a convention for Cutters United. She called it an art as if it were understood.

"You become an expert in anatomy and physiology," she continued, running the blade lightly over her scars. "Avoid the veins and arteries. Walk the path between the two. The first cut of the night is the best. It carries with it the anticipation of a full day waiting. For me, to be in control of my blade, letting out the first thin, red line. Some call it blood, but to me it's cum."

She touched the blade to a smooth spot on her forearm. Hayden didn't think, he lunged, grabbing the knife by its handle.

"I love making the first cut myself," she said, "but I prefer to have it done by a stranger. It's unpredictable. He has the power to kill me, if he wants to. It makes it all so much more intense."

He pulled the knife from her hands. She breathed slow, anticipating his move. He returned the knife to its case, closed and latched the lid. "You're sick," he said.

She didn't flinch. "A sick society calls this a sickness. But in some cultures it's sacred. There are Native American rituals—"

"You're not an Indian. Sounds like you're from the Midwest, found yourself in Los Angeles, probably stuck on crack or smack, started hooking to feed your habit. Might be a rite of passage to some; to *you* it's a sickness."

"He said you'd resist."

The comment silenced him. It was what he had been waiting for, but still there was a part of him that wanted to forget the reason he was in this room. "You said you hadn't met him."

"We spoke on the phone."

"Has he paid you?"

"He left some money, behind *Tweedle-Dee*."

"How did he find you?"

"I've got a hell of a Web site."

Hayden sighed. He should have guessed that Rufus would be too shrewd to meet with him at a public place.

"What did he tell you? About me."

"He said we were a lot alike. You and me and him. He said that it might be a tough transition for you. He said you were conflicted."

"Did he sound young? Old? Did you hear an accent? Any unusual sounds in the background?"

"He said you would ask a lot of stupid questions. But that you would calm down, after a while. You'd turn off this . . . mechanism, he called it. And then slip into a bubble, a place where the rules don't exist. He's concerned about you."

It bothered Hayden that Rufus presumed to know his thoughts and feelings. He could feel Rufus trying to manipulate him, using program talk to get under his skin. Hayden wasn't going to play his game. It was time to break the cycle.

"How much are you in for? What do you need to get out from under?"

"I don't know what you mean," she said.

"Tell me," he insisted.

"He said you'd be irrational."

"Don't fucking tell me what he said, what he thinks he knows about me. He doesn't know me. And we're not at all like him."

"You don't know if I'm like him. For all you know he could be my lover."

"That's not possible."

"Really. How can you be so *cock* sure?" Emphasized the word "cock" to regain control of the conversation.

"Because you're *alive*."

She stared at him blankly.

She looked a lot like another girl he had recently known. A girl lying on a shelf in the coroner's office. And now Tina would be his responsibility.

Hayden pulled out his wallet. He counted tens and twenties. Her interest peaked as she tracked the different denominations passing through his hands.

"I've got about three hundred dollars here," he said, looking her hard in the eye. "I'll give this to you at the bus station."

"Bus station," she repeated. She didn't understand.

"When we get there I'm going to buy a ticket. I'm going to send you someplace, I don't know where yet. You'll know when you board the bus. And when you get there, I want you to call me."

Hayden handed her his LAPD business card with his cell phone number listed at the bottom.

"And I'll wire you five thousand dollars."

It was all he had in his savings. He would have to take a loan against his 401k to pay Kennedy for the profile and Hempel for Charlie's security. He'd be in the hole for a long time after this.

"But you got to stay there," he continued, "wherever I send you, for a few months. Maybe longer."

She gave him a dubious look. "Are you for real?"

He held her stare, unwavering.

She grew quiet, staring at the floor. "Man, you're scaring me," she whispered. There was a flash, a moment where the face of freckles outweighed the sack of scars.

"You *should* be scared." Hayden pulled out the keys to his Jeep. "It's time to go," he said.

She hesitated, taking in the room around her, considering. Hayden reached out his hand.

"Do one right thing," he said. "Save yourself now, and the rest of the bullshit will work itself out."

His eyes were sincere. She reached up and took his hand.

He checked his rearview as he ran red lights and stop signs. He glanced her way occasionally. She stared down at the floor of his Jeep. He came to a screeching stop in front of the downtown Greyhound bus station. Dark shapes like bushes hugged the sidewalks and oily brick walls of the ancient building. The shapes revealed themselves as homeless encampments— sleeping bags, dirty towels and blankets, cardboard boxes, torn army tents, overturned shopping carts. Some shapes moved to meet other shapes, to exchange hidden artifacts before shuffling on. Hayden could see into the station and it was busy, even at this hour. Harsh fluorescent lights illuminated the worst attributes of a citizenry too poor to travel by plane, train, or car.

Hayden killed the engine. "You still with me on this?" he asked.

She nodded.

Inside the Greyhound terminal, Hayden stood in a line overflowing with travelers. Tina leaned against a nearby wall, her arms folded across her stomach. She studied the unsavory characters that peopled the terminal. She managed to avoid their hungry stares, projecting a "fuck you" attitude to all. Hustlers, vagabonds, drifters, runaways, college students, Marines. Each with his own way of vying for her attention. Only the most handsome Marine received her smile.

Hayden stared at the choice of destinations on the board above the ticket counter. Omaha, Chicago, El Paso, Baton Rouge, Detroit, Cleveland, Syracuse. She watched him with casual interest as he tried to decide. The line behind him grew longer and split in two with the arrival of a second ticket seller coming off her break.

He reached the counter still undecided and in an instant he thought of Omaha, because it sounded like a place she might stick to, a place that might heal her wounds. Omaha, the home of *Boys Town*. A place where upstanding citizens helped their wayward kin.

He paid with his credit card and tucked the bus ticket inside his wallet. Stepping away from the ticket counter, Hayden looked up, expecting to see Tina where he had left her. She was gone. He scanned every face in the room as he ran from the ticket counter. He glanced into every empty corner as he dashed from the terminal waiting area and out the front doors. He found her as soon as he stepped outside. She was leaning against a dusty brick wall, sharing a cigarette with the young Marine. Her blond hair reflected the pink neon of the Greyhound bus sign above her. She smirked devilishly when she saw his panicked expression.

"What, you thought I took off on you?"

He grabbed her wrist and walked her back into the station as she playfully waved good-bye to her new friend.

They sat side by side in curved plastic seats. Hayden fought sleep, his head falling forward with a snap that opened his eyes for a few minutes before the process repeated itself. Tina sat, arms crossed, watching the second hand of the large white and black clock that seemed to regulate the lives of everyone in the terminal. She turned toward him as his head began the downward nod. He woke with a snort when she elbowed his ribs.

"I gotta pee," she declared.

Hayden looked at his watch. "You're boarding in ten minutes," he warned her.

He followed her to the women's room, beside a gift shop just opening for business. Before entering, she turned and leaned into him.

"I can see what you're all about," she said earnestly. "You're a good person."

Her comment caught him off guard. She was an entirely different person outside the context of the Slough. She wrapped her arms around him and looked into his eyes.

"Thank you," she said.

She kissed his lips softly. She still tasted like lime. It felt like prom night to Hayden, after all the adventure, the kiss at her front door.

She pulled away slowly, squeezing his hand before stepping back.

He folded his arms and watched her walk away. This was worth it, he thought. The right thing to do. He could track Rufus later, after he'd seen Tina safely off.

Hayden saw the shelves of magazines and candy beside the cash register in the gift shop. He kept his eye on the bathroom door as he slipped into the store. He picked up *Newsweek, People, Entertainment Weekly, Vogue,* and the latest Grisham paperback. Anything to distract her, he thought. He grabbed bottled water, Planters Peanuts, sunflower seeds, and a half dozen granola bars. He dumped everything on the counter beside the cash register.

Hayden's demeanor changed when he reached for his wallet. Remembering the feeling of her hands around his waist, then only her lips and the smell of lime. She was as smooth as any pickpocket he'd ever met.

Hayden bolted into the women's rest room. He pushed open the doors of empty stalls, caught sight of the open window by the sink. He looked through it and saw an empty alley leading to a wide, dark boulevard that stretched a dozen miles north and south.

54

On his drive home Hayden plugged the flat-screen GPS tracker into the cigarette lighter and switched it to the "on" position. The unit came to life with a blue glow. A satellite map of downtown Los Angeles appeared on the screen, with a little red marker indicating the beacon's location at the Slough.

Hayden drove in silence through the mostly empty early morning streets. He was tired, too tired to concentrate after all he'd been through. His crusade to save another errant girl had been a waste of time. Now he'd have to sneak in a few hours of sleep before returning to the Slough to interview the bar's owner, the only person who might have actually met Rufus in the flesh.

Although Hayden hadn't come away with what he had wanted, which was Rufus in handcuffs or Rufus in a body bag, the morning's events still felt like a breakthrough. A connection had been established. Rufus wanted a relationship and Hayden had showed he was willing to provide him with one. And now, with the GPS tracker, Hayden had a shot at catching him. The artwork would eventually find its way back, and Hayden wanted to be there when it arrived. As for Tina, well, she could take care of herself, Hayden surmised. She was three hundred bucks and four credit cards richer. Maybe she had enough sense to lay low for a while.

Hayden thought back on the events of the past few weeks. He had lost almost everything he valued. The only great, mysterious good that seemed to come from it all was his introduction to Kennedy. He hated having to end it the way he did, but he knew it was for the best. He knew that his actions would save her life. And she would forgive him in time.

She was also the brightest investigator he had ever met. Hayden wondered if it would be possible to recruit her into the RHD. He had never imagined himself with a female partner, but then again, he had never imagined Kennedy.

55

Hayden woke before his alarm, took a long shower, shaved, and ate a breakfast of granola, non-fat milk, strawberries, and bananas. He did two hundred sit-ups, seventy push-ups, and twenty-five pull-ups. He had managed to get four hours of fitful sleep, his hand cupping the GPS tracker plugged into the wall. He had the feeling that today would be his day.

He left his apartment, driving his Jeep with the top down. The late morning sun warmed the crown of his head. He plugged the tracker back into the cigarette lighter in his dash and the beacon's image appeared again on the map in the location of the Slough.

As he closed in on Main Street he heard the helicopters above. Police cars dotted the intersection as he turned. He parked just outside the police line. They had the Slough surrounded, a Channel 7 News van out front with their buxom brunette on mike. Hayden heard fragments of sentences as he walked by. ". . . gruesome murders plaguing our city . . . Los Angeles Police Department seems stalled . . . the two men arrested for the murder of Councilman Pete Jackson's niece were released after DNA samples proved them innocent of the crimes . . ."

Hayden felt a hand on his shoulder.

"What are you doing here?" It was Wallace.

Two Divisional detectives were in conference by the Slough's entrance. Both looked over at Hayden.

"I saw the news reports," Hayden bluffed. "Seemed like this was right up our alley."

Wallace eyed him suspiciously. "You shouldn't be here."

Hayden took Wallace by the elbow and walked him to a more secluded spot near the trash bins where he had parked the night before.

"I know Forsythe doesn't have a lot of confidence in me right now," Hayden said in a hushed tone, "but I'm owed a chance, here. Let me just get a sense of the scene. I won't get in your way."

Hayden imagined him contemplating their future relationship, working together as partners, each trusting the other with his life. Hayden's departmental suspension was temporary—their partnership might last another ten years. Wallace would have to consider this.

"You can stay for a while, but I can't let you inside," he said finally.

"Fair enough," Hayden agreed.

Wallace glanced at the news reporter, who was conferring with her sound tech over a malfunctioning mike.

"What are they saying in the news?" Wallace asked. Hayden could tell that Wallace was the lead on this one. His first since joining RHD.

"Just a lot about the recent murders, the . . . prostitutes. They're saying that this one was a prostitute," Hayden lied, trying to justify his arrival at a fresh murder scene. He figured it was Tina in there. That she had left the bus station, returned to where she felt most comfortable. Three hundred dollars bought a lot of crack in Los Angeles.

"Christ," Wallace spat under his breath. "How did that leak?"

So Hayden had guessed right. He started to feel that weight in his head again. It felt like failure. Rufus was everywhere. Every place Hayden had been, every place he would go. Every time Hayden marveled at his own improvisations he discovered that Rufus wrote the script.

Wallace was called away by one of the crime scene techs. Hayden paced the grounds, nodding here and there to a patrol officer or investigator he knew. The scene had a strange vibe that Hayden couldn't quite make out. Maybe it was just the odd sensation of being at a crime scene and not being in charge. He chewed his lower lip as he walked, chewed until his jaw throbbed from the pain. *I should have held a gun to her head and forced her onto that bus. I should have handcuffed myself to her wrist and sat with her all the way to Omaha.*

Wallace returned to his side. "Coroner's taking their time," he said, distracted.

"What's it look like in there?" Hayden asked, trying to make it sound like the answer didn't matter as much as it did.

"This poor fucking girl," Wallace said, eyeing the activity on the street, "she's, like, twenty years old. Got these scars all over her body. But controlled, you know, in a fetish way. A lot of self-inflicted wounds."

"How'd she die?"

"Clean slice across the jugular. Nothing else. A lot of blood. We're lucky, though, lifted a big, fat print off the knife."

Hayden swallowed. Wallace looked him over.

"You look like shit, Hayden. What if the captain shows? Don't make me look like a pushover."

Hayden nodded, acquiescing.

As he turned to leave he realized what had bothered him about the scene—the detectives, the uniformed officers, even the ident guys, stood around aimlessly, looking restless and bored.

"What's everyone waiting on?" he asked.

Wallace looked at his crew.

"Coroner's short. Charlie's on light duty, Abbey's in the hospital. And three examiners quit, just like that. We've been waiting two hours, don't even have an ETA."

"How *is* Abbey?"

"In and out. They say she'll make it. Can't get anything out of her, though. She's the only one who can ID the guy."

"Yeah, maybe. A beating like that, she might not remember a thing. The key is those skin samples. How are we with the DNA results?"

"Another casualty of the system. The Scientific Investigation Division can't find them."

Hayden felt what must have been a claymore mine detonate inside his head. He stared at Wallace, incredulous. "Don't fuck with me."

"Lab loses crap all the time, if you don't walk it through the system—"

Hayden's hands were all over him, grabbing his shirt, knocking him off balance, pushing and shoving Larry hard until his thick frame smacked against the stucco wall.

"*You* were supposed to walk it through the system, Larry! That's your fucking *job*, goddammit!"

Two officers tackled him and struggled to pry him off. Wallace landed a solid jab into Hayden's ribs before the officers managed to separate the two. Just then the coroner's van arrived.

"Enough," Wallace spat, seeing the van. He pushed himself away from the cops who had come to his aid. He straightened his tie and tucked in his shirt, noticing that two buttons had been torn off in the scuffle. Hayden watched him with contempt, seething. The two officers held Hayden tightly, each gripping an arm.

"You're out of control," Wallace said. "No wonder you need a handler—"

"Yeah, fuck you, you blew the only evidence we had on the case—"

"Get the fuck out, Hayden. Don't ever show up at my crime scenes unannounced."

Wallace adjusted his jacket and walked away, signaling for the coroner to follow him. The two cops holding Hayden released his arms. One gave him a healthy slap on the back.

"Always count on you for a good time, Glass."

"Don't encourage him," said the other as they walked away.

Hayden, angry and out of breath, watched the group of them disappear inside the Slough.

56

Abbey Reed was still on a respirator. The swelling had gone down in her face. She seemed thin now, her frame fed by I.V. He reached down to touch her forehead. Warm, moist. Her eyes fluttered, then opened. He kneeled into her field of vision. Her pupils were wide, unseeing. The eyes closed again. He squeezed her hand. She squeezed back.

"I won't let it be wasted, Abbey."

Hayden left the hospital to visit the coroner's office. He stood in the room where Abbey had been beaten and almost killed. The department had suffered a tremendous blow with the loss of four examiners in less than a week. But at least Charlie was back now, and overwhelmed with new cases.

Hayden stood quietly, remembering the night. It was the closest he had come to meeting Rufus in the flesh. He canvassed the room looking for an angle. He tried to wrap his mind around the reason why Rufus had taken such a risk. Why he felt compelled to attack a woman at the coroner's office, a building that was open twenty-four-seven. All the previous scenes had been meticulously sculpted. The sloppiness of this one suggested that he had been caught off guard. Abbey must have discovered something that Rufus wanted concealed.

Hayden thought back to the call he had received from her that night. She said there was nothing there. That's what frightened her, that's why she had called. Hayden needed to know what "nothing there" meant.

He went downstairs. The hallways were cluttered with bodies on gurneys. Forensic techs and EMTs wandered in an exhausted daze. He peeked into autopsy rooms until he found Charlie hunched over a scale with a silky red liver cupped in his hands. The body of a fifty-five-year-old man lay on a gurney beside him, a giant flap of skin hanging like an unfurled flag off his chest. The man appeared to be leaning comfortably on an elbow, his head tilted to the side. Hayden half expected him to open his eyes and wave.

"Charlie," Hayden said, panting from the rush down the stairs. "I need you take me to the Crypt, now!"

The cadavers were rolled and tied in plastic, lying on racks stacked five high. It was cold in the Crypt, and it smelled like sour meat. Charlie and Hayden stood before a rack with a nametag that identified the body as Darla Sykes. They loosened the clear plastic sheet that covered her.

Charlie shone an ultraviolet light over her naked limbs. "She's decomposing," he said.

"Abbey was working off the notes from your initial exam," Hayden remarked, then stopped when he saw the expression on Charlie's face. "What?"

Charlie's fingers scampered across Darla's limbs like wild rats. They tugged and pulled at the chalky skin on her thighs and the backs of her arms. "Jesus Christ . . ."

"What is it?" Hayden demanded.

"It's gone, it's all gone . . ." Charlie's eyes were wide with fear.

"What's happening?"

"I had identified seven complete or partial prints on her body." He pointed out a half dozen discolored marks on her inner thigh, ankles, and arms. "The body's been scrubbed with bleach. They're all gone!"

Hayden felt his jaw tighten. "Is there *any* evidence?"

Charlie shook his head, "It's gone."

Hayden stared at him in disbelief. "Don't you see what you're telling me, Charlie?"

"But I . . . I made my notes at the scene. The prints were *there* . . ." Charlie stammered, realizing the significance of his words.

"So the bleaching either happened in the van—"

"Or it happened here, in the coroner's office," Charlie said. His voice cracked and Hayden noticed that he was holding his right hand with his left to keep it from shaking.

"What the fuck is going on, Charlie?"

Charlie seemed unable to move.

"It doesn't make sense," Hayden insisted.

Charlie began to teeter. He grabbed hold of one of Darla's ankles to steady himself. Hayden pulled away and began moving frenetically about the room. Charlie watched him, his eyes begging Hayden for answers.

Hayden paced beside the body racks in the cold, silent room. He read the names on the tags to himself as he passed. "Dimitri Sokolov." "Juan Gonzalez." "Jane Doe."

He tried focusing his thoughts. He had to put the pieces together. He knew that Charlie had seen and documented the fingerprints on Darla's body. The killer had to destroy that evidence and any record of it. Abbey discovered the tampering. But Hayden couldn't see the killer's urgency. Abbey only discovered that someone had *tampered* with evidence. A bleached body wouldn't lead to the killer. Any evidence would be circumstantial—the connection would die in the jury room. He realized that Abbey must have been more of a threat. She must have seen Rufus. She must have confronted or surprised him. It made sense to Hayden now; the scene was sloppy because Rufus hadn't planned on running into anyone.

Hayden came to the last nametag in the row as he turned back to Charlie. He hadn't read the name, not consciously. But it hovered in his peripheral vision. He looked closer. "Kennedy Reynard."

Wrapped tight in plastic and identified by her nametag was the body of an eighty-year-old black man.

"Charlie!" Hayden yelled.

Charlie jumped to his side. He stared at the nametag, baffled. "I don't know what to make of it," he admitted weakly.

Hayden's mind seized. It was getting hard to concentrate now, and he needed clarity in his thoughts.

The killer had to work at the Los Angeles County Coroner's Office. It fit the profile. The job gave him access, providing him with updates on the investigations. It kept him close to the police, to the detectives. It enabled him to fix whatever mistakes he made in the field. It gave him valid cover for revisiting the crime scenes. And then, like boomerangs, *his victims returned to him.*

So Rufus had left this as a message for Hayden. He had faith that Hayden would follow the path, that he would arrive at the Crypt to discover it.

Hayden dialed Kennedy on his cell. Reception was low, but he got through to her voice mail. He tried the home number and got her machine.

"Kennedy, you fucking call me back the second you hear my voice, got it?"

It was hard to release the line. He could hang up and call a thousand times again and he knew she wouldn't pick up. *He knew she was with him.*

Hayden turned back to his ashen-faced friend. "Charlie, I need your help."

It was after hours and the Administration offices were closed. Charlie swiped his ID through the magnetic reader and the door unlocked. They entered and closed the door behind them.

They passed empty cubicles on a path that led to the file room, row upon row of old files; the last chapters of thousands of lives told in precise, often violent detail. A graveyard of paperwork with each file a headstone. Charlie, still shaken, led him to a locked cabinet marked "Employee Records."

Hayden found a paper clip and picked the lock. Inside the cabinet were twenty-six employee files. He rifled through them quickly, saw "Charlie Dawson," "Abbey Reed."

"I'm taking everything," he told Charlie, as if asking permission.

"Do whatever you need to do."

Hayden grabbed a wastebasket, dumped the trash and took the liner. He lifted all twenty-six files from the cabinet and dropped them into the garbage bag, then threw the bag over his shoulder.

"You gonna be around?" Hayden asked.

"You need me, just call."

They shared a quick hug. Hayden smelled the sweat from the long hours of work. And the smell of death that settled into Charlie's clothes.

Hayden took a step back and looked him over. He never really *looked* at Charlie anymore. He would, though. He promised himself that, if he made it through this ordeal, he would never take Charlie for granted again.

57

Hayden was in his Jeep, heading to the Slough.

"Detective Glass. Get me Wallace. Tell him it's an emergency."

Hayden waited on hold.

"Hayden, that you? Where are you?"

"I'm heading back to the Slough of Despond. Meet me there. Get me an SID investigator, a police photographer, and a couple patrol units." Hayden explained that Kennedy had disappeared, that he thought the killer had her and that now was the time to mobilize their team. "Time to earn your stripes, Larry."

There was silence on the other end.

"Larry?"

"Just a minute, Detective." Wallace's response was too formal. Hayden heard muffled commands. Wallace was consulting with the captain.

"Okay, Glass, I'm sending everyone over. We just need you to come into the station first. So we can head to the scene together."

Wallace never was a good bullshitter.

"Larry, tell the captain that we're meeting at the Slough. That you left evidence behind. I've got employment records that'll lead us to the killer, but we've got to act fast. Everyone's a suspect and we've got to bring them all in now."

There was a long pause. "Ten-four, Hayden."

Hayden felt an uncomfortable coldness envelop his limbs. "What's going on, Larry?"

"Hayden," Wallace sighed, "it's over. We found your wallet at the scene." Wallace paused for a moment, as though it were difficult for him to proceed. "We've got your fingerprint on the knife that killed her," he finished.

Hayden swallowed. He tried to think of the things that could explain this. He tried to think of anything he could say that would put him in the clear.

"Why don't you come downtown now," Wallace said, "and we'll turn this process as quietly as we can. Don't make us come after you."

Hayden finally got some air in his lungs. "You've known me long enough, Larry. I'm not this guy. You can't possibly think that. Shit, we don't have time for this."

He heard the muted voice of Captain Forsythe asking for thirty more seconds. Hayden terminated the call. Verizon generally did a piss-ass job triangulating signals, but when the captain of Robbery-Homicide called in a favor, it was likely they'd pull out the stops.

Then he heard it; a beeping from the GPS tracker. He looked at the monitor. *Tweedle-Dum and Tweedle-Dee* was on the move, leaving the Slough to catch a ride on the 110 North. Hayden threw a U-turn. He was at least fifteen minutes behind it.

Traffic was slow and there was a line for the on-ramp. He debated whether to throw the cherry on his roof and use the emergency lane to pass the crowd. But he knew he'd attract a cruiser and then every LAPD unit on duty would swarm in. He gritted his teeth and waited, watching double-occupancy vehicles glide past using the carpool lane. He watched the little blip on his GPS tracker cross from the 110 North to the 10 West. Now twenty minutes behind.

By the time he merged onto the 10 West his package was merging onto the 405 North. When Hayden passed La Brea, the package had exited the 405 and was already two miles east on Santa Monica Boulevard. By the time he took the Santa Monica Boulevard exit the beacon had stopped moving. It was now a steady pulsing light at the corner of Little Santa Monica Boulevard and Beverly Glen.

Hayden found himself parked in front of an eight-story apartment building just off Beverly Glen. He stepped into the street and looked up at the white building with its angular terraces overgrown with ferns and ivy. Every balcony faced the ocean and promised a glimpse of the great Pacific, some five miles away.

The painting had been sitting motionless for fifteen minutes. Hayden popped the glove compartment, pulled his .38 and holster. He took the GPS tracker from its cradle and disconnected it from the charger. It would last half a day on a full battery.

The building's front door was locked, but a small gap in the gate that led to underground parking allowed Hayden his entry. He found a stairwell and began to climb. The tracker signal grew brighter as he drew closer to the beacon. Halfway between the seventh and eighth floors Hayden noticed that the signal was fading. He returned to the seventh floor and entered the hallway.

At this distance the tracker read the beacon's location in feet. The display screen read forty feet to target. Hayden pulled the .38 from its holster and inched forward with his back against a wall. The tracker read twelve feet when he approached the fourth door. The door was locked. He pulled his keys from his front pocket. Mixed with the half dozen keys that opened everything he owned was a set of lock-picking devices that opened everything else. He chose one and picked the lock with ease.

When he entered he heard a voice from another room. An anchorwoman delivering a TV newscast. Hayden was in a stylish, modern living room that was nothing like the lion's den he imagined he would find. The tracker led him toward a slightly open bedroom door where the newscast could be heard more clearly.

He placed the tracker on a teak armoire and noticed a group of framed photographs lined in a neat row on the wood. Hayden recognized a younger Kennedy arm in arm with two college-age girlfriends against the backdrop of Kauai's Fern Grotto. He reached for the photograph instinctively, knocking the tracker to the floor where it landed with a crack. He jumped back, raising his gun at the bedroom door. He stood still for a moment, waiting.

There were other photographs. Some featured Kennedy alone in playful poses. One had her dressed in a Bureau-blue pantsuit, her service revolver held across her chest in homage to James Bond.

Hayden felt his trigger hand shaking. He tightened his grip to steady it and stepped into Kennedy's bedroom.

The painting was there, set on a chair beside the TV. The local news continued, and Hayden flinched when he saw his official LAPD photo broadcast in the corner of the screen. An anchorwoman warned the citizens of Los Angeles to beware, ". . . Detective Glass should be considered armed and dangerous. Any information on his whereabouts should be directed immediately to the Los Angeles Police Department . . ."

He checked the bedroom and cleared it. He went back into the living room, then the kitchen. The apartment was empty. The killer knew the beacon was on the painting. He probably knew Hayden was close behind. He knew to get in and out quickly.

Hayden tightened his gun hand into a clenched fist to mollify the shaking. Landing in Kennedy's apartment had been a shocker. He thought he had been following the painting to Rufus's home.

He returned to the bedroom and turned off the TV. He was officially homeless now, so he'd have to make her apartment his base of operations. The painting, left alone in her bedroom, seemed to mock him. *Tweedle-Dum and Tweedle-Dee*. The grotesque marriage of their brains intertwined, gummy at the center but growing vinelike as it met the parameter, where the two profiles blossomed into an ominous black iris.

Hayden reached behind the painting for the beacon and found a wadded message wedged beneath it: three Zig-Zag rolling papers taped together. A note handwritten in a fine, soft lead that barely held to the paper. A little accidental rustling and the writing might lift off like charcoal dust blown through a straw: "She followed you, into the Slough. The shame of it."

He let the note fall like a teardrop. He felt alone, truly alone, for the first time in his life. There had always been something before. A wife, the LAPD, Rich, Sol. Not anymore. Nothing now.

Sol would have told him to turn to God. God was always there for him, always there *with* him, attentive and kind. Let Him guide you, Sol would say. Hayden fell to his knees, leaned his head against Kennedy's bed.

God, though I walk in the valley of the shadow of death . . . give me strength . . . give her strength. Please don't let him hurt her. Take me in her place, if that's the way it works. Let me trade my life for hers. I'm a miserable shit anyway. I'm sorry for cursing. Although you've heard me say worse. I'm sorry for all the shit I've said. Let me make it up to you, let me be your . . . angel of death. Help me take out this motherfucker . . . let me be your instrument. Please, God. Thank you. Amen.

He was a terrible servant of God. Prayer was so foreign to him that the best he could muster was a jumble of childhood birthday wishes mixed with confirmation speeches and leftover scraps from SAA affirmations. His detachment from all things spiritual embarrassed him, even alone in the presence of God. He was ashamed.

Which was what the killer wanted. To shame him. Because the killer had no shame. He was at ease, content, at one with himself.

As he kneeled on the carpet, hovering over the killer's note, Hayden saw in the handwriting an attempt to impress. The writing wasn't pretty, there was a sloppiness that couldn't be shaken. But the lines, the loops, the letters were manicured in their imperfection. Behind all the taunting and bravado, the killer sought his approval. He cared what Hayden thought.

There was hope. Kennedy might still be alive. He knew if the killer wished to impress him, if he hoped to gain an ounce of Hayden's respect, he would have to keep her alive. At least that was the way Hayden saw it.

He stood back for a moment and looked at his surroundings. Rufus had led him here. There had to be a reason. He studied Kennedy's bedroom, treating it like a crime scene. The painting. The note. The TV set. Nothing stood out. He thought it might be the bed itself. A reference to sex, to SAA, to his addiction to Kennedy. To the things they shared in common, *Tweedle-Dum and Tweedle-Dee.* Another brother in the program.

But there was something else in the room calling his attention. He closed his eyes.

He felt a pulse. Pulsating red, against his eyelids. He opened his eyes and found the source. Kennedy's answering machine, the little red light pulsing on, then off, then on.

He stood over the machine, studying it. He pressed the "speaker" button, then "messages."

Messages poured out. Hayden. The *L.A. Times* new subscriptions department. Dolores from her office. Hayden again. Verizon Wireless. Citibank. Roger from the office. Hayden, the message he left from the coroner's office.

A long pause. Then a voice, soft, subdued. It was Kennedy.

She sounded stiff, as though she were staring down the barrel of a gun. As if she knew this would be the most important call of her life.

"Hayden . . . he says that you have all you need. He'll give you one day. *One day he'll stay* for you—"

The message cut off. Her last words made no sense. He rewound the machine, played the message again.

"One'daiy he'lls-tay for you—" She drew the words out unnaturally, as if she were giving him a clue, some thread to follow.

He played it again.

". . . you have all you need . . ."

It would be easier to list what he *didn't* have. He thought about the things he had. His Jeep. A gun. This painting. Her message. The killer's note. His experience. Her profile. The employment records.

He found the key card that opened the gate to her underground parking and pulled his Jeep into her space. Too many cops knew his Jeep and it wouldn't be long before someone found it on the street. He returned to her apartment with the employment records in his hands.

He dumped the files onto the bed. He set Charlie's and Abbey's files aside. He sifted through the rest. Day receptionist and night receptionist he set aside. Two janitors out. This left twenty records. Six examiners, four coroner investigators, three forensic technicians, five part-timers, two drivers. He eliminated the drivers and the part-timers.

Of the six examiners and four investigators, three had been terminated within the past five years and one had retired. That left four examiners, two investigators, and the three forensic techs.

Hayden took out Kennedy's profile. Lined up the employment applications for the examiners, coroner investigators, and forensic technicians.

"A single white male between the ages of thirty and forty."

That eliminated the one black examiner of the group, and the senior citizen. Three examiners, two investigators, two forensic technicians.

From here out the profile described most anyone working for the coroner's office. Went to college. Excelled at sciences. Meticulous. Drove an official vehicle for work. Worked odd hours. A loner with a quiet personality. A deceased father.

He searched the employment applications and found two examiners, one investigator, and one forensic technician listing their father as deceased.

He went to the phone, dialed the coroner's office.

"L.A. County Coroner's."

"Hi, could you put me through to Donald Spiegel's voice mail, please?"

"I'm sorry, Dr. Spiegel no longer works here."

"Really, I just spoke with him last week."

"He left us two days ago. Can I get someone else?"

"How about Lance Elliot?"

"I'll put you through . . ."

Dr. Elliot's voice came up on a recording. Hayden hung up. He put Elliot's file to the side. He doubted the killer would remain employed at the coroner's office after the attack on Abbey. The place was too hot and it would only be a matter of time before every employee ended up in an interview room.

Hayden left Speigel's file in the pile. He dialed back.

"I'm sorry, Dr. Elliot isn't the one I'm looking for. Maybe it was an investigator. How about Tyler Apollyon?"

"I'm sorry, Mr. Apollyon resigned from the coroner's office last week."

"You've had two employees leave in a week?"

"Gloria Nihlson left, as well. We're shorthanded. Can I get your name, sir?"

"Thanks just the same," he said, and hung up.

Gloria Nihlson, a woman, was not the killer. That left Tyler Apollyon and Donald Spiegel. Hayden compared the employment applications.

Both were typed. Spiegel, an examiner, had been with L.A. Coroner's for seventeen years. He was forty-three years old, just out of the range of the profile. Apollyon had transferred from the County Coroner's Office in Sacramento six months ago. He had been there eight years, hired as a forensic technician after having first served as an intern from Sacramento State University. Tyler was thirty-five.

As a student intern Apollyon was required to provide an essay, which had remained with his employment records:

> My preparation to find employment in the Office of the Coroner comes after years of rigorous mathematical analysis and anatomical research. I have always purported to have a strong interest in anatomy, and even growing up in California's Central Valley I was fortunate to find a mentor in the person of a local taxidermist who himself introduced me to the basic techniques of taxidermy and animal dissection. My formal education in the biological sciences began in high school, where I encountered the work of the medical examiner during a field trip to the Sacramento County Coroner's Office. I eventually found my way to the School of Forensic Studies at Sacramento State University. My grade point average alone should qualify me for the internship of my choosing and it is my firm belief that the Los Angeles County Coroner's Office is the best place to get the experience I need. Finally I would like to conclude by saying that your office would benefit from my extreme dependability and accuracy, my organizational

skills, and my pride at a job well done. Please consider me for
this internship.

Hayden compared Apollyon's and Spiegel's signatures to the handwriting in the note left by the killer. It was a tough comparison—both signatures were little more than squiggly, looping lines. But Apollyon's leaned
forward by about twenty degrees, which resembled the slant in the killer's
note. Spiegel's signature was much smaller, a tighter construction, the
letters packed close like infantrymen on the march.

The applications yielded yet another clue—the applicant's weight.
Spiegel was 172, Apollyon 141. Kennedy's profile set the killer's weight at
145. The files also held photographs of each employee. Spiegel he didn't
recognize. But Tyler, yes, he recognized Tyler.

Hayden remembered the nondescript assistant who seemed to be
everywhere the bodies were. He remembered the smug, nonchalant way
he had asked Hayden to help lift the severed torso off Sol's body. He
must have savored the look on Hayden's face when the moment arrived.

Hayden knew this was Rufus. Thirty-five-year-old Tyler Apollyon, an
investigator with the Los Angeles Coroner's Office. This was the man who,
for whatever reason, had targeted Hayden and had torn his life apart.

Kennedy had been right, Rufus had not attended Hayden's home
meeting. It must have been the intergroup meeting. He either went because he knew Hayden would be speaking, or he went on his own, then
recognized Hayden as the detective he'd seen hanging around the coroner's office with Charlie.

Hayden stepped over to Kennedy's computer, pressed a letter on the
keypad. The screen crackled to life. The computer had been left on,
prompted to Google Maps. Another stepping stone.

Hayden Googled a map of the California Central Valley. A world of hills
and valleys appeared. From Bakersfield on up, little towns dotted east and
west of the 5 Freeway. Tulare, Coalinga, Paso Robles, Hanford, Fresno,
Madera, Merced. Bedroom communities, suburbs, and farmland outposts.
He followed the route right up to Modesto.

He magnified the map around Fresno. Kerman, Caruthers, Hanford,
Windy Hills, Tranquillity.

Kennedy's message could have been lines fed to her. Or they were her invention alone. He forced himself to evaluate all that she said. A prisoner did what his captor instructed to avoid punishment. A normal kidnap victim was expected to be the tool of his oppressor. But he knew Kennedy was far from normal. She knew the psychology of her subject. As a victim, as a woman under the microscope—or under the scalpel, as the case might be—she might be terrified. But as a profiler she would be fascinated and compelled to draw him out, to find and exploit his weaknesses, to communicate them forward to Hayden for help.

He returned to her voice message.

"Hayden . . . he says that you have all you need. He'll give you one day. One day he'll stay for you—"

It was as though she had suddenly acquired an Irish accent.

"One'daiy he'lls-tay for you—"

Hayden speculated on the line's disconnection. It seemed like Rufus had been caught off guard, that Kennedy had strayed off script. Maybe Rufus understood the hidden meaning of her words. Hayden took this as a good sign, that the world Rufus had crafted could be upset so, that it might rise and fall on the turn of a phrase.

Hayden rewound the tape. *"One'daiy . . ."*

It sounded like "windy." *"One'daiy he'lls-stay . . . "*

"Windy hills-stay."

Hayden ignored the "stay." Windy Hills. He saw it there on the map, seven miles northeast of Tranquillity.

". . . as a youth growing up in California's Central Valley . . ."

Windy Hills.

". . . mentorship in the person of a local taxidermist . . ."

Hayden went back to the computer, Googled "taxidermy and Windy Hills."

An address appeared in Tranquillity, "adjacent to the charming suburbs of Windy Hills."

Hayden grabbed the keys to his Jeep, then thought again. He figured there was an All-Points Bulletin on his car. He would never make it out of the city. Hayden lifted his cell phone, thought again. He tossed his phone on the bed and used the phone on Kennedy's bed stand instead.

"Charlie."

"Hayden, have you been watching the news? You're a fugitive," Charlie said, concerned.

"Even the cops make mistakes, Charlie. Do you trust me?"

"I trust you." There was no hesitation in his voice.

"I need your car. How fast can you get to Westwood?"

"Pretty fast, if I can sneak past the rent-a-cop you placed in my driveway."

58

Charlie arrived and Hayden told him about Tyler Apollyon. Charlie found it both impossible to believe and entirely plausible. It absolutely made sense to him that Tyler had the access necessary to move freely within the coroner's office, and that Tyler had motive to attack Abbey Reed. Hayden walked him through the other crime scenes and Charlie agreed that Tyler seemed to be the most likely suspect. But the fact that Charlie had worked alongside this individual for six months disturbed him. He couldn't believe his radar was so off that he had not suspected a serial killer in his presence.

"It might just as well have been six years," Hayden said. "A guy like this lives many lives."

Charlie still seemed disappointed in himself.

"I'll take those car keys," Hayden said, checking the .38 in his ankle holster.

Charlie hesitated. "It looks like you've got a good case against this guy," he said carefully. "I think you should explain everything to your captain. I think he'll get it."

Hayden locked the revolver into place and covered the holster with his pant leg. He stood up and took a step toward Charlie. Charlie cowered a little, but managed to hold his own.

"I could call Forsythe right now," Hayden agreed. "Tell him everything I just told you. The door to this apartment would be torn down before I got off the phone. They'd drag me into an interrogation room where I'd sit for eight hours before they even started asking questions."

He walked over to Kennedy's computer, studied the map of Central California.

"I think I could convince them," he said. "Eventually. They'd have to check my story. LAPD doesn't have jurisdiction over the Central Valley, so they'd have to work through channels to coordinate a rendezvous. They'd need a judge, a warrant. It would be days before a cruiser made its way to Windy Hills. This fucker has given me one day to get her. *One day*. I'm not leaving it up to the LAPD."

He stepped away from the computer and got into Charlie's face.

"How 'bout those keys, Charlie?" It was almost menacing, the way he said it.

"I'm driving," Charlie said, turning to go.

"Bullshit. You're staying here."

"You've hardly slept," Charlie countered. "It's at least a four-hour drive and you're not going to be a hero if you crash along the way. Unless you want to wrestle me to the ground right here, you'll shut the fuck up and let me drive."

Hayden looked him over, shaking his head. "Fuckin' Charlie."

It was a long drive up the 5 Freeway and Hayden was on the edge until they passed Magic Mountain. He knew they would be clear once they slipped from the noose of L.A. County. Only once did Hayden see a sheriff's cruiser, which drifted behind, then pulled ahead to tag the red Corvette that passed them at ninety miles an hour.

Charlie's four-cylinder PT Cruiser crawled the Grapevine's steep incline as fog rose through the asphalt beneath the tires. Fog lit like sparklers off the car's grill, multiplying in mass to land like a thick white comforter on the windshield.

He felt the road beneath the tires and the spaces between the cracks in the asphalt and the rounded edges of the bumps raised on the street to divide traffic north from south.

The fog reeked of bad intent, seeming to relish the luring of its prey into harm's way. It came from a source, and the source had a scent that Hayden recognized.

This same scent had permeated the first of the crime scenes Hayden visited the day the killer made himself known. It was the hot and sticky scent in the West L.A. apartment, a scent that misted the walls, preserving the acrid smell of murder on the ground, saturating the carpet with its spray. It appeared at each murder, heavier at times, depending on the size and shape of the room, the amount of victims, the splatter of body parts and fluids, the purge of adrenaline and fear that had been released before the act.

They were enveloped by the fog and it parted in swirls as an invisible paternal hand appeared to tug them safely along. He let his map drop between his knees.

They were two hundred miles from Windy Hills and Tranquillity, but Hayden knew that the damp fog would lead to the killer's doorstep, and like the foot denied circulation then suddenly wriggling free, Hayden was receiving the first waves of onrushing blood from the killer's impatient heart. He tried to sleep, but could not, and he finally convinced Charlie to let him take the wheel.

Hayden veered off the 5 to the 33 North and it was automatic, not even conscious of navigation. A small freeway sign flashed by with the message, "Tranquillity, 4 Miles, Pop. 1280."

They turned left on S. James Road into Tranquillity and the asphalt suddenly coughed and collapsed under the tires into a combination of pothole and tar. The jostling woke Charlie.

Hayden became aware of shabby single-family homes dotting the road-side. The sporadic neighborhood became "downtown," a stretch of ancient wood and brick buildings. Schoolhouse, firehouse, library, post office, mortuary, diner, feed store. Taxidermist. It was 11 P.M. and the town was deserted.

Hayden parked in the dirt beside Pat's Taxidermy. Charlie had fallen asleep again. He snored loud with sleep apnea, his head balanced against the cold window.

Hayden pulled the .38 from his ankle holster and left the car. He walked the ten steps to the taxidermy entrance. The door was ajar. He took a breath and stepped inside.

It was a dusty overstuffed trophy room featuring heads of deer and elk on the walls and wooden platforms that carried the frozen expressions and fighting stances of bobcat, raccoon, coyote, deer, badger, rattlesnake, and hawk. The smells of preservatives wafted up from tubs on the floor and from hidden cubbyholes where animal parts bobbed in chemical solutions. It smelled like the Crypt at the coroner's office.

There were ancient books piled on desks and tabletops, medical texts and reference books stolen from bankrupt libraries. Newspapers and magazines were piled in bulging towers that spilled onto the floor, some left in spots to cover pooled blood or spilled chemicals. The proprietor was a pack rat.

Pat, of Pat's Taxidermy, had a special interest in space and the orbital journeys of astronauts on the International Space Station, which was represented in newspaper articles tacked to the walls. There were local stories, too, glimpses of small-town life in the Central Valley, of giant pumpkins and fine chili competitions and the election of each year's homecoming queen. And the history of Pat's Taxidermy itself, with photos from the early 1900s to the present, with three generations of proprietors standing at the entrance. Recent photos showed a man of advanced age at work tanning the hide of a large cougar.

Hayden lost his olfactory sense as the room's odor and invisible, infinite dust invaded his sinuses. He heard the far-off gentle dripping of a faucet. Holding his gun before him he moved cautiously toward the sound, which led him to an open door that led to another room. He reached around the doorframe and found a wall switch, which he flipped. Nothing. Only the watered-down glow from the sodium vapor streetlight that filtered through the window.

His echoing footsteps on the tiled floor suggested a sparse room with stainless steel countertops and aluminum vats. The dripping sounded of a liquid thicker than water. He moved in the direction of the sound, avoiding clutter on the floor. His foot descended onto a carpetlike ripple and he knew it instantly to be the tail of a cat. He danced quickly off, expecting to hear the screech and feel stiletto claws on his legs. But the cat had been dead and stuffed long ago.

The dripping came from a large tublike shape against a back wall. A thin balloon-headed ghost stood beside it, which he took to be a lamp. He reached up and pulled a metal chain. A circle of yellow incandescent light emerged from the hard white 60-watt bulb under a mustard yellow metal lampshade. It illuminated a circle large enough to see the metal tub containing the body of the naked old man sitting upright, his arms held out before him by two armatures that allowed the blood in his veins to drip, pooling into an inch of coagulating blood at his feet.

Hayden recognized the man from the recent photos on the trophy room wall. It was Pat himself, being bled out for the purpose of his own taxidermy. The boy he mentored had left his mark.

Hayden guessed the murder to be about two hours old. It wasn't the bleeding that killed the old man, but the scalpel stuck into his brain at the base of his skull. There was evidence of cauterization around the wound—the killer didn't want to lose any of the blood through the victim's head. Apparently there was a very specific way of letting the blood for purposes of taxidermy, and the killer was intent upon proving his worth.

On the wall beside the body, the only other thing clearly seen in the light was another newspaper article: "Local Boy Makes Good with Scholarship to Sacramento State U."

There was a photograph of a younger Tyler Apollyon obscured and made unrecognizable by the grease of solvents and preservatives and maybe even a little recent blood. He was pictured beside the charming country cottage in Windy Hills where he had spent his youth.

Hayden snatched the article from the wall.

He left the building to find Charlie deep in conversation with Tranquillity's local lawman. The sheriff had his back to Hayden and his attention firmly fixed on Charlie, who was doing his best to spin a tale tall enough to explain his presence.

Hayden stepped silently in the soft dirt, staying in the darkness of the shadows. He was within a few feet when Charlie's surprised look gave him away, and the sheriff turned to face him. Hayden lunged, knocking the gun from the lawman's grip, landing with all his weight on top of him. The sheriff went down hard and Hayden coldcocked him. The man lifted his arms to cover his face, but Hayden pummeled him with his fists until he slipped into unconsciousness.

Hayden felt Charlie's hands tugging at his neck and shoulders and he spun around, grabbing his friend by the collar, slamming him against the car. Charlie's eyes grew wide with fear. Hayden cocked his elbow, prepared to land a solid right, then hesitated. Charlie cowered.

Hayden swung his arm around Charlie's neck instead and pulled him close, holding on as he had never held on to Charlie before. He felt his own wet tears on his cheek, and the vibrating of his chest as he sobbed. He wanted to knock Charlie out. It had seemed the simplest way to release him from this madness. If he took him to this meeting with Rufus he was sure that Charlie would die.

He held Charlie with the knowledge that this might be his last memory of Charlie, or this might be Charlie's last memory of him.

Hayden pushed with all his strength and Charlie fell down a four-foot drop into the woods that bordered the road. He heard Charlie grunting as he tumbled, coming to a stop against the trunk of a tree. Hayden ran to the car and turned the engine over.

"Hayden, wait! Wait for me!" Charlie called. Hayden gunned the engine to drown him out. By the time Charlie found his footing, Hayden had sped off into the night.

59

Windy Hills. The PT Cruiser made it to within a half mile of town before running out of gas. Hayden had never run out of gas before. He knew that when his Jeep's gauge hit empty he had another sixty miles to go. Not so with the Cruiser. Empty was empty.

He stood atop one of the windy hills, above the fog and looking down into it. There were small clumps of light in the haze, hugging close to a central dark line, which he took to be the main thoroughfare. He checked the .38 on his ankle and started walking.

After twenty minutes of weed and cactus and snake and scorpion, Hayden arrived at an old rotted-out barn that sat like the upturned skeleton of a beached whale. A dog in the home nearby barked incessantly at Hayden's approach. Hayden ducked out of sight and found the dirt road that was Main Street.

He searched his pockets for the newspaper article he had lifted from the taxidermy business. He supposed he had lost it in his struggle with the sheriff. But Hayden remembered the photograph, and he felt the pull of Rufus toward the house.

He had walked a few acres in the dark when a bright orb appeared through the hazy fog, hovering around a grassy hill like the moon peeking from eclipse. His pace quickened. He felt the energy, smelled its presence. As he neared, the light separated into many lights, and then into landscape lights and lamps on posts, a gas lamp on a front door, and lights under eaves. Hayden found himself standing before a beautiful country cottage with a white picket fence and lemon trees. The photograph. French windows glowed from within. He ascended three steps to the front porch and reached for the door. Unlocked. He pulled his revolver.

Inside a fire burned in the fireplace. A bearskin rug lay on the oak wood floor, next to ancient tan leather chairs. The house was warm and inviting, with Amish furniture and Americana knickknacks. There was nothing kitsch about it either; it was *Architectural Digest* country cottage all the way. The living room could have been a cigar lounge with its manly earth tones and leather armchairs. Branching off the living room were the kitchen and dining room, bright in light yellows and deep reds, with white wood molding around every arch and doorframe.

It appealed to his nose, too. Cedar burning in the fireplace. Scent of lavender and jasmine outside the windows. Basil and other herbs in pots on windowsills. Then something more—something that brought warmth and a sense of security. Hayden walked slowly into the kitchen, his gun held firmly before him. He found the source of the smell—a plate full of freshly baked chocolate chip cookies, still warm, atop a wooden kitchen table. A cardboard note sat folded beside the cookies, like a seating notice placed next to the silverware at a wedding reception.

The note said, "Relax. Take a load off. You must be hungry."

Hayden circled the kitchen, more cautious than ever.

"I'm here, you motherfucker! Come on out!" Hayden was angry; he wanted to finish this thing. His challenge was met with silence.

There is another scent here, he thought. *There is something beneath the chocolate and the potpourri in this Hansel and Gretel house.*

He checked every crevice and closet in the kitchen and living room and cleared the front of the house. He continued into the hallway that led to the bedrooms.

"Tyler!" He was losing his patience. Or losing his nerve. He was jumpy, tired, hungry. He didn't know what he was going to find here, what he would see when he stepped into the master bedroom. He didn't want to see Kennedy's body splayed out before him.

He wondered if Rufus was even here. Hayden imagined the rest of his life, moving from one crime scene to the next, always one step behind him. Witnessing the deaths of Kennedy, and Charlie, and Abbey.

He entered the master bedroom. A polished brass bed. No bloody wrists cuffed to the posts. The room was dignified and bright. It looked like a room in a bed-and-breakfast, waiting for its first visitor. Hayden checked the closet, the bathroom, under the bed.

He continued on to the guest bedroom, checking linen drawers and closets along the way. It was the only door in the house that was closed. Out of habit he checked his gun. Anything could happen on the other side of that door, and Hayden's reflexes and the dependability of his weapon were the only things he could count on. He wished he had the Glock now. He had put in more range time with the Glock.

Hayden tried the knob but the door was locked. He stepped back, took a breath, then kicked.

Another charming Victorian domicile. A flowery comforter on the bed. Rose wallpaper. Statuettes of fairies and frogs. A crystal decanter half filled with port. Hayden checked the closets and under the bed. He had cleared the entire house. There was nothing now, nothing. He wondered if this was the wrong house, if the note by the cookies had been left for a visiting neighbor.

He slumped on the bed, the .38 in both hands, finger on a hair trigger.

He heard a sound. Clanking, metallic. He thought it came from outside. He stood and moved to the window. The sound came again, from inside the room. He turned, wondered what he had missed. He took careful steps toward the door until the sound of metal was behind him. He turned again, saw an old, metal heating coil attached to the wall beside the bed. *Clank.* He heard scraping and dragging. Metal against concrete.

Hayden stood above the heating unit, observing the coils that twisted and spun into the floor, where they disappeared into and under the floor. *Under the house.*

He rushed outside and circled the perimeter. He found a set of steps recessed into the ground behind a hedge of jasmine, leading to a half-size metal door. He approached and turned the handle, and the door opened with a loud *click,* like the sound of a heavy wall switch being flipped.

The smell came from here. This was the scent beneath the calm. Like cold wet meat and chemicals. It reminded him of the basement he used to sneak into at summer camp when he was twelve. He and the other boys used to sit in the dark, on damp, moldy stone floors, telling ghost stories until the younger kids pissed themselves or screamed. He went back to that same camp as a counselor, fifteen years old, and he took a fourteen-year-old junior counselor into the same basement, where he touched her developing breasts. She squeezed his penis under his jeans and he came. As he looked down into this pit Hayden wondered if these memories were the first of the stream of memories to flash before his eyes in the moment of his death.

The floor was made of rock and dirt, more like a cave than a basement. The walls were uneven cinderblock and loose gravel. He could tell it was a huge room from the sound of his feet against the dirt floor. In the distance, around where the living room met the hallway above, there was a bleeding of light against the wall, coming from another subterranean cove. Hayden made his way towards the light. He saw shapes on the floor and bookcases and shelving built into the walls. It was almost a replica of the taxidermy business he'd visited in Tranquillity.

But the trophies boasted a style of their own. The animals were stuffed in tortured poses. Animals fused with other animals. Bobcat and deer as one—the head, chest, and paws of the bobcat turned around on itself, attacking the lower half of the body, which was deer. Another form took the shape of a coyote on its back, biting and clawing at five kittens erupting from its belly. A wild pig with the legs of a dog and antlers piercing its sides like skeletal wings. They were grotesque works of art. They led the way in, yet guarded the sanctum like gargoyles at the entrance of a church.

Here and there were paintings he recognized from the Slough. Leaning against the shelving, scattered haphazardly on the floor, collected with seeming carelessness.

And on the shelves were objects in bottles of formaldehyde. Globs of tissue recognized as liver or bladder or heart. By their sizes and shapes they looked like animal parts. But as Hayden approached the light at the end of the cavern the objects in the bottles took on different forms. A human hand, male, floated in a milky solution, its fingers clawing eternally at the glass. A female breast bobbed in the next one. A small jar of human eyeballs, like martini olives, in another.

Hayden felt his stomach rising. The dull damp feeling returned to his head, like wet wool on the surface of his brain. It was getting hard to concentrate. *Stay on target,* he told himself. His lids weighed heavy on his eyes.

There was an arrow on the ground ahead, arcing to the left, toward the room and the light. As he neared he saw that it was made of severed human fingers placed in a line. Long, bright red nails. He tried to remember the color of Kennedy's fingernails.

He took breaths to calm his nausea. The air was stale, a cauldron of rotting human and animal tissue. He steadied himself, steadied his gun, bit his lip to stay alert. He tasted the blood; it brought memories of his childhood, the nervous biting of his lips and inner cheek and tongue. The way he picked at the gums beneath his front lower teeth until the flesh was almost gone, requiring the skill of an orthodontic surgeon to repair. More early memories. The memories of his life in a flash. Hayden took his step and turned the corner into the light.

This was a completely different room. Stainless steel from floor to ceiling, like the autopsy rooms at the coroner's. It stretched out beyond the pool of light that hung from a pendant over the steel table in the center. There was the hint of hallways and other rooms in the shadows beyond.

Hayden walked to the table and found papers and documents illuminated in the light. A United States passport sat on top, opened, with a photograph of Hayden. A different name appeared under his photo. The passport was current. A manila file folder sat next to the passport. Hayden opened it. A birth certificate, sharing the name from the passport.

Travel brochures. Thailand. The Philippines. Amsterdam. Black market pamphlets depicting foreign brothels advertising young girls and boys. Photos of abuse done to children by masked men.

"I myself have only read about them, seen photos in pamphlets and magazines."

Hayden turned toward the voice, his gun raised. There was only darkness, and the voice seemed to come from many different places at once.

"I've seen some of it on the Internet, but the Internet's a dangerous place. One click on the wrong URL means an FBI trace to your desktop."

Hayden turned in a slow circle, the .38 wavering in front. "Where is she?" he demanded.

"In Thailand, we roam free. Women, boys, girls spill into the streets. There's a life for every day of the week, every day of the year. I know you like the Asian girls. In Buenos Aires we make a fortune harvesting organs. It's not hard. If you've ever carved a Thanksgiving turkey, you can do it."

Hayden followed the voice down a darkened hall. A dim light was visible as he edged near.

"What is this, a partnership?" Hayden asked.

"Of sorts," the voice responded. "I always thought I would do this alone. *My* little secret, see. But it's hard to carry . . . alone. You feel the need to *share.*"

"Why would I be interested?" Hayden asked. He squinted at an object illuminated at the end of the hall.

"Oh, you're interested. You can't deny the man you are, Hayden."

As Hayden neared the end of the hallway he saw that the object was a large metal tub, like the one he saw at the taxidermy business. He saw the naked shoulders of a woman with her back toward him. Naked through a mass of thick, red hair that fell past the rim of the tub.

Hayden ran the last few yards and came around to meet her. Her eyes widened, in shock, relief, disappointment. Her mouth was duct-taped shut and a crude mechanism held a straight blade to her throat. She was naked in the tub, and her arms, held before her, were strapped to a pair of armatures like the ones he saw at the taxidermist's office earlier that night. Each wrist displayed three erasere-size wounds where blood drained slowly out and into the tub. Hayden reached but she groaned in warning as the straight blade went taut against her neck. She braced, awaiting the cut that didn't come. A tear escaped the corner of her eye, traveled the length of her cheek, and fell to mix with her blood in the tub.

"The blade is radio-controlled," Rufus continued. "When you opened the door to the basement you sent a signal that caused the device on her arms to puncture the skin, which began the bleed-out. She has you to thank for that, Hayden. It's a slow and painless process. She'll be unconscious in an hour, a half hour after that the coma cannot be reversed, and a half hour later she's dead. Of course, at any moment I can speed the process by flipping a switch, activating the knife at her neck." He spoke matter-of-factly, as if he had done this a hundred times before.

Hayden suppressed a reckless urge to grab the knife and wrestle it loose. But he knew the risks. A slight laceration at the jugular would be fatal. Even if Hayden could reach a phone he wouldn't see an ambulance out this far for at least an hour. He hated this helplessness. He had charged recklessly forward without thought of consequence, and now he was as much a prisoner as Kennedy. He didn't feel much like a savior.

"I suggest you drop your gun into the tub and turn around."

Hayden turned but saw only darkness in the hallway.

"Come on, now," Rufus continued. "I'm just another brother in the program."

Hayden peered back into Kennedy's eyes. He knew he could click off six rounds in three seconds, pepper the hallway with gunfire, with one or two shots taking Rufus down. Or he might miss entirely. Either way left enough time for the killer to flip the switch that would cut her throat.

Hayden dropped his gun into the tub and turned to face the darkness.

A moment of silence, then soft footsteps. His hands came into view first, extended, carrying the small radio transmitter. His thumb rested on a toggle switch. As he stepped further into the light Hayden saw Tyler Apollyon. He remembered his face, the smirk it wore on the day Sol's body was discovered. The sight of him ignited something in Hayden's soul. For a moment Hayden felt a cold terror that set his hands to shaking. It was a feeling he recognized, from some place, some time before. He could not recall it now.

"I've only been to a couple of your meetings," Rufus said. "Not. Much. Fun." He released a wry half smile.

He wore the mark of Abbey's scratch across his face.

"Tyler." Hayden struggled to maintain control. "Why don't we let her go now. It's just you and me. Let's drop her off along the highway."

"Don't patronize me, Detective. I've got things in store for you."

Hayden looked back at Kennedy. The blood fell in slow droplets from her arms. Her eyes betrayed her fear. He returned a look of assurance. *I will get us out of here. Don't worry.* She seemed to understand and trust him.

"The meetings you go to," Rufus continued. "They talk about this thing, this evil. They call it *addict.* It's not *me,* you say. It's my *addict.*"

He spoke as if he were a professor lecturing his class. Dispassionate, removed.

"Well, I'll tell you what I've learned," he continued. "There is no part of us from which we can separate. The addict *is* us, it's what we're made of. If you do a thing, if you fuck a whore, then that's you. You're a whore-*fucker.* If you kill someone, then that is you. You point to the addict and you point to yourself."

"You might have been at those meetings, but you weren't *present,*" Hayden said with venom.

"Ah, Twelve Step programming. Stop feeling shame, Hayden. There's no room for shame in what we do. Shame is for those who *want* to stop." His words were monotone, emotionless.

"I'm not like you."

He laughed. "No? Where is your badge, *officer?* Where is your *one-year chip?* You think perverted thoughts, you do terrible things to women. You have been brutal and you have killed."

"In self-defense, in the line of duty."

"Drop the pretense. You can be honest with me. It doesn't matter what she hears. Don't you know? She's dead already."

Hayden saw her eyes, growing tired now. Her face losing color, pasty white with sweat. The blood pooling around her feet. If there was a chance to save her it would have to be now.

The nausea came suddenly, and Hayden gripped the tub and leaned over and vomited. Kennedy's eyelids fluttered, her head bobbing back.

"There is a difference between us," Hayden managed between breaths.

"Tell me," Rufus said, his voice indignant.

"I've left a door open."

Rufus didn't understand. Hayden swooped the gun from between Kennedy's feet and fired five shots through the tub wall. Rufus fell and Hayden lunged at him. But a sound from the tub made him stop. He turned back to see Kennedy's knees in the air, writhing. Muffled screams from under the duct tape, the sound of screaming through the channels of her lungs.

The blade touched her neck but hadn't cut. Hayden dove forward, shoving his hand between the blade and her neck. He felt a hollow thud as his knuckles hit her larynx, pushing her neck as far as possible from the oncoming blade. The mechanism was crude but efficient. He tore at the aluminum box that hid the coils and wires that controlled it. The fingers of his right hand felt the razor sharp edge rip into his skin. He wrestled all but two fingers out. He tried to wrap them around the dull side of the blade. His mind told him that it was there, that his fingers were on it and the blade was bending backwards from his grip. He smiled and felt himself laugh, a real belly laugh that emerged with the realization that he had managed to save her. In his mind he saw the blade retracting. He heard Kennedy's desperate gasp for air, her sob of relief now that the danger was over.

Then he heard two distinct cracks as the blade severed the tips of his fingers. He felt the release of blood from his clenched hand, accompanied by the drenching of his arm and shoulder and his face blinded by warm liquid, with the taste of salt, and Kennedy's legs pounding the sides and bottom of the tub, pounding against his arms and shoulders, and the sucking sound of air through an open windpipe. When he wiped the blood from his face he saw her eyes wide and alive for one brief moment, looking deep into his own, devouring his soul, stunned by the broken promise he'd made in the look they had shared a moment before. She moaned, convulsed, slammed her head into the back of the tub. Her legs cycled out from under, her feet kicking the gun he had dropped in his attempt to save her. The wet lungs collapsing sounded like hell licking an open portal.

"I'm sorry," Hayden cried, holding his ears, trying desperately to bury the sound of her struggle. He grabbed his revolver from the tub and put the barrel to her head. The wound in her neck flapped wet and violent with the out-rushing air and her eyes stared wide and fearful and brave and Hayden closed his eyes and pulled the trigger. The gunshot silenced the room.

Her still eyes remained on him, though a portion of her head was gone. He was holding her neck, trying to stem the flow. But it was *his* blood that flowed. The top digits of his right hand middle and index finger were sliced clean off. He removed his shirt and wrapped his hand in it, pulling it tight against his knuckles. He took his belt off and fashioned a tourniquet around his wrist.

Then he heard something that set his head on fire. Echoing through the stainless steel hallways. Laughter.

There were drops of blood on the ground. A bloody handprint on the wall. He followed the laughter.

Hayden turned the corner to find Rufus leaning over the metal table that held Hayden's false passport and birth certificate. Rufus with a scalpel in his hand, using it to pick a bullet from the fleshy part of his forearm. He looked up as Hayden approached.

"Now *that's* been done," Rufus said, satisfied.

Hayden lifted the gun to Tyler's forehead and pulled the trigger. *Click.* His last bullet spent on Kennedy. Rufus didn't even flinch. He stared at the cross around Hayden's neck.

"Do you wear it all the time, then?" he asked.

Hayden touched the cross absently.

Rufus looked into Hayden's face, as if he were searching for some unspoken truth. He winced as he worked the scalpel into the wound, digging deep under the muscle. He came out with the slug.

"There she is," he said.

Hayden stared past him in a daze. Rufus reached for a bottle of hydrogen peroxide.

"Let's talk about Tobias Stephens," Rufus said.

"He was your first," Hayden whispered.

Rufus dabbed the peroxide on his arm. There was a sizzle as it worked its way into the wound.

"This thing, I've been doing a long time," Rufus began. "It's just what I do. If I didn't, well, I wouldn't be *alive* if I didn't. My first was this kid in high school. I smashed his brains into the toilet seat in a public rest room. I was ashamed at first, until the weeks went by and no one came for me. It just became easier after that. The rush justified everything."

Hayden stood very still. He felt no rush in ending Kennedy's life. He felt only pain. And he *did* feel shame.

Rufus found a sterile bandage and taped it to his arm.

"That first kid had a brother. The brother searched for his brother's killer for years, never stopped. He finally hanged himself. Now that's a bond. He couldn't live with himself. And I thought, two for the price of one."

He smiled, as if sharing a private joke.

"A couple years ago I thought back on that and I wondered if it wouldn't be nice to have a brother of my own. I wondered how I might find someone like me. I read newspapers and searched the Internet. All the good ones had been caught—in jail or on death row. Then there were the ones who had never been caught. But . . . how was I supposed to find them when a thousand FBI agents couldn't do the job, right?

"Then it came to me . . . cold cases. Perfect. A murder here, a murder there, no incentive to solve the thing. I found this one, just terrible. Some random killing of this black guy in Watts. A *minister*. He was mutilated, torn apart mostly by the killer's *bare hands*. There was *rage* behind it. It was . . . *beautiful*. But it didn't make sense—it looked like a robbery, but nothing was taken. Nothing but the necklace the guy always wore. And that wasn't in the police report. I found out about the necklace from the victim's sister." His eyes fell once again on the cross around Hayden's neck.

The nausea came in waves. It began in Hayden's gut and vibrated through to the rest of his organs. His dry tongue weighed against the back of his throat.

"The police could never solve the case," Rufus surmised, "because the police weren't looking in the right places. They knew it wasn't random—the rage made it personal. They figured it had something to do with the guy's background, the gangs he hung out with. It wasn't that hard for me. No big mystery. I just figured, who would want to kill him, *really* kill him, and why? I learned everything I could about this man, Tobias Stephens. I went to his church, talked with his family. Everything came up zero, just like it did for the cops. Then one guy, some homey who had found religion, *he* knew Tobias. Real well. Told me about the thing that turned Tobias to God. The thing that nobody knew, but Tobias and God, and *this* guy. He told me about the freeway shooting. Some bullshit, random, stick-the-gun-out-the-window-kid-and-shoot-somebody type of killing.

"I knew this was it, and this was the *only* guy who knew. I had to kill *him*, of course. But I followed that trail and it lead to the guy who got killed, on the freeway. *And I found out that he had a son.*"

In Hayden's memory it all came back. How he felt, at age fifteen, when the lead detective told him they had done everything they could, that the case would not be solved. These things happened. It wasn't fair and you couldn't explain it, the detective said. The best thing to do was let it go. We did everything we could. *It's in God's hands.*

It took years for Hayden to get in. To know the kids in the different gangs, to hear the bullshit and rumors, to finally get his lead. Things happened fast once he had the name. Tobias. The guy who lives in Watts. Doesn't bang no more, took the righteous way out. *Tobias.*

His rage led him to the man's doorstep. He remembered the thrill, the adrenaline as he jimmied the sliding glass door. And then there he was, in his kitchen, eating a bowl of Froot Loops in his underwear and a T-shirt. He heard Hayden's footsteps. Looked up. Faced him without fear. His fingers quietly searching the table for a weapon, for a fork, his eyes on Hayden. He had been waiting, it seemed, for years. He had known that his end would come this way. His fingertips touched the fork and Hayden lunged. Hayden found the chain around Tobias's neck and pulled.

Hayden was nineteen. He was younger and stronger and more determined. In the end all Tobias could do was grasp at the chain. And in his eyes the knowledge that, while still alive, he was already dead.

And then what? What had Hayden done after that?

Hayden reached down now, to feel the cross around his neck. The cross that was not his father's, but was *for* his father.

"That was *your* first time, Hayden," Rufus said.

Rufus moved his injured arm in a circle. The bandage showed a deep red stain.

"It really isn't hard, to find things out about a man," Rufus claimed. "Whatever you've covered can be *un*covered. I'm sure you felt it was justified to kill the man who killed your father. Twenty-three bones broken. His eyes gouged out with a fork. An ear torn with such force that half the scalp came with it."

Hayden felt the weight of his skull against his spine. Numb, his head, his very thoughts. A low, pulsating thump . . . thump . . . a thump behind and or maybe above his ears. His lungs processing air and formaldehyde and dust.

Rufus put his hand on Hayden's shoulder.

"Can't you see what I've done?" he said. "I've removed *the crutches*— your sponsor, the friendships upon which you judged *yourself*, your job, your women. You're free, Hayden."

Of course, Hayden thought. The addict thinks only of the addiction. A man in recovery builds a support system in his friends, his sponsor, his therapist, his *brothers*. The addict waits patiently for the opportunity to destroy this network. Rufus wants *all* the attention. Rufus is a patient but a jealous lover. Tyler is Rufus incarnate and Tyler had set Hayden's Rufus free.

"You'll stay here a few days," Rufus said. "Rest. Prepare for your new life. Don't worry about the girl, I'll take care of that. You need to get well, in body and spirit. In a few days we'll slip across the border. We'll fly out from Mexico. I'll take care of the rest."

Hayden had been gripping his bloody shirt in his fingers. The nubs of his two severed fingertips throbbed. He let the shirt fall to the ground. The tourniquet he made from his belt held true. The bleeding was just a trickle now, leaving his hand a bloated, blue-gray balloon.

"I'll take care of that, too," Rufus continued. "It's a clean cut. The blade was sharp and sterile. You're lucky it didn't slice vertically. I'll cauterize the tips. I've got antibiotics, of course. What doesn't kill us makes us strong—"

His last word silenced by the scalpel stuck through the roof of his mouth. He grabbed Hayden's wrist, tried with tremendous force to pull the scalpel out. But Hayden's will was greater. Hayden charged, forcing the scalpel deep, knocking Rufus backward onto the ground. He pushed him across the room as Rufus struggled, moving crablike on his heels and elbows, his hands like a vise around Hayden's wrist. Rufus knew too well what the result would be if that scalpel rose another inch up the base of his skull.

Hayden's momentum took them into the hallway. They stopped when Rufus's head hit the wall, cracking the glass jar that held the bobbing, severed hand. Shattered glass showered down and the hand dropped between their faces. Hayden brushed it aside, held the scalpel firm, Rufus's head wedged into the bookshelves.

Rufus was stuck. He stopped resisting, looked into Hayden's eyes. Of course, he thought, Hayden was only proving his point. The two of them would be equal. All the best partners were. No one would hold sway above the other.

The wound in the roof of his mouth could be mended. A thimble full of sterile gauze would stem the bleeding and an intern at the urgent care center in Fresno could do the stitching. Even Hayden could do it, with Rufus's instruction. It was a love bite, really. Each of them would have their marks now, physical reminders of the sacrifices they made to enjoy their new life together. It really was perfect.

He smiled into Hayden's eyes. Hayden relaxed his arm. Rufus tried lifting himself from the scalpel. Hayden switched hands. Things felt awkward in his left hand, but he would have to get used to it. He pushed again, driving the scalpel three more inches into the base of Rufus's brain.

There was a gurgling scream, a tearing at the scalpel. Rufus's palms rapped the sides of Hayden's head. But Hayden held true, staring back at Rufus with cold resolve. And then the realization in Rufus's eyes. The knowledge of what was.

Rufus pulled and twisted, tried to gouge Hayden's eyes with his thumbs. Too little, too late. His hands shook as his body convulsed, as the life, or that which had been living, was sucked down through the hole in his skull, into the depths of hell.

He held Hayden's stare as he drained away. What appeared first as surprise settled into dull disappointment. In the end it was disappointment for plans undone. Until now everything had gone according to plan. The addict hated a surprise.

Hayden still held the scalpel firmly in place. He couldn't seem to let it go. He leaned into the blade, pushing up simultaneously. It slid smoothly through brain tissue, and the pressure he applied to the base of the scalpel and the roof of the mouth caused Tyler's skull to split. He worked the scalpel right and left and, like a coconut, the break in the skull separated, releasing the gelatinous pink tissue inside.

He couldn't remember what happened after that. The bubble consumed him. He tried to walk when he came to, but slipped and fell in the mess that had once been Tyler Apollyon. His feet were tangled in . . . *what? Intestines?* Stretched from the naked torso and draped around the room, tied here and there around a chair or table leg in a Boy Scout knot. He was drenched in Tyler's blood and he smelled like the fuming gasses and yellowing acids released from a freshly opened corpse. He heard helicopters in the distance. He heard helicopters coming close. He blacked out.

There was activity around him when he came to. There were people in the room, walking in the shadows. No one approached.

He heard Detective Wallace's voice, like an echo. "Was that Hayden's bullet, from his gun?"

There was a pause and a murmur in the room. Then he heard Charlie's voice.

"The gun didn't kill her," Charlie said. "The blade did."

He could make out figures passing through shadow and light. Patrol officers. There must have been ten of them. They circled, but kept their distance. He heard Detective Wallace again.

"Jesus," Wallace said. "What the hell did he use, a grenade?"

More shuffling of feet. Hayden wanted to lean against something but his hands touched soft tissue that gave way when he put weight on it. He couldn't seem to dislodge himself from the mess at his feet. He heard footsteps, Charlie approaching Wallace and Captain Forsythe.

"It doesn't matter," Forsythe said. "Hayden took him out. That's *all* that matters."

It seemed settled between the three of them. Hayden wriggled his right foot free. He took a step. He lifted his left foot and wet suction nearly took off his shoe. He leaned back toward his heel, shifted weight, and pulled out with ease. He took another step and cleared it. He saw their shoes in front of him. They stood in a close-knit group. Their discussion ended as he approached.

Hayden stared at the floor. Dust hovered everywhere. Too much activity in too small a place.

After a moment he heard Wallace clear his throat.

"How are we gonna ID this guy?" Wallace asked. "Charlie?"

The question sparked something in Hayden. He had prepared for this. He reached into his pocket and removed an object. He presented it to the others in the open palm of his hand. The three stared silently back. Their stances shifted as they tried to remain composed. Finally, Charlie reached out and took Tyler's severed finger from Hayden's hand. Tyler Apollyon's index finger, from the bottom knuckle up, with its perfect print, its undamaged set of whorls and loops and arches.

It was unnaturally silent for a room filled with police. He heard Wallace cough, suppressing a sneeze. Captain Forsythe seemed in a distant place. Charlie stepped forward and into Hayden's field of vision. He felt Charlie's hands on his shoulder and elbow, guiding him from the scene of the crime. They passed a gallery of mute officers averting their eyes.

Charlie draped his arm around Hayden's shoulder like a brother, like a partner. He pushed Hayden's head down gently to help him through the small door that led to the surface. Hayden smelled jasmine in the night.

"You're gonna be okay, Hayden," Charlie assured him.

Hayden stopped at the stairs. He turned back to observe the crime scene. Warm steam rose like yellow fog from Tyler's remains. Limbs and organs were intertwined and spread across the room. It looked like a scene from one of Tyler's paintings. Or a sketch that Hayden would never draw.

Hayden took Charlie's outstretched arm and turned back to the stairs. He smiled to himself as he ascended, realizing for the first time in his life that he didn't feel the shame. Not any shame at all.

ABOUT THE AUTHOR

Stephen Jay Schwartz grew up in New Mexico and traveled the United States extensively before settling down in Los Angeles with his wife and two sons. There he became the director of development for film director Wolfgang Petersen, helping develop films such as *Outbreak* and *Air Force One*. *Boulevard* is his first novel. His website is www.stephenjay schwartz.com.